Abby Green spent her teens reading Mills & Boon romances. She then spent many years working in the Film and TV industry as an Assistant Director. One day while standing outside an actor's trailer in the rain, she thought: *there has to be more than this*. So she sent off a partial to Mills & Boon. After many rewrites, they accepted her first book and an author was born. She lives in Dublin, Ireland and you can find out more here: www.abby-green.com

Sandra Marton is a *USA Today* Bestselling Author. A four-time finalist for the RITA®, the coveted award given by Romance Writers of America, she's also won eight Romantic Times Reviewers' Choice Awards, the Holt Medallion, and Romantic Times' Career Achievement Award. Sandra's heroes are powerful, sexy, take-charge men who think they have it all – until that one special woman comes along. Stand back, because together they're bound to set the world on fire.

Cathy Williams is a great believer in the power of perseverance as she had never written anything before her writing career, and from the starting point of zero has now fulfilled her ambition to pursue this most enjoyable of careers. She would encourage any would-be writer to have faith and go for it! She derives inspiration from the tropical island of Trinidad and from the peaceful countryside of middle England. Cathy lives in Warwickshire her family.

The Mistresses

COLLECTION

Mistresses: Seduction in the Boardroom

ABBY GREEN

SANDRA MARTON

CATHY WILLIAMS

MIX
Paper from
responsible sources
FSC   FSC C007454

This book is produced from independently certified FSC™ paper
to ensure responsible forest management.

For more information visit: www.harpercollins.co.uk/green

Printed and bound in Spain
by CPI Barcelona

MILLS & BOON

First Published in Great Britain 2020
By Mills & Boon, an imprint of HarperCollins*Publishers*
1 London Bridge Street, London, SE1 9GF

MISTRESSES: SEDUCTION IN THE BOARDROOM © 2020
Harlequin Books S.A.

Ruthless Greek Boss, Secretary Mistress © 2009 Abby Green
Not for Sale © 2011 Sandra Marton
Hired for the Boss's Bedroom © 2009 Cathy Williams

ISBN: 978-0-263-28119-4

0420

RUTHLESS GREEK BOSS, SECRETARY MISTRESS

ABBY GREEN

CHAPTER ONE

'YOU'RE the coldest man I ever met. If you have a heart it's made of stone. You're cruel and contemptible. I *hate* you.' The woman's strident voice quivered dangerously on the last word and came through the heavy oak door with effortless ease.

There was silence, and then the ominously low rumble of a man's voice. Short, sharp, succinct. Lucy could imagine only too well the glacial look that was most likely accompanying those indistinct words. She sighed as she heard the woman splutter indignantly, but then she was off again, her voice rising so high now that Lucy feared for the crystal decanter on the drinks board nearby. While Lucy was new to these scenes first-hand, she had to reflect that the rumours she'd heard over the past two years hadn't been a myth after all. The voice was drawing her attention back to the present moment.

'Don't think that you can seduce your way back into my bed after treating me like this!'

Lucy had just enough time for a cynical smile as she reflected that if her new boss was to so much as arch an eyebrow this woman would undoubtedly be back in his bed in a heartbeat before the door was suddenly flung open. She looked studiously at her computer screen, trying to sink down in her seat and be as unobtrusive as possible.

Being unobtrusive was her trademark: it was what had got her this coveted job, along with her impeccable credentials and references. There was a lull, a pseudo-calm in the middle of the storm. Lucy didn't look up, but could visualise the woman standing dramatically on the threshold of the palatial office. Tall, sleek and blonde. Stunningly beautiful, from the top of her shiny head to the tip of her expensively manicured toes, evident through the peepholes of a pair of sky-high heels. She was reputedly one of the most alluring women in the world, but apparently hadn't managed to hold his attention for longer than a few weeks.

'Needless to say you won't be hearing from me again.'

The door slammed shut with such violence that Lucy winced. He wouldn't appreciate that. Even though Lucy had only been working for him for two months she already knew that he hated scenes. A cloud of noxious perfume lingered in the wake of the tall woman's exit. She hadn't even glanced Lucy's way.

Lucy breathed a sigh of relief and then heard a loud thump, as if a fist was connecting with a hard surface. She counted to ten, and on the count of ten the door opened. She looked up and willed any emotion or reaction from her face. Her boss stood there, filling the frame easily. Veritable sparks of energy crackled from his body.

Aristotle Levakis, CEO of Levakis Enterprises which encompassed all aspects of a dizzyingly successful global imports and exports business.

Tall, broad-shouldered, lean hipped. Every hard-muscled, dark olive-skinned inch of him adding up to a—currently bristling—Greek alpha male in his potent and virile prime.

His distinctive light green eyes skewered Lucy to the spot, almost as if the last ten minutes had been *her* fault. Instantly she felt breathless; her heart hammered. She hated that she was aware of him. But the best part of two years spent viewing him from a distance, along with every other ogling female in his thousand-employee-strong company, had done little to help diminish the devastating impact of working in such close proximity to him. A memory surfaced and familiar heat flooded her. If only she *had* been kept at a safe distance he might not be having this effect on her now—but there had been that moment in a lift, almost a year ago…Lucy ruthlessly crushed that memory stone-dead. Now was *not* the time.

But, much to her chagrin and dismay, she couldn't halt her reaction. It was something about the way he'd obviously just raked a hand through his unruly ink-black hair, leaving it even more dishevelled, and the way his jaw was so defined and hard it looked as if it was hewn from granite. His cheekbones and that full lower lip softened the hard edges, giving him the look of a master of sensuality—which by all accounts he was. Yet dark brows drawn together over those deep-set, amazing eyes took away any lingering pretty edges.

'Lucy,' he rapped out, distaste for the recent dramatics etched all over his handsome face. 'Get in here. *Now.*'

Lucy blinked and landed back to earth with a bump. What was she doing? Sitting here mentally listing her boss's attributes as if he wasn't standing there looking at her as if he wanted to throttle someone. Caught short, which she never was, she scrambled up somewhat inelegantly from her chair and walked towards him, but then, to add insult to injury, she dropped her pad and pen from suddenly nerveless fingers. She bent down to pick them up, cursing herself in her head, *and* cursing the fact that her skirt was too tight when it resisted her movement. She'd put it in the wrong wash and it had shrunk about two sizes; with no time to shop for a replacement it had had to do, but now she was terrified it might split at the seams. The thought of that made her go hot all over.

If Aristotle Levakis so much as guessed for a second that he had any effect on her she'd be out on her ear and replaced so fast her head would be spinning. She didn't have to remind herself that was exactly what had happened to his last two unfortunate assistants.

Speed had been of the essence as his in-house headhunters had scrambled to find the next best person. Lucy had since discovered that Levakis Enterprises was involved in a top secret series of merger meetings, and the luxury of extending the search to outside the company hadn't been an option.

As luck would have had it, Lucy's boss, Levakis' senior legal counsel, had retired the very day of the last unfortunate PA's demise. Lucy had been vetted and promoted within twenty-four hours to the most terrifying and yet exciting position of her career so far: Levakis' personal secretary, heading up a team of five junior administrative assistants, not to mention staff in Athens and New York.

When she straightened up, taking care to breathe in, all this raced through her brain and she felt thoroughly flustered. She pushed her glasses higher on her nose and felt her cheeks grow even hotter. Aristotle moved back to let her precede him into his office, and she caught the look of exasperation that crossed his face as he articulated her own thoughts out loud with narrowed eyes,

'What is wrong with you today?'

She burned inside with humiliation at her lack of control. She was no better than the swooning legions of girls who gathered in the kitchens on each floor of this impressive London headquarters to eulogise over his mythical sexual prowess and inestimable wealth.

'Nothing,' Lucy muttered, and called on every bit of training she had to regain her composure. When she heard him shut his door behind them and follow her in she closed her eyes for a split second and took deep breaths. She chastised herself roundly. This job was so important; the sharp increase in wages meant that she was finally able to take care of her mother properly.

She couldn't jeopardise all that now by turning into a bumbling, stumbling, mooning idiot—no matter how gorgeous her boss happened to be. A voice mocked her inwardly. It wasn't as if she even *wanted* a man like him to notice her. She *had to* control these wayward thoughts. They disturbed her more than she cared to admit, making her think of long-buried memories of her childhood.

It should be easy enough to do after witnessing that last little scene. Evidently Aristotle Levakis went for quivering, highly strung thoroughbreds, all lean and sleek with good bloodlines. Lucy Proctor was more along the lines of a…a placid cart horse, and her bloodline was considerably less blue than he was used to. More of a murky brown.

She watched as Levakis came back around the other side of his desk and gestured impatiently for her to sit down and take notes, not even glancing her way. Lucy willed her heart-beat to slow down and sat, legs tucked under the chair demurely, pen poised over a blank sheet of paper, and prayed that her skirt wouldn't split open.

Aristotle Levakis stood behind his desk, hands deep in the pockets of his trousers, and looked at the demurely bent head of his new assistant. It was most irritating to be faced with the fact that Augustine Archer had forced him to reject her by demanding more of a commitment than he was prepared to give right now. To any woman.

His assistant shifted in her seat minutely, making Ari's eyes narrow on her. That ripple of awareness ran through him *again*. It was faint, elusive, yet irritatingly insistent, and had been ever since she'd walked into his office two months before in a primly structured suit.

An uncomfortable suspicion made him tense inwardly;

was it this *awareness* that had had an effect on the lessening and ultimate annihilation of his desire for Augustine Archer? Her shrieked words still vibrated in the air, but at that moment Aristotle would be hard pushed to bring her image to mind. Immediately as he realised the import of what he was thinking he rejected the notion as utterly absurd.

Lucy Proctor, his relatively new assistant, was as far removed from his habitual choice of lover as could be humanly possible. He couldn't believe he was even giving a second of his time to this subject, or putting those two words *Lucy* and *lover* in the same sentence, but almost against his will his eyes flicked down from shiny, albeit non-descript dark brown hair to where her knees were tight together, legs tucked under the chair.

His almost contemptuous regard stopped for a moment to take in what could only be described as wantonly voluptuous thighs encased far too snugly in the confines of a pencil skirt. Irritation prickled stronger. He would have to have a word with the head of Human Resources and tell her to pass on a discreet message about the code of dress he expected from his assistant. And yet his expert eye hadn't missed the surprisingly small waist, cinched in by a belt. That realisation stung him.

He tried to reassert his self-control. She was big…all over… His eyes flicked back up to the line of more than generous breasts under her silk shirt. And yet, prompted a little rogue voice, she looked as firm as a succulent peach. And her face…that was something he realised now he hadn't really given much time to study, seeing her only as someone employed to do his bidding, but now, much to his chagrin, his gaze wanted to stop and linger. Look properly. Take in the surprisingly graceful curve of a well-defined cheekbone. Aristotle's blood was starting to heat up; with a kind of desperation he noted that she wore glasses, as if that might have the effect of a cold douche on his suddenly raging hormones.

It didn't. He battled with his libido but it seemed determined to confound him, and he wondered what on earth was precipitating this reaction when Lucy had worked for his company for two years already. He'd only met her intermittently in that time, as she'd worked for his legal counsel, and she certainly hadn't had any discernible effect on him then. But now she was his assistant, and a welcome relief after dealing with a succession of simpering, moon-eyed idiots.

With that in mind, he called on all his powers of logic to explain the bizarre anomaly of his physical reaction, and finally felt some equanimity return: he was a red-blooded male, he was bound to respond arbitrarily to some women, even only passably attractive ones.

Except this wasn't the first time: he uncomfortably recalled one morning when he'd stepped into the staff elevator, because his own private one had been closed for repairs. Someone had run to stop the doors closing and launched themselves into the lift with such force that they'd careened into him. He'd felt every contour and curve of a very lush female body plastered against his for a second. It had been Lucy.

The memory seared him now. She'd been as curvaceous as something brought to life from a painting by Rubens, and the minute she'd walked into his office to interview for this job he'd remembered that moment in annoyingly vivid detail. Right now all he could think about was how she'd felt pressed against him. Especially when compared to the more sparingly built Augustine Archers of this world.

Lucy Proctor had shown no hint of remembering the moment in the lift, though, and Aristotle certainly wasn't going to admit to such a chink in his own legendary control. But when she sat in front of him now, the vision of her thighs straining against that too-tight skirt on the periphery of his vision, he could feel his body responding to her with a strength that disturbed him—a strength almost beyond his control…

The object of his uncharacteristic pondering looked up then quizzically, clearly wondering why he wasn't saying anything. Irrational rage rushed through him. He wasn't used to being rendered speechless like this. But in that moment, as if to compound every other revelation, he noticed she had the most unusually coloured eyes: a dark slaty grey that was almost blue, framed with the longest blackest lashes. Her mouth opened, as if to speak, and entirely against his will his eyes moved down. He'd not noticed until now that she had a sizeable gap between her front teeth. It was all at once innocent and unbelievably erotic.

Shocking and out of nowhere Aristotle had a sudden vision of those lips wrapped around a part of his anatomy, those almond-shaped eyes looking up into his as she— Lust exploded into his brain and turned everything red.

Lucy looked up at her boss and her mouth went dry. Her pulse, which had finally started slowing down, picked up pace again and she could feel herself grow hot. He was looking at her with such intensity that for a moment she thought— Instantly she shut down those rogue thoughts, and as if she'd imagined it the lines in his face tightened. He was positively glowering at her. Inwardly she quivered, outwardly she clung onto her poise and acknowledged that it was no wonder his adversaries hadn't ever got the better of him.

'Sir?' she said, thankful that her voice sounded cool and calm, unruffled.

He kept glowering at her for another long moment, and Lucy felt inexplicably as if some sort of battle of wills she was unaware of was going on.

Eventually he bit out, 'I think you can start calling me Aristotle.'

His voice sounded rough. She guessed it must be the remnants of his anger at the recent scene, but even so Lucy's belly quivered. She knew some close colleagues called him Aristotle, and she'd heard the beautiful blonde requesting breathily to speak to 'Ari' when she'd phoned before the dramatics this morning, but the thought of addressing this man by his first name was having a seismic effect on her whole body.

'Very well,' she finally managed to get out. But couldn't bring herself to actually say it.

Aristotle sat down as if he hadn't just invited her to call him something far more intimate than *Sir*, or *Mr Levakis*, and proceeded to dictate with such lightning speed that it took all of Lucy's wits and concentration to keep up. In truth she was glad of the distraction, but by the time he was done her head was ringing.

He dismissed her with a brusque flick of his hand, his head already buried in some paperwork, and Lucy stood up. She was at the door when she heard a curt, 'Oh, and see to it, please, that Augustine Archer is sent something...'

Lucy turned around, and the look of dark cynicism she saw on Levakis' face made her draw in a breath.

'...*suitable.*'

Lucy looked at him, nonplussed for a moment. Her previous boss had never made such a request. Did he mean...?

As if he could read her mind, Aristotle said ascerbically, 'That's exactly what I mean. I don't care who you call, just make sure it's expensive, anything but a ring, and send it over with a note. I'll e-mail you the address.'

Lucy's hand was clutching the door, and she didn't know why this feeling of something like disappointment was curling through her. Anyone with half a brain cell would have been able to tell her this was exactly how a man like him operated. And wasn't it confirmation of another rumour about him?

How well he compensated his lovers? But still…he wasn't even taking the time to compose a note himself.

She forced herself to sound non-committal. 'How would you like the note to read?'

He shrugged one broad shoulder and smiled sardonically, cruelly. 'Make it up. What kind of platitude would *you* like to hear from a man who has just dumped you?' His mouth twisted even more. 'I think it's safe to say that someone like Ms Archer will throw away the card and move straight to the main prize, so I wouldn't worry about it too much. Just keep it as impersonal as possible.'

Shock at his cold words impacted Lucy right in her belly. Her face must have given something away, because Aristotle lounged back in his chair and looked at her with a dangerous gleam in those fascinating green eyes.

'You don't approve of my methods?'

Lucy could feel a tide of heat climb up from her chest. She alternately shook and nodded her head, and some garbled words came out. 'Not at all…' She realised what she'd said and groaned inwardly when she saw a flash of something dark cross his face. She could not let her own personal opinion of his behaviour jeopardise this job. Too much now depended on her wages.

She gestured clumsily. 'I mean, I have no problem doing as you suggest. Your methods…are your methods. It's not for me to judge.'

He sat up and raised a brow, and Lucy wondered dismally how on earth they had got onto this. She wanted to be back outside, with a wall and door between them, catching her breath and restoring her equilibrium, not discussing how best to let his mistress down.

But he said, 'So you admit there is something to judge, then?'

Lucy shook her head, drowning in heat now. 'No—look,

I'm sorry, I'm not being very articulate. I'll do as you ask and make sure that the accompanying note is appropriate.' She added hurriedly, 'I can show it to you before I send it…?'

He shook his head and his face became impassive, hard. Lucy stood there for another moment, not sure what to do and then he bit out,

'That'll be all.'

Stung, and more than mortified, Lucy mumbled something incoherent and fled, shutting the door behind her. Amidst the embarrassment, anger surged—why was she surprised or, worse, disappointed? She'd seen this kind of behaviour from men all her life.

But still, what an *absolute*— She halted her racing thoughts as she sat behind her desk and fought to steady her breathing and hammering heart. The last five minutes was the closest she'd come to a personal discussion with her new boss. She should have just bowed her head and walked out. She cursed her expressive face. Her mother had always told her it would get her into trouble. And hadn't it just? Her inherent distaste for his coldly generous dismissive treatment of his ex-mistress hadn't been well hidden enough. But the truth was it had tapped into a deeply buried pain, a very familiar pain. She'd witnessed the other side of someone on the receiving end of that treatment. Over and over again.

Lucy shuddered inwardly when she woke her computer from sleep and struggled to concentrate on work. Aristotle's cynical view of how Ms Archer would receive his gift was no doubt spot-on; hadn't she witnessed her own mother reduced to that level after years of similar treatment? Although Augustine Archer didn't strike her as the kind of woman who had to survive on hand-outs. No, this was a different league. Lucy's soft mouth tightened as bile rose from her belly. That kind of so-called *main prize* would have been just the kind of thing her mother would have used to pay for Lucy's school uniform for another year—the sort of thing that had financed their lives.

Lucy forced her anger down. She had to think of her boss purely in professional terms. What he did or how he acted personally was none of her business. She didn't have to like him; she just had to work for him.

Thank goodness she'd forged a different path. She would never be beholden to any man or, worse, held in his sexual or financial thrall. She'd worked too hard and her mother had sacrificed too much to make sure she avoided exactly that scenario. Just as her computer screen came back to life and she saw her bespectacled face momentarily reflected on the dark surface she felt unmitigated relief that she need never fear the kind of attention her mother and women like Augustine Archer courted. She was safe from all of that.

Aristotle watched the closed door for an inordinate amount of time. Heat still coursed through his body—heat that confounded him and every effort he made to try and dampen it. All he could see in his mind's eye was the sway of that well-rounded bottom as she'd stopped by the door, and how he'd blurted out the first thing that had come into his head, as if he'd had to stop her, not let her leave.

He flung himself back in his seat and raked a hand through unruly hair, unusually diverted from work. He cursed the fact again that he'd had to let Augustine go at this point in negotiations. He briefly considered wooing her back, but his fists clenched in rejection of that idea. He would never debase himself by grovelling to a woman—not for *anything*.

He considered the request he'd just made of Lucy; he'd always made the call to a jewellers himself before, and would instruct them to compose a suitably impersonal note. Usually it wasn't even a note—just his name. A clear indication that whatever he and the particular woman had shared was over and she shouldn't come calling again. And invariably they knew not to. Few were as impertinent as Augustine Archer, confronting him directly. His mouth twisted in recognition of the fact that as he got older and remained single he represented some kind of irresistible challenge to those women.

He diverted his thoughts from an area he didn't want to investigate: that of having to contemplate giving up his freedom, which he knew would be inevitable at some stage. The future was unavoidable. He would have to find a suitable wife and produce an heir, purely to protect all that he was now putting in place from the greedy clutches of others.

The prospect evoked no more emotion in him than mild uninterest and irritation. He'd long ago learnt the lesson of what marriage really meant—at the age of five, when his father had introduced Helen Savakis as his new stepmother and she'd quickly shown him the cold hatred she had for a son who wasn't her own. Whatever dim and distant memories Ari might have had of his mother, who'd died when he was four, and a halcyon time that might never have existed except in some childish fanciful memory bank, had long been quashed and buried.

The fact that those nebulous memories rose to haunt him in dreams so vivid that he sometimes woke in tears was a shameful weakness he'd always been determined to ignore. It was one reason he'd never spent a full night with a woman.

As if drawn by a magnet his thoughts again went to his assistant, who was fast assuming a place in his imagination that he did not welcome. Why had he felt goaded into saying all he just had? And then been surprised by the blatant look of distaste on her face—annoyed by it? And he had not left it at that but engaged her in a dialogue about it. As if he even cared what her opinion of him was! He was aware of a niggling desire that he'd wanted to see her somehow...rattled. Since she'd been working for him she'd always seemed to fade into the background, barely noticeable.

But he *was* noticing her and she *had* just reacted, her cheeks flushing prettily. He frowned at that. Since when had he started thinking of her as pretty? And since when had he been interested in *pretty*?

And, not only that, what on earth had compelled him to tell her to call him Aristotle when he'd always preferred his PAs to call him Mr Levakis? It was something in the way she'd looked up at him and said *sir*.

In a bid to restore some order to his life, which seemed to be morphing out of all recognition, he rang through to Lucy and gave her the name and number of the latest English socialite who had been chasing him, instructing her to set up a date for that evening. He ignored the way even her voice seemed to send a frisson of reaction straight to his groin. With that done he felt some semblance of calm wash over him. Life would return to normal. He would forget all about this bizarre obsession with his secretary's far too provocatively well-built body and concentrate on the merger.

The following morning, when Lucy was walking the short distance from her bus stop to work, she still burned with mortification. In her hand she carried a small overnight bag which held a change of clothes and some evening wear. She'd taken a call from the head of Human Resources the day before and been informed stoutly that she needed to think a little more thoroughly about the way she dressed, and that it might be a good idea to have a change of clothes in the office at all times to cover for emergencies. Like too-tight skirts, she thought churlishly. The fact that Levakis had gone over her head and asked someone to speak to her made her skin crawl with humiliation—not to mention the fact that he'd obviously noticed her bursting out of that skirt.

With getting her mother settled in her new home she simply hadn't had time since she'd started working for him to kit herself out with a new wardrobe, despite being given a generous allowance to do so. It had been full-on from day one.

Luckily last night had been late-night shopping, and Levakis had left relatively early for the date Lucy had set up for him. Her belly clenched at the thought of that. The woman she'd rung hadn't been in the slightest bit fazed that Aristotle himself hadn't bothered to call, and of course she'd been free at a moment's notice. A wave of disgust washed through Lucy and she pushed it down along with bitter memories. She didn't care what he did or who he did it with. A voice mocked her inwardly: who was *she* to judge anyway?

Just at that moment the heavens opened from a slate-grey sky and Lucy yelped as torrential rain poured down, comprehensively drenching her in seconds. *No*! She ran across the road towards the refuge of the huge gleaming Levakis building, her mind filled with the fact that they had an important meeting to attend in less than an hour on the other side of London.

Aristotle strode through the reception area, raking a hand through rain-wet hair, and mentally cursed the inclement English weather which had momentarily darkened the enormous glass atrium. He stepped into his own private lift—no possibility of a lush, curvaceous body colliding with his today—and stabbed at the button to whisk him all the way to the top of the building, irritated beyond belief to be thinking of that *again*. Was he actually hoping for it? he asked himself derisively.

His starkly handsome face was reflected back to him in the steel surface of the door, but he didn't see that as the lift zoomed skyward. No, what he saw and what he relived was the fact that last night he'd taken a beautiful *available* woman on a date and she had done nothing for him. His mouth twisted. It hadn't been for lack of trying on her part, or even on his, which had been a novel sensation.

In a bid not to be dictated to by his malfunctioning hormones, he'd escorted Arabella—*or had it been Mirabella?*—up to her apartment, but had realised with sickening inevitability that nothing would be happening. With her, anyway. He'd been rendered impotent from the waist down. She'd become petulant and increasingly desperate, seeing correctly that she hadn't managed to snare Aristotle's interest, and he'd had to extricate himself with more diplomacy than a head of state during peace negotiations.

So now, as he strode out of his lift and towards his main office, he was thoroughly disgruntled. Ignoring the assistants sitting meekly at their desks in the ante-room that preceded his and Lucy's offices, he opened the door and took a breath, preparing to fire a series of commands at the woman who had been the singular cause of his unsatisfying night.

But the office was empty.

He had the most curious sensation of his belly hollowing out before he heard movement coming from the door which led into the bathroom just off their offices. While he had a private bathroom too, this more communal bathroom had a shower and a dressing room, which Aristotle availed himself of whenever he was required to go straight to a function from work.

Closing the main door quietly behind him, without really being aware of what he was doing, he walked silently into the office. He heard a muffled curse and then something drop.

Feeling like a voyeur, and not liking it, he halted by the door which lay slightly ajar. Through the crack he saw Lucy, and when his eyes registered what he was seeing his whole body locked, every muscle taut. Unable to move, all he could do was take in the sight with widening eyes. Lucy's wet hair hung in long dark tendrils over luminously pale shoulders. She was bending over to pull trousers up over long, surprisingly slender legs. Her legs led upwards to those shapely thighs, which curved out to a lushly rounded bottom encased in some kind of black lace and silk concoction.

She wriggled her bottom and her hips as she pulled the trousers up fully, and then twisted towards Aristotle to tie the fastening at the side. Heat engulfed him. His blood hummed and his heart picked up an unsteady beat. Facing him as she did, both hands to one side, her perfectly formed breasts were enticingly pushed together and towards him with unknowing and unbelievably erotic appeal. Her bra looked hardly adequate to contain the generous mounds of alabaster flesh—he wondered dimly if any of her clothes fitted properly. And who would have known that she'd have such exotic tastes in undergarments underneath that prim exterior? Arousal soared.

Another muffled curse came as an even longer tendril of dark hair swung over her shoulder and clung wetly to the slope of one unashamedly voluptuous breast. Aristotle's gaze moved up with supreme difficulty, and he saw that gap in her front teeth as she bit her lip, a hectic flush across her cheeks.

As if entranced by a siren song, he couldn't move. His gaze slid down again and took in that small waist, which he'd only noted yesterday, and her belly, which was sucked in to help with the obstinate fastening. It was soft but gently contoured, as if she fought some kind of battle to keep her body in check but it was determined to thwart her efforts and retain its inherently seductive softness. Her hips flared out generously from that waist with such hourglass perfection Aristotle felt momentarily dizzy.

Abruptly she moved, having at last managed to fasten her trousers, and straightened. Her belly was still sucked in, pushing her breasts out even more as she reached for something else which Aristotle could see was a shirt.

His brain wouldn't function. He couldn't move. All he could see was Lucy and her half-naked body, that long dark hair clinging provocatively to her skin like wet skeins of silk.

That thing that he called *awareness* had just exploded into full-on lust.

Lucy yanked the tag off her new shirt and pulled it on impatiently, all fingers and thumbs on the buttons of the slippery grey silk material. She'd never have gone for something like this normally, but after being hauled over the coals the day before she'd known that she had no choice but to buy the kind of uniform that someone like Aristotle Levakis would expect—and that meant expense, and things like silk as opposed to cotton. She breathed out thankfully. At least she'd had that change of clothes. No way could she have faced him this morning looking like the drowned rat she'd been just moments before.

With the shirt finally closed she tucked it in hurriedly and desperately listened out for a heavy footfall or the door opening. She knew he was due in any minute—he was more punctual than any boss she'd ever known. That had to be the reason her heart was thumping so hard: the fear of being caught like this. She raked a brush through her hair, wincing as it caught on the still-damp strands, and quickly twisted it up into a chignon of sorts. It would have to do.

Slipping her feet into flat shoes, she stuck her glasses back on, gathered up her wet things, looked up—and stopped breathing. In the crack of the open door her boss was just standing there, looking at her.

CHAPTER TWO

How long had he been standing there? The words barely impinged on Lucy's consciousness. She was too full of raging heat, embarrassment, and something more disturbing.

On some self-protective level she refused to believe he had seen her yanking her clothes on with all the grace of a baby elephant. He wasn't moving. He looked slightly shell-shocked, and mortification rushed through Lucy. She managed to move and opened the door fully, gabbling something she hoped was coherent to fill the awful silence.

'I got caught in the rain shower. I was just changing.'

She stepped out and past Aristotle, who turned to follow her with his eyes as she retreated to the safe zone behind her desk, not even sure why she needed to feel safe.

When she could bring herself to look at him, she registered that his hair was damp, his suit slightly wet. She met his eyes, and in that instant something passed between them, something electric and elemental, and Lucy knew that he *had* seen her dressing—even though stubbornly she still refused to believe it. She recoiled from the uncomfortable awareness deep within her. It scared the life out of her.

Still babbling, she said, 'Looks like you got caught too. Do you want to change before we go? I've instructed Julian to have the car downstairs in fifteen minutes, and I can have your suit sent out to be cleaned.'

Aristotle, seemingly completely unconcerned about the meeting or changing his clothes, lounged back against the doorjamb and crossed his arms. His gaze swept down over Lucy's outfit and she cringed, wondering if she'd left a tag on somewhere. She fought the urge to check herself.

He just continued to look at her with that disturbing intensity before saying, 'Tell me, did you wear that skirt yesterday on purpose? Aware of how provocative it was?'

Shock, disbelief and cold horror slammed into Lucy. Her mouth opened for a moment but nothing emerged. She couldn't articulate, but finally managed a strangled, 'Of *course* not. I would never be so…' Words failed her again and she closed her mouth helplessly.

Aristotle could see injured pride straighten her spine, the shock on her face. He had the absurd impulse to apologise, but couldn't help remembering the way she'd looked so wantonly luscious in it, straining against the material. He could imagine inching it up over those pale quivering thighs as she stood with her back against him, how the full globes of her bottom would press into him as he pushed her forward over his desk, reaching down between them to hitch her skirt higher and free his own— *What the hell was wrong with him?* His mind never deviated to lurid sexual fantasies with so little provocation.

He stood away from the door abruptly and curtly informed Lucy to make sure she had all the necessary papers and documents required for the meeting ready. He then went into the dressing room and breathed deep, as if he could inhale some common sense. But instead an evocatively feminine scent teased his nostrils and brought the last few minutes vividly back. Along with his libido.

With a growl of intense irritation Aristotle yanked a clean

suit from the well-stocked wardrobe and stripped off to step into the shower, turning it onto cold. It did little to help.

Lucy flinched minutely and scowled at her computer when she heard the phone being slammed down in her boss's office. He'd just taken a call from his half-brother in Athens, and while he never seemed to welcome those calls he usually acted with more restraint than that. She shook her head. He'd been in a foul humour for two weeks now. *Ever since that morning.* Heat still crawled over her skin when she thought of the way he'd lounged against the door and looked at her, and mentioned that skirt. *He believed she might have worn it like that on purpose.*

And yet since then he had proceeded to treat her either as if a) he couldn't bring himself even to mention her name, or b) as if he might turn to stone if he so much as looked at her for longer than two seconds.

Lucy had to assure herself that nothing *had* happened, and if anything this was just a normal working relationship. Aristotle was famous for his brusque, no-nonsense approach. What had she expected? Warm and fuzzy? She shifted in her seat uncomfortably, the fact was she did feel inordinately *warm*—especially when he was around. She also felt constantly on edge, as if a kind of prickly heat lay just under the surface of her skin. She felt achy and jittery, but no symptoms of a flu or a cold had developed, so she couldn't put it down to that. She was beginning to despair of ever having any sense of equilibrium again. At times like this she longed for the uncomplicated working relationship she'd had with her last boss. Her mouth quirked wryly. But then, he had been nearing seventy, well past retirement age, and had a huge typically Greek family.

Lucy nearly shot out of her chair when she heard a coolly drawled, 'Something funny on the internet today?'

She quickly pressed a key so that her blank document disappeared, and took a breath before looking up, steeling herself. She had to steel herself a lot around this man. She smiled brightly, but it faded when she saw something dark cross his face.

'No… I was just…going over the latest mail from the Parnassus Corporation.'

She mentally crossed her fingers and breathed a sigh of relief, because that was exactly what she *had* been doing—*before* she'd been looking at a blank document for minutes on end like some moon-eyed idiot.

Aristotle emerged from his office and prowled towards Lucy. Her blood-rate shot up.

'Liar,' he said softly.

Her back straightened. 'Excuse me?'

He came to her desk and rested on his hands over it, looming over her. She fought against shrinking back as his eyes bored into hers. It was making her dizzy after days of only the most cursory eye contact.

He arched one slashing dark brow. 'If that's the case, tell me what Parnassus proposes we do in the final stages of sealing the merger?'

Lucy looked up, spellbound. As if from a long way away her more rational and professional self, the one that wasn't melting into a puddle in her chair, came back. Miraculously, information came into her brain, and she clung onto it like a life-raft.

Unable to break eye contact, and feeling as if her voice had been dipped in rust, Lucy said, 'He…he suggests that the final stages take place in Athens, as that's where the two companies originated one hundred years ago. He thinks it should be there that the merger is finally revealed. He wants it to be a triumphant homecoming to the country he and his family fled from when he was young, and for Athens to be the symbolic and actual birthplace of the greatest merger in Greek shipping and industrial history.'

Silence lengthened and tautened between them. Electric awareness quivered in the air until finally Aristotle just said quietly, 'Good. And I presume you have everything in order for you to travel to Athens for three weeks?'

Lucy just blinked stupidly for a moment as numerous things impacted her brain. Primarily the fact that she hadn't actually considered the fact that *of course* she'd be expected to go to Athens too, in little over a week from now.

All she could say was, 'Yes, I do,' when in actual fact for some reason—even though it had been talked about for weeks—she'd never considered for a moment that she'd be accompanying Aristotle on such a prestigious engagement.

Her lack of foresight mocked her; of course it had to be her, no one else had had access to all the vital and top secret information—information so secret that she'd had to sign a contract the day she'd been hired, forbidding her to divulge any information to anyone. If she committed such an offence it could see her being fired on the spot, and certainly ruined for any future employment within these circles...

The full enormity of the size of this merger and the importance of the man in front of her started to sink in very belatedly. Mortifyingly, Lucy knew that a large part of her distraction had to do with finding herself working for someone who had reached into a secret part of her and shaken her up so much that she had to spend an inordinate amount of time just denying it to herself. Even now, as he still loomed over her, she denied it to herself.

She reassured herself desperately that she was just reacting to Aristotle Levakis' undeniable charisma, like any other red-blooded human being.

With that in mind she took a sheaf of papers that needed filing off her desk and stood up, clutching them to her chest.

It was a blatant attempt to put some distance between them. Aristotle straightened too, and with arms folded surveyed her closely. That treacherous heat pooled within her again, but now she knew what it was she could deflect her own reaction to it.

She hitched up her chin. 'Was there anything else?'

He shook his head slowly and a lazy smile curved his lips. Lucy felt like clinging onto something.

'No, that's all for now.' He turned to go back to his office, but just when Lucy was about to let out a sigh of relief he turned back. With his forearm resting high on the doorjamb, drawing her eye to his long and hard muscled body, he said, 'Don't forget we have that engagement tonight. Be ready to leave at six-thirty. I'll get dressed in my office; you can use the dressing room.'

He disappeared into his own office then, shutting the door behind him, and Lucy all but sagged onto the floor in a heap. She *had* forgotten all about the function they were to attend that night. She cursed herself as she sank down heavily into her chair. What was wrong with her? Forgetting the function, not realising she would have to go to Athens... Her brain was turning to mush. And in this job that was not a luxury she could afford.

How could she have forgotten that terse conversation just days ago, when he'd said to her with a grimace on his face, 'You're going to have to come to the Black and White Ball with me.'

Lucy's belly had clenched. She'd expected that she might have to accompany her boss to some functions, but with Aristotle's extremely healthy social life she hadn't considered it would become a reality so soon. And did he have to look so reluctant at the prospect?

She'd ignored the ridiculous feeling of hurt and asked hopefully, 'But surely there must be someone else...' *anyone else* '...you could call?'

After all, as she'd restrained herself from pointing out, last-minute dates were not something he shied away from. He'd had more than a few since the Honourable Augustine Archer and then the even more Honourable Mirabella Ashton, each one well-documented in the press that gloried in his playboy exploits. And yet the morning after each date he'd appeared taciturn and as irritable as she'd ever seen him.

He'd curtly instructed her to send each night's delectation a disgustingly expensive bunch of flowers. Lucy had cynically assumed that none of the women were performing well enough to hold his interest and merit a piece of jewellery.

It was then that she'd realised that she hadn't arranged a date for him in at least a week. The thought had unsettled her more than she'd liked to admit.

He'd looked at her with narrowed eyes. 'As I am currently partnerless, not that it's any of your business, I've decided that *you* will accompany me. Do you have a problem with that?'

Feeling sick, Lucy had shaken her head rapidly. She had to stop reacting to this man and provoking him. 'No. Not at all. I'll put it in the diary now.'

Lucy came back to the present moment. She was still holding the sheaf of papers clutched to her chest like some kind of shield. She looked at the open diary beside her and there in stark letters was written *'Black and White Ball, Park Lane Hotel. Seven p.m.'* The thought of spending any more time than was absolutely necessary with this man was causing nothing short of sheer panic inside her.

She put down the papers and picked up the phone to make a call to the home where her mother was resident. She asked them to pass on the message that she wouldn't be able to visit that evening.

The matron on the other end said gently, 'I'll pass on the message, Lucy love, but you do know that it won't make any difference, don't you?'

Lucy felt very alone all of a sudden. She swallowed back the ever-present guilt, pain and grief, and nodded even though the other woman couldn't see her. Her voice was thick with emotion. 'I know…but I'd appreciate it all the same, if you don't mind.'

Lucy could hear Aristotle moving around in his own office as she changed in the dressing room. This was a formal event, so she had to wear a long dress, and the one she looked at now in the mirror was perfectly respectable—if completely boring. It was black, which meant it was slimming, and it had a high neck which covered her breasts adequately. Anything that did that was fine with her. And anyway, she told herself stoutly, she wasn't dressing to impress, she was dressing to accompany her boss in a work capacity.

She left her hair up and put on some make-up: mascara and a little blusher. Then, slipping her feet into a pair of plain black high heels, she picked up her weekend bag stuffed with her work clothes and took a deep breath before walking out, feeling ridiculously nervous and hating herself for it.

That breath hitched in her throat and her brain stopped functioning when she saw Aristotle emerge from his own office, resplendent in a traditional tuxedo. The black made him look even darker, and very dangerous. Lucy fought back the wave of awareness, her hands gripping her bag.

He looked up from adjusting his cufflinks then, and the snowy perfection of his shirt made the green of his eyes pop out. He ran quick eyes over Lucy, making her squirm inwardly before quirking a brow and saying mockingly, 'Well, if you're trying to fade into the background it's already working.'

Lucy swallowed past a dry throat. 'I'm your assistant, not your date.'

More's the pity, Aristotle surprised himself with thinking as he took her in, just a few feet away. Although not in that dress. It was basically a sack: a black sack covering her from neck to toe. It might as well have been a burkha for all he could see of her body, and he knew with a hunger that had been growing day by day and minute by minute that he very much wanted to see her body showcased in something much more revealing and *tight*. Like that skirt which had assumed mythic proportions in his fantasies. He beat back an intense surge of desire, in spite of the awful dress, and noted the hectic flush on her cheeks, the wary glitter of her eyes.

She was intriguing him more and more—not only with her luscious curves, but in the way she reacted to him, his spikily quick responses. Every expression was an open book as it crossed her face. She wasn't afraid of him, and that was heady in itself. That she didn't approve of him was glaringly obvious, and it was a novel sensation to have that from a woman.

Aristotle was looking at her far too assessingly. Lucy's belly quivered in response and she told herself sternly that she *wasn't* responding to him; she was just responding to the charisma of the man.

But then he strolled towards her nonchalantly and she had to fight the urge to turn tail and run. He walked around her as if inspecting a horse, and she turned around, unable to bear the thought of him looking at her too-large bottom. She cursed her genes again and felt acutely self-conscious. Why couldn't she be a slim, petite little thing like her mother?

Her voice was high and defensive. 'Is there something wrong? This dress fits perfectly well. It's not too tight, if that's what you're afraid of.' She wouldn't be making *that* mistake again.

Aristotle's eyes flicked to hers. They glittered with something dark and indefinable.

'The dress is fine. For an old lady.'

Lucy sucked in a shocked breath. She'd spent a small

fortune from her allowance on this dress. But before she could say anything he was gesturing to her head.

'It's too late to do anything about the dress, but leave down your hair. You look like you're going to work.'

His normally accentless voice had lapsed into something unmistakably Greek, and it resonated within Lucy. Her mind blanked and her hand went up instinctively in a protective gesture. Her hair was part of her armour, she suddenly realised. No way could she take it down. She might as well just strip off the dress and stand in front of him in her underwear. Treacherous heat licked through her again, making a mockery of her attempts to rationalise it. She shook her head dumbly.

His eyes held hers and he just said quietly, 'Take it down Lucy.' It was so utterly shocking to be standing in front of her boss and have him speak to her like this, that Lucy found herself obeying him. With extreme reluctance she took out the pins from the back. She could feel her hair loosen and fall with annoying and heavily layered predictability around her shoulders and down her back.

Aristotle fisted his hands in his trouser pockets to stop them reaching out to feel the texture of that heavy silky mass of hair. It was darker than he'd originally thought, and luxuriously unruly, reaching down as far as her shoulderblades. He had an image of her reclining back on a sumptuous divan, tendrils of that glorious hair over her shoulders and trailing over her the tops of her bare— *Get a grip, man*! With a supreme effort of will Aristotle reined himself in and said gutturally, 'That's better. *Now* you look as if you're ready for a function. Let's go.'

With an easy and automatic courtesy which surprised Lucy, and she wasn't sure why that was, he took her case from her white-knuckle grip and led the way out of the office. She stumbled as she followed his graceful stride down the corridor to his private lift. She had a moment of dithering, stupidly wondering if she should take the staff lift just a few feet further down, but as if reading her mind *again* Aristotle flicked her an impatient glance and she stepped in.

It was only when they were ensconced in the lift that the memory of the last time she'd shared such a space with him came back in all its glory.

She couldn't help her reaction flowering. Too much had happened since then. Now she stood there, with her hair down, feeling as exposed as if he'd just run his hands over her naked flesh—especially when she recalled his look from moments ago, a look that had to have been some projection of her own awful, twisted feelings. The tall man beside her oozed with sexual heat. She could smell him and feel him. Suddenly she had the strangest sensation of holding something huge back… Wanton images hovered tantalisingly on the periphery of her mind and threatened to burst through, mocking her for a control that was beginning to feel very shaky.

Lucy gritted her jaw and looked resolutely up at the display as the lift seemed to inch downwards, willing it with every fibre of her being to go faster.

The effort it took to stay apart from Lucy in that lift, amidst a rush of memories of how she had felt pressed against him, which once again stunned him with their vividness, washed away Aristotle's last resistance where this woman was concerned. He'd never experienced this level of sexual awareness before, and in truth frustration was a novel sensation when he was so used to getting what he wanted, when he wanted. He didn't stop to question his decision or his motives for a second.

It was quite simple. He had to have this woman in his bed—and as a soon as possible. He would sleep with her. Then she would lose her allure and this bizarre spell she held over him would be broken. In three months he could let her go. Or less, if he got bored. According to her contract he could terminate employment with due notice; she, however, could not walk away unless she wanted to seriously sabotage her career. Because of the top secret nature of the merger she was tied to Levakis Enterprises until the whole thing became public.

Work, which he'd always strictly compartmentalised as separate from pleasure, would become pleasure—*his* pleasure. And Lucy's too. He wanted her with him every inch of the way as he took her again and again to sate this burning ache. Somehow instinctively he knew that one night would not be enough, and it made him uncomfortable to acknowledge it.

Nevertheless, as the lift descended the final few floors, a fizz of anticipation ran through Aristotle's veins and he felt truly alive for the first time in a long time. Even thoughts of the merger were receding into a background place. A dim and distant alarm bell sounded at the back of his mind, but he was too fired up to notice or dwell on it.

The lift juddered softly to a stop and the doors swished open. He stood back and gestured for Lucy to precede him, looking at her carefully as she did so. She was avoiding his eye with all the finesse of a guilty-looking six-year-old caught with her hand in the cookie jar.

She stumbled slightly stepping out of the lift, and Aristotle took her bare silky smooth arm just above the elbow. The frisson of pleasure that went through him nearly made him sway. He could feel the swell of her breast tease his fingers and a primal instinct to possess this woman coursed through him. The fact that she held herself so rigidly at his side didn't put him off. She was as unmistakably his as—for now—he was hers.

A colleague of Aristotle's had just walked away. Lucy watched him go with a feeling of mounting terror. She did not want to be alone with her boss.

They were standing side by side under the seductively soft lighting of the main ballroom in the exclusive London hotel when she heard his drawling query, 'You don't need your glasses? Or are you wearing contacts?'

She nearly choked on her sparkling water and lowered the drink carefully, realising without even making a reflex gesture to check that she had indeed forgotten her glasses. She could picture them right now, sitting on the vanity cabinet in the dressing room of the office. She flushed guiltily and sent a quick, fleeting look to Aristotle. Standing here in this milieu, with his tall, hard body just inches away, was making her nervous. It made her so nervous, in fact, that she didn't stop the truth from spilling out.

'They aren't prescription glasses.'

She saw him frown from the corner of her eyes. 'So why do you wear them?'

He sounded aghast, and Lucy had no doubt that he could not understand why any woman would knowingly want to make herself any less attractive than she already was. A sense of extreme vulnerability washed through her.

She shrugged minutely and avoided his eye. 'I started wearing them when I was looking for work after college.' She squirmed inwardly. How could she explain to this man that she'd grown sick and tired of prospective bosses ogling her sizeable assets rather than her CV? A memory made her shiver with distaste: her first boss, whispering lasciviously on more than one occasion that he liked *big girls*.

Ever since then Lucy had made sure to be covered up at all times, hair pulled back and glasses firmly on. Yet, uncomfortably, she had to acknowledge that she'd found working with Aristotle Levakis something of a relief in that she knew there was no way on this earth a man like him would look twice at her. That assertion suddenly seemed shaky.

As if to compound the feeling, from the corner of her eye

she could see Aristotle turn subtly, so that he had his back to the room full of people. She even saw one person in the act of approaching falter and turn away, as if he'd sent off some silent signal she couldn't see. She couldn't resist sending him another quick look. He had an expression on his face that caught and held her, and she couldn't look away.

His eyes flicked down to her breasts—in exactly the way she'd seen men do all her life, ever since she'd developed out of all proportion in her early teens. But instead of her usual feeling of disgust and invasion, to her shame and horror she could feel herself respond. Her breasts grew heavy, their tips tight and hard. For a cataclysmic moment she actually felt the novel desire to know what it would feel like to have this man touch them. Shock at the sheer physicality of her reaction made her feel clammy.

Aristotle's eyes glittered. A whisper of a smile hovered around his mouth and then he said, 'And did it work?'

Shame and chagrin rushed through Lucy. Was she really so weak? With one look this man was felling all her careful defences like a bowling ball sending skittles flying.

Her voice sounded strangled. 'I found that, yes, it did work.'

Until now.

Lucy felt like a trapped insect, flat on its back and helpless in the face of a looming predator. Determined to negate her disturbing reaction, she looked away and said crisply, 'Plenty of people wear glasses for cosmetic reasons. I would have thought that you'd approve.'

His voice was curt. 'Your CV and your work ethic speak for themselves, Lucy. You don't need to bolster your image by making it more businesslike.'

Too-tight skirts, yes. Glasses, no. Aristotle swallowed a growl of irritation at his wayward mind.

Lucy looked back. She was more than surprised at his easy

commendation of her ability. So far it was only the fact that she hadn't been let go that had given her any indication of how well she was doing her job. She had to fight the urge to cross her hands defensively over her chest, but that was ridiculous. He wouldn't be looking at her like that. He'd just been making a point.

She inclined her head and said, 'Fine. I won't wear them.' She bit back the reflex to say *sir*. The last thing she needed now was for him to repeat his request to call him Aristotle. What she did need was for this evening to be over as soon as possible and to have a whole two days away from this man, to get her head together and clear again. Especially when the prospect of spending three weeks in Athens with him loomed on the horizon like a threatening stormcloud.

A few hours later Lucy breathed a sigh of relief when the car drew to a smooth halt outside her apartment block in south London. She'd tried to insist on taking a cab from the hotel, but Aristotle wouldn't listen. Then she'd tried to insist that he be dropped home first, but again he'd been adamant.

She reached for the door on her side and looked back to say a crisp goodnight. Her ability to speak left her. Aristotle was lounging in the far corner like a huge, dark avenging angel. A surge of panic gripped her and she felt blindly for the door handle, all but scrambling in her haste to get out and away. But just as she opened the door, extending one leg out of the car, the awful sound of ripping material made her heart stop. An ominously cold breeze whistled across the tops of her thighs.

She looked down and her jaw dropped when she saw a huge rip extending down the side of her dress from mid-thigh to hem. Only peripherally was she aware that it must have snagged on something. Her white thighs gleamed up at her in the gloom.

As all this was impacting on her brain, she heard a coolly sardonic, 'You don't seem to have much luck with clothes, do you?'

The sensation of wanting the ground to open up and swallow her whole had never seemed more strong than at that moment. She heard Aristotle say something unintelligible to his driver and then he got out. Lucy couldn't move. She was terrified that if she did something else would rip and her entire dress might fall off. But then Aristotle was standing there, looking down at her with a mocking smile and extending a hand.

With the utmost reluctance she put her hand in his and felt the world tilt crazily as he pulled her up. With her other hand she scrabbled to hold her dress together. Her face felt as red as a traffic light. Aristotle now had a light grip on her arm, and Lucy noticed that he held her bag in his other hand.

That, and the way he was looking at her now, made her feel extremely threatened. *It was the way he'd been looking at her that morning in the office.*

She felt jittery and stiff all at once, and tried to get her arm back.

'It must have caught on something. I'll be fine from here. You must be impatient to get home.'

But Aristotle ignored her and easily steered them towards the path, not letting go for a second. Lucy's blood was starting to fizzle and hum in her veins. She tried again while keeping a desperate clasp on her ruined dress. 'Really, Mr Levakis, my door is just here.'

She even dug her heels in, but he called back to the driver, 'That's all, Julian. You can go. I'll get a cab from here.'

'You're sure, sir?' The driver's surprise was evident in his voice.

'Yes. Goodnight, Julian.'

And with that, before Lucy could formulate a word or acknowledge the escalation of pure mind-numbing panic in her breast, she was being led to her door and Aristotle was looking down at her with his trademark impatience.

'Your keys?'

Lucy spluttered. The driver was pulling away from the kerb, making her even more panicked. 'Mr Levakis, *really*, you don't have to do this. Please. Thank you for the lift, but you shouldn't have let Julian go. You'll never get a cab from here…'

He looked down at her, those green eyes utterly mesmerising. 'I thought I told you to call me Aristotle. Now, your keys? Please.'

Much like earlier, when he'd told her to take down her hair, Lucy found herself obeying. She knew on some dim, rational level that it was just shock. She awkwardly dug her keys out of her handbag, while trying not to let the dress gape open, and watched wordlessly when Aristotle took them and opened the door, leading them into the foyer and to the lift. He looked at her again with a quirked brow and Lucy said faintly, 'Sixth floor.'

As the lift lurched skyward Lucy felt somehow as though she must be dreaming. She'd wake any moment and it would be Monday morning and everything would be back to normal. But then the lift bell pinged loudly and Aristotle, *her boss*, was looking at her again expectantly. She had no choice but to step out and walk to her door a few feet away.

Her brain was refusing to function coherently. She simply could not start to pose the question, even to herself, as to what he was doing here. She turned at her door with a very strong need to make sure she went through it alone and this man stayed outside.

She held out her hand for her keys, which he still held. She couldn't look him in the eye. The bright fluorescence of the lighting was too unforgiving and harsh. Although she knew that it wouldn't dent his appeal.

'Thank you for seeing me safely in.'

'You're not in yet.'

With more panic than genuine irritation Lucy sent him a fulminating glance and grabbed her keys. She opened the door with a hand that was none too steady. She could have wept with relief when the door swung open. She turned back and pasted on a smile.

'There—see? All safe. Now, if you just take a right when you go out, the main road is about a hundred yards up the street. You should be able to get a cab from there.'

CHAPTER THREE

ARISTOTLE leaned nonchalantly against the wall, hands in the pockets of his trousers. At some stage since they'd left the hotel in town he'd undone his bow tie, and it hung rakishly open along with the top buttons of his shirt. Dark whorls of hair were visible, and Lucy felt weak with shock again at his bizarre behaviour. Belatedly she wondered if he might be drunk and she looked at him suspiciously. But then she recalled that, like her, he'd barely touched alcohol all evening. So if he wasn't drunk… Her belly fluttered ominously.

'I thought you said I'd never get a cab from there? Would you let me wander the mean streets of south London alone and defenceless? I can call a cab from your apartment…and I could murder a coffee…'

This man and the word *defenceless* did not belong in the same sentence. He smiled and her world tipped alarmingly for a second. Lucy had to swallow her retort, along with the stomach-churning realisation that she was being subjected to her boss's teasing and charming side. She heard the lift jerking into life again. More people arriving home from a night out. Suddenly she was terrified that it might be her very bubbly but very nosy neighbour Miranda. She could just imagine trying to explain this: a gorgeous, lounging six-foot-four

Greek tycoon in their mildew stained hallway. Her dress was suddenly the least of her worries.

'OK, fine. I'll call you a cab and get you a coffee.'

Lucy walked in and stood back to let Aristotle through. Immediately the air seemed to be sucked out of the room and replaced with his sheer dynamism. Lucy closed her door just as she heard the very drunken-sounding laughter of her neighbour and gave a sigh of relief.

As Aristotle started to prowl around her humble sitting room Lucy spied a lacy bra hanging over the chair nearest the kitchen. She dived for it while he was turned away and hurriedly balled it up. Aristotle turned round and Lucy's belly spasmed.

'Coffee,' she babbled. 'I'll get the coffee on.'

She turned and fled into the small kitchen off the sitting room and stuffed the bra into a cupboard, taking out coffee and setting the kettle to boil. She kept looking surreptitiously into the sitting room. Aristotle was still prowling around. Except now he'd taken off his jacket, and she could see the broad line of his back tapering down into an impossibly lean waist. Her gaze followed the line down over taut buttocks and long, long legs…

The shrill, piercing scream of the kettle made her jump, and she winced when drops of boiling water splashed on clumsy hands. She gathered her dress together and walked back into the sitting room, noticing that Aristotle had put on some lights. Their glow of warmth lent an intimacy to the scene that raised her blood pressure. She had the vague thought of going to get changed out of the dress, but couldn't contemplate the idea of removing a stitch of clothing while he was anywhere near. She noticed then that he was studying a photo in his hand, with a slight frown between those black brows. Lucy was terrified he might recognise the woman in the picture. She handed him the coffee, forcing him to put the picture down and take the cup.

He just gestured with his head. 'Who is that? You and your mother?'

Lucy looked down at the photo in the frame and fought the urge to snatch it out of sight. It was a favourite one of her and her mum, taken in Paris when Lucy had been about twelve. They were wrapped up against the cold, their faces close together, but even from the picture you could tell that Lucy hadn't taken after her mother's delicate red-haired beauty. She'd already been taller than her mother by then.

She nervously adjusted it slightly and replied, 'Yes,' clearly not inviting any more questions.

Aristotle looked at Lucy. She was as nervous and skittish as a foal—avoiding his eye, her hand in a white-knuckle grip on that dress. That was what had pushed him over the edge. Seeing those soft pale thighs exposed to his gaze, one long leg already out of the car. It had taken every ounce of restraint not to reach out and run his hand up the soft inner skin of one gloriously lush thigh.

Especially after an evening that had been a form of torture, trying to focus on work while she'd stood beside him. Following her out of the car and up to this apartment had felt as necessary as breathing. But now he forced himself to take a step back, sensing her extreme nervousness.

She gestured jerkily to a seat. 'Please, sit down while you have your coffee. I'll call a cab. It may take a while to come at this hour.'

Aristotle sat down on a springy couch under the window and watched as Lucy went to the phone on the other side of the room and made the call, turning her back firmly to him. He tried to bank down the intense surge of desire even her back was igniting within him and thought back to the function.

She'd been a surprisingly pleasurable and easy date,

offering intelligently insightful comments on more than one person, showing snippets of dry humour. At one point she'd caught him off-guard entirely, when she'd seamlessly switched to accentless and fluent French. He'd become accustomed to people *saying* they were multi-lingual and meaning they had the basics, like hello and goodbye. Something dark lodged in his chest. He'd also been inordinately aware of the keen male interest she'd generated and how seemingly oblivious she'd been to it. He wasn't used to that.

Fighting the sudden surge of something very primal, he let his eyes drift down over her body and long legs; a vivid image exploded into his head of the moment her dress had split. He wondered how those legs might feel wrapped around his waist as he thrust deeper and deeper into her slick heat. Arousal was immediate and uncomfortable. He shifted on the seat, and even the evident relief in Lucy's voice when she got through to the cab company did little to dampen it.

When Lucy put the phone down, she could finally turn and look her boss in the eye. Escape was imminent. She just had to make some small talk. 'Ten minutes for the cab.' She sat down gratefully in the chair beside the phone, relief making her feel weak. She was still clutching the torn dress over her legs, hanging on to it like a lifeline.

Aristotle leant forward and put down his coffee cup. He had an intense gleam in his green eyes. 'We're going to be spending a lot of time together in Athens.' He looked around her apartment, and then back to her. 'I thought this might be a good opportunity to get to know each other a little better.'

Something treacherously like disappointment rushed through Lucy, but everything within her rejected it. Had she been so blind? Had she truly suspected for a moment that Aristotle had been rushing her up here to try and make love to her? She felt very brittle all of a sudden.

'Of course. I mean, I could…' She racked her brain. Evidently she had to find some way of giving some information to Aristotle, so he didn't feel as if he had to follow her up to her apartment to talk to her. 'I could fill out a questionnaire…?'

He arched a brow.

'A personal questionnaire…if you want to get to know more…about my history.' A leaden weight made her feel heavy inside. She'd become an expert at putting a glamorous spin on her life with her mother. On her history. Glossing over the reality.

But Aristotle was shaking his head and standing up, coming towards her. He came and stood right in front of her, and Lucy realised that she was in a very vulnerable position, her eye level at his crotch. She stood too, so suddenly that she swayed, and Aristotle put out his hands to steady her. They were on her waist. Immediately it was an invasion of her space—especially when she was so self-conscious about her body.

With one hand she tried to knock him away but his hands were immovable. Her other hand was still clinging onto her dress with a death grip. She looked at him and her brain felt hot, fuzzy. He was too close. She could smell his fresh citrusy scent, mixed in with something much more male, elemental. All she could see were his eyes; all she could feel were those hands, like a brand on her body.

He was talking. She tried to concentrate on his words.

'…more along the lines of this…'

And then, as realisation exploded inside her, Aristotle's head was coming down, closer and closer. Everything went dark as his mouth covered hers, warm and firm and so exotic that she couldn't move.

It was so shocking that Lucy continued standing there like a statue. Through her mind ran the comforting words, *You won't feel anything. You're cold inside. You're not your mother.*

You don't react to this. You don't crave men...sex... You've proved this to yourself...

But, as if disconnected from her mind, a radiating heat was taking over, spreading upwards from a very secret part of her. A core she'd never acknowledged before. A core that had never been touched.

Aristotle was pulling her closer. Those big hands were still around her waist, spanning it now, fingers digging into soft, yielding flesh. He was warm and firm, and as he brought her flush against his body she realised just how hard he was. How tall, and how strong. He was huge, and she had the distinct impression for the first time in her life of being...somehow delicate. No one had ever made her feel like that.

He moved one of his hands upwards from her waist, skimming close to her breast which tingled in reaction, the peak tightening almost painfully. But then he speared that hand through her hair, around the back of her head, angling her towards him more. She was aware of the rush of disappointment that his hand hadn't lingered, cupped the weight of her breast.

His mouth was insistent, but something inside Lucy was like ice amidst the heat, still protecting her from fully feeling. It was a wall of defence she'd erected over a long time...and yet even as she thought that she suddenly visualised that defence crumbling.

As sensation got stronger, igniting an alien urgency, panic surged. Aristotle could have no idea of what was happening inside her, how cataclysmic her reaction was, but at that moment he took his head away and looked down into her wide eyes. Somewhere Lucy was dimly aware that she wasn't pushing him away...which she could. But she felt so heavy, so deliciously lethargic, and she couldn't think when he was so close and looking deep into her eyes like this.

He said gutturally, 'Lucy...I can feel you holding back. You're shaking with it.'

And then she became aware that she *was* shaking—like a leaf, all over. Reality exploded around her. She was in her boss's arms and he was kissing her! The feelings rippling through her were intense to the point of overwhelming her completely, more intoxicating than anything she'd ever experienced, or thought she could experience. With that thought sanity tried to break through: she didn't respond to kissing in this way. And yet...she was.

Aristotle chose that moment to kiss her again, and Lucy was caught between two worlds, defenceless and vulnerable, conflicting desires whirling in her head, making her dizzy. Making her weak against this far too seductive attack on her senses. One hand was curled against Aristotle's chest, and as his mouth moved over hers once again her fingers unfurled, like the petals of a flower opening to the sun. When his tongue traced along the seam of her tightly closed mouth the sensation made her open her lips minutely, some dark and distant part of her wanting this, wanting to experience this, and Aristotle took immediate advantage, opening her mouth, forcing her to accept him. And to respond.

When his tongue-tip touched hers it set off a chain reaction in her body. Suddenly she was *feeling* for the first time, and it was too strong to resist—like a flash-flood carrying her downstream. She moved closer to Aristotle's body and felt his growl of approval. His tongue stabbed deep, exploring and coaxing hers to touch and taste. The hand at her waist brought her even closer, and the evidence of his arousal pressing into her soft belly elicited a deep craving feeling not of disgust, but of desire to experience *union*.

Her fingers tangled in surprisingly silky hair; she could feel her back arch wantonly towards him. He shaped the indent of her waist and hips and Lucy didn't feel self-conscious, she felt exultant. When his hands moved to cup her buttocks and pull her even tighter into the cradle of his lap her breath caught.

Aristotle tore his mouth away and looked down at her. Their bodies were still plastered together. Their breath came swift and uneven, and he didn't take his eyes off hers as he reached one hand down between them and found where her hand was still tightly clenched over the rent sides of the dress. He loosened her fingers and, helpless, Lucy could only look deep into his glittering eyes as she felt the dress fall apart and his hand smooth up over her thigh, then between her legs, climbing higher and higher.

He was looking at her. His eyes were on her…studying her. While his hand—

'You're so beautiful. Why do you hide yourself away, Lucy?'

It wasn't his hand climbing to such an intimate place but his words that broke her out of her sensual stasis: *so beautiful…*

She wasn't beautiful. She'd heard those words a million times before. Not directed at her—never at her. But at someone else. Someone who had craved them; someone who had spent her life being defined by men's opinion of her.

The shock of everything suddenly hit her, and made Lucy jerk back violently, knocking his hand away and pulling her dress together again. She had the mortifying image in her head of wantonly pressing as close as she could, and the shame of her reaction to that made her feel nauseous. Between her legs she throbbed and tingled.

Her voice was shaking and thin, too high. 'This is completely inappropriate. I'm your *assistant*.'

Aristotle's face was uncharacteristically flushed. 'You're also the one woman I can't stop thinking about and wanting. And it's a bit late to put on the injured virgin act.'

He raked a hand through his hair in frustration, leaving it gorgeously unruly.

Lucy shook her head in rejection of that, trying to ignore the way her mouth felt so full and plump. She felt anything but virginal right now. In a few seconds he'd managed to blast to smithereens the knowledge that she'd comforted herself with ever since she *had* lost her virginity: she was frigid.

'No. I'm your assistant. This is not possible.' More shame rushed through her as she said, 'If you think I gave you some indication that I might welcome…' She couldn't even say it. 'You're just…bored or something. You can't possibly—'

'Can't I?' he interrupted harshly. He stood with hands fisted at his sides and glowered at her. 'I saw you changing the other morning and I felt like a schoolboy watching a naked woman for the first time. No woman has ever reduced me to that. And you want me too, Lucy. You've just shown me that.'

Embarrassment washed through her in a wave of heat. He *had* seen her. She'd known it…but to hear him confirm it nearly made her mind short-circuit. And along with the embarrassment came another feeling, one of illicit pleasure, when she remembered seeing his face. She shook her head again, even fiercer this time, both hands clutching the dress.

Just at that moment the phone rang shrilly. Lucy jumped. She was starting to shake; reaction was setting in. 'That's the taxi. Get out right now.' When he didn't move she said, *'Please.'*

Aristotle finally strode over to pick up his coat and, flinging it over one shoulder, he walked to the door. He looked back at her for a long moment, hugely imposing and dark in her plain little apartment. Men like him weren't meant for scenes like this, she thought.

The phone had stopped, but now started again.

'I'll see you on Monday, Lucy. This isn't over—not by a long shot.'

And then he was gone. Lucy stood stock still and could barely breathe. When the phone impacted upon her consciousness again she went over and picked it up. 'He's on his way down,' she said.

When she was certain he had gone, Lucy undressed and had a steaming hot shower, thinking perhaps it might eradicate the painfully intense feelings Aristotle had aroused in her when he'd touched her and looked at her. She dressed in her oldest and comfiest pyjamas and made herself a hot chocolate, dislodging the bra she'd hurriedly hidden as she did so from the cupboard. Heat rose upwards again, but she resolutely ignored it and went into the sitting room and sank onto the couch, cradling the hot cup in cold hands.

She reached up and took down the photo of her and her mother and tears filled her eyes as emotion surged upwards. She felt incredibly raw after what had just happened.

Her mother had been diagnosed with early onset Alzheimer's two years ago. It had come on the back of her growing ever more forgetful and irritable, prone to mood swings and dramatics. It had been so unlike her usually sanguine mother that Lucy had insisted she go to be checked out by a doctor. They'd run some tests, and as soon as a diagnosis had been made her mother's condition had worsened by the day—almost as if naming it had allowed it to take hold completely.

At first Lucy had been able to look after her in their small townhouse near Holland Park, but when she'd come home one day to find her mother wailing inconsolably in a flooded kitchen, with all the gas rings of the cooker on and alight and no idea how or why she'd done it, Lucy had known she couldn't fight it on her own any more.

She'd started with home help—the cost of which had rapidly eaten up all their savings. Her mother had never worried about money too much beyond making sure Lucy was provided for, and there had invariably been a new rich lover more than happy to provide. However, in recent years Lucy's mother had been coming to terms with the harsh realities of aging in a world where youth and beauty were a more potent draw to powerful men. The protection of rich lovers had all but disappeared.

Lucy's mouth compressed as her finger ran over her mother's image in the picture. She supposed in the nineteenth century her mother might have been considered one of the most famous courtesans of her time. But in this lifetime she'd been a famous and much sought after burlesque dancer—a true artist. Lucy's mouth tightened even more; her mother had simply got used to the attention of very rich, very powerful men.

She'd craved the control she'd had over them—her ability to reduce them to ardent lovers, desperate to please her in any way they could. Her allure and beauty had been legendary. Her powerful lovers had funded their lives, and unwittingly helped put Lucy through the best schools all over the world. She couldn't denigrate her mother's memory now by judging her over where that money had come from. Her mother had simply used all the tools at her disposal to survive.

Her father had been one of those men. When he'd found out Maxine was pregnant and refusing to give up her baby, he'd paid some maintenance but hadn't wanted anything to do with Lucy. When Lucy was sixteen he'd died, and maintenance had stopped abruptly—because of course he hadn't told his family about her.

What had upset Lucy more than anything else was the lack of confidence and self-esteem her mother had suffered that only she, as her daughter, had been privy to. While on the one hand her mother had been in control, using those men as they used her, on another, much more vulnerable level she had craved their affection and approval. She'd used her beauty to enthral her lovers, but she'd been broken in two every time they'd walked away, leaving behind nothing but costly gems, clothes—*things*.

It had been shortly after finding her mother so distraught in the flooded kitchen that Lucy had discovered the house they'd lived in—a generous present from another lover—had never been signed over to her mother, despite assurances at the time. The man was a prominent politician who'd just died. Lucy's mother's solicitor had advised that Lucy should not contest ownership of the house when the family had discovered its existence, as obviously they had no idea of their father's secret affair. The family had debts to clear on the death of their father, and Lucy had had no option but to let the house go. The precariousness of their situation had forged within Lucy a deep desire for order and her own financial independence.

About a year ago they'd moved into her current small apartment. Lucy had still hoped that home help would be enough, but the cost of it had barely left her with enough to buy food at the end of each week. Her job at Levakis Enterprises was the only thing that kept them afloat. And now with her increase in wages, it was the only thing giving her mum the opportunity to have decent care.

Lucy stared unseeingly down at the picture, and suddenly an image broke through—Aristotle standing right here in this room, holding her close, his hand between her legs. She could remember the way she'd throbbed and burned for that hand to go even higher, to where she ached. *To where she still ached.* Lucy shifted so violently in reaction that the picture fell from her lap to the wooden floor and the glass smashed in the frame. With a cry of dismay she put down her cup and picked it up carefully. As she did so, something hard solidified in her chest.

She knew exactly how to handle this situation, how to

handle Aristotle Levakis and make sure everything returned to normal. She couldn't contemplate how her decision would impact her mother just yet. All she knew was that she had to protect herself—because she'd never felt under such threat in her life. She would make sure her mother was safe and cared for. *She would.* She just couldn't do it like this.

On Monday morning, early, Ari stood at the window of his huge office, with its commanding view out over the city of London and all its impressive spires and rooftops. From the moment he'd been placed in charge of Levakis Enterprises at the age of twenty-seven, on the death of his father five years previously, he'd moved the power centre of the business here to London, his adopted home.

He'd told himself it was for strategic reasons, and certainly the business had thrived and grown exponentially since he'd moved it here, but it was also a very distinct gesture from him to his family, to say *he* was in control, not them. They'd shunned him enough over the years. No way was he going to play happy families back in Athens. And while he had left the original office there, which his half-brother now oversaw, they all knew that it was just a symbolic front for the business. Ari controlled its beating heart, and it lay here, under the grey and rain-soaked skies of London.

But today his main focus was not on business; it was on something much more personal and closer to home. On something so exquisitely feminine and alluring that he didn't know how he'd managed to control himself for the past weekend and not go back to that small dingy apartment, knock down the door and take Lucy hard and fast, before she could draw up that *faux* injured virgin response again. He could still feel the imprint of every womanly curve as he'd held her close to his body. She'd been more lusciously voluptuous than any fantasy he could have had.

His hands were clenched to fists deep in his pockets now, and his jaw was gritted hard against the unwelcome surging of desire. His assistant was causing him frustration of the most strategic kind.

She wanted him. And he couldn't understand where her reticence came from. No woman was reticent with him; he saw, he desired, he took. It was quite simple and always had been. An alien and uncomfortable feeling nagged him as he acknowledged the dominant feeling he'd had the other night. He'd felt *ruthless* as he'd coaxed and cajoled a response from Lucy. When she'd finally capitulated, even for that brief moment, it had been a sweeter conquest than any victory he could remember. He didn't usually associate ruthlessness with women—that was reserved for business—and the fact that such a base emotion was spilling over into his personal life was—

Ari heard a noise come from the outer office—Lucy's office—and his body tensed with a frisson of anticipation, all previous thoughts scattered to the winds.

He wanted Lucy Proctor and she would pay for making him desire her by giving herself up to him, wholly and without reservation, until he was sated and could move back into the circles in which he belonged. He vowed this now, as he heard a sharp knock on his door, and waited for a moment before turning around, schooling his features and saying with quiet, yet forceful emphasis, 'Come.'

Lucy took a deep breath outside the heavy oak door. As soon as she heard that deeply autocratic *'Come'* her nerves jangled and her heart started racing. Just before she opened the door, her hand clammy and slippy on the round knob, she prayed that the make-up she'd put on that morning would hide the dark circles under her eyes. She hadn't slept a wink all weekend.

Steeling herself like never before, she opened the door and stepped in. Aristotle was standing with his hands in his pockets and his back to the huge window. Waves of virile masculinity seemed to radiate from him and Lucy's throat went dry. For an awful second her mind seemed to go blank and be replaced with nothing but heat…but as her hand clenched on the envelope she gave an inward sigh of relief and reminded herself that she'd soon be out of this man's disturbing orbit.

She walked further into the office and tried to ignore the way Aristotle's narrowed gaze on her was making her even more nervous. She came to a halt just a few feet from the desk.

She cleared her throat. 'Sir, I…' Heat washed into her face. 'That is…Aristotle…' She stopped. She was already a gibbering wreck.

'I thought I told you there was no need for you to wear your glasses.'

Lucy's hand went reflexively to touch the sturdy frames. She cursed herself for having told him she didn't need them, and bristled at his high-handed manner. The sharp edge of the envelope reassured her.

'Well, I feel more comfortable wearing them. The fact is that—'

'Well, I don't.' He was curt, abrupt. 'You work for *me*, and I don't want to see them again. And you can also stop tying your hair back as if you're doing some kind of religious penance.'

Lucy gasped. She could feel the colour washing out of her face, only to be swiftly replaced by mortified heat.

Knowing that she had nothing to lose, she didn't curb her tongue, but her voice when it came was slightly strangled. 'Is there anything else you'd like to comment on while you're at it?'

Aristotle leaned back against the window and negligently crossed one ankle over the other, crossed his arms over that formidable chest. His eyes took on a slumberous quality that made Lucy's breath falter and a tight coil of sensation burn down low in her belly.

'Have you thrown out that skirt yet?'

Lucy's hands clenched. She didn't feel the edges of the envelope any more, or remember what she was here to do. Right now she was being subjected to the lazy appraisal of a man who, she told herself, was just like every other man who had traipsed in and out of her mother's life. The fact that her predominant emotion wasn't the anger she'd expected made her feel very vulnerable.

'It's none of your business where that blasted skirt is. You can rest assured that you won't have to be subjected to seeing me wear it again, because I'm here to—'

'That's a pity.'

Lucy's mouth was still open on the unfinished part of her sentence. She blinked as his words sank in. She shook her head. She had to have misheard. Distracted, and hating herself for it, she asked, 'What did you say?'

He stood then, and even though he didn't come towards her she took a step back.

'I said, that's a pity. You'd be surprised how much of my mental energy that skirt has been taking up. I think I may have been too hasty in my judgement of it.'

Lucy shook her head again and could feel herself trembling inwardly. She felt as if she were in some twilight zone. What about the Augustine Archers of the world, impeccably groomed to within an inch of their skinny designer lives? Surely he couldn't really mean that he preferred...? Her mind shut down at that, but the words slipped out and she watched herself as if from a distance as she said faintly, 'But...it was just a high street skirt that shrank in the wash. I didn't have time to get a new one. You thought it was inappropriate enough to have me taken to task for it.'

'That was a mistake.' His eyes flicked down over her body, and Lucy's flesh tingled as if he'd touched her. Even though she wore perfectly fitting and respectable trousers, a high-necked shirt and a jacket, she felt undressed.

When his eyes rose to meet hers again she registered the dangerous gleam in their depths. The bubble of unreality burst. Self-preservation was back. The envelope. She held it out now, with a none too steady hand.

Aristotle looked from her face down to it and then back up. He arched an enquiring brow.

Lucy stammered, 'It's—it's my letter…of resignation.'

Ari's hands clenched. Something surged through his body—a primal need not to let this woman go. No way was she walking out of here. That ruthless feeling was back.

He shook his head. 'No, it's not.'

'Yes, it is,' Lucy replied automatically, a little perplexed.

'No. It's not.'

Anger started to lick upwards as it dawned on Lucy that this wasn't going to be the quick result she'd hoped for.

'Yes, Mr Levakis, it is. Please accept my resignation with the grace with which it's tendered.' She held out the envelope further. 'I am not available for…extra services outside work, and your behaviour the other night was not acceptable.'

Lucy's eyes had turned to a dark slate-grey and they were flashing. There was a resolute tilt to her chin. Ari marvelled that he hadn't noticed it before now, but this woman had passion oozing from every pore of her tightly held body. She had backbone. Far from fading into the background, as he'd so misguidedly believed her to have done from day one, she'd been there under his nose the whole time. He could see now that her appeal had been working on him subliminally, bringing him to the point he had now reached: the point of no return, unless this woman was with him.

Ari moved around the desk and perched on the edge, arms

still folded. When he saw Lucy's eyes flick betrayingly down to his thighs he smiled inwardly, and smiled even more when he saw a flush stain her cheeks. *How* had he ever thought of her as plain or unassuming? He ignored her outstretched hand and the white envelope.

Lucy refused to show how intimidated she was by moving back, but she wanted to—desperately. Her breath was coming in shallow bursts. She felt as if she wanted to reach up and undo the top button of her blouse.

Aristotle cocked his head and asked enquiringly, with a small frown, 'Now, exactly what part of the other night would you say was not acceptable?' He answered himself. 'The part where I escorted you safely to your door? Or perhaps the part where I accepted the coffee you made me?'

Lucy's other hand balled into a fist and she bit out, 'You know exactly what I'm talking about.'

His face cleared, the frown disappeared and he said, 'Ah! You mean the part where I proved just how mutual our attraction is?'

CHAPTER FOUR

LUCY flushed even hotter, mortified heat drenching her in an upward sweep. Much to her utter humiliation she knew it wasn't *all* mortification. Some of it was pure...*thrill*. This man was doing nothing short of creating a nuclear reaction within her, comprehensively threatening everything she'd protected herself with for years.

She dropped her outstretched hand without even realising what she was doing and shook her head, finally taking a step back, pretending she wasn't as affected as she was as if her life depended on it.

'You mean the part where you mauled me? That wasn't mutual attraction.'

Immediately he tensed, and his eyes flashed dangerously. Lucy swallowed. She knew she'd just said the worst thing possible. Most bosses in this situation would sense the potential danger of having a sexual harassment suit landed against them and back off. But Aristotle Levakis was not most bosses, and Lucy guessed belatedly that no woman, *ever*, had accused him of mauling them. Certainly her dreams over the weekend hadn't been of someone mauling her—quite the opposite, in fact.

Aristotle stood to his full height, power and pure sexual charisma bouncing off him in affronted waves. He arched a brow, his arms still folded tightly across his chest, the biceps of his arms bunching even through the material of his silk shirt.

'*Mauled*?' he repeated softly, dangerously.

Lucy swallowed again, her throat suddenly as dry as parchment. She nodded, but felt herself curling up inside with humiliation.

Aristotle came and stood very close Lucy had to tip her head back and look up. She clenched her jaw. He was looking down at her with an expressionless face, those light green eyes glittering. Dark slashes of colour highlighted his cheekbones. He was livid, she recognised, and a flutter of fear came low in her belly, along with another flutter of something much more dangerous.

He started to walk around her. Lucy held herself rigid.

From behind her she heard him say, 'When I put my hands on your waist you didn't stop me or push me away.'

'I—' She began, but stopped as the memory of his hands on her waist speared through her. How his fingers had dug into her soft flesh. How she'd wanted them to dig harder.

'Then, when I kissed you, you also didn't pull away.' His voice was low and sultry. 'I know when a woman is enjoying being kissed, *moro mou*, believe me.'

He was still behind her, and Lucy was finding it increasingly difficult to concentrate. His voice was so hypnotic, resonating with something that pulled on her insides and left her weak.

'I…I…didn't like it.'

'Liar.' It came so softly from close behind her head that she jumped minutely, her skin breaking into goosebumps.

He moved to her side. Lucy fought against closing her eyes and wondered dimly why she just didn't walk away, but she knew on some level that she was afraid if she moved she might fall down. She stayed rigid.

'You did like it…when my tongue touched yours…when you let me explore the sweetness of that mouth. Did I tell you that I'm fascinated by the gap in your teeth? Right now all I want to do is kiss you again until you're so boneless in my arms that all I'd have to do is carry you to the couch over there…'

Lucy's breath had stopped. Her brain had certainly stopped functioning. The couch was in her peripheral vision, and Aristotle was right in front of her again. For a big man, he moved as silently as a panther.

She closed her eyes in a childish gesture to block him out, but quickly realised what a mistake that was when he continued, 'I'd lay you down and remove those glasses and let your hair out of its tight confinement…'

At that moment Lucy's head throbbed unmercifully, as if in league with him.

'Then I'd start to undo your buttons, one by one, but I probably wouldn't be able to resist kissing you again, coaxing you to bite down on me too, so you could feel how I might taste.'

The sensation of what it might be like to bite into the sensual curve of his lower lip was shockingly vivid. Lucy was starting to quiver badly now. Her eyes still closed tight, she felt hot and flushed all over, and between her legs… Her mind seized.

'Stop…' she said threadily. 'Please…'

'But you see you wouldn't want me to stop, as your shirt fell apart, baring those gorgeous breasts to my gaze… Is the lace of your bra chafing you now, Lucy? Are your nipples tight and tingling? Aching for my touch? Aching for my mouth? I would take those peaks and suck them into my mouth, hard, until they're aroused to the point of pain. And then I'd cover your body with mine, so that you could feel how turned-on I am. *Even right now* I'd lift up your leg and let my hand slide over the silk of your stocking, all the way to the soft pale flesh of your thigh. You'd be moaning softly, willing my hand even higher, to that secret place between your legs where you're aching for me to find the silk of your pants drenched with desire. You'd beg for me to slide them aside so that I could feel for myself—'

'Stop!' Lucy's eyes flew open and in an instant she was jerking away—only realising at the last second that he wasn't even holding her. He held up his hands to prove the point. Her breath was coming in short, shallow gasps, her breasts felt heavy, their tips tight and tingling, exactly as he'd described, and between her legs seemed to burn a molten pool of something dangerous and unwelcome… It was that that had finally woken her out of this awful, *delicious* dream.

But it wasn't delicious—it *wasn't*, she told herself desperately as she looked anywhere but at Aristotle. She felt disorientated, dizzy, as if she could almost believe she *had* been on that couch. Her upper lip felt moist. Her hands clenched and she realised that she no longer held the envelope. In that instant she saw that it was in one of his hands and he was ripping it in two.

She put out a hand. 'Wait! What are you doing?'

Lucy also realised, along with everything else in that moment, that contrary to her own state of near collapse Aristotle looked cool, calm and collected—a million miles away from the man who had been just whispering in her ear how *aroused* he was. She was a quivering wreck and he hadn't even touched her.

His cool voice cut through her like a knife as she watched him turn on his heel and walk back around his desk. 'I'm putting this letter of resignation where it belongs—in the bin.' And he promptly did just that.

Lucy was a mess, still reeling from the way his voice and words had affected her, and how utterly unaffected he clearly was. He was sitting behind his desk now, for all the world as if nothing had just happened, and as if he was waiting for her to sit and take notes.

'Mr Levakis—'

His voice was curt. 'We've been through this before. I told you to call me Aristotle. I don't want to tell you again.'

Lucy all but exploded. 'I am resigning. There is nothing you can do or say to stop me. I will not stay and be subjected to the kind of treatment you just…just subjected me to.'

Aristotle was looking down, flicking through papers, and he said easily, 'Lucy, I didn't even have to touch you to turn you on, so when the time comes and I do touch you for real can you imagine how good it's going to be? Why would you deny yourself that?'

For a million and one good reasons! Lucy saw red spots dance before her eyes. His words had impacted upon her so deep, and in a place so visceral, she nearly screamed with frustration. But she swallowed it down and said, as coolly and calmly as she could, 'It's clear that your arrogance is clouding your ability to assimilate this information. Perhaps it'll become more clear once I've gone. I can send you another copy of my resignation. Good day, Mr Levakis.'

She turned on her heel and was almost at the door when she heard him, deadly soft. 'If you walk through that door, Lucy Proctor, you'll be hearing from my lawyers within the hour.'

Lucy stopped in her tracks, her hand still in the act of reaching for the doorknob. She turned around slowly and saw that hard green gaze spearing her on the spot. Her stomach felt as if she was in freefall off a huge cliff.

'What are you talking about?' But dread was already trickling through her as her professional brain went into overdrive and she had a sickening memory of signing that other contract along with the one for her job. She really hadn't thought this through with her usual clear rationality at all.

'Well, for a start, you're obliged to give me at least four weeks' notice, as per your standard work contract, and if you leave before the merger is completed you'll be sued. It's quite simple.'

*And utterly devastating...*Lucy realised with mounting horror.

He sat back in his chair. 'We leave for Athens in a week. You know far too much, and have been privy to all the top secret discussions. Quite apart from that, if you left now you'd be leaving me without an assistant for the most important joining between two Greek companies in years. That is something I will not allow to happen. If it means I have to threaten you with legal action to get you to stay then so be it. I won't hesitate to use the full force of my power.'

He sat forward then, and he had never looked so intimidating. 'Lucy, I don't think I need to tell you that your career would be comprehensively ruined if you insist on leaving. You could be crippled financially for years.'

Lucy wasn't sure how she remained standing. She'd known all this—she'd *known*. She'd been smart enough to read the fine print of both contracts, and at the time it had given her a sense of security to know that Levakis wouldn't be able to turn around and get rid of her at a moment's notice. It was what had given her the confidence to put her mum in that home— the confidence to go to the bank and take out a loan which would assure her mother's place in that home for at least a year. Lucy had known that as long as she could keep up the payments everything would be secure for the short term, and hopefully for the long-term future.

But now...if she walked out of here and incurred Aristotle Levakis' wrath she'd be kissing all that goodbye. She could well imagine the loan from the bank being called in. Losing her job would quickly mean that she'd have no source of income with which to pay for her mum's accommodation. She'd be back to square one, becoming the primary carer, and without a job that would be impossible.

She said now, in a small voice, 'You would do that...' It wasn't a question.

'Without a doubt,' he answered grimly. 'This merger and this company are too important to me. They are everything.'

So what am, I then? Lucy wondered a little wildly. Just a convenient plaything because you happen to be bored with all the usual sycophants?

He stood again then, but Lucy was in too much shock and distress to move as he came closer, hands in his pockets. He looked smug. He knew he had her effectively trapped. Suddenly she longed to have no responsibilities, so she could just disappear. But she did, and she couldn't.

He stopped a few feet away and looked at her. Her world had been reduced to this room, this man and those eyes. And that voice.

'Lucy, I don't want to be ruthless about this, and I certainly don't relish the thought of taking action against you. I want the merger, yes, and I'll do whatever I need to to protect it and make it happen. But I also want *you*, and I will do whatever I need to in order to make that happen too.'

Lucy shook her head dumbly, even now fighting. It made something in Aristotle's eyes flash dangerously. She had thought that someone like him would give up when faced with obstinate resistance, although that assertion was now fast losing ground. She had to acknowledge that he'd most likely rarely, if ever, faced resistance from any woman.

'You've made it quite clear that it is impossible for me to leave.'

That was the understatement of the year. Her conscience mocked her. She should have realised all this at the weekend, but he'd had her head in such a tizzy all she'd been able to think of was getting away from him. She realised now that if she had thought it through she could have done her best to keep him at arm's length for the duration of the merger and *then* given her notice—instead of these dramatics, which were so unlike her.

'I'll stay for the merger and then I'll be giving you my notice.'

She would just have to worry about her mother when that happened. She hated the fact that she wasn't strong enough to try and stay and resist this man indefinitely.

Aristotle just looked at her for a long, heated moment. Lucy saw a muscle throb in his temple and it made her insides quiver like jelly. He reached out a hand and cupped her jaw. Shock and instant heat paralysed her at his touch.

'Say what you want, Lucy, if it makes you feel better, but know this: we *will* be lovers. It's as inevitable as the inclement English weather. There's something raw and singularly powerful between us and I've no intention of letting you go—either in the boardroom or in the bedroom.'

Lucy swallowed painfully. His hand still cupped her jaw, his thumb moving lazily against the sensitive skin under her chin. One thing was certain: if, in some parallel universe, she actually gave in to this man, she had no doubt that far from being given the luxury of giving notice *he'd* be the one saying goodbye—and so fast that her head would be spinning. Something like four weeks' notice would be reduced to a mocking sham of a professional nicety.

She hated the fact that it was the thought of *that* right now that made her feel more vulnerable than even the prospect of the battle to come. One other thing was sure: with every bone and last breath in her body she would resist the seduction of this man. Yet, she had to ask herself inwardly, for someone who prided herself on being frigid, why did it suddenly seem like such an uphill struggle?

A week later.

Lucy sat opposite Aristotle on his private jet as it winged its way to Athens from a stormy London. She could almost believe for a moment that she'd imagined what had happened in his office last week, when he'd declared so implacably that he was determined to have her in his bed.

Since that day when she'd been so firmly put back in her place, her letter of resignation torn up, Aristotle had been utterly consumed with business and preparations for the merger. They'd worked late into the night almost every night, and she'd been in the office most mornings as the cleaners were still finishing up. She'd never been so tired, yet so contentedly exhausted. Despite her trepidation at the undercurrents flowing under the surface, professionally speaking she'd never worked at such a heady pace, nor been entrusted with so much responsibility. The sense of pitting her wits against Aristotle and keeping up with him was exhilarating. She blocked out the snide voice that mocked her with the assertion that *work* was the only exhilarating thing.

Thankfully she hadn't had time for much more than falling into bed, snatching some food, and getting up again. The weekend had been a blur of last-minute visits to the office, packing, and a bittersweet visit to her mum, before she'd been collected by Aristotle's driver that Sunday afternoon. The visit to her mother had been bittersweet because she'd had one of her brief lucid moments, recognising Lucy as soon she'd walked into the private room at the home.

'Lucy, darling!'

Lucy had had to swallow back a lump as she'd watched her

still beautifully elegant mother rise out of her chair by the window to greet her with her usual warm and tactile affection. Lucy had missed it so much. On Maxine's good days, and obviously this was one, she took care of her appearance. On her bad days Lucy would come in and, if not for the care of the attentive staff, her mother could look as unkempt as a bag lady. It made her heart ache with sadness as her mother had always been so fastidious about her looks.

Lucy had been careful not to let the emotion overwhelm her; these moments of lucidity were growing further and further apart, and she'd have her mother with her for only ten minutes before the inevitable decline came. The sentences would stop and falter, her eyes grow opaque, until finally she'd come to look at Lucy with a completely blank expression and say, 'I'm sorry, dear, who are you?'

It broke Lucy's heart to know that there was no point in even trying to explain where she was going, or that she was going to be out of the country for a few weeks. At least she could give thanks for the sterling round-the-clock care she could now afford. It made her attempt to resign from her job seem all the more childishly impetuous now. How could she jeopardise her mother's security? And yet how could she keep working for Aristotle once this merger was completed?

'*Lucy.*'

Lucy's head jerked round from where she'd been looking out of the window at the sea far below. Aristotle must have called her a couple of times; she could hear impatience lacing his voice. He was looking at her sternly, and at that moment Lucy realised how little space was between them—just a small table. Even as she thought that she felt Aristotle flex a leg and it brushed hers. She froze, all that heat and awareness rushing back, mocking her for believing it might have disappeared under a pile of work.

'I'm sorry. I was just thinking about something.'

He quirked a brow. 'Something more interesting than me? Or this merger? Not possible, surely.'

Lucy froze even more, she couldn't handle Aristotle when he was being like this…flirty. Yet with a steel edge. She couldn't imagine him ever being truly light, free and easy. Smiling. He was too driven, intense.

She smiled brittlely, determined that he shouldn't see his effect. 'Of course not. How could I?'

At that moment the steward arrived to serve them lunch. Lucy automatically went to clear the table and her hands brushed against Aristotle's. She flinched back but tried to mask her reaction, a flush rising up over her chest. It would appear their tenuous 'work truce' had ended. Tension was a tight cord between them.

Lucy studied her food, a delicious-looking Greek salad and fresh crusty bread.

'Would you like some wine?'

She looked up to automatically shake her head. Wine on a plane with this man was a recipe for disaster.

'Some water will be fine, thanks.'

She watched as Aristotle's lean dark hand elegantly poured himself wine, and then water for her. She muttered thanks and took a deep gulp, hoping it might dampen the flames that were licking inside her.

They ate companionably in silence. It was one of the things that perplexed her about this man. They had moments like this when she could almost imagine that they might be *friends*. She'd noticed in general that he didn't feel the need to fill silences with inane chatter, and neither did she. It surprised her to find that in common. In all honesty, if it wasn't for the great hulking elephant in the room, Lucy had to admit that so far she'd enjoyed working for Aristotle and admired his work ethic.

She was finishing her final mouthful of salad when she

sensed him leaning back in his chair. She could feel the brush of his leg against hers again and fought not to move it aside. She was aware of his regard and it made her self-conscious.

'You really don't approve of me, Lucy, do you?'

She looked up, surprised. It was the last thing she would have imagined hearing him say. She gulped and wiped her mouth with a napkin, a flare of guilt assailing her.

'I…I don't think one way or the other. I'm here as your assistant, not to form a personal opinion.' She wondered wildly what had brought this on.

He folded his arms across his chest, supremely at ease.

'I've seen those little looks you dart at me—those little looks that have me all summed up. And when I asked you to send a gift to Augustine Archer, you most certainly didn't approve of that.'

Lucy was so tense now she thought she might crack. 'Like I said before…it's not my place to judge—'

'And yet you do,' he inserted silkily.

Lucy's face flamed. Yes, she did. She had him wrapped up, parcelled and boxed as being exactly like the men she'd seen court her mother, and no matter how she'd seen him treat women, the inherently unfair judgement of that made her feel unaccountably guilty all of a sudden.

It goaded her into saying, 'All right. Fine. I don't think it was particularly professional of you to ask me to send a parting gift to your mistress. It's not my business, it made me uncomfortable, and I felt that it crossed the boundaries.' *Not to mention that it made me feel angry and disappointed too.* But Lucy held her tongue. She couldn't go that far, and those revelations made her feel far too vulnerable.

She felt as prim as a mother superior, and couldn't look Aristotle in the eye, sure he had to be laughing his head off at her.

'You're right. I won't ask you to do that again.'

She looked at him in shock. His face wasn't creased in hilarity, it was stone cold sober.

'To be honest, Lucy, I did it to get a reaction out of you…and you gave it to me.'

She frowned and shook her head minutely. 'But why?'

He shrugged one broad shoulder nonchalantly, not at all put out to be discussing this, his gaze on hers not wavering for a second. 'Because I sensed something about you, under the surface…' His gaze dropped to where she could feel her breasts rising and falling with her breath. He looked back up and her heart stopped. 'And I suddenly realised that you were causing me an inordinate amount of…frustration.' His mouth tightened. 'I blamed you for the fact that it had become necessary to say goodbye to a perfectly good mistress.'

His words caused little short of an explosion of reaction within Lucy. She tried desperately to block it out—the realisation that even then—Her brain froze at that implication. Her hands clenched tight on the table and she hid them on her lap.

'Look, Aristotle…' She knew she was all but begging. 'I've already told you, I'm not interested in anything…like that. Really, I'm not. If I've given you that impression I'm really sorry.'

His eyes flashed and he leaned forward, hands on the table, starkly brown against the surface. 'Don't patronise me. You give me that impression every time you look at me. It's there right now. You're desperately aware of where my leg is—how close it is to yours under this table—'

'Stop it,' Lucy all but cried out. 'Don't do that words thing again.' She wouldn't be able to handle it.

Triumph lit Aristotle's eyes. 'See? You want me, Lucy. I can smell it from here. But don't worry. I'm not some lecherous boss who is going to force you into some compromising position. You'll come to me. It's just a matter of time before we see how long you can hold out against it.'

Between Lucy's thighs she felt indecently damp. She coloured even more hotly. Could he really smell that? Did desire have a smell? And since when had she admitted it *was* desire and not just sheer banal human reaction? The thought made her squirm, but also made her feel weak and achy. She scrambled out of her seat. She had to get away.

As she pushed past his chair he snaked out a hand and caught her wrist. She looked down, and he was looking right up at her, trapping her. She watched as he took her wrist and brought it to his mouth. He pressed his lips against the sensitive skin on the underside. And then she felt his tongue flick out to taste her there, right against her pulse. With a strangled cry that spoke more of desire than disgust, she yanked her hand away and ran, aiming for the toilet at the back, his mocking chuckle following her all the way. Any complacency she'd felt in the past week was blown sky-high to smithereens. He'd just been biding his time.

She locked herself in with shaking hands and looked at herself in the small, unforgiving mirror. She had to fatally and finally accept the knowledge that she desired this man. It wasn't just his indisputable charisma, it was *him*. And his effect on *her*. She wanted him with a hunger that she'd always intellectualised as something she'd never experience. Except now she was. And it was ten million times worse than anything she could have ever imagined.

This was nothing short of catastrophic when she'd happily devoted herself to a life that had promised to offer up only the sort of passion she could handle. Safe, staid, unexciting. She hadn't committed herself to being celibate—she did hope to one day meet someone and settle down, perhaps even have children—but at no point had she ever hoped for the kind of fulfilment that was a deep throbbing ache within her right now.

She'd unconsciously left her hair loose, and now she

bundled it up again, tight, digging out some hairpins from her pocket to hold it in place. Then she searched for and found the comforting frames of her glasses. She'd kept them close by but hadn't worn them all week, as she'd been genuinely afraid of what Aristotle might do, but now she needed to send him a message once and for all. Lucy Proctor was not available and not interested. And never would be. If she told herself that enough, she might actually believe it.

Even though Aristotle might be laughing at Lucy's reaction, his body most certainly wasn't laughing. His body had never felt so serious and intent on one thing: carnal satisfaction, and with that woman. He burned from head to toe with it. The past week had been pure torture. They'd worked in such close proximity that it had taken all of his strength and will-power not to sweep aside the paperwork, throw her across his desk and take her there and then.

The only thing holding him back—apart from the very real need to prepare for the merger, and it irked him that that hadn't been enough—had been Lucy's own reaction. Any other woman, knowing that he desired her would have happily laid herself bare for his delectation. But not Lucy. She'd avoided his eye—she'd avoided *him* at all costs. She'd scurried out every night and been there quietly, studiously working every morning. Buttoned up and covered up to within an inch of her life in shapeless boxy suits.

It inflamed him and perplexed him. He'd genuinely never had to deal with this before. But what it was doing was raising the stakes, and raising his blood pressure. He was too proud to force her, even though he knew she wasn't far from tipping over the edge, but damned if he'd do it.

No, she would come to him, just as he'd declared. When she was weak with longing and stir crazy with desire she'd come to him, and this build-up would finally explode in a blaze of mutual satisfaction. He heard the bathroom door click open behind him and shifted in his seat to ease the constriction of his trousers. He picked up some work papers resignedly and it chafed—because he was not a man used to *resigning* himself to things.

For now, though, he'd use work to drown out his clamouring pulse. He would not let her see the roiling waves of frustration that gripped him and tossed him like a tiny boat in a thundering storm. When she came and sat down opposite him, and that sensual womanly smell that was so at odds with her prim appearance teased his nostrils and made his arousal even more acute, he almost groaned.

He looked up for a second. Predictably, she was looking down, immersed in papers. He saw what she'd done to her hair and the firmly reinstated glasses. He felt a surge of adrenalin and thought to himself, *Fine, if that's the way you want it.*

He pulled out his laptop and fired off a curt but informative e-mail to his assistant in Athens, instructing her to have everything ready by the time they landed in two hours. For someone with his wealth and resources, what he'd just asked for shouldn't be hard to pull off, and as he sat back he realised with a jolt that once again he felt more alive than he'd done in months.

The fact that the merger was once again relegated to second place raised just the dimmest clanging bell in his consciousness.

CHAPTER FIVE

A FEW hours later, Lucy sat on the bed of a palatial suite in one of the most expensive hotels in Athens. She'd never seen such opulence and luxury in her life. Everyone here seemed to talk in hushed tones. She'd even found herself almost whispering *thank you* to the concierge who'd shown her to her room.

Her mouth quirked dryly. Needless to say, the manager himself had shown Aristotle to *his* room. She'd seen that they were more or less next door to each other, he in the Royal Suite and she in a smaller adjoining one, although she had no intention of using the interconnecting door that had been pointed out to her. She was already far too close to her boss for comfort.

Feeling antsy, she got up and wandered about the room for a bit, looking out of the window, taking in the view of Syntagma Square and its elegant lines and trees. She hadn't expected Athens to be so…elegant. She'd seen the Acropolis in the distance and felt a lurch of joy; even though she'd travelled extensively due to her peripatetic childhood, she never tired of seeing famous monuments.

Her thoughts went inward. She hadn't failed to notice that the closer they'd got to Athens, the more tense Aristotle had grown—until by the time they'd been walking through the airport, his hand tight on her elbow, he'd been positively radioactive. She knew it had nothing to do with her. She suspected it had something to do with the way that, whenever he had to deal with his stepmother or half-brother, he always seemed to go inwards and become monosyllabic. Clearly there was no love lost between him and his family or his ancestral home, and it made Lucy wonder about that—before she realised what she was doing and put a halt to her wayward thoughts.

She checked her watch. They were due to have informal drinks with Parnassus and his team in one hour and she had to wash and change, but there was still no sign of her luggage. Lucy called down to Reception, and what the girl said made her frown.

'I'm sorry? You say my clothes are here? But I'm still waiting for my case.'

The hotel receptionist's tone was smooth, as if she was used to dealing with recalcitrant hotel guests. 'I think if you check your wardrobe, Miss Proctor you'll find everything hanging up and ready for your use. The chest of drawers is also full.'

Lucy thanked her faintly and put the phone down. She knew that Aristotle's wealth could just about do anything, but surely it couldn't magically conjure up her suitcase, unpack and store all her clothes without her even noticing? With a snaking feeling of *something* slithering down her spine, Lucy threw open the ornate door of the wardrobe in the corner and gasped.

It was full, heaving with a myriad assortment of every piece of clothing any one woman could possibly hope for. Day-wear, casual wear, evening-wear. Lucy flicked past dresses and suits and trousers and shirts and wraps and capes, feeling more and more dizzy as she did so. All sorts of shoes were lined up below the hanging clothes.

She backed away from the wardrobe with something like horror in her chest, and went to open the drawers of the chest beside the wardrobe. She pulled out T-shirts, shorts, casual trousers, capri pants… They all fell from nerveless fingers. There was thousands of euros' worth of clothes in front of her and not one stitch was hers. A deeply scooped-neck T-shirt fell from her hands and she looked at it and shuddered at the thought of how much cleavage *that* would expose. Suddenly realisation struck. *Aristotle.*

Without thinking, galvanised by pure anger, she marched over to that adjoining door between their rooms and yanked it open. To her surprise his own door was already open, leading into a room that made her own opulent one look like a prefab.

He strolled out at that moment from what she presumed must be his bedroom, naked except for a small towel around lean hips. All Lucy could see was a magnificently bronzed muscled chest, a light smattering of dark hair and long, long muscled legs. His hair was wet and slicked back, making him look somehow more approachable, vulnerable.

Seeing him like this completely scrambled her brain and defused her anger.

'I…' She realised she was breathing hard.

He stopped and looked at her enquiringly, and then she watched him lift his wrist to look at the heavy platinum watch.

'A little longer than I thought it might take, but still…not bad.'

It took a few precious seconds for what he said to sink in. He'd planned this. He'd orchestrated this and had been waiting for her to react exactly as she had. Sheer fury and impotence rushed through Lucy in a wave so strong she shook.

'Where is my case, please?'

Aristotle folded his arms and that was worse—because where his shirt might have hidden those biceps, now she could see them in all their olive-skinned, bunched glory. Lord, but he was beautiful, and her body was reacting like the Road Runner, seeing his mate in the distance.

'Your case is somewhere safe. I've taken the liberty of removing the items I think you'll need, like your toiletries. I didn't want to presume to know what products you like to use.'

'Yet you can presume to know what clothes I may like and my size?' Her voice fairly crackled with ice.

His gaze drifted down over her body, and she cursed herself for inciting him. His eyes met hers again and he drawled, 'I think you'll find that everything…fits.'

She cursed him under her breath. She wouldn't be surprised to find them all a size too small, and if they were…

But he wasn't finished. 'I also decided that from what I've seen you're more than capable of choosing your own underwear. You'll find the items I've taken out there, in that bag.'

He gestured to a table nearby, where one of the hotel bags was sitting, a lacy bra strap dangling provocatively from the top. Blind rage and humiliation at the thought he'd handled her intimate clothes, and at remembering that he'd seen her changing, almost made Lucy stumble as she stalked over to get it. But in that instant she vowed she would not react as he was expecting her to. She would not give him the satisfaction.

So she merely walked back to the door, turned and, avoiding his eye, said grimly, 'I'll see you in the lobby in forty-five minutes.'

'I'm looking forward to it, Lucy.'

It took an awful lot of restraint not to slam both interconnecting doors as Lucy went back into her own room, but under a steaming hot shower minutes later she vented her anger with no holds barred.

* * *

Some forty-five minutes later Lucy paced in the lobby and in-effectually tried to pull the dress down again. It felt indecently short, even though it came to just above her knees. She hated the fact that otherwise it fitted like a glove. And she'd never worn shoes with heels so spiky they looked like a lethal weapon, but it had been them or flat shoes, and even *she* had enough fashion pride not to make a complete fool of herself. She also hated the fact that they made her feel some-how…powerful. She couldn't say the word *sexy*. Her brain seized at the mere nebulous thought.

Aristotle watched Lucy from behind a plant for a moment, feeling curiously protective—and something else: surprised at her obvious reluctance to embrace her innate sexiness, es-pecially when she oozed such voluptuous femininity. She'd chosen one of the least revealing dresses, but even that made his blood boil over with lust.

It had a high neck but, unlike her other sack of a dress, this one was cut to define a woman's body, to hug and emphasise its curves. When she turned to the side he had to draw in a breath. Her breasts were so beautifully shaped and enticingly full that he noticed more than one man falter as he saw her.

That galvanised Aristotle to move. Possessiveness was an alien emotion, but it was coursing through him now as he took in the way the dress drew the eye to those stupendously long and slender legs, a discreet slit showcasing their shapeliness. And those shoes…

Lucy turned away abruptly. She'd noticed a man nearly tripping over himself as he'd seen her and she flushed with mortification. He probably thought she was a call girl. She felt like one. This was ridiculous. She was going to demand her own things back—

Suddenly Aristotle was right in front of her and, as was becoming annoyingly familiar, her brain emptied of all rational thought. He was dressed in a black suit, white shirt and royal blue tie. It somehow made his eyes pop out, even though they were a dark slumberous green. But weren't they normally light green? As Lucy was wondering this, as if it had become the most important question in the universe, Aristotle moved so fast that she didn't even notice until he'd whipped her glasses off her face and removed the pins from her hair.

'Hey!' she cried out, too late, only to see him calmly snap her glasses in two and feel the heavy fall of her hair around her shoulders. He took her by the arm and marched her out towards the entrance, handing her broken glasses and hairpins to an unsurprised-looking doorman, who took them obsequiously, clearly not fazed by such behaviour. It made Lucy even madder. Those glasses had been her last bastion of defence and he'd merely ripped it away, like removing a toy from a cranky child.

She barely noticed the pleasantly warm early evening air caressing her skin between the hotel and the luxury car. When they were ensconced in the back, Aristotle curtly ordered the driver to put up the privacy partition, which he duly did. Lucy's mouth was opening and closing ineffectually, steam practically coming out of her ears as Aristotle rounded on her, blocking out any daylight coming through the tinted windows. Absurdly, in that split second Lucy thought how unbearably intimate it seemed to make the space.

'Enough,' he growled out, and before she knew which end was up Aristotle had reached out, hauled her into his chest and his mouth was over hers. He was kissing her as if his life depended on it, one arm like steel across her back, one hand in her hair, clasping her head. There was no hesitation. Lust exploded in a blaze of heat.

All of Lucy's reflex denials melted away in a flame of desire so profound and deep that she couldn't question it. All she knew was that Aristotle's mouth was on hers, his tongue stabbing deep, with ruthless precision, and she was *craving* it. Her breasts were crushed against his chest, her hands trapped against those hard contours, and the beat of his heart was an unsteady tattoo that made her own beat faster.

She forced her hands free to twine them around Aristotle's neck, fingers pushing upwards into the thick, silky hair that brushed his collar. He groaned deep in his throat, their mouths not parting for a moment, lost in a dark, lustrous world of tasting and touching, of sensation heaping on top of sensation so acutely delicious that when Lucy felt herself being lowered back onto the seat behind her, and Aristotle coming over her, she too gave a deep moan of approval.

All she knew was here and now. Sanity had ceased to exist.

The outside world? Gone.

This was her world, and this man was the only thing in it. His huge hard body crushed hers to the seat beneath her, but her arms were free and she explored and spread them under his jacket to feel the latent strength of his broad shoulders.

His mouth left hers to blaze a trail of hot kisses along her jaw and down her throat, where he nipped gently and then sucked, making her squirm as an arrow of pure lust shot to her groin, making her wet.

As if he'd read her mind, she felt his hand encircle her ankle and start to travel up her leg. He breathed into her mouth, 'Remember what I said the other day?'

Words couldn't impinge upon her mind in this drenching of desire. Lucy couldn't function. She was finding it hard to open her eyes, finding it hard to breathe as she looked up and drowned in dark green oceans. She didn't recognise the man above her. The expression on his face was so raw and elemental. All she knew was that he looked exactly how she felt. Her breasts were tight and aching, tips chafing against the confining bra and dress. And slowly, so slowly, his hand was climbing with relentless precision, until its heat was wrapped around her upper thigh, where her sheer stockings ended. His fingers spread wide to encompass as much as he could touch. Any second now they'd be on her bare skin. She stopped breathing in earnest.

'Please…' Was that voice hers? Who was she anyway? She was suffering from temporary amnesia. Somewhere distant, where a bell was ringing, she felt something wanting to intrude, but more than that she wanted *this*. It felt so right and so necessary. Too right to question.

'Please… *Ari*…'

With a muffled groan of something that sounded Greek and almost painful, he lowered his head, took her mouth again. Their tongues connected feverishly just as his hand hovered and tantalised at the tender place of her soft inner thigh, on the edge of her silk pants. Lucy tore her mouth away and arched herself towards him, gripping his shoulders. She could feel the heavy stabbing weight of his erection against her leg and she moved experimentally, exulting in his answering growl of unmistakable torture.

And then he was *there*, fingers pushing aside the barrier of her pants to slide into hot slickness, where she ached most. She sucked in a breath, shocked eyes opening wide. She looked up and his fingers began to move, finding the secret spot and pressing it, flicking it. Blood roared into Lucy's head, drowning out everything but the clamour for satisfaction which was coming towards her like the mirage of an oasis in the desert.

And then suddenly, as quickly as this insanity had taken over, it was gone. Aristotle was taking away his hand, moving back, his features harsh and unbearably tight. Cold seeped into Lucy as she realised where she was. She was supine on the back seat of a car, her legs spread, and her boss had just been—

Oh God.

She also realised what Aristotle had realised way before her: they had stopped, obviously at their destination, and the driver was patiently knocking on the privacy window. They hadn't heard him because—

Oh God.

More shame and mortification and self-disgust than she could ever remember feeling coursed through Lucy in a tidal wave of heat so intense she felt feverish. She scrambled to sit up, hands shaking as she pulled her dress down to cover her thighs.

A large brown hand came over hers, and she had to stop herself flinching back.

'OK?'

The huskily asked question surprised her. *It was almost as if he really cared.* But she couldn't look at him, just nodded jerkily, a curtain of hair hiding her face from view. She could give thanks for once that it was down. She didn't think she could ever look at him ever again. In the split seconds they had as they gathered themselves and she heard Aristotle— *Ari*—speak to the driver, Lucy tried to assimilate what had just happened.

The fact that she'd all but drowned in an instantaneous pool of lust in his arms was evident enough. She'd deal with that in a darkened room on her own later. But it was the fact that it had happened without hesitation, with not even a flicker of rejection or desire to draw back. Was it simply because after weeks of denying this to herself, weeks of this desire building and building, the merest touch had sent her up in flames and she'd been unable to draw up even the flimsiest of defences? She'd turned into a complete wanton.

When Aristotle climbed out of the car, and Lucy readied herself to step out too, she realised that any vulnerability she'd felt before had paled into pathetic insignificance. The truth swirled sickeningly in her breast. She truly was her mother's daughter, and that knowledge jeered her for all her efforts to deny it for so long.

There was no going back now, not after that little performance, and she quaked when she saw the huge looming shape materialise on the other side of the door. That everything she feared most lay outside that door right now was obvious, and also the fact that she'd just kissed goodbye to any pretence of a defence she might dream up to excuse her behaviour. The door opened abruptly and Lucy was compelled to step out, taking the hand that was offered and forcing down the frisson of electricity at even that innocuous touch. She felt as though the entire world had changed, and suddenly her place in it.

It was while they were standing alone for a moment, in the luxurious salon of the palatial Parnassus villa on the outskirts of Athens, that Lucy felt Aristotle turn towards her. She closed her eyes momentarily and pleaded silently, *Please don't look at me...please don't say anything.* But since when were her prayers answered? She opened her eyes and gritted her jaw.

Aristotle looked down at Lucy and felt completely out of his depth. He still couldn't quite believe what had happened in the back of his car. He'd never, *ever* been so consumed with lust like that—that he'd laid a woman down in the back seat and all but made love to her there and then. When he thought of it now, of how close he'd been to unzipping his fly—his hand clenched around his drink and he had to force it to unclench.

Lucy hadn't looked at him since she'd stepped out of the car and he couldn't blame her. What was it he'd said? That he wouldn't be a lecherous boss? And then within seconds of getting into an enclosed space... But she'd been so responsive, dammit. Like his most potent dream, his hottest fantasy. She'd been hot, willing, passionate...*wet* for him. His body tightened again. She'd shown him the woman she was hiding under all that primness.

It was hard to equate the woman who'd paled at seeing her bra strap hanging out of a bag earlier to the woman who'd almost come apart in his arms less than a couple of hours ago.

'Lucy?'

He could see her grit her jaw, and it was only then that he noticed the faint pink mark on her neck. Shock coursed through him—and self-disgust. He'd given her a love bite? The last time he'd given a woman a love bite it had been a *girl*, and in a boarding school in England, probably at the age of thirteen. All of a sudden Aristotle felt anger for what this woman was reducing him to.

He took her arm and tried to ignore the way her skin felt, tried to ignore the way he wanted to caress it, tried to ignore the way she looked almost green.

'Lucy, look at me.'

With the utmost reluctance Lucy turned her head and looked up, willing her reaction far down. She even pasted a smile on her face. 'Yes?'

Aristotle looked angry. 'Lucy…' He sighed with exasperation and ran his other hand through his hair, leaving it to flop back in such sexy disarray that Lucy felt her knees tremble.

'I had no intention of kissing you like that, and I'm sorry. It shouldn't have happened—'

'No, it shouldn't.'

His eyes narrowed dangerously. He turned so that the room was blocked out and it was just the two of them facing each other.

'That's not what I meant. I was going to say it shouldn't have happened *like that.*'

'Well, it shouldn't have happened at all.'

Aristotle's brow went up. Lucy hated that brow.

'Are you going to try and tell me that you didn't like it? Or that I was mauling you again? What was it you called me? *Ari*?'

'Stop it,' Lucy hissed, a crimson tide washing into her face when she remembered that passionate entreaty, how easily it had fallen from her lips. 'Of course I'm not going to say…that. But it shouldn't have happened, and it's not going to happen again.'

Aristotle moved closer, and Lucy realised that she couldn't move back as there was a plant behind her. His heat and that innately musky scent came and wrapped itself around her, binding her into the memory of what had happened, making longing rush through her. And she hated it.

Aristotle's face was a harsh mask of self-recrimination as he said, 'It *will* be happening again, Lucy—just not in the back seat of a car. Somewhere infinitely more comfortable, where we won't be constricted by space and hampered by clothes.'

Just then someone approached, and Aristotle smoothly turned to deal with the newcomer, stunning Lucy with his ability to morph from intensely demanding alpha male to urbane businessman. And for the rest of the evening, as she accompanied him around the room, meeting and greeting the people involved in the Parnassus side of the merger, she could almost be forgiven for thinking she'd imagined the whole thing.

While they were in Athens Lucy was to be Aristotle's executive assistant. She'd met Martha, his Greek PA, a pleasant older lady who she'd spoken to on the phone before. She met them at the hotel earlier. *She* was going to deal with the day-to-day office stuff. Martha wasn't aware of the merger. In fact none of his family seemed to be—something which had perplexed Lucy.

Mr Parnassus approached them now, distracting her from her thoughts. He and Aristotle had already gone to his study for a private meeting as soon as they'd arrived. Now this old and stooped man, who walked with a cane, looked Lucy up and down with a wink. They'd been introduced earlier.

He said to Aristotle, 'Well, Ari, do you think we can trust her?'

Aristotle's voice was deep and authoritative. 'Absolutely. She's been with my firm for over two years now.'

As they continued to converse, Lucy decided that she liked Parnassus. He had a friendly twinkle in his eye. Suddenly he declared that Aristotle should go and mingle so that he could 'take this beautiful young woman outside for a turn around the patio'.

At a pointed look from her boss that Lucy couldn't really fathom, she gave her arm to Parnassus and led the way outside. It was night and the sky was clear, stars twinkling over a commanding view down into Athens. Momentarily relieved to be out of Aristotle's disturbing orbit, Lucy breathed in. 'It's so beautiful here. You have a lovely home, Mr Parnassus.'

'Please, call me Georgios.'

Lucy smiled. 'Very well. Georgios.'

He looked at her with shrewd eyes. 'He must trust you very much. This merger is very important. Not even his own family know about it.'

Lucy's belly clenched painfully. It wasn't so much about trust as necessity and desire, but of course she couldn't explain that. She frowned slightly. 'I'm aware of that.' She didn't want to say more. She didn't know Aristotle's reasons for not divulging this to his family, and she knew the only reason they were here in Athens was because Parnassus had requested it.

'He's driven.'

Lucy was lost in her thoughts for a moment. She almost didn't hear what the man said. But he was continuing, looking down at the view laid out before them.

'He reminds me of myself when I was his age.' Parnassus

smiled, but it seemed sad. 'He reminds me of my own son. In exile. Driven to succeed at all costs. And for what?'

Lucy was nonplussed. Parnassus caught her look and chuckled. 'I'm sorry—you don't want to hear an old man's ramblings. We should go back inside.'

She put out a hand. 'Oh, not at all… I just… I don't know Ar—' She blushed. 'That is, I don't know Mr Levakis all that well.'

Parnassus stalled and looked at her closely. He gestured with an arm to encompass the view and the villa. 'See all this?'

Lucy nodded and sat back against the balustrade, captivated by this wizened man, by his deeply ingrained accent which he obviously hadn't lost despite living in the US for decades.

'It's taken me years to build it up. My family left this country in shame, and all I've ever wanted was to come back in a blaze of glory.'

Lucy frowned. 'But…that's what you're doing with this merger, isn't it?'

He shrugged one bony shoulder. '*Ack*. In some ways. It's not how I imagined it, even though I'll get what *I* want for my children, whether they want it or not: re-introduction and acceptance into Athens society. But the ultimate glory will belong to that man in there, and he's welcome to it.'

They both looked to where Aristotle stood, surrounded by a fawning crowd. Lucy shivered slightly despite the treacherous heat curling down low in her abdomen. He reminded her of a lone wolf. Head and shoulders above everyone else, supremely confident, supremely sexy and yet…*alone*. She hadn't really thought of him like that before, and didn't like the tender feelings it aroused.

At that moment a very glamorous-looking middle-aged woman came out to the terrace. Parnassus introduced her as his wife, bade Lucy goodnight and went back inside. Lucy turned to face the view again, her mind full of questions. She wrapped her arms around herself, feeling a sudden cool breeze. What did Parnassus mean about Aristotle? Did he somehow see him heading for an empty life, driven by a need to succeed? Clearly he wasn't far wrong. Aristotle had said himself that this merger was the most important thing, and yet—

She jumped when she felt a warm blanket of heat settle around her shoulders and heard a deep, 'We should get going. We've got a busy day tomorrow.'

His jacket was warm with his body heat and scent. It enveloped Lucy, making her sway a little as they went back in. She didn't say a word. Every nerve was twanging at the thought of sharing a car with him again, and her head was bursting with all the enigmatic questions Parnassus had posed.

But she needn't have worried. Aristotle couldn't have made it clearer he had no intention of touching her. Lucy sat in her corner and watched as they were driven down the hill towards the city centre. Feeling somehow compelled, she turned to face Aristotle and asked, 'Don't you have a family home here?'

She sensed him tensing, but he just said, without looking at her, 'Yes, it was my father's home, but I prefer to stay in a hotel.'

And then, before Lucy could halt her runaway mouth, she heard herself asking, 'Why don't your family know about the merger?'

His head whipped around so fast that she nearly flinched back. The lines in his face were stark. 'What makes you ask that?' The thread of warning was explicit.

Lucy shrugged. 'I just…wondered.'

'None of them are aware,' he said curtly. 'And I've already told you they must not know. As far as they're concerned I'm here for three weeks to check up on the Athens side of the business.'

Lucy's jaw clenched. 'I know all that, and of course I won't be telling them anything. I'm well aware of the terms of my *contract.*'

She turned her head away, stunned to feel a welling of emotion and discover that she had sudden tears stinging the backs of her eyes. What on earth was *that* about?

When she felt her hand being taken by a much larger, warmer one, her heart tripped. She looked around warily. She couldn't really see Aristotle's face in the dark gloom.

He sounded weary all of a sudden. 'Look, it's complicated, OK? It's family stuff between them and me and they just don't need to know. It's for security reasons…'

'That's all you had to say.' Lucy took her hand from his and took off his jacket, handing it back to him. 'I'm warm enough now, thanks.'

Boss/assistant. The lines of demarcation were unmistakable. Aristotle cursed himself again for having lost control earlier. In all honesty the depth of that desire still shook him up. He took the jacket and watched as she turned her head to look out of the window again. The curve of her cheekbone, the fall of her hair was an enticing temptation to turn her face back, seek out those warm lips, sink into her yielding soft body again.

He swore under his breath. He'd vowed he wouldn't take her like some randy over-sexed teenager, but here he was mentally stripping her, moments away from trying to seduce her all over again. He sat rigid in his seat the whole way back to the hotel. *Never* had a woman caused him this much frustration.

When they got back to the hotel Lucy skittered away from him like a scared foal. He let her go, bidding her goodnight, then went into the bar and ordered himself a shot of whisky. It was going to be a long three weeks.

* * *

Towards the end of that first week, Lucy half heard a question from Aristotle as they sat in his office in the centre of Athens. In essence they were conducting separate lives: presenting a benign face to his Athens-based company, and conducting top secret meetings with Parnassus at the same time. The meetings with Parnassus' side were complicated and technical, calling on all of Lucy's skills and much of the small amount of legal training she'd done.

She'd met his stepmother Helen and half-brother Anatolios, at a general board meeting that morning. The stepmother was tall and thin and cold, effortlessly supercilious. His half-brother was nothing like Aristotle. He was blond, shorter and had a spoilt, weak-looking face. It hadn't taken Lucy much to deduce that his brother had a serious jealousy complex as he'd frowned sulkily throughout the meeting, clearly hating having Aristotle back to remind everyone who the *real* boss was. After meeting them, she didn't entirely blame Aristotle for wanting to keep his distance.

'…to put in an appearance at the charity ball tonight.'

Lucy realised she was being spoken to and looked up. 'I'm sorry…?'

Her voice drifted away as she was caught by the gleam in Aristotle's eyes. They were sitting close together, side by side at a table, with papers strewn everywhere. For the whole week, ever since the night they'd arrived and that earth-shattering moment in the car, she'd been rigid with tension, happily throwing herself into work to try and escape from dealing with…*this*.

But it hummed around them now, this awareness. She'd been so careful not to let it catch her unawares, but she had failed in this instance. And in all honesty she knew that it was largely to do with Aristotle's own restraint. He'd been cool and solicitous all week. Not a hint of what had happened in his behaviour. At first it had thrown her, she'd been absurdly suspicious, but now… She realised it had been there all along. She knew it and he knew it, and much to her utter shame a flutter of dark excitement erupted deep in her belly.

She tried to ignore it. 'I'm sorry—what did you say?'

Aristotle looked at her and stifled a groan. Her eyes were huge pools of swirling grey, like a stormy ocean, with lashes so long and dark he could already imagine them fluttering against his cheek. *How* he'd managed not to touch her all week he couldn't really fathom. It had taken super-human restraint, but he'd been determined to prove to himself that she didn't exert that much control over him. Except it had been an exercise in failure, because she did. His mind had constantly been taken from business.

It didn't help that because of the wardrobe he'd provided, which was perfectly respectable, she was unwittingly displaying more of her luscious body. He knew she was deliberately choosing the most *un*revealing clothes, but conversely they were making him want to unwrap her like a delicious parcel.

At the board meeting earlier, when he'd seen his own half-brother's eyes riveted to Lucy's cleavage, he'd wanted to reach across the table and punch him in the face. Being driven to violence by a woman was a very novel experience, and he had to put it down to sexual frustration.

He cleared his throat and dragged his eyes back up, vowing silently to himself that he'd have her in his bed within twenty-four hours. He couldn't take much more of this.

'The charity ball tonight. Everyone will be there—including Parnassus. Needless to say it'll be seen entirely as a co-incidence that we're there too. When we meet any of his people we'll affect no knowledge of having met before.'

Lucy had seen the extent of the security detail that both Aristotle and Parnassus commanded, so there had been no chance of a leak. Again the size and importance of what they were working on stunned her.

She asked abruptly, '*Why* is it so important that nobody knows of this, exactly?'

Aristotle's mouth thinned. 'Because our two companies merging will put a lot of noses out of joint. We'll effectively be blowing any competition out of the water; the only companies who will remain safe are the ones who are huge enough to withstand the pressure—people like Kouros Shipping, for instance.'

Lucy nodded, she'd heard of Alexandros Kouros. 'But…your family?'

His eyes flashed at her persistence, but he answered tightly, 'My stepmother and brother would oppose this absolutely. Helen would see it as a dilution of my father's name and a threat to her security. If my brother had even an inkling of this happening he'd do his best to derail it just to get at me. That's why we have to be vigilant. And they'll be at the ball tonight too.' His mouth twisted. 'Although I wouldn't worry about *him* too much—no doubt he'll be more concerned about scoring the best drugs and the best women.'

Lucy hid her shock at this evidence of little love lost. She quashed her immediate questions. She had no desire to know about Aristotle's family history. None at all.

CHAPTER SIX

THAT evening, after they'd eaten a sumptuous dinner, Lucy found herself separated from Aristotle. She was feeling almost relaxed, which she knew had something to do with the fact that she'd been seated apart from him, even though she'd felt the weight of his gaze from across the table, periodically.

She'd been seated next to Kallie Kouros, the wife of Alexandros Kouros, who'd proved to be down to earth and utterly charming, giving Lucy hilarious tidbits of information about Athenian society. When her gorgeous husband had come to whisk her away they'd looked so in love, and he'd been so innately protective, it had made a very secret part of Lucy ache... It surprised her, as she'd never found herself envious of happy couples before.

Lucy craned her neck to try and find Aristotle, not even sure why she felt compelled to do so when he was clearly only too happy to leave her to her own devices. Finally she saw him across the room, with his head bent towards a very blonde and very beautiful woman. She saw him smile and it impacted her deeply. He'd never smiled at *her* like that. *Yes, he did*, reminded a little voice. *That night outside your apartment.*

Immediately she could feel her blood cooling, the colour draining from her face. A strange falling feeling made her feel shaky all of a sudden. On a complete reflex, to deny her reaction and the fact that it might possibly be stemming from feeling *jealous*, she whirled around and made blindly for the ladies room.

After collecting herself she went to the sink and splashed some cold water on her face. When she stood up again she nearly jumped out of her skin to see Helen Levakis, Aristotle's stepmother standing beside her, reapplying her blood-red lipstick.

She looked at Lucy and said, 'Lizzie, wasn't it?'

Lucy shook her head, fascinated by this woman's brittle shell. 'Lucy.'

The woman smiled insincerely. 'My apologies. Ari seems to have a new assistant every time he comes home.'

Lucy washed her hands briskly. 'It's no problem.'

Helen Levakis turned and rested back against the ledge. 'You're sleeping with him, aren't you? I saw that little look outside, when you saw him with another woman.'

Lucy tried and knew she was probably failing to keep the shock from her face. This woman had stuck a knife right into the tender heart of her, and to realise that was huge.

She found her voice. 'Excuse me, but I really don't think it's any of your—'

'You're right,' the woman dismissed cuttingly. 'However, I thought I'd do you a favour. Ari may *sleep* with a woman like you, but he'll never marry a woman like you. That's more than likely why he's home. He'll be looking for a suitable bride soon. A man like him? He'll want to have an heir to secure his inheritance. He'll do anything to stop his brother getting what's rightfully his.'

Lucy watched the tall thin woman disappear back out into the bustling throng with a last glacial glance. She turned to face the mirror, realised that she was holding her breath and let it out in a big whoosh. What on earth had precipitated that? And what did she mean about his brother? And was Ari really looking for a suitable bride as well as the merger? And was she really that transparent?

Lucy forced herself to stand tall and looked at herself critically. She'd chosen one of the less revealing dresses, but still she wanted to yank it up and pull it down. One-shouldered, silk, it cut across her bosom far too low for her liking, and showed a veritable acreage of pale skin, which she was very conscious of in this milieu of much skinnier, more sun-kissed people.

The dark grey seemed to make her eyes stand out too large in her face, and her hectic flush had nothing to do with make-up and everything to do with embarrassment that everyone in the room must have seen her mooning after her boss. Well, it ended here. For the next two weeks it was work only. She'd keep Aristotle at arm's length however she could. A dart of doubt struck her. How did she know he hadn't already transferred his affections to that blonde? Perhaps he'd finally grown weary of chasing his too tall and too buxom secretary?

Choking back a frustrated cry at her own awful weakness and feeling so vulnerable, she left the bathroom—every intention of going back to the hotel. She got out to the lobby and retrieved her coat. She'd just leave a note for—

'Where have you been?'

A hard hand whirled her around so fast she lost her balance and ended up plastered against Aristotle's chest, looking up, slightly winded. When she realised what she was doing she scrambled back, inarticulate anger rushing through her. 'I'm going back to the hotel. I'm tired.'

'Well, I'm not—and we're not finished here.'

'It's a social event. Surely you don't need me to work.'

'I…' Ari faltered. He'd been about to say, *I do need you.* But she was right. It wasn't for work, and if it wasn't for work then what was it? Had he got so used to her calm, insightful presence? Had he really missed her throughout dinner?

He made the only decision he could. 'Fine, then I'll escort you back.'

A huge neon danger sign flashed over Lucy's head. 'No!' She tempered her response. 'I mean—you stay. I don't want to drag you away…' *From that blonde you were obviously enjoying so much.*

But in his usual arrogant way he'd already taken her arm and was leading her outside, where as if by magic his car drew up in front of them.

She tried again in the car. 'Really, you should stay.'

He quirked a small hard smile, leaning back easily, studying her. 'Oh, really? Should I?'

Lucy's hands twisted in her lap. She felt something intangible shift between them. The energy was palpable. 'Yes…' Why did her voice sound breathy all of a sudden? 'Yes,' she said again, stronger. 'You should. You obviously have…people to talk to.'

Aristotle grimaced when he recalled trying to evade the clutches of Pia Kyriapoulos just now. A very beautiful and very wealthy divorcee, she'd made it quite clear what he could expect if he wanted to indulge in an affair while in Athens. Before, he might have been tempted—she was offering just what he liked, no-strings sex—but now…the only woman he wanted was sitting just a few inches away from him, and he couldn't contemplate sex with anyone else.

'You're wrong, Lucy,' he drawled in deep honeyed tones. 'There's no one I want to talk to, and I am only too happy to escort you back.'

Lucy stifled a retort and looked out of the window, a mixture of dread and excitement licking through her when she remembered the last time he'd insisted on taking her home.

Far too soon they were pulling up outside their hotel. Lucy scrambled inelegantly from the car before her door could be opened. But of course her attempts were futile. Aristotle caught up with her easily and took her arm again, leading them over to the gleaming lifts.

Once inside, standing apart from him, Lucy looked up resolutely. She nearly collapsed when she heard Aristotle say innocuously, 'Do you remember the first time we met in a lift?'

Shocked and aghast, she looked at him—and realised too late that it was a mistake. 'The first time we…?'

'Met in a lift,' he said easily, turning to look up at the display. 'Funnily enough, the day you walked into my office to interview for the job I remembered it.' He looked back down at her. 'In vivid detail.'

Lucy was barely aware that she was still standing. She wanted to put out a hand to hold onto something, but the only solid thing was *him*. She prayed she wouldn't collapse.

She shook her head. 'No,' she croaked…and then knew she couldn't lie. 'That is…yes. I remember you using the staff lift, but I don't remember much else.'

Her heart was thumping as all she could remember right then was how hard his body had felt underneath hers. A lot like it had felt *over* hers the other day in the car.

The lift doors opened and Lucy almost fell out. Aristotle walked alongside her easily. Her legs were trembling. As she tried and failed to stick her keycard in her door she felt it taken out of her hand imperiously, and watched helplessly when he effortlessly opened the door.

When she stepped in he said quietly, 'Who knew you were such a consummate liar, Lucy Proctor?'

She turned around, affronted. 'What's that supposed to mean?' She saw that he'd neatly stepped into the room too, and when the door closed behind him her heart seemed to spasm in her chest. 'And what do you think you're doing in here?'

'Proving what a liar you are, Lucy Proctor.'

And then he reached out, two big hands encompassing her waist, and pulled her inexorably towards him, towards that searing heat. Lucy, gripped by an awful feeling of inevitability, stumbled right into his chest.

'This is much better,' Aristotle growled as she fell against him, and he lifted his hands to cup her face and thread fingers through her hair. 'Now I have you exactly where I want you.'

Lucy couldn't help a groan of reluctant supplication when he bent his head and took her mouth. It felt as if he'd injected some kind of life force into her body. Every nerve came tinglingly alive, her heart-rate sped up, her skin seemed to glow…and down below, between her legs, she could already feel her traitorous body responding hotly, wetly.

His tongue swirled, sought hers, sucked it deep into his mouth. She felt fireworks explode in her head. Then he was nipping gently at her lower lip and sucking it, exploring the gap in her teeth and saying throatily, 'Bite me…'

A feeling of exultation took her over. She felt him push her coat off her shoulders to the floor and hardly noticed. Experimentally, shyly, she bit down on his sensual lower lip, feeling its cushiony springiness, soothing with her tongue where she'd bitten.

He growled something indecipherable, and then she felt him searching for and undoing the zip at the side of her dress, pulling it aside so that one lace covered breast was bared. He lifted a hand and cupped its weight. Lucy bit her lip. She felt heavy, aching with a pooling of desire, and it was such an alien feeling it held her in its grip.

One of his big hands reached down and cupped her round buttocks, drawing her up and into him, where she could feel his arousal digging into soft flesh. She felt more liquid heat and instinctively closed her legs against it.

He was palming her breast, a thumb hovering teasingly

over the puckered tip, Tension mounted until Lucy wanted to scream, and finally he lowered his head. Her own fell back when she felt that tight, aching lace-covered tip being drawn into the hot, sucking spiral of intense desire that was his mouth.

His hand gripped her buttock and she strained upwards, urging him to suck harder, her hips moving sinuously against his. She was seeking for a pinnacle that she'd never experienced before, but she knew it was there somewhere.

Something made Lucy open her eyes, and she drew in a shocked breath when she saw their reflections in the mirror across the room, highlighted by the one dim lamp in the corner. They must have moved from the door somehow, although Lucy knew that an earthquake might have happened and she wouldn't have noticed. The image shocked her to the core. It was so explicit…and so like something she'd witnessed as a child, when she'd walked in on her mother unannounced one day.

Sanity and reality didn't trickle back—they exploded in her face. In a second she'd pushed Aristotle away and was pulling up her dress to cover her heaving breasts. She shook violently.

'Get out of here—*now*.'

She spied something from the corner of her eye and moved, grabbing the hotel robe from the end of her bed and pulling it on, wrapping it tightly around her, belting it firmly. She went and stood near the window, her brain hurting and her body throbbing with unfulfilled desire.

'*Please* just get out.'

'No, Lucy, I won't.' Aristotle's voice was unbearably harsh.

She could only imagine how angry he must be with her. She knew what men called women who—

'Look, I'm sorry. I should never have let that happen—it's entirely my fault.'

'You didn't *let* it happen, Lucy. You weren't helpless. You wanted it as much as I did.'

She shook her head dumbly and felt tears threaten.

Aristotle stepped forward then, and stopped a few feet away. His face looked as if it was carved from stone and Lucy quaked inwardly. She wanted to say sorry again, but didn't. His bow-tie was askew, his hair ruffled. Had she done that?

He frowned, as if trying to understand. 'Lucy, did someone do something to you? Did someone hurt you?'

She shook her head quickly. 'No…nothing like that.'

He shook his head. 'Well, if it's not that…what is it?'

She felt like crying in earnest now. How could she get into her tangled emotional history? Into how threatened she felt by the way he made her feel?

'I just…I don't want this. I don't want to *feel* this way.' It was the closest she could come to an admission.

Aristotle was unsympathetic. 'Well, tough—because you do and I do. It's called chemistry and it's unavoidable.'

'What if I leave?' Lucy asked hopefully.

He shook his head. 'We've been through this. You're not going anywhere.'

Her shoulders slumped, and she missed the flash of something that crossed Aristotle's face.

'Look,' Lucy began awkwardly, 'I'm not experienced— I'm not like the women you go for. I won't know how to…'

'You already do, sweetheart, without even trying.'

She looked up. It seemed important to say it. 'I'm not a virgin…I've had sex before.' *Once.* 'But I didn't feel anything. So I know that…it won't do anything for me.'

He came close and tipped her chin up. Lucy tried to avoid his eye but it was impossible.

'Are you seriously trying to tell me that you think you won't enjoy having sex?'

She shrugged, feeling very silly.

'Lucy, in case you haven't noticed, you're a sensualist. That's the only word I can find to describe you. Even though you seem determined to deny it, and I've no idea why that is. Don't you know why you have a taste for exotic underwear?'

'It's because…' Lucy stopped, remembering all those shopping trips with her mother—how she'd had it drummed into her how important it was to buy decent underclothes. But of course other teenage girls hadn't had the privilege of shopping with the scandalous Maxine Malbec.

'It's because I developed too early. I'm too…' her face burnt and she was glad of the dim light '…big. To get the right sizes you have to pay more…'

His hand still gripped her chin. 'Lucy, there's a whole nation of women out there bigger than you who wear woefully fitting underwear. Can't you just admit that you're drawn to it? To the feel of it against your skin? How it fits and makes you look—'

She tore his hand away and stepped back further. 'No.' But she knew his words had made an impact. *Did* she instinctively like it? *Was* she a sensualist, despite everything—just like her mother? Well, she'd proven spectacularly that in all other respects their shared genes certainly seemed to be showing themselves.

'No. Look…I have my reasons for not wanting this. I just…want you to respect that.'

Ari fought the most intense battle of his life as he looked at her downbent head and the tightly drawn belt on the robe. His body burned and ached. He felt hard from tip to toe and couldn't believe she was denying them this.

But he found some strength from somewhere. He stepped close again and saw the way Lucy's body tensed even more. In that instant something inside him melted. He wanted this woman with a passion he'd never known before, but he didn't want to force her. He felt an uncomfortable level of concern grip him as he tipped her chin up to see her face. She avoided his eyes. He felt her grit her jaw against his hand and his stomach clenched. He rubbed his thumb back and forth over silky smooth skin. The bones felt unbelievably delicate. Her jaw finally relaxed, and something akin to triumph moved through him.

Suddenly the urge to take Lucy to bed was superseded by his wanting to reassure her. He had the insane impulse to pull her close and tell her everything was going to be OK. Something deeply ingrained within him kept him from making the move, but it made his voice husky.

'I'm going to leave, but I want you to think about this, Lucy. What's between us is more than a banal attraction that happens every day of the week. This is…' His own words surprised him, and so did the emotion he could feel behind them, but he told himself it was just because he wanted her so badly. ' This is something much stronger. I don't know what demons you're fighting, and I can't fight them for you. Only you can do that. I'm going to leave the interconnecting door to my room open. I'd like you to use it, Lucy…I want to explore what this is with you…'

His mouth twisted. 'I've no doubt it'll burn itself out, but it's not going to go away until we do explore it. It's just going to get stronger. It's up to you. If you're strong enough to resist this then by God I hope you have enough strength for the both of us.'

Lucy's breath had stalled, and because it was hard not to she found herself staring directly into his eyes. What she saw there made her heart twist. It wasn't the heated intensity she'd expected—well, *it was*—but it didn't make her feel threatened. It made her feel quivery and achy, as if she wanted to throw caution to the wind and say *yes*.

For a long moment they stood like that, his words hanging

heavy in the air, and all Lucy's nerves seemed to centre on the hand which felt so warm and oddly reassuring on her jaw. But then Aristotle was taking that hand away and stepping back. He turned and walked to the door. In a second he was gone, and the room felt huge and cavernously empty. Bereft. In mere seconds she heard him opening the interconnecting door on his side and flinched slightly at the sound.

She went and sat heavily on the bed, feeling sick in her belly, his words swirling in her head. Was he right? Would this only get stronger? The ripples of sensation still pouring through her body mocked her. Who was she kidding? She'd fooled herself that it had receded this week, but he was right—especially if her reaction just now was anything to go by.

She'd also, she had to acknowledge, fooled herself into thinking she was frigid. Right now she felt like the least frigid person on the planet. She had to recognise that in losing her virginity she'd subconsciously gone out and deliberately chosen someone she didn't feel attracted to—as if to try and convince herself that she wasn't like her mother, that she wouldn't spend her life craving sex.

She frowned at that. It sounded wrong as she thought it now. She'd always believed her mother to have craved sex…but in actual fact it had been the men, their power and attention. She'd sought validation from *that*. When Lucy really thought about it, her mother had always been quite cool and clinical about sex. She'd never become so passionate about a man that she'd lost sight of practicalities.

The way Lucy felt about Aristotle right now had nothing to do with being cool and clinical. He could be the hotel doorman and he'd still have this effect on her. While Lucy knew for a fact that her mother would never in a million years have spared a mere doorman a second glance.

Seeing herself and Ari reflected in the mirror, the look on her face—it *hadn't* been the same as her mother's that day.

She'd never seen her mother look like that. So…desirous, so caught up in the moment.

The revelation stunned her now. Because of her mother's profession, and how overtly sexual it had been, she'd always assumed that Maxine's myriad liaisons had been all about sex. But they hadn't. They'd been about money and power and her mother's self-esteem. Not sex. That had merely been a tool she'd used. Lucy had *known* this, but it had taken the awakening of her own desire to really *see* it for the first time.

One of Lucy's biggest fears had to do with losing her independence by depending on men as her mother had done. But wasn't this a totally different situation? She was working; she already had a job. She wasn't hoping to get anything out of Aristotle—certainly not money or gifts. And he seemed to be as surprised by this flaring of attraction as she was. She had no doubt that if he had a choice he'd prefer this to be happening with someone in his own social group.

So didn't it stand to reason that once this thing had *burnt out*, as he'd said, things would get back to normal? Although Lucy had to concede she didn't know what it would mean to get back to *normal* in the office after something like this…her mind skittered weakly away from that.

She was pacing now, the thought of sleep impossible to consider. She bit at her nail, a tight feeling growing in her belly. For the first time in her life the fears she'd carried for so long about turning into her mother and all that meant seemed flimsy—they didn't hold water any more. *She was different*. The warm feeling of reassurance she'd imagined she'd felt just now surged back even stronger. And it scared her slightly, as she'd never in a million years have said that Ari was a *reassuring* type of man.

She stopped pacing. What if she could do this? Instead of running away, why not face this and vanquish the demons that had been plaguing her? Already she felt different; she had to admit she'd enjoyed the less restrictive wardrobe, and even though her reflex was still to cover up it was diminishing. She'd caught some of the men looking at her earlier in the ballroom, and instead of wanting to hide away she'd found herself straightening up, feeling a very fledgling sense of confidence trickling through her.

Had Aristotle helped her come to this? It didn't feel like the diminishing needy power that she'd seen her mother crave. It felt like an innately feminine power, pure and strong.

She thought about it again, tested the words: what if she did this? Just went over there to that door, opened it and walked through.

Before she knew her legs had even carried her Lucy stood at the door, breathing short shallow breaths, her heart thumping. She'd once read a book: *Feel the Fear and Do it Anyway.* Was she brave enough? To step across the line?

As if in answer to her own question, an intense yearning spread through her. She wanted this—wanted this man and what he promised more than she wanted to look at all the reasons for not doing it. He was right. The thought of repressing this desire was...inconceivable.

With a shaking hand she touched the doorknob, took a breath and turned it. She shut her eyes as the door opened silently. A lurid mental image of Aristotle lounging back against black silk sheets, hands behind his head with a mocking smile, nearly made her slam it shut. But she resisted the impulse and opened her eyes.

It took a second for Lucy's eyes to adjust, and the scene greeting her was as erotically charged as she could have imagined and yet surprisingly benign. Through the open bedroom door, across the wide expanse of opulent sitting room, Lucy could see the reflected figure of a sleeping Aristotle in his bed in a slightly open mirrored wardrobe door. Far from black silk, the sheets he lay on were white, like hers. He'd thrown off the main covers and lay now, half propped up, with just a sheet hitched up to his waist. She'd seen his naked torso the other day, but now she looked her fill. It was long and lean and bronzed and hard, and exquisitely muscled. More superlatives filled her head but she couldn't articulate them. He was simply the most devastating specimen of a man she'd ever seen—not that she'd seen many, she had to acknowledge wryly, but she felt fairly sure that Aristotle could take his place among some of the most beautiful men on the planet.

Unruly inky black hair flopped with incongruous youthfulness onto his forehead, making him look much less like the feared CEO of Levakis Enterprises and instead like someone altogether more vulnerable and human.

Lucy's breath snagged when her eyes rested on those lean hips and then moved down lower, to where the strategically placed sheet was tented slightly over his lap. Hot colour poured into her cheeks at the intense and immediate reaction to even such subtle provocation.

A sound made her eyes dart up, and suddenly the sleeping god of perfection was no more—he was awake, light green eyes darkening even as she looked at him. Lucy belatedly realised that, as if in a dream, she'd walked right into his room and was now standing at the foot of his bed, the dim light of one lamp imbuing everything with innate intimacy.

Her hands gripped the sides of her robes together, knuckles showing white. Reality slammed into her, and she suddenly wondered if she'd suffered some kind of paralysis as she couldn't seem to move.

'I…'

Aristotle was completely still, awake and watchful now. 'You…?'

The sound of his voice resonated deep within her.

'I…I don't think… That is…perhaps I should—'

'Come here.'

The words were uttered with deep implacability, and Lucy's legs felt shaky. She'd come too far to go back now, so she moved forward jerkily, around the bed, until she was standing just a few feet away, eyes glued to his, mesmerised.

He lifted a hand and gestured. 'Come closer.'

Lucy looked desperately for any sign that he mightn't be as *über*-cool as he looked. And at the last second, just when she was contemplating running while she still could, she saw it: the light sheen of sweat beading his brow and the pulse beating fast at the base of his neck.

But, even so, it was as if the old, safe Lucy was calling her back through the doors, willing her to slam them shut between her and this man and this craving, aching need within her. She even turned and looked, as if to judge the distance.

Immediately her hand was taken in a ring of heat. Lucy looked down to see her wrist dwarfed by his bronzed hand. She looked at him, and gulped.

'Lucy, are you sure you want this? Because if you stay there's no going back.'

And in that instant Lucy mentally shut the doors behind her. She didn't want to go back. She wanted to go forward and free herself of this unwanted baggage she'd been carrying.

She shook her head and felt her hair slip around her shoulders. 'I'm not going.'

He pulled her irrevocably towards him, and then she was there, legs leaning weakly against his bed, His eyes never left hers as he brought her wrist to his mouth and pressed a kiss against the pulse, his tongue flicking out. She gasped and felt as if he'd branded her, even with that small move.

And then he let her hand go and leant on one elbow. 'Take off your clothes.'

When he said the words, Lucy felt only an intense explosion of heat in her pelvis. She was far beyond disgust or shock. Without breaking eye contact she undid her thick robe and let it drop to the floor. She still wore the dress, which gaped open, and her shoes. She stepped out of the shoes and bent to put them neatly under the chair. Then she stood and looked at Aristotle again.

He had made no move, but his eyes had turned so dark with lust that the green looked almost black. His gaze burnt into her.

With a tremor in her hands she pulled the zip down all the way, and then slowly peeled the dress off her shoulder and down, baring breasts only just confined by a strapless lace bra. Her awful self-consciousness seemed to have faded away to another place. Another person.

Hands on her hips, Lucy wriggled slightly to ease the dress down and over her womanly shape. The veritable waves of heat coming from Aristotle as his eyes followed the path of her dress nearly had Lucy melting on the spot. The heavy silk pooled at her feet, and she stepped out with an innate grace she was entirely unaware of.

Seeing a heavily brocaded chair beside the bed, Lucy lifted one leg to rest her foot there and started to peel one stocking down, only belatedly becoming aware of the eroticism of her pose. She sensed it in the way Ari had stilled even more, felt it in the intensity of his gaze on her, and for the first time in her life, found herself glorying in her innate femininity.

Aristotle knew that the only thing keeping him from jumping out of the bed and burying his aching hardness into her as she bent like that over the chair was the knowledge that, given one touch of her skin, he'd lose all control. When he'd seen her standing at the foot of the bed like a vision, his feeling of pure desire twinned with what had felt suspiciously like joy had made him act gruffer than he would have liked. He gripped the sheets tight in both hands now. It felt hard to breathe. The fact that he also felt more out of control than he'd ever felt with another woman was uncomfortable. Finesse in this kind of situation was a distant memory.

A curtain of dark hair swung forward, restricting his view of the bountiful breasts threatening to spill from that completely inadequate bra, and instinctively he leant forward and brushed it back over one pale shoulder. She turned her head and looked at him, her lower lip caught by her teeth, sending a shudder of pure arousal through his body, tightening the erotic notch on his flimsy control.

She put down that leg and lifted the other, repeated the exercise. By the time she was done Ari could feel sweat rolling down his back from the effort it took to stay still.

Lucy registered the almost indecent bulge in the sheet covering his lap and her throat went dry.

'Your bra,' he said hoarsely. 'Take it off too.'

Lucy reached around behind her and felt for the clasp. She had to pull the bra tighter in the motion it took to undo it, and she saw Aristotle's Adam's apple move convulsively as he registered the movement. The clasp was undone, and Lucy held it for a long moment…*this was it*. And then, with an almost defiant movement, she pulled it away and threw it down, releasing her heavy breasts. She stood before him in nothing but her silk and lace pants. In some dim and distant part of her still-functioning brain Lucy had *no idea* how she was doing this—the enormity of the moment was too huge to contemplate—but the beat of her blood was drowning out everything but the need to be here right now, *with him*.

His eyes seemed to glaze over as he looked at her, making her skin tighten and tingle all over, especially her breasts. She could feel the tips puckering and growing unbearably tight. She didn't have time to feel self-conscious. Aristotle reached out with two hands and grabbed hers in both of his, pulling her close to the bed. The sheet moved down. Lucy had a stomach clenching view of narrow hips and dark hair just above—

With a smooth move she never saw coming he tumbled her down, so that she lay flat on her back. He loomed, huge and dark over her, his hands still capturing hers, held against her belly, his knuckles brushing the sensitive undersides of her breasts. Her heart was beating so fast she felt dizzy, but then his head was lowering to hers, his mouth slanting over hers, and within seconds dizziness had been replaced with heat and sensation. His naked torso crushed her chest. He released her hands and she instinctively wound them around his neck as she arched voluptuously towards him.

Never had she imagined feeling like this. This rightness. She fitted him; he fitted her. The moment she ached for him to touch her somewhere he touched her; the moment she wanted him to deepen the kiss he deepened it—sucking her tongue deep, biting her lip, pressing fiery kisses down over her jaw and further, until he hovered teasingly over her breasts.

He cupped one and then the other, caressing their firm smoothness. Lucy's breathing was fractured, jerky. She looked down but couldn't bear the eroticism of seeing her breasts in his hands like that. So she closed her eyes and cried out when he took one burning nipple into his mouth and sucked hard, rolling the tip, flicking it with his tongue, grazing it with his teeth before suckling hard again.

Lucy was burning up, her hands in his hair as he cupped both the voluptuous mounds together, his mouth tasting and testing each peak until they were throbbing with arousal.

'Please…' she begged brokenly.

Her hips moved in a silent and primeval rhythm, her lower body on fire. She looked down to see Aristotle looking up at her, eyes dark green, cheeks flushed. His huge broad shoulders blocked out the light as he finally released her breasts and came over her on strong arms, lean and awe-inspiring.

'Are you ready?'

She nodded jerkily. She wanted to say yes to anything this man said, not even caring what he meant.

'Are you sure? I think we should check, just in case…don't you?'

'Yes,' Lucy gasped. 'Whatever—just do it…'

He smiled down at her even as she registered that the sheet had fallen away and his powerful erection nudged her belly. On pure instinct she reached down and covered him with her hand, heat suffusing her face and neck as she registered the size of him—fully aroused.

He grimaced as her hand tightened on him and he took it gently away. 'That's why we have to see if you're ready Lucy, *mou*…patience.'

She didn't know what *mou* meant, but then he disappeared, and Lucy gave a yelp when she felt him drawing her pants down, over her hips and down her legs, before he spread her legs apart with big hands. Lucy tried to resist the movement, which felt far too intimate, but he was ruthless, eyes on hers, holding her, *telling her to trust him* as his head lowered. She closed her eyes and put a fist to her mouth to hold back the groan when she felt his breath feather in the intimate space between her legs, and then the sensation of his mouth and tongue on her nearly sent her shooting into the stars.

He licked her, exploring her secret folds, thrusting deep into her, circling and sucking on her clitoris until her hips were lifting off the bed, wantonly jerking towards him, her teeth biting down on her fist.

When she felt two fingers slide deep into her slick heat everything in her body teetered on an edge that she'd never known before; every nerve pulled tight. But then he was withdrawing for a moment. She heard a drawer slam shut, a foil wrapper, and then he was back over her, strong, hair-roughened thighs parting her own smoother ones even more.

She could feel his erection nudging her down there, where she burned. He moved back and forth, drawing his penis along the moistened and plump folds of her sex, eliciting a deep groan from somewhere deep within her. She was almost mindless for the need for *something*…she wasn't sure what it was…it hovered just out of reach.

Lucy put her hands on his shoulders. They glistened with sweat, and the feeling of something so earthy made her rejoice.

'Ari…' she breathed. 'Please—I'm ready.'

And that was when Ari's control broke. He heard her husky words, felt her tip her hips up towards him, reach down to take hold of him, forcing him to impale her slightly. And then he drove in deep and hard, knowing instinctively that this woman was made for him alone and they would fit like a glove.

Ari stilled his movements—both of them did. Lucy's eyes were wide with shock at the sensation of him filling her, but it wasn't painful…it was delicious.

She moved again, experimentally, and Aristotle sank into her even more, pushing her down into the bed. Lucy wrapped one leg around his waist and threw her head back, hands still clinging onto his shoulders as he slowly withdrew and then impaled her again. He continued with his slow, voluptuous rhythm, the pleasure building and building. Lucy could feel her body starting to shake as he took her other leg and bent it back, opening her up to him even more, changing the angle slightly, going even deeper, and as his movements started to get faster and more urgent Lucy could feel the onset of something so huge, so terrifying as it came hurtling towards her, that she tensed—even though everything in her was urging her to meet it head-on.

Aristotle bent his head, his body holding her suspended

with his movements, and kissed her deeply. Her breasts were crushed against his chest, her arms clasping his neck. 'Let go, Lucy… It's OK…let go.'

Holding on tight, she took the final, terrifying leap and let go…and was thrown so high and so far on the wave of her orgasm that she was hardly even aware of Aristotle's own explosive loss of control as his big powerful body jerked and still rhythmically thrust into hers as the never-ending ripples of her orgasm held him suspended in a halfway world he'd never known before.

CHAPTER SEVEN

ARISTOTLE was running away. And the fact that he was aware of what he was doing made him nearly incandescent with rage. He didn't *run away*. And yet after last night, with Lucy, all he'd known was that he needed space—and fast. His brain was still too hot and far too tangled to even pretend he could deal with a banal morning-after scenario. He'd received a call from his New York PA while Lucy lay sleeping, and on the flimsiest of pretexts had declared he'd fly over for the weekend to take care of something that ordinarily he wouldn't have touched with a bargepole.

Lucy had woken to find him dressing that morning. He'd seen her wake through the reflection of the mirror as he'd knotted his tie with unsteady hands. Unsteady because he'd wanted to strip off all his confining garments and go over to where she lay in such gloriously voluptuous naked abandon and take her all over again. But the truth was he wasn't sure if he could take that intensity of experience again.

Wasn't sure if he could take that intensity of experience again? Ari's hand clenched around the crystal glass, the design digging into his palm as he looked unseeingly out of the plane window. Since when had sleeping with a woman been too intense for him? *They* were the ones left weak and dizzy and sated. Not him.

He closed his eyes and threw his head back. And then opened them again abruptly when all he could see was Lucy's passion-glazed eyes as she'd looked up at him the moment he'd filled her, the moment he'd been completely sheathed in her hot moist warmth… It had felt…it had felt like nothing he could have imagined. He could remember the feel of her breasts pushing against him, their peaks as hard as bullets against his chest, could hear their heartbeats even now, thudding slow and unsteady, and then, as he'd started to thrust deeper and deeper, the beats had got faster…until—

Aristotle swore softly. He needed to numb that *intensity*.

His mouth twisted and he called himself all sorts of a fool for running away. So it was the best sex he'd ever had? That was it. It didn't mean anything. It hadn't touched any part of him that hadn't been touched before. *So why did it feel as if it had*?

Ari blocked out that assertion. He was immune to feeling, immune to emotions. He'd started to shut them away when his mother had died, and then when Helen Savakis had come into his life, and then finally on that first night in a cold boarding school in England at the age of five. It was the last time he'd cried and now… His gut clenched. *Now he only cried in his sleep*. He reiterated it to himself: he didn't *do* emotions.

Perhaps he'd sensed that Lucy did, and that was why he'd run. A sense of calm stole over him. That was it. She wasn't like the women he went for…she was bound to be less versed in how this would work. He'd seen the look on her face that morning, slightly nervous, biting her lip… And suddenly he was right back to square one—a raging erection pushing against his trousers, thirty thousand feet in the air, and the only chance of alleviating it far behind him on Greek soil.

He just had to lay it on the line with her, that was all. Make sure she knew what not to expect. And then...then he would take her again, and these demons would not be hovering over his shoulders. Ari smiled cynically. Who would have thought he'd be growing a conscience now, after all these years?

Lucy had got over Aristotle's abrupt and cold departure yesterday morning. She told herself stoutly that she was back on an even keel. But if she allowed images to surface for a second— She stumbled slightly in the street and a kindly old woman caught her arm and smiled up at her, saying something in Greek. Lucy smiled weakly and mumbled something back. So much for an even keel. If she even *thought* about the other night for a second she lost her balance... Self-disgust ran through her.

She spied a taverna on the other side of the street and made her way there, sitting gratefully in an empty chair. She ordered sparkling water and fanned herself with a menu, thinking that perhaps it was the heat getting to her. Who was she kidding? The heat was getting to her all right, but it had nothing to do with the sun.

And along with the heat was a lingering hurt—Lucy brutally cut off her thoughts there. She wasn't hurt. *She wasn't.*

She tried to focus on her surroundings, the pretty and quaint area of Anafiotika, a hidden gem of old Athens within touristy Plaka, just beneath the Acropolis. She'd climbed up there earlier, the exertion doing little to clear her head of the tangled knots. She took a sip of water, but with annoying precision her mind slipped back again to that excruciating moment when she'd woken the day before.

She'd felt so heavy, so lethargic, so replete. She'd lazily stretched and opened one eye before realising that she was naked, and that muscles ached where no muscle had been before. In an instant she'd been alert, and staring into the cool, wide-awake green eyes of Aristotle as he'd knotted his tie in the mirror.

She needn't have worried about the embarrassment of the morning after as he'd coolly informed her he had to go to New York urgently on business, that he didn't need her, and that he'd be back late on Sunday. It was almost as if nothing had happened. Lucy had even wondered for a paralysing moment if she'd sleep-walked into her boss's bed and he was merely being diplomatic and ignoring the *faux pas*.

And then he'd gone, leaving her there, shell-shocked, the only evidence that anything had happened in the tremors that had started through her body along with the ache when she moved.

After he'd left her mind had gone to some numb place where she wouldn't have to process what had happened, answer the questions that were piling up. Was that it? Had he just been scratching an itch? Would things revert to normal now? Was he that cold with everyone? Lucy had remembered the way he'd treated Augustine Archer and she'd doubled over in her steaming shower, feeling sick. *How could she have let this happen with a man like that?*

Because, she realised now, as the everyday hustle and bustle went on around her, she simply had not had a choice. He'd overwhelmed her—her response had overwhelmed her. And she was grateful for the space and time to process what had happened.

At that moment a group of handsome young Greek men passed her table, and they all turned to look Lucy over appreciatively as they backed down the street. One of them cheekily wolf-whistled. The shock of the attention when she wasn't used to it made her freeze. She felt acutely self-conscious in her khaki shorts and V-necked black T-shirt. The waiter in the restaurant bustled over and shouted something at the boys. They ran, laughing, and he started apologising to Lucy, but she assured him smilingly that it was fine and put some money on the table, getting up to go.

She had to acknowledge as she walked away that it wasn't an entirely unpleasant experience to be noticed like that. She'd hidden away for so long that she'd never had a chance to just play with situations like this.

The sun beat down and she tipped her head up to it for a moment. She felt an alien sensation of lightness, as if she were finally letting go of a weight. It was also a sense of freedom, and she desperately wanted to cling onto it. One thing she knew: *if* Aristotle thought they could take up where they'd left off when he returned, that sense of freedom might disappear. She'd indulged in the experience once; it would have to be enough. She knew too much about him, about his cold methods, and she knew that she didn't have the hide of someone like Augustine Archer to be able to take it.

But she had a mortifying, sickening feeling that he'd had enough already, and it killed her to admit to feeling other than overjoyed at the prospect.

She set off back in the direction of the hotel. Just before she rounded the corner a flash of movement caught her eye, and she looked over to see Aristotle lounging against an ancient wall, hands thrust deep into jeans pockets, a faded white T-shirt making him look indecently handsome. Dark glasses hid those amazing eyes, but added to the overall devastating package.

It was so like something she might have conjured up out of a fantasy that she blinked and blinked again. *Was* it a mirage? He was dressed more casually than she'd ever seen him. He moved, strolled towards her. Stopped in front of her. Her heart stopped and kick-started again with heavy thuds.

This was no mirage.

'You're…back.' Despite the drink of water, Lucy's mouth felt like a desert.

Ari smiled a hard smile and in that second Lucy knew it was him. Despite his hardness something melted inside her, all her good intentions of moments ago disappearing like pathetic wisps of cloud.

He lifted his glasses onto his head. 'I left New York in the middle of the night.'

The shock of seeing him like this and the force of those eyes on hers made her brain feel fuzzy. 'But you…you had to work.'

'I sorted it out. I needed to get back here.' *I shouldn't have left,* he surprised himself thinking, as lust slammed into his gut.

'You did?' Lucy was mesmerised by his mouth, remembering what it had felt like on her skin. Heat bloomed between her legs. People jostled past them and Aristotle took her arm and led her to the side, to the wall. He pushed her back against it and stood close—far too close. She could feel him, smell him… God, she wanted to taste him.

'Ari…'

He bent his head, feathering a kiss to her neck. 'Yes, say that again. That's why I came back.'

'Ari.'

His hands rested on either side of her head, his pelvis was tight against hers, and she could feel how aroused he was— right here in the middle of the street, with people passing by.

'I'm going insane for you, Lucy.'

Lucy opened her mouth, but her words were stolen by his lips coming down hard and swift, demanding and eliciting a flash-fire of response. After a long drugging moment Ari lifted his head, his eyes glittering down into hers. Amazingly, she could see herself reflected in his eyes, looking up, dazed, and that sent sanity rushing back. Somehow, with superhuman strength, Lucy found the will to put her hands against his broad chest and push.

He budged only minutely, a frown drawing those black brows together.

'*No.*' Lucy was starting to panic. The speed with which he'd appeared and made her conveniently forget all logic was making her burn inside.

He quirked a devilish smile. 'You're right. Here isn't the place.'

He took her hand and started to pull her away, clearly misinterpreting her reasons for wanting to stop. Lucy dug her heels in and pulled her hand back. He didn't let go, just looked back impatiently when she wasn't moving.

'What—?'

He took one look at Lucy's mutinous face and it sent something cold through him. 'I'm sorry—did I misunderstand? Maybe you *want* to be made love to in front of Athens strollers and their families?'

'I don't want to be made love to, full-stop,' Lucy hissed, very conscious of the stares they were getting—primarily from admiring women.

Ari gripped her hand tight and Lucy, very reluctantly, let herself be pulled towards him.

Ari was frowning again slightly, something like ennui trickling through him, making him feel absurdly disappointed. 'If this is about the way I left…'

Lucy emitted a sharp laugh that disguised the dart of pain and the surge of anger at how easily she'd given in to his charm and fallen into his bed the other night. Faced with him now, the fact that she desired him even more acutely was making her regret it all the more fiercely. 'Of course it's not. I'm well aware of how you conduct yourself… I guess—oh, I don't know—I expected at least a bunch of flowers. After all, isn't that what you give all your one-night stands?'

He stood stock still, staring down at her, the lines in his face tightening and growing harsher by the minute.

'Well, let's make this more than a one-night stand, and then you'll get a priceless piece of jewellery. Is that what it'll take, Lucy?'

He looked around for a moment and spotted something Lucy didn't see. With that tight grip on her hand, he began hauling her away again. Trepidation slithered down her spine. He'd looked ready to throttle her.

He growled back, 'Tell you what—why don't we cover all bases now? That way we're clear, left in no doubt as to where we stand, because to be perfectly honest I don't think I'm going to be satisfied with just two nights.'

'What—?'

Ari stopped abruptly at a flower stall and picked out the biggest bunch of flowers the man had. Then, to Lucy's horror and the flower stall man's delight, Ari presented it to her with a mocking flourish.

Lucy took them purely because she couldn't *not*. She pasted a smile on her face for the benefit of the flower seller, and after paying Ari was leading her away again. The flowers were huge and cumbersome. Lucy tried to get his attention, pulling on his hand, but it would have been easier talking to a block of wood. He led her relentlessly through a veritable maze of streets until they emerged into a charming square and Lucy spotted shops with designer names.

Again without pausing for a moment, Ari tugged Lucy along until she found him leading her into an exclusive jewellery store, the iconic name of which made horror slam into her. As the door hissed quietly closed behind them, and the security guard clearly recognised Aristotle Levakis, Lucy tugged fiercely on Ari's hand—but to no avail. He led her over to where an eager assistant, already smelling a large sale, stood.

He drew Lucy in close to his side with an arm of steel and sent her a devotedly loving look. Only Lucy was aware of the hard glitter behind it. Hardly breaking that eye contact, he said, 'I'd like to buy something for this beautiful woman.' He flicked a glance at the sales assistant and smiled urbanely. 'Although I'm sure you'll agree that there couldn't possibly be anything in this shop to rival her beauty.'

The sales assistant cleared her throat obsequiously and looked Lucy up and down, taking in the T-shirt and shorts, the flat gladiator sandals and dusty feet. Lucy cringed from head to toe under the snooty woman's scrutiny, and right then she hated Ari more than she'd ever hated anyone in her life, hearing his well-practised patter.

Hellbent on proving *something*, Ari was still so incensed that he dragged Lucy from display to display, forcing her to look at priceless bracelets, necklaces, earrings and brooches. Every now and then she tried to entreat him, to tug on his hand, but he ignored her. A heavy mass of dark, twisted emotion was weighing him down inside.

Why hadn't her eyes lit up when they'd got in here? And *why* had he felt that punch to his solar plexus in the street when he'd believed her to be exactly the same as every other woman? And *why* was she contradicting that now, insisting on leaving? Making him feel confused and out of his depth. He heard her speak again.

'Ari. *Please.* Let's just go. I don't want anything here.'

He turned to look down, and the stunning natural beauty of her face and those stormy grey eyes nearly floored him. He could feel the thrust of her soft breasts against his chest. She looked pale. But he did not know how to get himself out of this situation except by saying, his voice harder than he'd ever heard it, 'We're not leaving until you choose something, Lucy. There's not a woman in the world who would say no to that, so please don't play the wide-eyed innocent with me. It won't work.'

Lucy's belly clenched at the look of pure cynicism that

crossed Ari's features, twisting them. Suddenly her anger dissolved, and all she felt was sad. She tore her eyes away and looked around futilely, hating every single item of jewellery on display. This whole scenario was making her skin crawl. But she knew he meant it. They would not leave until she'd chosen something.

She tugged her hand, and for the first time Ari let go. Moving away, feeling tears film her eyes, Lucy searched and searched, barely even seeing the glittering gems arrayed in glorious profusion.

But then something did catch her eye, hidden away at the back of one of the cabinets. It was a necklace of such stunning simplicity that it took her breath away. It was a butterfly design; she'd always had a sentimental thing about butterflies, and her mother had used to buy her presents with butterfly motifs. Seeing this now was like some kind of sign, and Lucy had to fight back the tears.

The wings of the design glistened with what she could only assume were tiny diamonds, and three delicate silver strands linked it on each side to the catch.

She pointed with a trembling finger. 'I like that one.'

A startled gasp of disbelief came from the sales assistant, clearly seeing her month's worth of commission disappearing down the drain.

'*That* one?'

Ari had heard the exchange and was behind Lucy, looking over her shoulder. She tensed as the fine hairs stood up on the back of her neck.

The sales assistant couldn't keep the pain out of her voice. 'Well, yes, it is a nice piece…' She laughed nervously, 'If you like something more…subtle…and the designer is local. But *really*…'

Lucy heard a scathing, 'Less than one thousand euros? I don't think so…' come from behind her, and then she felt his mouth close to her ear, so only she could hear which he said. 'I think I want a lot more than a two-night stand Lucy, *mou*, so I think you're worth a lot more than that…'

Before she knew it Ari had arrogantly picked out a completely different necklace, with a huge sapphire stone surrounded by diamonds, and the ecstatic sales assistant was wrapping it up efficiently before they changed their minds.

Outside the shop, Lucy broke desperately from Ari's grasp, but he caught her again effortlessly and swung her round. She closed her eyes and to her utter horror could feel tears welling. She couldn't stop one from slipping out. She felt a tense stillness come into his body.

'Lucy…' He sounded exasperated now. Lucy didn't doubt that he'd moved women to tears after buying them jewellery before, but for entirely different reasons.

Ari took hold of Lucy's arms. They felt slender and fragile under his hands. He saw the tear slip down the pale softness of her cheek and cursed himself silently, feeling like an absolute heel when he didn't even know why. He'd just spent a fortune on her! And in his experience money equalled a satisfied woman. He was floundering badly, had never been in this place before, and had certainly never expected a reaction like *this*. She looked almost green.

Seeing her still holding onto that crazy bunch of flowers, Ari grabbed them out of her hand and passed them to a woman strolling past. He was unaware of her gasp of delighted surprise as she took them, entirely focused on Lucy again. More tears were slipping down her cheeks. He was used to women's histrionics, but this was different. She was doing it so silently. And he could tell that she hated that she was crying.

'Lucy…look—'

She seemed to come to life and lifted a hand, knocking aside one of his as she wiped her cheek. Finally she opened her eyes, and their swirling depths made him want to pull her close. But everything about her screamed *stay back*.

Her voice was heart-achingly husky. 'I've never been so hu…humiliated in all my life.'

Ari raked a hand through his hair. He wanted to go back to when he'd seen Lucy in the street, taken her in his arms and kissed her, and start all over again. But when she'd pushed him away and then said those things about the flowers he'd lost all perspective. Without wanting to look too closely at why, he just knew it had something to do with her reference to those other women. That this was exactly the same… A small voice crowed, *Wasn't it?*

Lucy couldn't look up at Ari any more. She broke free and started to walk back towards the hotel. She could see it in the distance; they were closer than she'd thought. She felt numb.

When she felt Ari take her hand again she stopped dead and took a deep breath before turning around. 'Look—'

'No, *you* look.'

She did—right up at him, emotion still swirling danger-ously in her breast. She'd never felt so vulnerable, like every one of her childhood fears was being taken out and exposed to the harsh sunlight.

Ari felt tight. 'Those women in London—the flowers… They weren't one-night stands. They were pathetic attempts to negate your effect on me and to keep up appearances.' His mouth twisted. 'I'd agreed with Parnassus that it might help distract people from investigating the merger if I was seen to be out and about as usual.'

Lucy's head went into mind-melt.

'I'm sorry for leaving you so abruptly the other morning. I'm sorry for the flowers, and I'm sorry for dragging you into that shop and forcing you to choose something you didn't want.' *Even now he couldn't understand her reaction, or why he was explaining himself when he never had before.* And he couldn't really believe he'd felt compelled to defend his actions in London. But he wanted Lucy more than he wanted to understand right then…

Fresh tears threatened and Lucy wailed inwardly, *Don't be nice!* I can't handle nice.

She pursed her lips even as her anger drained away spectacularly. *He hadn't slept with those women?* She felt very wobbly and vulnerable, and knew her words lacked impact. 'Your behaviour was unforgivable. Spending that kind of money just to make a point is disgusting.'

His face tightened. He held up the bag. 'What do you want me to do with it?'

Lucy felt wrong-footed by his immediate response. The Ari she'd thought she knew was morphing out of all recognition. She thought for a second. 'I don't think that lady in the shop deserves commission when she couldn't be bothered to promote local talent. I don't know…it'd be nice to give it to someone who'd really appreciate…'

She looked around. In the thronged square, back at the jeweller's shop, she could see a young couple clearly in love, looking wistfully through the window at the engagement rings. Lucy could see the pain on the young man's face at his girlfriend's quickly disguised yet crestfallen expression as they walked away. She glanced up at Ari and could see that he had followed her gaze and witnessed the little exchange.

She saw his jaw clench. He let her hand go and strode through the crowd to the young couple. Lucy saw the conversation, saw Ari gesture back to her with a rueful smile and hand the young man the elaborately wrapped box. The young couple's faces were shocked as Ari walked back to Lucy and took her hand again.

He led her away, but looked back for a moment and said, 'Satisfied now?'

Lucy nodded jerkily. She couldn't quite believe he'd done

that, and asked a little shakily, 'How…how much was it worth?'

He tossed back a figure and she felt the colour drain from her face. She bit her lip and said quietly, 'Oh, well, it'll buy them a nice engagement ring…or three.'

She felt the earth shift as she realised she was seeing a completely different side to Ari. She was very much afraid that she'd stuck her head into the lion's mouth and he was about to bite down—hard.

By the middle of the following week Lucy was as drunk as she'd ever felt, and all without touching a drop of alcohol. She couldn't stop her mind drifting back to last Sunday afternoon, now as she sat waiting for Ari to come out of a private meeting with Parnassus being held in his villa in the hills above Athens.

When they'd got back to the hotel an unspoken inevitability had vibrated between them, intensifying the closer they'd got to her room. Once inside, as if to stave it off, as if she could save herself from the burning flames, Lucy had said breathlessly, 'Wait…what is this now? What are we?'

Ari had rested back against the door, hands behind him, those lean hips in the low-slung jeans making Lucy's mouth dry and her head ache with the effort it took not to look down.

'We are two consenting adults, exploring a strong mutual attraction, and this is…the second time we make love.'

Heat had exploded all around her. He'd pushed off the door and come towards her. Lucy had put out a hand, as if that could stop him, and had watched as he'd nonchalantly stripped off his T-shirt.

She'd swallowed. 'But…what about us…working together? How can we do this…?'

He'd caught up with her effortlessly and pulled her into him, tight. She had felt the bulge of his arousal pressing against his jeans, pressing just above the apex of her thighs, and her legs had nearly buckled.

He'd bent his head and whispered at the corner of her mouth, '*This is* how we do this…'

Things had escalated swiftly. Clothes pulled and yanked, they'd stumbled and staggered towards the bed, Lucy falling back into the softness, somehow naked except for her under-wear.

She'd watched as Ari yanked down his jeans and briefs in one go. She'd gazed at him in all his bronzed, aroused glory, she'd realised in that moment that ever since that day she'd bumped into him in the lift *this* image had been hidden deep in the recesses of her darkest fantasies. A fantasy she never might have acknowledged if this man hadn't wanted her too.

Was that why he'd got under her skin so thoroughly from the start? The revelation sent her pulse soaring, pounding through her veins and under her skin, even now, as she sat on the chair with her legs tight together and Parnassus' own as-sistant sitting just feet away.

Even that couldn't halt the images, though. Ari had come towards her like an avenging god and pushed her legs apart, where they dangled over the bed. On two hands he'd rested over her. After looking down at her for an intensely long moment, he'd pushed down one bra strap and then the other, and then pulled down the cups of her black bra so that her breasts were exposed, upthrust by the confining underwire.

When he'd bent his head to blow softly Lucy had groaned deep in her throat, in between her legs a deep, endless ache. When his tongue had flicked out and teasingly licked around the rapidly hardening peak of one breast she'd arched her back, willing him to suck it deep, like he had before.

When he hadn't, she'd looked at him, felt sweat breaking out on her brow. He'd smiled devilishly, and she'd cursed him silently, her eyes flashing in a mute appeal.

He'd shifted her back onto the bed and with far too practised ease managed to dispense with her bra. His big hands on her thighs had held her apart. He'd looked at her with such desirous intensity she'd felt trepidation lick through her, feeling that she *had* to be imagining this.

She'd spoken huskily, and winced now at the memory. 'How can you…how can you find me attractive? I'm not like… I'm too big…I'm *plump*…'

He'd merely hooked fingers into the side of her pants, said throatily, 'You're perfect…' and started to pull them down, dropping them summarily on the floor. He'd stood again, blatantly aroused, making a mockery of her words. Making her feel as if she was all woman and the only woman for him.

He'd bent over her and she'd felt his erection teasing her, hot and hard against her desire-drenched sex. She'd felt so *wanton*, but had bitten her lip and forced herself not to move her hips towards him as she'd wanted to do so very badly.

Lying right over her, so she could feel his chest against her, he'd stretched her arms above her head, the movement causing her breasts to rise as if offered to him like succulent desserts.

Holding her hands captive with one of his much larger ones, he'd trailed his other hand down the side of her body, teasing the side of one breast, and whispered in her ear, 'You are quite simply the pure embodiment of my every fantasy of what the perfect feminine form is… I didn't know it till I saw you, and now I can see nothing else…'

Lucy's heart had stopped altogether. She'd searched his eyes as he'd lifted back and looked down, so dark and hot they'd scorched her alive.

'You…really mean that?'

Lucy hoped desperately now that she hadn't sounded as vulnerable as she'd felt in that moment.

In answer Ari had bent his head and laved one of her nipples with his mouth and tongue, before sucking it deep, causing her back to arch again helplessly.

Releasing her hands for only a second while he'd put on protection, he'd come back and captured them high again. Lucy's hips had bucked of their own volition.

He'd then slid into her, inch by torturous inch, and when he was in as far as he could go, when she didn't know where she started or he ended, he'd leant close to her mouth and kissed her deeply, before saying, so quietly that she almost didn't hear, 'Yes…I really mean it.'

And then, with slow, deep thrusts which built and built to a stunning crescendo—

The door in front of Lucy opened suddenly, and she jumped up at the same time as Parnsassus' assistant, a guilty flush staining her cheeks, breathing as if she'd just been running. A pulse throbbed between her legs and she was caught by a pair of glittering green eyes.

She saw Ari smile sardonically, as if he knew *exactly* what she'd just been thinking about, and Lucy flushed even redder. He strolled over and took the file she was holding out of her hands, his fingers caressing hers underneath for a lingering moment, making her pulse beat even faster.

Lucy nearly groaned out loud, and then he said *sotto voce*, 'Have Helios bring the car round. We'll be out of here in less than ten minutes… I'll tell Parnassus we can work from my office for the rest of the afternoon.'

Lucy just nodded, not capable of much else, and certainly not capable of anything like *work*. She felt feverish, distracted, more elated than she'd ever felt, and knew that right now she had neither the strength of will *nor the inclination* to resist this man.

* * *

'We've been invited to my father's house for dinner on Friday night.'

'You mean *you've* been invited for dinner.' Lucy shuddered inwardly, she didn't fool herself for a second in thinking that Helen Levakis had included her in that cosy little invitation.

Ari shook his head and marvelled at this woman in front of him. They were having a private dinner in her bedroom at the hotel, late in the evening. She looked so beautiful in just a bathrobe, with her dark hair spread around her shoulders, not a scrap of make-up, that delicious cleavage just visible in the gap of her robe. When he thought of how they'd barely made it back to the office the afternoon before— He stopped his rampant mind. He was far too susceptible to this woman. And, worryingly, he didn't feel at all complacent or triumphant about the fact that he'd got her into bed. If anything he just felt a growing sense of hunger. The fact that that was not the usual way for him and women was conveniently pushed aside. He reminded himself that Lucy was different, from a different class—world. It was the novelty of that, *that* was all. And for now he was loving the novelty.

Reaching for her hand, he tugged her up and over until she fell into his lap, making a spasm of lust arrow straight to his groin.

He shook his head, and before he bent to kiss her said, 'Where I go, you go.'

Lucy accepted the kiss, drowned in the kiss, but a sense of guilty anticipation made her shiver slightly. No matter that they were spending time together like this. Ari was still as open as a closed book when it came to anything but the most general conversation. And now the thought of getting a chance to learn more about this man, who was fast tangling her head into one big knot of confusion and reducing her body to little more than a slave to his, was proving to be far headier than was healthy for her heart.

When the kiss deepened, and as Ari carried Lucy over to the bed and came down on top of her with his delicious weight and told her how beautiful she was, how desirable, she conveniently blocked out the clamour of voices in her head telling her to be careful, not to be weak, and not to be so easily seduced—and above all *not to fall in love*.

On Friday evening Lucy was sitting ramrod-straight on a rigid divan in the main drawing room of the grossly opulent Levakis house. Tonight had to be one of the most excruciatingly uncomfortable evenings of her life. From the moment she'd arrived, with Ari's hand on her arm, it had been clear she wasn't welcome.

Lucy had held her head high and thanked her lucky stars for her chaotic but expensive education; every time Helen had directed some snide comment her way, or had tried to undermine her, Lucy had answered with the utmost dignity. Helen had even been so rude as to conduct some of the conversation between the few guests in French, but her eyes had almost popped out of her head when Lucy had replied fluently.

Lucy felt inordinately proud of her mother's legacy.

Ari was now on the other side of the room, talking to the same beautiful blonde who'd captured his attention at that function the first week. Lucy tried to ignore the poisoned darts that seemed to be arrowing into her heart, and tensed even more when she saw Anatolios, Ari's half-brother, head her way.

He sat down, far too close for comfort, obviously drunk, and Lucy tried to edge away, smiling weakly. He merely moved with her, crowding her. She felt intensely vulnerable.

Anatolios's blue eyes followed where her gaze had just been and he said, 'Beautiful, isn't she?'

Lucy flushed. 'I'm not sure I know what you mean.'

She looked at Anatolios reluctantly. She guessed she couldn't be much older than her own twenty-three years, and hoped the revulsion she felt didn't show on her face.

He smiled sleazily, and then, shockingly, ran a fleshy finger up and down Lucy's bare arm. She flinched, but couldn't move, hemmed in as she was.

He gestured with his head. 'That's Pia Kyriapoulos. She used to be a famous model, and now she's famous for being wealthy and divorced and looking for a new husband.'

Lucy swallowed painfully and looked across the room. They did look amazing together—blonde contrasting with dark. Pia had her hand resting on Ari's arm, and he certainly didn't look in a hurry to move it. At that moment he looked up and straight at Lucy. Feeling inordinately exposed, Lucy smiled brilliantly and looked back at Anatolios as if he'd said something funny. Not as if he'd said something to make her heart feel as if it was being ripped, still beating, out of her chest.

When she felt Ari's gaze move again Lucy ripped her arm away from Anatolios, who glowered sulkily at her. His eyes dropped to her cleavage and Lucy screamed inwardly. The guy was a total creep.

Just then Helen swept into the room and said something to Ari who, after a moment's hesitation, followed her from the room, his face hard. Sensing a chance to escape, Lucy mumbled something about needing the bathroom and fled, vowing to get out of there even if she had to leave on her own.

Wherever I go, you go. Ari's words resounded mockingly in her head. At least until the next available, infinitely more beautiful woman came along, she surmised grimly.

She was coming back from the bathroom and passing a partially opened door when she heard raised voices. *Ari and Helen.*

Without being conscious of what she was doing, she slowed down and heard Ari say, a low and blistering voice,

'I'll never marry someone like her; she's completely inappropriate. And anyway, don't you think it's a little late to be doing the concerned mother act?'

CHAPTER EIGHT

LUCY's heart froze like ice in her chest as the words registered. Was Helen afraid that their affair was more than just a fling? She had to swallow back a semi-hysterical cry, putting a hand to her mouth. Well, Ari had certainly reassured her of that.

The next words from Helen were indistinctly shrill, and then Ari's voice came again. Lucy stood rooted to the spot in some kind of sick, paralysed fascination, and heard him say something along the lines of, '...useless waste of space of a brother...'

There was an awful silence, and then the sharp crack of what could only be a hand across a cheek.

Knowing that it wouldn't have been Ari, and acting on a surge of adrenalin that was pure primal instinct, Lucy pushed open the door and flew into the room, aiming herself straight at Helen, who still had her hand raised, her eyes glittering almost feverishly.

Lucy was unaware of their shocked looks. She saw only Ari's proud stance, the livid handprint and the trickle of blood from the corner of his mouth. She saw red, and for the first and only time in her life considered striking another person. It was only Ari's quick reflex action, pulling her back behind him, that stopped her.

Helen lowered her hand and her eyes took on a malevolent glow. She smiled cruelly. 'Well, well—if it isn't the quiet little secretary, come to save her lover.' The woman's obsidian eyes flicked up and down and she added cuttingly, 'Or perhaps I shouldn't say *little*.'

Lucy made to move again and Ari held her firm, glancing back with a hard expression, 'Leave it, Lucy.'

He turned back, and Lucy could feel the ice in his gaze even though he wasn't looking at her.

'She wouldn't balk at striking you too. After all, you never had any qualms about striking a five-year-old—did you, Helen?'

Helen's focus moved back to Ari, and Lucy could see the older woman's face grow mottled with anger. Abruptly Ari turned and pulled Lucy with him, and within a blur of minutes they were sitting in the back of his car, leaving the house behind.

Lucy was still shaking, a mixture of powerful anger and shock coursing through her. She glanced at Ari. He was looking resolutely out of the window. When she saw his mouth her heart lurched painfully.

'You…you're bleeding.'

He turned abruptly, and the dead look in his eyes scared her. He smiled harshly. 'Want to kiss it better for me, Lucy?'

He flicked out a handkerchief nevertheless, and dabbed at the blood. Overcome with an emotion she couldn't name, Lucy reached out and put her hand to his cheek, where it still felt warm.

'How could she have hit you when you were so small?'

A surge of emotion so powerful that it made him tremble caused black spots to dance before Ari's eyes. His breathing grew shallow. The feel of Lucy's hand like a cooling balm on his hot cheek, the look on her face… He'd never, *ever* had someone rush to his defence so unreservedly. He'd felt the fine vibrating tremors of her anger as he'd held her back, and he didn't doubt that if he hadn't stopped her she might very well have struck Helen. The realisation was cataclysmic, earth-shattering.

A hardness entered him. He certainly wasn't going to shatter along with it. Everyone wanted something out of him—especially women. Lucy was just taking advantage of a vulnerable moment.

Lucy's wrist was gripped and pulled down. Ari's eyes glittered at her, but at least some life had come back into them. 'Quite easily,' he bit out. 'I was an easier target then.'

He kept hold of her wrist, almost painfully, but Lucy didn't say anything.

'Don't pity me, Lucy Proctor. I don't need anyone's pity.'

The fierce pride on his face nearly made Lucy weep. She shook her head and managed to pull her hand back, cradling it with her other one. He saw the movement and sighed deeply, raking his hair with barely concealed anger.

Lucy looked away for a long moment. The rest of the evening was coming back—what had happened just before she'd gone to the bathroom, and then the words she'd heard. *What was wrong with her?* Sitting here mooning over a man who quite patently needed no one and was biding his time with her until he flitted to the next woman.

She started hesitantly, 'I didn't mean to... I was just passing and heard her...'

'How did you know it wasn't me hitting *her*?' came the sardonically amused question.

Lucy turned around, a fierce expression on her face. 'Because I know you would never do anything like that.'

His belly clenched. It was harder not to touch her than to touch her and risk that emotion rising again, so Ari reached out and tugged a resisting Lucy onto his lap. He felt an unusual peace steal over him. He buried his head in her neck and after a moment felt her relax, her curves softening into him with delicious inevitability.

But then he felt her tense again, and he looked up and said with a growl, 'Stop it. Relax, Lucy, *mou*.'

She was biting her lip and avoiding his eye. He turned her jaw so that she had to face him, and she said, almost defiantly, 'I saw you with that woman. I won't…won't be some substitute. If you'd prefer to be with her, then please…just go back.'

The thought of going back to that house made Ari shudder. He'd known it would be a mistake to go at all, and hated the fact that he had done so. Hated the fact that after all these years there was still a tiny sliver of yearning left for something he'd never experienced. Harmony. Even as that thought materialised in his head he blocked it ruthlessly, focused on the woman on his lap, reducing his world to the here and now.

He shook his head, amazed that Lucy could have seen him and Pia together and not have known that he'd all but itched to go back across the room to *her*. Then he remembered the moment before Helen had come into the room and asked to speak to him. Lucy had been with Anatolios, looking at him and laughing gaily. Anatolios had been practically sitting in her lap.

Dark anger surged. 'From what I saw of you and my brother, you looked very cosy also… Are you sure it's not you who wants to go back to him?'

Lucy couldn't help the shudder of disgust run through her as she said quickly, '*No*. I was just—we were just…talking.'

The relief that surged through Ari made him feel weak. He pressed a kiss to Lucy's bare shoulder and she shivered again, but this time he recognised desire and it was heady.

'Then, please believe me, I too have no desire to go back to that house. Pia Kyriapoulos is a woman who is looking for her next wealthy protector. She thinks I could be it, but this evening I told her in no uncertain terms that I have no interest in signing up for the job. And anyway…' Ari brought Lucy's hand between them to his lap, where she could feel the stirrings of his growing arousal. 'She doesn't have this effect on me.'

Ari felt Lucy's fingers flutter over him and held back a low groan as his arousal soared. In that second he had a flash of an idea. Without stopping to consider what he was doing, he said, 'When we get back to the hotel, pack some things for the weekend. We're getting out of Athens…'

When Lucy woke the next morning she knew immediately that she was alone in the strange bed, but she was too deliciously lethargic and sated to worry about it. She heard nothing except beautiful stillness and the gentle lapping of water nearby.

They had travelled here, to this island, which Ari had told her was called Paros, by helicopter last night. It had all been a little overwhelming to Lucy. When they'd arrived Ari had driven them in a Jeep to this place, which Lucy hadn't been able to make out in the dark.

Now, without opening her eyes yet, as if superstitious for a moment that it might disappear, Lucy knew that there were doors open nearby. She could feel the warm breeze, could smell the tang of the sea and feel the bright sunlight.

Finally she opened her eyes. They took a second to adjust, and then as if in a dream she got up, blindly threw on a T-shirt and walked to the open French doors and the tiny balcony. She simply could not take in the beauty of her surroundings for a moment. The balcony seemed to be perched right over the Aegean Sea, which stretched out in glittering blue before her, other islands visible as shapes in the hazy distance under a clear cerulean sky.

The modest house was whitewashed and all but clinging onto the rocky coast, nestling alongside equally bright houses either side. Lucy frowned slightly. She'd seen Ari's portfolio of extensive properties around the world, and knew he had a luxurious villa on Santorini, but she'd never seen pictures of this house. She looked around. Admittedly, it was more humble than anything she might have expected of him. And all the more intriguing.

She heard a sound behind her and turned to see Ari, shouldering his way in through the door with arms full of supplies. Her breath snagged at remembering how he'd stripped her bare last night and taken her to heaven and back on the modest double bed. He was wearing long shorts and a faded T-shirt, and looked impossibly young and handsome at that moment—a million miles from the proud, successful, arrogant billionaire.

He pressed a lingering kiss to her mouth and proceeded to spread out a veritable feast of a breakfast on an ancient wrought-iron table. Bread, jams, fruit… Then he disappeared, presumably to the tiny kitchen downstairs, and came back with steaming fragrant coffee in two cups.

'Cat got your tongue?' he asked lightly as they sat down and Lucy still hadn't said a word.

She shook her head and tried to communicate with him what she was thinking, feeling. She made a half-gesture around them, encompassing the view. 'It's so beautiful… I can't even begin to describe…' She looked at him then. His face was shuttered, dark glasses shielding his eyes. 'This property isn't listed with your other ones…'

Ari's jaw clenched. He looked out towards the glittering Aegean. When he'd made the decision to come here he hadn't stopped to consider Lucy's reaction to the basic nature of the house. He knew very few women who wouldn't have turned up their noses and shuddered disdainfully. A ridiculous feeling of disappointment ran through him and he drawled, 'You'd prefer to be on Santorini? The villa there certainly is…larger.'

Shock coursed through Lucy. 'No! That's not what I meant at all. I'd much prefer to be here…' She hated that he'd jumped to that conclusion. 'I just mentioned it because I hadn't seen it. That's all.'

Ari flicked her a glance. 'It's not listed because I've deliberately kept it private. It was my mother's house—where she grew up.'

'Oh.' There didn't seem to be anything more to say, and Lucy could feel a wall spring up between them. Clearly he wasn't going to elaborate. It seemed important to make him believe so she leaned across and took his hand. 'Ari, I'm glad you brought me here. Really.'

After a long day in the sun, exploring the island's beaches and eating a basic picnic, drinking sparkling wine in the shade on an empty beach, making love until their bodies seemed boneless and sated, Ari couldn't stop thinking about Lucy's words and expression from that morning. She'd seemed sincere. He'd believed her to be sincere when she'd professed to liking the place.

He held her hand in his now, as they wandered through the ancient winding streets of his mother's birthplace. He repressed the urge to ask her if she'd really meant what she'd said—if she really loved this humble little place as much as she seemed to—because he hated how important it felt to him that she did.

A little later Ari sat back in his chair in the small taverna he'd brought her to, and Lucy's belly flipped over at his expression. He was looking at her so intensely she had to ask, 'What…? Have I got something on my face?'

He shook his head and smiled, and her heart turned over. She had once thought he was incapable of smiling, but the younger-seeming, softer side of this man was altogether far too enticing.

'Just a lot of freckles. Who would have known you'd freckle so easily?'

Lucy grimaced. 'I have celtic ancestry.'

He smiled wider, lounging back, cradling a half-empty wine glass. 'They're cute.'

Lucy scowled at the word. 'Unfortunately we can't all go a deeper shade of bronze in the sun.'

She tried to stop her eyes roving over his powerful form but couldn't resist. His T-shirt strained over broad shoulders and clung to that lean torso; low-slung jeans were so low slung that she could see a sliver of taut dark flesh just above the button, the dark shading of hair making her heart trip.

'Stop devouring me with your eyes, or I'll carry you back to bed over my shoulder, Lucy Proctor.'

She looked up again and blushed. He leant forward and captured her hand.

'It's amazing that you can blush when you're so incredibly sensual…when you wear such decadent underwear…'

Lucy groaned.

'…and have a body to put the Venus de Milo to shame…'

'I don't… *Stop*.' Lucy glanced around, mortified, in case someone had heard him. He laughed out loud.

'Yes, you do—and it's entirely appropriate that we're here, because this is the island that supplied the Parian marble for the sculpture.' He kept her hand and asked then, 'Tell me, Lucy, why is it that you have these two different sides? And why did you fight not to fall into my bed? Was it all a game?'

His voice had hardened, his hand had tightened, and Lucy looked at him and felt nervous. It suddenly seemed very important to be honest with him.

Even more so when he added, 'And how is it that you speak at least two other languages fluently and can hold your own in the snobby dining rooms of Athens?'

Lucy was silent for a long time. She looked out of the window that they were seated beside and saw the dark ocean, and fishing boats twinkling under a moonlit sky. And then she said haltingly, 'My mother was one of the most celebrated burlesque performers in the world…'

And before she knew it she was telling him everything, and he was listening, as rapt as she'd ever seen him. She told him about living in Paris, and before that Rio de Janeiro, New York…London. The ever-changing schools, the nomadic nature of their lives.

Lucy wrinkled her nose. 'Her real name was Mabel Proctor, but she changed it to Maxine Malbec.'

Ari frowned. His thumb stopped making little circles of sensation in her palm.

'*The* Maxine Malbec?'

Lucy nodded, feeling slightly sick. Was he going to judge her now or, worse, judge her mother? She started to pull her hand back, but he gripped it again.

He was shaking his head. 'Lucy, that's an amazing story… The picture I saw in your flat—I thought there was something familiar about her.'

She smiled wryly. 'That's what I was afraid of. And it's not a story—it was my life.' She shrugged, feeling self-conscious. 'Having a mother who was so overtly…sexual made me wary, I think, of that side of me.' Her mouth tightened. 'It's also why I have an aversion to expensive jewellery…trinkets… Seeing my mother fobbed off by so many rich men over the years… My father was one of those men, married with his own family. He had no desire for a love-child.' Lucy's voice trailed away. She was shocked she'd revealed so much so quickly.

She didn't elaborate on how precarious her life had been until she'd grown older and taken control of herself and her mother. She also didn't elaborate on the fear she still had of becoming dependent on a man, on how her father's rejection had fostered a deep feeling of insecurity she was only just beginning to let go of.

Ari winced inwardly when he recalled her reaction to his asking her to buy something for Augustine Archer, and then dragging her around that jewellery shop. He remembered the innately sexy way Lucy had stripped for him that first night. 'You've obviously inherited her natural sensuality—*that's all*. She sounds like she was an amazing woman, and it must have been hard, raising a daughter on her own.'

Lucy was struck somewhere very vulnerable by his easy understanding. She nodded and smiled weakly, feeling emotion rise. 'She was...*is* an amazing woman.'

Ari frowned. 'She's still alive?'

Lucy nodded. 'Yes, but...' She told him about her mother's illness and the home that she was now in.

He said quietly, 'It must be hard to see her like that...diminished.'

Lucy just nodded, terrified she might start crying. 'It is.'

To her relief he seemed happy to let it drop there, and discreetly paid the bill before tugging her up and leading her back down the quiet winding streets to the humble little house.

A few hours later Ari lay on his back, his arms around Lucy's sleeping form, her breasts rising and falling gently against his bare chest. Even though he was recently sated, that subtle movement made him hard again. He shifted minutely and bit back a groan when Lucy moved too, and he felt her nipples against his side like two hard berries.

For the first time in his life he'd put himself in a situation where he couldn't just get up and leave a woman behind—after all, where could he go? And for the first time it wasn't sending that usual feeling of suffocating claustrophobia into his belly.

* * *

The following evening Lucy was changing while Ari had a shower in the small bathroom downstairs. The house *was* tiny, and rustic and beyond basic, but she loved it. Ari had told her earlier of how his mother had grown up there with her sister and her mother, his grandfather having died when they were small.

She went to the balcony and smoothed the plain dark red sundress over her hips. Her skin tingled from being in the sun, and she felt freer than she'd felt in a long time. She'd called her mother's home earlier, and she was obviously having a good day—although Lucy had had to explain again why she wasn't able to visit for another week. It seemed as if her mother was making friends with some of the other residents, and the matron had assured her again that she was being well cared for. The relief was enormous.

A sound made her whirl around from where she was leaning against the balcony rail, watching the sun go down over the sea. Ari stood in the doorway with just a towel around his lean hips.

She looked up, throat dry, and met his eyes. They glowed with dark, decadent promise. He put his hand to the towel and with a flick of his wrist it was gone. Lucy's body flamed.

'Come here…' he said softly.

Lucy tried to resist the feeling of hot insanity. 'Ari, I've just changed…'

'Come *here.*'

On shaky legs and bare feet Lucy walked over and said, 'Has anyone ever told you that you're extremely bossy and arrogant?'

He shook his head and pulled her right into him, reaching for her dress and pulling it up, at the same time pulling her pants down. Excitement made Lucy shiver uncontrollably.

'Only you seem to have the nerve to say these things…' he growled, mock angrily.

And then talking stopped for a long, languorous moment.

* * *

Much later, when the moon had risen and the stars were out, they headed out for dinner. Lucy had put on a light cardigan as the late spring evening had a slightly cool edge. Her eyes drank Ari in as she trailed him, her hand firmly clasped in his. She never would have imagined him to be so tactile, but he was always reaching out to touch her, to take her hand, rub the back of his hand down a cheek… She sighed inwardly. He was wearing black trousers and a snowy white shirt, and he was more gorgeous than any one man had a right to be.

This part of northern Paros was a sleepy fishing village. The summer hordes hadn't descended yet, but in the distance Lucy heard music and recognised a traditional Greek tune as they rounded the corner into an idyllic little square where a taverna was all lit up. A mad profusion of flowers erupted from every windowsill and around the door.

Lucy heard shouts and laughter, and as they went in Ari ducked his head to avoid hitting the doorframe. An even bigger shout went up, and suddenly a crowd was thronging around them and a huge man was dragging Ari's face down and kissing him soundly.

When he could, Ari pulled Lucy forward, feeling an incredible lightness in his chest. He'd missed coming here. A gut-wrenching sense of homecoming nearly floored him with its intensity. London and the merger and Athens and Helen all seemed to be light years away from this moment.

But as if he couldn't hold it down the thought rose up like a spectre: *the emotion…* The threat of it was rising up to swallow him whole. That was why he hadn't been back.

He felt for Lucy's luscious curves and let her distract him from those dark thoughts, introducing her to his mother's old friends and even to some distant cousins. He could see a few of the young bucks eyeing her up, but with one warning look from him they retreated, shamefaced. Ari kept her close when they were seated in the corner with Costas, the owner, who pulled up a chair and ordered a veritable feast on their behalf.

Lucy sat back a while later and groaned, wiping her mouth with a napkin, 'I've never eaten as much as I have these last two days. And I do *not* need any extra padding.'

Ari looked at Lucy from under hooded lids, his eyes drifting down to that delectable cleavage in her red dress. It made him remember taking that dress off her only hours before, unhooking her bra and letting those voluptuous mounds spill into his hands. His body tightened and grew hot with annoying predictability. She turned him on with such ease…

She caught his eye and smiled and leant forward, crossing her arms so that her breasts were pushed together and forward. 'See something you like?'

Ari's green gaze glittered and darkened. He leant forward too and said softly, 'Witch. I'll punish you for that.'

They looked at each other, everything fading into the background for a long intense moment, until Costas came over and pulled Ari up, breaking the spell. It was only then that Lucy saw the tables and chairs had been pushed back, the volume of music had been raised and Ari stood now with Costas, arms high, as they started to do a mesmeric Greek dance.

Lucy's breath caught in her throat. It was so beautiful. It should have made Ari look effeminate, but it did the opposite. A couple of the older ladies dressed in black got up and danced with the men, their steps in sync as the music started to increase in tempo. As more people, young and old, joined in and linked arms, the music got faster and faster. The next thing Lucy knew she was being hauled up to join in.

She hissed at Ari. 'Don't you *dare*.'

But he didn't listen, just drew her into the melee, and Lucy found herself laughingly trying to keep up with everyone else. The women were showing her the complex steps, it was frantic and captivating, and as the last evocative chords died away she stumbled right into Ari's arms.

Something potent and silent was vibrating between them, and without further ado Ari grabbed Lucy's cardigan and they left, a silent intensity surrounding them all the way until they returned to the small house. Barely had the door closed before their mouths were fused, hands seeking desperately to touch bare flesh. They didn't even make it up the stairs. Ari took her there and then, fast and furiously.

It was only later, after they'd made it to the bed and made love again, that Lucy woke from a tangled dream to a strange sound. She was curled close to Ari's big body and she looked up to see that he had an arm flung over his face. His breathing was fast and shallow and he was speaking in Greek.

Lucy put her hand on his arm, tried to draw it down, and it was only when she did that she saw the tracks of tears on his face. Her heart turned over.

At her light touch, he was awake in an instant, eyes alert, straight on hers. Lucy's voice was incredibly husky. 'You were…' She faltered, nearly saying *crying* but instinctively stopping herself. 'You were having a dream…you sounded upset.'

He did nothing for a moment, and then his face closed over and became so cold she nearly shivered. His expression was quite clear in the bright moonlight streaming in through the open doors.

In an instant he'd jackknifed off the bed to go and stand with his back to her at the balcony railing, looking out to the dark expanse of the sea. He was naked, and his physique was so gloriously powerful that it took Lucy's breath away for a moment. He was also extremely tense.

She got up and pulled on a T-shirt, went over silently to stand next to him. She noticed that his hands were wrapped so tight around the railing that his knuckles shone white.

Instinctively she put her hand over his nearest one, and he flinched minutely as if he'd been unaware of her presence. When Lucy looked up at his face it was unbearably harsh, and she knew instantly that this man was worlds apart from the one-dimensional playboy tycoon she'd first believed him to be.

She didn't say anything, just kept her hand on his, and after a long moment he said, so quietly that she had to strain to hear, 'I remember being here…in this house…with my mother and father on holiday, just before she died. Ya-ya was still alive too, and my aunt…and we were happy. Really happy.'

Lucy didn't interrupt.

'My father had met my mother when he'd come here on a day-trip with some friends. They were typical Athenians—cocky, arrogant, rich… But he saw her, and within a month he'd taken her back to Athens to be his wife.'

'He must have loved her a great deal.'

Ari jerked his head to look down at Lucy. She felt tension spike in his form as if he'd just realised that he'd spoken out loud and had a witness.

'Loved her so much that after she died he married again within the year? *Please.* My father left me here with my grandmother, and the next time I remember seeing him he had Helen Savakis with him. His new wife.' His lip curled. 'She convinced him to send me to boarding school, where I was conveniently out of the way, so that she could have her own son and raise him to be my father's golden child.'

Lucy's shock at Helen's cold-hearted ruthlessness was palpable. 'But your father left everything to you…?'

Ari nodded, looking back out to sea. 'Which is why Anatolios hates me and Helen despises me even more now than she did when I was a child. She hates the fact that she needs me for her security. She hates the fact that I'm not in Athens, where she can try to make me marry a woman of her choosing to control me even more…'

Lucy winced reflexively at his mention of marriage and re-membered his caustic response to Helen's obvious fear that what was between *them* might be serious. She guessed in that moment that Ari's memory of this place and that time when his parents were together ran deep for a reason. If they'd had a halcyon time here, only for his mother to die so suddenly and his father disappear, it must have been heartbreakingly confusing for a small child. How would someone so tiny make any sense of loving a place when it was also the scene of such sorrow?

But from the sounds of it, if his father had been a success-ful young man, with the world at his feet, it must have been love for him to marry Ari's mother, who would have been very poor.

'I can only imagine how hard it must have been for your father to leave you behind…perhaps that's why he married again so soon…'

Ari turned then, and looked down at Lucy properly. She felt very exposed in the face of his deep hurt and unmistak-able cynicism.

'Yes—and why he found it no chore to send me away to school on his new wife's recommendation.'

'Ari, I've seen the way a woman can enchant a man. Maybe he was just—'

Just enchanted the way you're being enchanted right now? The revelation made Ari's voice harsh. 'What, Lucy? Please don't try and feed me some psychobabble nonsense. This subject is closed for discussion.' His eyes flashed a warning in the silvery light. 'And you're far too overdressed.'

Ari picked Lucy up with an intensity that sent a flutter of fear through her. Instinctively her hands tightened on his shoulders. And then something happened. Almost instantane-ously she sensed a different intensity run through him. The mood altered. He looked down at her and she could see feral desire mixed with something almost like confusion in those dark green depths, and her heart ached with a mirror emotion.

The fact that she could sense his need to dilute the emotion he'd just revealed with physicality made her reach up and touch her mouth to his. She felt him tremble slightly, and as she wrapped her arms around his neck and deepened the kiss he responded.

He took her over to the bed and laid her down with a gentleness Lucy would have bet he hadn't been feeling just moments ago. The fact that she was so aware of him, aware of what was going on inside his head, made her reel anew. His body covered hers with a delicious weight and Lucy brought a shaky hand to his face. When he turned to press a kiss to her inner palm she felt another flutter of fear—but this time it was because she knew for certain that she'd fallen in love with this complex, proud man who presented one face to the world and another here with her.

When Lucy woke the next morning she wasn't surprised to see Ari up and dressed and sitting on the balcony. Dark glasses shielded those amazing eyes. There was a stillness to his body and a sternness to his features that told her the sensual cocoon they'd inhabited last night was gone. The revelation of admitting she'd fallen for him made her feel intensely vulnerable in the harsh light of day. She pulled the sheet up over her body and Ari's head turned. Her skin prickled when she imagined the slow appraisal he was giving her from behind those shades.

She came up on one arm and pushed her heavy mass of hair back, feeling very rumpled and lethargic. Ari had been ruthless in his pursuit of pleasure last night, *hers and his,* surprising her with the depth of passion he'd incited within her. It had seemed as if their lovemaking had gone to another place, and Lucy cringed inwardly now to remember that she'd been moved to tears after one shattering climax after another.

Now Ari just uncoiled that long lean body from the chair and said coolly, 'We need to get back to Athens. We've got work to do and a heavy week coming up.'

Lucy felt as if he'd slapped her. Her body went cold. Boss/assistant. Back to work. Back in her place. The intense vulnerability made her feel slightly sick.

'Of course,' she said through numb lips, when she felt like saying something like, *I never asked for this, you know, and I certainly never expected to be brought here to this idyllic little hideaway where you couldn't contain your emotions.*

When Lucy stood under the shower a short time later her belly clenched painfully. She could see exactly why he'd brought her here now: no possibility of paparazzi catching them out, no one who knew him apart from the locals he'd known as a child...*no chance for her to be getting any ideas*.

There was a knock on the door that made her jump, and Lucy heard a curt, 'The helicopter is on stand-by. As soon as you're ready we're leaving.'

'Fine,' Lucy called casually, belying the unsteady beating of her heart and the sick feeling gripping her gut. His words and cool manner were an all too mocking confirmation of her fears and her own stupidity. He was hustling them out of here as if there had just been some kind of dire weather warning, making it patently obvious how much he regretted bringing her there in the first place.

As she switched off the shower and stepped out, she knew that she would have to start distancing herself. She couldn't go on like this. She was being served a timely reminder of what she could expect out of this relationship—which was nothing but a very bruised heart.

That evening, when they returned to the hotel from Ari's Athens office and Lucy felt Ari take her arm as they stepped out of the lift, she drew on all her strength to pull away from his touch.

They approached her hotel room door and she prayed silently that he wouldn't try to come in. She sent him a quick glance, while swiping her door open at the same time, thanking God that her hands were steady.

'I'm tired. I'm going to go to bed...'

Her door opened and she heard a drawling, 'Not a bad idea.'

Lucy turned in the door and looked up. '*Alone*. As you said yourself earlier, we have a heavy week. And I—I am tired.'

Ari looked down at Lucy and felt the knot of frustration which had started the minute he'd left their bed earlier this morning intensify. Every moment he spent not touching this woman meant dealing with a level of frustration he hadn't experienced before. He looked at her properly for the first time. He'd tried to avoid looking directly at her all day—if he was honest since last night, when she'd— His belly flipped over and he ruthlessly quashed the memory of such weakness. He still couldn't believe it had happened...

But now she did look tired, with faint circles of violet under her eyes. She also looked a little strained, and a dart of guilt struck him when he remembered the urgency he'd felt to get off Paros and back here, bringing them straight to the office and working them both like dogs.

Lust was a force within him, crying out for satisfaction...but he would not admit to that. She wanted to go to bed alone? Well, he was damned if he was going to let her see that the notion of that went against every clamouring instinct to throw her over his shoulder and carry her to his own bed.

So he backed away, and did not like the visible look of relief that crossed her face. He almost stopped and gave in to his primal urges—had to clench his fists not to.

'We leave for Parnassus' villa at nine a.m. I'll see you in the lobby.'

She nodded and then disappeared into her room, shutting the door between them with a firm click that seemed to resonate all the way through Ari's body right to his feet.

On Thursday evening Lucy thought back to the gentle exhaustion she'd felt the previous Sunday and could have laughed. Since then it had been like the first week—a frenetic blur of work, whizzing from Parnassus' villa, back to Ari's office, and back to the hotel. Ari had been out late nearly every evening, having private meetings with Parnassus and their legal teams, and much to Lucy's relief hadn't thought it necessary for her to be there too.

She'd carefully locked the interconnecting door on her side each night, even though all she'd fantasised about was slipping naked between Ari's sheets and awaiting his return.

Instead, as she'd thumped her pillow, she'd told herself that this was the best way. Nip it in the bud now, and when they got back to the UK she'd calmly inform him that this brief moment of madness was over. Her mind froze at the thought of calling women for him, arranging dates, seeing him come in in the morning with that satisfied look on his face, slight shadows under those amazing eyes from not sleeping—

'Lucy, what are you doing hiding over here? Has Ari told you to stay out of sight in case people realise he's sleeping with his PA?'

It took a moment for Lucy's focus to return to the room and realise that Anatolios was standing in front of her, with a smarmy look on his face. She could almost feel sorry for him now that she knew he'd been rejected in the end, despite his mother's vast efforts to secure him number one place in his father's affections.

'I'm not hiding.' She felt defensive. She *had* been guilty

of hiding, hoping to get a glimpse of Ari and compose herself before going over to him. 'I've just arrived and I was looking for Ari.'

They'd come separately to this, another charity ball which was being held in their hotel in honour of Parnassus' contribution to helping the homeless in Athens. It was going to be the precursor of the announcement of the merger, which would be made the following morning, with the papers being signed at a press conference.

Lucy felt a prickle of unease skate up her spine when she saw how Anatolios's eyes were all but devouring her breasts, and she realised she was hemmed in between him and a wall. She moved to try and edge past him, but he moved too, surprising her with his agility.

He came and stood close, effectively blocking her from the room, and Lucy was very aware of how intimate it might look. She was plastered against the wall behind her now, could feel Anatolios's breath, smell the alcohol. Her belly spasmed.

'Anatolios, I have to go and find Ari. Would you excuse me, please?'

He laughed, and it was nasty. He didn't move. 'You English, you're always so polite—please and thank you. You're not going anywhere until you tell me what Ari is cooking up with Parnassus.'

Lucy flushed, and her eyes were immediately caught by Anatolios's. He couldn't hide his look of triumph.

'I *knew* it. I knew there was something big going on.' He grabbed Lucy's arm then, making her wince.

'Tell me what it is *right now,* I have a right to know what my brother is—'

Abruptly Anatolios was moved out of the way bodily, and then Ari was standing there. Lucy felt weak with relief.

He gestured with a hand for her to come with him, and she went gratefully, her legs feeling like jelly. She didn't look back, and when Ari said to her, 'What was going on there?' she avoided his eye and shook her head, saying, 'Nothing. He just…we were just chatting, that's all.'

The whole scene, with its air of menace, was making her feel sick, but she didn't see the point in rising Ari's ire now, when the deal was all but done.

Lucy made sure to stick close to him after that, figuring the devil she knew was better than dealing with Anatolios or Helen, who she'd also seen in the distance.

Just before everyone started to disperse Ari pulled her aside and took a sheaf of folded documents out of his inside jacket pocket. He handed them to her and they were still warm from his body heat. Even that made her tremble.

'Put these up in the safe in my room, would you, please? They're the official merger documents for tomorrow.'

She just nodded, avoiding his eye, and hurried out of the ballroom, glad of the respite and a chance to get herself back under control.

Ari watched Lucy leave the room, his eyes drawn helplessly to her glorious body in the figure-hugging strapless dress. His hunger for her was like a wild thing within him— a beast clawing to get out.

He rationalised it: it had to be because she'd been holding him at arm's length all week, her door firmly closed by the time he'd come back each evening. His mind had been helplessly distracted, despite the fact that he'd told her *not* to come to those late-night meetings, but now— His body tightened unbearably. The thought of her right now, in his room… He glanced around and knew he wouldn't be missed for a few moments. His blood surged at the thought of tumbling her onto his bed and sating this demon desire inside him.

* * *

Lucy was walking over to where the safe was hidden in the wardrobe of Ari's bedroom when she heard something at the door. She turned and went back, thinking it might be the turn down staff. When she saw Anatolios slipping into the room she froze.

'What are you doing here? How did you get in?'

He smiled nastily, and she saw his eyes take in the documents in her hand. She hurriedly put them behind her back.

He kept coming towards her, and she started to back away into the bedroom.

'Oh, let's just say I'm in Athens a lot more than Ari these days, so I have my contacts. Now, why don't you show me what you have hidden behind your pretty back?'

He was coming straight at her and Lucy froze for a second, fear gripping her like a cold, clammy hand. He was almost on her before she turned and stumbled, making for the safe before he could get the documents from her.

She felt her arm grabbed in a merciless grip and cried out, tipping off balance. Anatolios jerked her back painfully.

'Let me *go*.'

He was reaching around her, trying to get the papers, his face red and flushed. In a bid to get away, though his arms were wrapped tight around her now, Lucy dropped the papers behind her and used her hands to try and push him off. He saw the papers and lunged, knocking them both to the ground. He fell as a heavy weight on top of her, reaching underneath her for the papers.

Lucy was struggling in earnest now. She could feel her dress riding up her leg, her chest being squashed by his heavy weight. 'You… Get off me. I can't…*breathe*…'

'What the hell is going on here?'

CHAPTER NINE

BEFORE Lucy knew which way was up, the heavy weight of Anatolios was being plucked off her by Ari, as if he weighed no more than a bag of sugar. He literally held Anatolios by the scruff of his neck. The man was spluttering now, clearly terrified of his much stronger older brother.

'She told me to come up here. She told me she had something for me. *There!*'

He pointed to the papers, now strewn on the ground.

'Is this true?' Icy green eyes and an even icier voice were directed down at Lucy, who realised that she was still on the floor, dress hitched up, breasts heaving with her breath. She scrambled up, but then had to subside onto the side of the bed when her legs wouldn't hold her. Reaction was starting to set in.

She shook her head. She couldn't look at Ari—or *him*. 'No, of course it's not true. He followed me up here. He must have seen you give me the papers.'

Anatolios spluttered even more. 'Come *on*. Why on earth would I want to see some stupid papers? It's not as if there's anything going on—is there?'

Ari stilled. Right until that moment his vision had been blurred because he was so angry. When he'd seen Anatolios on top of Lucy he'd felt an awful weakness pervade his limbs before he'd kicked into action. And then, when he'd seen the papers… His heart was telling him one thing, but his brain was refusing to listen.

He dragged Anatolios to the door of the suite and said blisteringly, 'If I find out that you were the instigator of this incident you can kiss goodbye to working for Levakis Enterprises once and for all.'

And with that he threw his brother out of the suite and faced back to the bedroom, thinking to himself, *If, on the other hand, I find out it was Lucy…* His brain seized.

She appeared at the bedroom door. She looked unsteady on her feet, one shoe on, one shoe off. Her dark hair was tumbled in glorious profusion around her milky pale bare shoulders, the curve of her breasts outlined by the top of her strapless dress. As if seeing the direction of his gaze, she put her hands there and hitched the dress up. He noticed they were shaking, and yet he couldn't give in to his overwhelming instinct which was to go to her, to take her into his arms. He *couldn't*—because she might very well have just tried to betray him in the most heinous way.

He suddenly thought of the way he'd seen her earlier, backed into a corner talking to Anatolios as intimately as if they'd been lovers. And thought too of all the distant warning bells he'd ignored in his pursuit of her. The fact that work had taken second place, especially at such an important time, was starkly clear now.

Lucy sucked in a sharp breath. Ari clearly wasn't leaping to see if she was all right as he stood there, all but glowering at her. The fact that he believed she *might* have led Anatolios up here with a view to giving him or showing him the documents was screamingly obvious. Her hand gripped onto the doorframe as sheer hurt at his fundamental lack of trust nearly floored her.

He moved suddenly, and she flinched, but he just went over

to the drinks board and poured a measure of what looked like whisky into a shot glass and brought it over to her.

'Here—drink this.'

She looked up as she took the glass. 'Ari, please let me—'

'I don't want to hear it. Not right now anyway.'

And he stepped past her and into the room, where she looked back to see him pick up the papers and put them in the safe.

Feeling numb, Lucy bent to take off her one shoe and went into the sitting room to sit down. She took a sip of the liquid, wincing as it burnt its way down her throat.

Ari came back out and stood with arms folded, all but towering over her. She refused to cower back into the chair, and put the glass down jerkily on the table beside her.

'Ari—'

'Did he see the papers? Does he know about Parnassus?'

'Of course not. How can you think that?'

'Because tonight is the second time I've seen you deep in conversation with my brother, and now, the night before the biggest merger in Greek history is announced, he happens to be conveniently in the same room as you when you're putting the papers in the safe.' His mouth thinned. 'Although obviously you both got distracted—'

Lucy stood, quivering from head to toe. 'Stop that right now. That's not how it happened. He followed me up here and got in somehow. He must have got a key from someone on the staff. Before I knew it he was…' She shuddered convulsively as she remembered the instant panic at feeling him crowding her, all over her.

Lucy stopped talking and looked into those devastating and yet icy green eyes, that harsh face. Her words might as well have been addressed to a marble statue. He was so remote, so *untouchable*. And something slammed into her consciousness. It was cold and stark reality. Despite his cool behaviour that last morning on Paros, had she really fooled herself for a second into believing that something amazing had happened between them? That against all the odds they'd gained some sort of mutual trust and respect? She was just the secretary and he was her boss… She gasped audibly as it became even more clear, her hand going to her chest as if to stop the lancing pain. But it didn't.

Even Ari frowned. 'What is it?'

Lucy figured dimly that all the colour must have drained from her face. She felt icy cold all of a sudden, and tried to formulate words through numb lips. 'That's why you appeared—you didn't even trust me to come up here and do this. You suspected something all along.'

She watched as his face flushed a dark red, and found herself sinking back down onto the chair.

'All this time you've thought that I might do something like this.' She shook her head and looked up, pain shattering her insides as she had to ask, 'Is that why you slept with me? Because you thought it might be easier to control me?'

His lack of response and that stony visage was confirmation enough. As if watching a movie in slow motion, Lucy went all the way back to when she'd tried to resign and Ari had told her she couldn't. It must have been then. He must have decided at that point that she might be a liability and planning some kind of revenge.

She somehow found the strength to stand again. She felt even clammier now. She'd always known what Ari was, the kind of man he was, but somehow in the past few weeks she'd let herself forget it.

He put out a hand towards her but Lucy flinched back, moving behind the chair,

'Lucy—'

'No. I don't want to hear it. I know it's over. It's all over. That's the only reason you slept with me. I've been really—'

She stopped and bit her lip before she could say *stupid*. She lifted dead eyes to his. 'Blood really is thicker than water, isn't it?' She smiled a small harsh smile. 'Perhaps this is a step forward in fostering a new regard for your half-brother?'

Her smile faded. 'Anatolios doesn't know about the merger. It happened exactly the way I said it did. The reason I passed off the conversation earlier as nothing was because he was beginning to suspect something and asked me about it. I didn't tell you because I figured he'd never find out before the morning and you didn't need the hassle.'

She hitched up her chin. 'I intend to resign once the press conference is over, I can't see why you wouldn't agree to that now.' She smiled with brittle brightness. 'After all, I can't imagine you want to be faced with an assistant you had to sleep with for business every day.'

Lucy turned and walked stiffly to the door, then looked back, somewhere in his general direction. 'I can organise my own flight home tomorrow after the press conference. I'd prefer that, and I'm sure you would too. I'll work out my notice if you insist, but I'm happy to collect my things from the office on Monday too.'

And, opening the door, she slipped out.

Ari watched the door for a long moment. The earth was shifting underneath him. He *had* been about to refute her reasoning behind why he'd slept with her, but then, when she'd interrupted him and obviously decided that that had to be the case, he hadn't spoken up.

He could have stopped her from leaving. He could have told her. *Why* hadn't he?

Ari sat down heavily onto the ornately brocaded sofa behind him. Without the awful stomach-churning red mist of anger that had gripped him, he had to concede that of course he trusted Lucy over his opportunistic brother any day of the week. This whole scene had all the clumsy and unoriginal hallmarks of Anatolios. But he'd just seen them together and…his mind had imploded.

His fists clenched when he saw how easily he'd misinterpreted the situation. She was wrong in this case. Blood was most certainly not thicker than water. If Lucy had been guilty she'd never have jumped to the conclusion she had. She'd have defended herself vociferously, she'd have cajoled and enticed, perhaps even tried to seduce him into bed to distract him. But he didn't need reminding that she hadn't come near him since Paros. His mouth twisted. And could he blame her? When he'd all but hustled her off the island like a fugitive. But he had just been so…so overwhelmed that she'd witnessed his excruciating weakness. *She'd seen him cry.* And she hadn't turned away in horror, she'd been gorgeous, sympathetic, understanding… It had been too much.

He couldn't deal with that. No one had seen that side of him. It had been locked away for so long—he'd been alone against the world for so long…

And that was why he'd let her stand there and believe he'd seduced her deliberately. His life hadn't been on an even keel since he'd started noticing her, desiring her. That had been part of his knee-jerk response tonight—the knowledge that he'd been so hungry for her that he'd followed her to the room for *that* and not because he might have suspected her of espionage. He'd felt intensely vulnerable for the brief moment when he had contemplated that that could have been the reality.

He stood abruptly and made for the door. He had to go back downstairs, had to smile and pretend everything was OK, when he felt as if his insides were twisting tight in his gut. Lucy was right. It was over. Where could it go from here anyway? He would not let her see him be weak one more time. No woman was worth that.

* * *

The next morning, when the press conference was over, Lucy avoided the scrum of shocked and chattering press and went up to her room. She picked up her one small bag, she was leaving all the bought clothes behind, and went down to the lobby to check out.

She was just arranging for a taxi to take her to the airport when she felt her arm taken in a spine-tinglingly familiar grip and a smooth voice spoke over her to the concierge. 'My driver will look after her, thank you.'

She stiffened under his touch, her whole body crying out shamefully for more.

'That's really not necessary.'

He smoothly moved them away, his hand still on her arm. Lucy fought not to pull it free, afraid he might guess how badly he was affecting her.

'Lucy—' he sighed heavily '—about last night—'

'Please. You don't have to say anything.'

'I do.' His hand tightened, and she looked up against her better judgement. His eyes were so green that she felt pole-axed.

'You were wrong, I never slept with you because I thought you were capable of espionage. I read the situation entirely wrong and I'm sorry. But you're right…it's…this—*us*—is over.'

Lucy tried to school her features, even though she felt as if someone had just stabbed her in the belly. Relief that he *had* trusted her was eclipsed by sheer pain that she shouldn't even be feeling. 'What about…your brother?'

Ari grimaced. 'I'll deal with him. It's not for you to worry about.'

No, thought Lucy faintly, still reeling and hating herself for it. Because she wouldn't be working for Levakis Enterprises any more.

'Look, I'm leaving for New York from here for about ten

days, to make sure the merger goes smoothly over there. If you still intend to resign—'

For a second Lucy heard nothing but a roaring in her ears— *what other option did she possibly have?* It cleared just in time for her to hear him say, 'That should give you time to sort yourself out.'

Lucy nodded dumbly. Even though she *wanted* this, had asked for this, to be faced with it now was like no other devastation she'd ever felt. But how on earth had she thought it might play out? she admonished herself. Aristotle Levakis would never keep a discarded lover hanging around like a bad smell. And of course they couldn't go back to a benign working relationship, no matter how she'd thought it might happen.

Ari walked her out to the entrance, where his car was waiting. He handed her in and said, 'I want to thank you for all your work. This merger wouldn't have happened nearly as smoothly without you.'

Oh, please just don't, she almost said. Their affair was reduced to this—trite thanks for her work on the project and for pleasuring her boss in bed in between meetings. The glaring cliché of it all nearly made her want to be ill. Before she could lose control, Lucy grabbed the door handle and pulled it closed firmly, shutting Ari out, but not unfortunately, the pain.

She didn't look back as the car pulled away, so she didn't see Ari standing there, his features drawn and almost grey in the glorious Athenian sun. And anyway, even if she had she wouldn't have believed it.

It was Friday evening, a week later, and Lucy was packing her final bits and pieces into a box, looking around the now empty office. It had been infinitely easier to do this without Ari here, though it had been heart-wrenchingly painful to talk to him on the phone every day, when he'd called to check in or give instructions and hear how interviews were going for a new assistant.

'I trust you. After all, you've been the best assistant I've had,' he'd said when she'd protested that she couldn't be responsible for hiring someone new.

He'd made no effort to ask her to stay, and even though Lucy didn't even want that, couldn't contemplate that, she'd found it nauseating to shake the hand of the best candidate just the other day and had forced a brittle smile when the girl had said, 'Is it true what they say? Is he really that astoundingly gorgeous?'

Lucy shook her head now, to try and clear it, and pulled on her beige trenchcoat. She'd dressed down today, not having seen the point in making an effort, and was wearing jeans, an oversized black jumper and battered sneakers. Her thoughts in that moment went guiltily to her mum, and she bit her lip as she hefted up the box. She had to find another job, and soon. She'd be OK for the next few months or so, but after that—

'*Lucy.*'

Lucy whirled around at the familiar deep voice. It tugged on her insides and made a fire of sensation race across her skin. Her movement had been so sudden that the full box wobbled precariously out of her arms and fell to the floor, upending everything in a big mess.

She barely registered Ari standing at the door like a huge, dark and threatening presence, and bent down to start picking the things up, her hands shaking. He moved fast and crouched down. Lucy put out a hand. 'Please—don't. I can do it.'

But he ignored her, picking up books and stationery, putting things back in the box. Lucy had to break the taut silence. 'I thought you weren't coming back till the weekend.'

Had he been wining and dining some new woman already in New York? She slammed a book more furiously than she'd intended into the box, in reaction to her wayward thoughts and the jealousy that spiked through her gut.

Ari didn't seem to notice, calmly packing the box. His scent reached out and wrapped her in a heat haze of lust.

'I wrapped things up early. I wanted to get back here.'

His voice was cool, devoid of emotion.

Lucy's movements became brisker. She just wanted to get out of here—right now. 'I think you'll like Gemma, your new assistant. She was far and away the most qualified person.'

Everything was back in the box, and there was an awkward moment when Lucy and Ari went to pick it up at the same time. Lucy had to let him take it, or it would have fallen again.

'I thought I told you I don't like your hair tied back.'

Lucy's eyes flew to his in shock. He sounded almost *flirty*. And his eyes were dark, glittering in a way she hadn't seen since— Once again she cursed her fevered brain. 'That's hardly relevant any more.' She took the box firmly out of his hands and held it to her like a shield. She stepped neatly around him, her breathing feeling short and jerky. 'Well, I'd better—'

'You haven't found a new job yet, have you?'

Lucy turned around. When would this torture end? She longed to be able to say yes, feeling inherently ashamed that she hadn't found a job, as if it made her look unemployable. But every single company she'd approached had stone-walled her—hadn't even allowed her an interview. She couldn't understand it. With a glowing reference from Ari himself, she'd have thought it would be at least easier than it had.

She shook her head and could feel her low ponytail move as she did so. 'Not yet.' She lifted her chin. 'But I'm sure I will, sooner or later.'

Ari sat back on the edge of her desk and fire raced into Lucy's cheeks as she remembered one day in his office in

Athens, when he'd perched her on the edge of his desk, spread her legs and— She nearly dropped the box again.

'Look, I have to get going. I have to visit my mother.'

'How is she?'

Lucy wanted to scream. What was this? Twenty questions? Her throat felt constricted. 'She's fine…well, as fine as she can be. She's comfortable—that's the main thing.'

Ari stood up then, hands in pockets. 'Lucy, I want to offer you another job here in the company. You don't have to work for me, you can work for the legal team again. A position has become vacant.'

She shook her head immediately, panic gripping her at the thought of not being able to escape from this man's devastating orbit. 'No, I don't want— That is, I'd prefer to seek employment elsewhere.'

He said nothing for a long, ominous moment, and then said quietly, 'You might find that more difficult than you think.'

Sick realisation sank in. The box slipped precariously in Lucy's arms but she gripped it tight. She thought of all the jobs she'd gone for in the past few days. The dead ends when she'd known that they were seeking people yet had turned her away.

'Did you—have you stopped me from getting jobs?'

Ari's jaw clenched. He didn't have to answer—he saw the dawning realisation on Lucy's face. 'I've changed my mind. I want you to stay here with Levakis Enterprises.'

His jaw clenched even harder. He'd changed his mind as soon as he'd seen his car pull away with her in it that day in Athens. 'I want to see you again, but I know it can't happen if you're my assistant. It wouldn't be fair on you. But this way it'll be much more acceptable.'

Shock, horror, *heat*—a complete mix of emotions rushed through Lucy with such force that she nearly fainted. She saw black spots before her eyes, but through them she saw Ari—

tall and proud and hard and implacable. And as ruthless as ever. Because he hadn't finished with her. *Yet.*

'You've changed your mind, you say? Well, I'm sorry,' she bit out, 'but I'm not available for the position of convenient mistress.'

He stood straighter, his face flushing. 'It doesn't have to be like that, Lucy. I'm asking you to be my lover. We were good together. I can't get you out of my mind…'

She shifted the box. Her arms were starting to ache. But when Ari saw the movement and made as if to take it out of her arms she jerked away. *'No.'*

This moment was so important to her—how she acted right now. Because if she followed the craving call of her body to give in she would be going the way of the doomed, of her mother. She would have learnt nothing. Her heart was bound up inextricably with this man, and he would crush it completely.

She felt a deep sadness well within her that she'd fallen for someone who could never love her as she now knew she ached to be loved. She ached to find the fulfilment she'd never seen as a child. To have the security that came from being in a committed, equal and loving relationship. The kind of thing she'd seen in Kallie and Alexandros Kouros.

'I don't want that, Ari. I don't want you…not like that. I'm worth more than a sleazy work affair, and, no matter how you try and pretty it up, that's all it would be.'

'There is another option. You don't have to work here. It could be much easier than that. I could show you the best that this world has to offer, take care of you and your mother—'

Lucy felt bile rise. She shook her head vehemently, her ponytail slipping over one shoulder. 'I won't be set up like that. I grew up with that, and it's something I just won't settle for. I can look after myself and my mother just fine. We don't need you or any other man.'

Lucy saw Ari's fists clench at his sides at her rejection of his offer. His voice had a rough quality that somehow jarred with his autocratic behaviour, but Lucy didn't have time to dwell on the meaning of that. 'Well, good luck finding a job, Lucy…I'll be waiting for your call when you realise you won't get one. I've marked you as exclusive to this company—no one will touch you with a bargepole.'

Lucy felt tears prick the backs of her eyes when she thought of what a precarious position that would put her mother in. '*Why* are you insisting on doing this?'

He said something guttural in Greek, his face unbearably harsh. 'I told you. I want you. This isn't over between us. I'll expect you to be in Theo's office on Monday morning. I know you can't move from London without jeopardising your mother's treatment.'

Right then Lucy hated Ari, and yet even as she thought that her heart clenched—because she knew she didn't. She couldn't. She tried to make her voice sound as cool and calm as possible, and prayed that for once her every emotion wasn't showing on her too-expressive face.

'I will not be manipulated like this, and I *won't* be falling back into your bed. You'd have to knock me out and drag me there like the neanderthal you're behaving like now.'

His face flushed again, but she didn't mistake the glint of triumph, despite her petty barb. He thought he had her right where he wanted her, but Lucy vowed not to succumb—no matter what he might try or what he was threatening. She turned and stalked from the room, realising that she'd never see him again, at least not in person, and the pain that ripped through her nearly made her stumble and fall.

It was only his softly spoken mocking words that came from behind her that helped her to keep going.

'See you on Monday morning, Lucy.'

CHAPTER TEN

ON MONDAY morning Ari strode authoritatively through his own building. The gasps and shocked murmurs as he passed people by merely bounced off him. Aristotle Levakis never frequented any office or floor of the building but his own. His blood was humming, anticipation a taut wire of need, and all because he was going to see Lucy any second now—and because seeing her the other day after a week's absence had shown him that even one day was too long. He vowed there and then to make sure it didn't happen again.

He was too far gone to try and deny the fact that she had him wound so tight around her little finger that he couldn't think straight. For the entire weekend his conscience had been pricking him but he'd quashed it down with a strength of will that was matched only by the strength of his desire for this woman. As he walked towards her office he finally had to acknowledge that he felt out of control for the first time in his life. One thought and one thought only had dominated since he'd seen her last: he wanted her, he needed her, and anything was better than her leaving—

He stopped in his tracks when he pushed open the outer door to his legal team's offices only to see an empty chair where Lucy should have been sitting—*where the hell was she?*

The immediate hollow ache in his solar plexus stunned him

with its force. Just then Theo strolled out of his office, a frown on his face.

'Ari? What's up?'

What's up? Ari felt dizzy for a second. He bit out, 'Lucy Proctor—where is she?'

He was hardly aware of Theo's frown and obvious confusion. 'I thought you knew…? She rang this morning and said she wouldn't be taking the position—said something about wanting some time off. I won't lie, I was delighted when you said she was going to be back working for us, but now…'

Ari didn't hear the rest of whatever Theo said. He left. When he got back up to his office he shut the door on his new PA's concerned face and found that he was shaking. Actually shaking. Aristotle Levakis—shaking like a leaf.

With a roaring in his ears he went over to his drinks cabinet and poured himself a drink. He downed it in one. For the first time in his life he did not know what to do. He sat down heavily in his chair and stared vacantly into the distance.

She'd gone. She'd not been playing coy. He'd not backed her into a corner with his threats to derail her chances of getting work. And, if anything, to remember what he'd done and said, the lengths he'd gone to to keep her near, made him feel ill. Especially when he thought of her mother and how much it meant to Lucy to have her taken care of. Immediately he went to reach for the phone, to call her and tell her that everything would be fine, that he'd look after her mother. He stopped.

He'd already done that. He'd already offered her his protection, the exalted position of his mistress, and she'd turned him down. Again bile rose as he realised he'd offered her the one thing she'd refuse even if her life depended on it. Ari sat back and closed his eyes, something awful like dread trickling through him, gathering force as it did so.

* * *

Lucy felt as brittle as a Chinese Ming vase teetering on the edge of a table. It had been two weeks since she'd *not* walked back into Levakis Enterprises to take the job that had been so ungraciously offered to her. She still felt sick to her belly to know that despite everything, despite all she'd shared with Ari of her life, he'd turned around and offered to *take care of her*.

And yet as she sat here now in her mother's bedroom, holding the book she'd been reading from aloud, she missed him with an ache that seemed to be growing more acute and stronger by the minute. She was constantly bombarded with images of their time together, and, worse, she'd even caught herself in a daydream of them together, *with a family*, before she could stop herself. Having never believed she was the slightest bit maternal, it was as if she'd suddenly tapped into some universal compulsion to have a baby. With him.

Her mother shifted restlessly and Lucy looked at her, smoothing some hair off her brow. She'd fallen asleep as Lucy had read to her.

Lucy hadn't had the heart to fight the uphill battle to look for a new job yet, so she'd spent the last two weeks coming to see her mum every day, but time was running out. She needed to get work fast. Her mouth firmed as the familiar pain rose. More than that, she needed to forget about—

'Lucy, love, someone here to see you.'

Lucy looked up and blushed. She'd been so caught up in her thoughts she hadn't heard the woman come in. She stood up, and as she followed the nurse out she wondered who on earth it could be…here of all places.

When she came out into the corridor the world swirled crazily. So crazily that she must have swayed, because before she knew it Ari was in front of her and holding onto her, looking down into her eyes.

With a deep inner cry of dismay Lucy wondered if she was

conjuring him up, and if it was in fact just her mother's consultant. She blinked. Ari. She blinked again. *Ari.*

From somewhere deeply welcome she came back to earth and pulled herself free of his touch. She stalked to a small empty waiting area nearby. She crossed her arms and turned around, feeling her cheeks grow hot as she took in the reality of facing him again. Those recent images of small dark-haired babies mocked her.

'What are you doing here?' She injected all the frost she could muster into her voice, but when Ari winced imperceptibly she treacherously felt nothing but remorse.

He looked awful. As if he hadn't slept in a week or shaved in days. He was wearing jeans and a sweater, nothing like the cool urbane businessman she'd first seen at a distance two years ago. He was more like the man she'd seen on Paros. Her heart clenched painfully.

He looked at her, and she quailed inwardly but tipped up her chin. When he spoke she had to strain to listen.

'I thought that here might be the only place you'd speak to me. Please forgive me for intruding on your personal space with your mother.'

One fire died in Lucy's belly and another started. Her arms relaxed fractionally. How was it that he still had the power to surprise her, damn him?

'Lucy, I want you to come back to Greece with me. Right now. I want to show you something. I need to talk to you but I can't…' He looked around for a moment. 'Not here…'

Lucy's arms tightened again. She shook her head fiercely. *Go back to Greece?* He had to be kidding. The thought of being in close proximity to this man was about as dangerous as sky-diving without a parachute.

He registered her reaction and Lucy saw something flicker in his eyes.

'Lucy, *please.*'

Something in the quality of his voice made her stop, but still she shook her head. Nothing on this earth would persuade her to set herself up to be hurt again. She crushed the treacherous need to know answers: why did he want her to go to Greece? Why wasn't he sweeping in here and demanding to know why she hadn't taken the job? It was what she might have expected. Why wasn't he acting like the proud, arrogant man she knew? And—the worst question of all—why had it taken him two weeks to come after her?

Ari's jaw clenched and something trickled down Lucy's spine. She saw a glimpse of the man she knew. Hard and implacable.

'Very well, if the only way I can persuade you to come is by threatening to reveal to the press that your mother is here, then so be it.'

Lucy gasped and went icy cold. On some level she was certain that Ari would never do such a thing, but on another level she wasn't absolutely sure, and the fact that he was even threatening such a thing made her feel acutely disappointed, and if she was disappointed what did that say about her own pathetically skewed judgment?

'You absolute *bastard.*'

He stepped forward and she stepped back, seeing colour flash through his cheeks. He held out a hand imperiously, and when she didn't move he just dropped it and said, sounding utterly defeated, 'I don't know where that came from. I'm sorry. Of course I wouldn't do that to you or your mother. I just want you to come with me so that I can show you something and talk to you…I promise that if you want to return after you've seen it and we've talked, I'll bring you straight back here.'

Lucy looked at him for a long moment. She was already starting to drown in those green depths. The real and awful truth was that she'd go to the ends of the earth if this man asked her. A very weak part of her was saying, *Go, go, go,* and she could already feel resistance washing away. He was confusing her with his behaviour, with the vulnerability she'd glimpsed but couldn't quite believe. Even so, she had every intention of keeping him to his word.

She said tightly, 'You promise? Then you'll leave me alone and let me find another job?'

He nodded. 'I'll make sure nothing stands in your way.'

Lucy waited for what seemed like an interminable moment, and then finally said, 'I'll get my jacket and bag.'

A scant few hours later they were landing at Athens airport, and Lucy still felt slightly winded at knowing that she'd been sitting at her mother's bedside just hours before. The steward opened the plane door and Ari stood and held out a hand. Lucy looked at it. They hadn't spoken a word on the flight. Ari had been sternly cold.

Feeling intense trepidation, she put her hand in his and let him pull her up. He led her out, and then they were climbing into a nearby helicopter, which was lifting into the clear blue sky within minutes.

Lucy's hands were tightly clasped in her lap, and she avoided looking at Ari as much as possible. After a while Lucy could see that they were circling an island, and she recognised Paros. A mixture of sheer pleasure and intense pain gripped her. If he'd brought her here just to—

But the helicopter was landing, and then they were out, and it was just Lucy and Ari, standing by the same Jeep they'd used the last time. Memories were too intense.

Lucy backed away and mocked herself inwardly for having such a weak and delayed reaction. He'd got her here by barely saying please. She was pathetic.

'Ari, if we're just here so that you can—'

He came and stood close—too close. 'Lucy, please, just trust me. A little further, that's all.'

Where could she go anyway? Lucy looked around. They were miles from anything. Silently she got into the Jeep. Ari got in too, and then they were driving. When she recognised the signs for his mother's tiny village Ari turned and went eastwards. After another ten minutes he took a sharp left turn down towards the coast, and they stopped at a set of ancient wrought-iron gates, nearly overgrown with vegetation.

Ari came round to meet Lucy. He helped her out but when he saw her open her mouth as if to speak he put a finger to her lips. He'd never been so terrified in his entire life; his heart was hammering painfully.

'This is what I wanted to show you.'

The feel of her soft lips against his finger nearly undid him, but he controlled himself.

He led her in through the gate, which was hanging off its hinges, then down an overgrown path and out into a huge clearing where an old and rambling villa, clearly dilapidated, stood on a bluff overlooking the sea.

Lucy's hand tightened reflexively in Ari's. It must have been stunning in its heyday, and the view was priceless. Already she could imagine what it might be like if it was done up, restored to its former glory.

'What is this place?'

Ari brought her over to the other side of the house and an unimpeded view of the sea to where a trail led down to a private beach.

'I bought it…signed the papers just yesterday.'

Lucy felt a little bewildered. He'd brought her here to show her his latest acquisition? 'Oh…well, congratulations.'

He turned and looked at her intently. 'You like it, don't you?'

Lucy frowned, feeling very vulnerable. 'Well, of course I like it. It's beautiful, idyllic, but what does it matter what I think about it?'

He didn't say anything for a long moment, and then he said, 'Because I bought it for you…for us.'

Lucy tried to make sense of his words, feeling a little spaced-out. 'You mean…?' Something struck her then, and anger flowered deep down. She took her hand from his. 'Ari, if you've bought this as some kind of…of love-nest, just so that I can be your mistress—'

He was shaking his head, a curious light in his eyes. 'No. I want it to be a home—a place where we can come…perhaps even with a family…'

Lucy was starting to flounder badly. His words were making all sorts of things bloom in her heart, making it beat faster. How could he know of her deeply secret daydreams? It felt as if he was looking straight into her head. 'Ari—I don't… What are you talking about…?'

He brought a shaking hand to her face, his eyes so intense it nearly hurt to look at them. 'Lucy, I brought you here because *here* is the only place I know how to be me, where I can say what I need to say. I've been going crazy these past two weeks. At first I told myself I didn't need you, that I wasn't devastated beyond belief when I found out you hadn't taken the job with Theo. And then one night, at three o'clock in the morning, when I found myself driving to your flat and sitting outside like a stalker, I had to face up to myself.'

He took a deep breath. 'I think I fell in love with you when you appeared like a whirling dervish to defend me against Helen. I've never had anyone stand up for me before—*care about me before*. I've never *needed* it. But you made me realise how lonely I've been all my life.'

His mouth twisted. 'I thought I had it all figured out. I'd keep you on in the company if you insisted on working, but essentially I wanted you as my mistress. It was only when I said the words out loud I realised what an insult it was—especially to you, after all you've been through. And it was then that I knew I wanted much, much more than that. I wanted everything. A life together. *A marriage.*'

He laughed harshly. 'Of course I denied it to myself. *Love?* I'd cut myself off from anything like that when I was sent away to England and it became my home. Helen effectively cut me off from my father, wouldn't even allow a normal relationship to develop between me and my brother. That's why I'd locked away my memories of here and my mother...I couldn't believe it had existed. But meeting you, falling in love with you, made me believe in them again. It made me remember the love I felt.'

Lucy was more than shocked. She was in danger of floating away from her body. But at the same time she felt welded to the ground, incapable of processing his words, because she realised just how badly she wanted this. And yet...

'But I heard what you said to Helen just before she hit you...about never marrying someone like me...'

Ari looked confused for a moment, and then his face cleared. '*Thee mou*, that wasn't about *you*. Helen was suggesting I marry Pia Kyriapoulos, which would have suited her ends perfectly and kept me marginalized. Pia is not exactly the epitome of the blushing Greek bride.'

'Oh.' Lucy tried to look down, away from his intensity, but Ari wouldn't let her budge.

He took something out of his back pocket and held it out to Lucy. It was a small velvet bag. She looked at him and he just said, 'Open it—please...'

She was all fingers and thumbs, so Ari helped her, and then it was open and something fell into her hand. It was the stunning butterfly necklace she'd seen all those weeks ago and it glinted up at her now. She felt her eyes film over with tears. Ari took it and placed it tenderly around her neck, making tingles run up and down her spine. He tipped her chin up again, forcing her gaze to meet his. His eyes blazed into hers.

'So will you, Lucy Proctor—marry me? Please? Because I cannot imagine going forward from this day or this place without you by my side.'

Emotion was cracking open inside Lucy, and it was the most gloriously painful thing she'd ever felt in her life.

'I never wanted to feel this much.'

Ari's mouth quirked. 'It's painful, isn't it?'

It was the sudden complicit feeling of mutual emotion and how similar they really were in their hearts that made Lucy's eyes water in earnest. Her mouth wobbled precariously. 'I thought I'd settle for someone boring—someone who wouldn't make me face up to myself, to the desires I kept hidden. But you made me believe I had nothing to be scared of... I love you, Ari. I fell for you the day you gave that stupidly expensive necklace to two strangers in the street. And it was when you brought me here that I knew I'd fallen in love with you. And, yes, I'll marry you.'

Lucy could feel the tremor in his hands as they framed her face.

'Thank God,' he said huskily, and bent his head to seal their vow with barely restrained passion.

When they broke apart she could still feel his hands trembling, and his face had such an endearing mix of expressions—pure Ari arrogance and then something she'd never seen before, sheer childlike *joy*—that she couldn't help smiling at him.

He returned her gaze, and for just a moment Lucy caught a glimpse of something achingly vulnerable cross his face before he said haltingly, 'That night I was sitting outside your flat, apart from lurid fantasies featuring a certain tight skirt, I found myself imagining you pregnant...having a baby...*our* baby. I suddenly wanted a family. And not just for an heir...but to create something—a secure foundation. It scared me to death, and it's the only thing that's held me back from coming for you sooner.' He quirked an unsteady smile. 'That and the fact that you might reject me. But the thing is…I've no idea how you feel about kids…'

Lucy looked up at him and wondered how her heart hadn't exploded into tiny pieces. 'Funny you should mention that…'

In more or less exactly the same spot where Ari had proposed to her three years before, Lucy shaded her eyes and looked down to the private beach, where her husband was holding their son high in the air before dunking him back in the glittering sea. The childish shrieks of delight made her smile and she sat down, rearranging the tiny baby in her arms so that she could feed her from the other breast.

'You're very happy, darling, aren't you?'

Lucy looked over to her mother, who was sitting in a wheelchair in the shade on the other side of the table, and smiled. 'Yes, Mum…I am.' Her mother looked away again, out to sea, with an enigmatic smile of her own.

Maxine had these moments of lucidity every now and then, ever since Lucy and Ari had moved her here to the refurbished villa on Paros permanently, with a full-time nursing staff to take care of her every need. Her Alzheimer's hadn't improved, but it seemed to have slowed its development, and sometimes when Lucy looked at her she knew her mother was imagining herself to be in this beautiful place being cared for by one of her besotted suitors.

Lucy had insisted on Ari keeping his mother's house nearby exactly as it was, and sometimes they went back for a night on their own, and revelled in their private space that no one knew about.

Just then a dripping wet Ari appeared, holding an exuberant Cosmo steadily on his shoulders. He smiled widely, his eyes flashing with secret promise and something much deeper and more enduring—*love*. Lucy couldn't remember when she'd once wondered what he'd look like if he smiled. She smiled back, for life was good.

NOT FOR SALE

SANDRA MARTON

CHAPTER ONE

LUCAS VIEIRA was mad as hell.

His day had not gone well. Not gone well? Lucas almost laughed.

An understatement.

His day had been chaos. Now, it was rapidly turning into catastrophe.

It had started with a mug of burned coffee. Lucas had not even known there could be such a thing until his P.A.—his very temporary P.A.—had brewed a pot of something black, hot and oily and poured him a cup of it.

One taste, and he'd shoved the thing aside, flipped open his cell phone to check his messages and found one from the same fool of a reporter who'd been badgering him for an interview the past two weeks. How had the man gotten his number? It was private, as was the rest of Lucas's life.

Lucas cherished his privacy.

He avoided the press. He traveled by private jet. His two-level penthouse on Fifth Avenue was accessible only via private elevator. His estate on the ocean, in the Hamptons, was walled; the Caribbean island he'd bought last year was festooned with No Trespassing signs.

Lucas Vieira, Man of Mystery, some wag had once called him. Not exactly true. There were times Lucas couldn't avoid cameras and microphones and questions. He was a multi-billionaire, and that stirred interest.

He was also a man who had risen to the top in a profession where lineage and background had significant meaning...

And he had neither.

Or, rather, he did—but not the kind Wall Street generally preferred. Not the kind he would discuss, either. The only questions he would ever consider were those that concerned the public face of Vieira Financial. As for how Vieira Financial had come to be such a powerhouse, how Lucas had come to be such a success at thirty-three...

He had tired of being asked, so he'd finally offered a response in a recent interview.

"Success," he'd said, in his somewhat husky, lightly accented voice, "success is when preparation meets opportunity."

"That's it?" the interviewer had said.

"That's it," Lucas had replied, and he'd unclipped the tiny mike from the lapel of his navy wool Savile Row suit jacket, risen to his feet, walked past the cameras and out of the studio.

What he would never add was that to reach that point, a man could permit nothing, absolutely nothing, to get in his way.

Lucas frowned, swung his leather chair away from his massive Brazilian rosewood desk and stared blindly out the wall of glass that overlooked midtown Manhattan.

Which brought him directly back to today, and how in God's name was he going to keep to that credo?

There had to be a way.

He had learned the importance of letting nothing come between a man and his goals years ago when he was a boy of seven, a dirty, half-starved *menino de rua*—a kid living on the streets of Rio. He picked tourists' pockets, stole whatever he could, ate out of restaurant trash bins, slept in alleys and parks, although you didn't really sleep when you had to be alert to every sound, every footfall.

There was no way out.

Brazil was a country of extremes. There were the incredibly rich who lived in homes that defied description, and the incredibly poor, the *favelados*, who eked out an existence in the *favelas*, the shanty towns, that clung to Rio's hillsides. Lucas was not even one of them. He was nothing. He was vermin. And what seven-year-old could change that?

All he had was his mother. And then, one night, a man she'd brought home took a look at Lucas, trying to make himself invisible in the corner of their cardboard shack, and said forget it, he was not going to pay good money to lie with a *puta* while her kid watched.

The next day, Lucas's mother walked him to the dirty streets of Copacabana, told him to be a good boy and left him there.

He never saw her again.

Lucas learned to survive. To keep moving, to run when the cops showed up because they'd as soon beat the crap out of you as not. Then, one night, somebody yelled, *"Bichos!"* but Lucas couldn't run. He was sick, half-delirious with fever, dehydrated after vomiting up what little was in his belly.

He was doomed.

Except, he wasn't.

On that night, his life changed forever.

Some do-gooding social worker was with the police. Who knew why? It didn't matter. What did matter was that she took him to a storefront that housed one of the few organizations that saw street children as human. There, they pumped him full of antibiotics, gave him fruit juice to drink and, when he could keep that down, food. They cleaned him up, cut his hair, dressed him in clothes that didn't fit, but who gave a damn?

The clothes were free of lice. That was what mattered.

Lucas wasn't stupid. In fact, he was bright. He'd taught himself to read, to do math. Now, he attacked the books they gave him, observed how others behaved, learned to speak properly, to remember to wash his hands and brush his teeth, to say *obrigado* and *por favor*.

And he learned to smile.

That was the hardest thing. Smiling was not a part of who he was, but he did it.

Weeks passed, months, and then there was another miracle. A North American couple showed up, talked with him for a little while—by then, Lucas had picked up passable English from one of his teachers—and the next thing he knew, they took him to a place called New Jersey and said he was now their son.

He should have known it wouldn't last.

Lucas had cleaned up nicely. He looked cute. Black hair, green eyes, golden skin. He smelled good. He spoke well. Inside, though, the boy who trusted no one was still in charge. He hated being told what to do and the New Jersey couple believed children should be told what to do, every minute of every hour of every day.

Things deteriorated rapidly.

He was not grateful, his would-be father said, and tried to beat gratitude into him. His heart was owned by demons, his would-be mother said, and demanded he seek salvation on his knees.

Eventually, they said he would never be any good. On his tenth birthday, they drove him to a hulking gray building and handed him over to Child Services.

Lucas spent the next eight years going from foster home to foster home. One or two were okay but most of them... Even now, as an adult, his fists knotted when he thought back to some of what he and others had endured. The last place was so terrible that at midnight on the day he turned eighteen, he'd tossed the few things he owned into a pillowcase, slung it over his shoulder and walked out.

But he had learned what would become the single most important lesson of his life.

He knew precisely what he wanted.

Respect. That was it, in a word. And he knew, too, that respect came when a man had power. And money. He wanted both.

He worked hard, picked crops in New Jersey fields during the summer, did whatever manual labor he could find during the winter. He got his GED—his General Educational Diploma—because he had never stopped reading and reading led to learning. He enrolled in a community college, sat through classes when he was exhausted and desperate for sleep. Add a helping of socially acceptable good manners, clothes that fit the long, leanly muscled body of the man he had become, and the way to the top suddenly seemed possible.

More than possible. It was achievable.

At thirty-three, Lucas Vieira had it all.

Almost.

Almost, he thought grimly, on this day that had started with bad coffee and an inept secretary, and he had no one to blame but himself.

Anger surged through him and he shot to his feet and paced the length of his big office.

A bad sign, that uncharacteristic show of fury. Learning to contain one's emotions was also necessary for success. Still, it wasn't as bad as his having missed the signs of his current mistress's unrealistic reading of what she'd called a relationship.

When he'd thought about it at all, he'd called it an affair.

Whatever it had been, he was on the verge of disaster.

He was going to lose buying Leonid Rostov's twenty billion dollar corporation. And the deal was close, tantalizingly close to finalization…

Everybody wanted the Rostov holdings but Lucas wanted them more. Adding them to his already formidable empire would validate everything he had worked so hard to become.

A few months ago, when word got out that Rostov might be selling, that he was coming to New York, Lucas had taken a gamble. He had not sent Rostov letters or proposals. He had not phoned the man's Moscow office. Instead, he'd sent Rostov a box of Havana cigars—every photo of the Russian showed him with a cigar in his teeth—and a business card. Across the back he'd written, *Dinner in New York next Saturday, 8:00 p.m., the Palace Hotel.*

Rostov had swallowed the bait.

They'd had a leisurely meal in a private room. There was no talk of business. Lucas knew Rostov was sizing him up. Rostov ate heartily and drank the same way, Lucas ate sparingly and made each drink last. At the end of the night, Rostov slapped him on the back and invited him to Moscow.

Now, after endless flying back and forth, negotiating through translators—Rostov's English was chancy but how could Lucas fault it when his Russian began with *zdravstvuj*—hello—and ended with *dasvidaniya*?

Now, Rostov was in New York again.

"We have one more meal, Luke-ahs, one bottle of vodka—and then I will make you happy man."

Only one problem.

Rostov was bringing his wife.

Ilana Rostov had joined them the last time Lucas was in Moscow. She had a beautiful if surgically altered face; diamond earrings dangled like Bolshoi chandeliers from her ears. She moved in a cloud of choking perfume and she was fluent in English; she'd served as her husband's translator that night.

She'd also had her hand buried in Lucas's lap beneath the deep hem of a crisply starched tablecloth.

Somehow, Lucas had made it through the meal, the translator he'd hired for the evening oblivious, Rostov oblivious, only Lucas and Ilana Rostov aware of what was happening. He had barely escaped with his dignity, never mind anything else, intact.

And Rostov was bringing her with him tonight.

"No translators," he'd said firmly. "Translators are functionaries of the state, *da*? You can, of course, bring a voman. But for talking, my Ilana will take care of you as good as she will take care of me."

Lucas had almost laughed. And he *could* laugh this time, because he had an ace up his sleeve.

Her name was Elin Jansson. Elin, born in Finland, spoke flawless Russian. She was a model; she was Lucas's current mistress. She would be his date, his translator…

And his protection against Ilana Rostov.

Lucas groaned, went to the window wall behind his desk and pressed his forehead against the cool glass.

It had all seemed so simple. He should have known better. Life was never simple, and today had proved it.

"Mr. Vieira?"

Lucas swung around. His temporary P.A. smiled nervously from the doorway. She was young and she made lousy coffee but far worse, no matter what he did to make her feel comfortable, she remained half-terrified of him. Right now, she looked as if one strong gust of wind might blow her over.

And well she should look exactly that way, he thought grimly. He had left orders that he was not to be disturbed.

"What is it, Denise?"

"It's Elise. Sir." The girl swallowed dryly. "I knocked but you didn't—" She swallowed again. "Mr. Rostov called. I told him you were unavailable, just the way you said. And he said to tell you that he and Mrs. Rostov might be a few minutes late to meet you and—"

Her voice trailed off.

"You've told me," Lucas said crisply. "Is there anything else?"

"I just—I just wondered if—if I should phone the restaurant and—and tell them there'll be only three for dinner.'"

Merda! This was going from bad to impossible. Did the entire world know what had happened?

"Did I ask you to do that?"

"No, sir. I just thought—"

"Don't think. Just do what you're told." The girl's face collapsed. Hell. So much for controlling his emotions. "Denise. I'm sorry I snapped at you."

"It's Elise," she said in a wobbly voice. "And you don't owe me an apology, sir. I just— I mean, I know you're upset…"

"I am not upset," Lucas said, forcing a smile the way he'd done when he was a boy. "Why would I be upset?"

"Well—well, Miss Jansson—when she was here a little while ago—" Another gulping swallow. "Mr. Gordon was at my desk. And we couldn't help but hear— I mean, I couldn't stop Miss Jansson from going by me and then, once she got inside your office…"

"So," Lucas said, through his teeth, "I had an audience." He attempted a smile but suspected it was more a grimace. "What about everyone on the other floors? Were they in attendance, too?"

"I don't know, Mr. Vieira, sir. I could ask around, if that's what—"

"What I want," Lucas said, "is that you never mention this again. To me or anyone else. Is that clear?"

The girl nodded.

Mental note, Lucas thought dryly. *Offer to quadruple regular P.A.'s salary when she returns from vacation if she swears never to leave her desk again barring death, disease, or God forbid, marriage.*

"It is, sir, and I want you to know how sorry I am that you and Miss Jansson—"

"Go back to your desk," Lucas snapped. "And do not interrupt me again or you'll find yourself at HR, collecting your final check. Understood?"

Apparently, it was. Denise, Elise, whoever in hell she was, slunk off, shutting the door behind her. Lucas glared at it for a couple of seconds. Then he sank into the chair behind his desk, tilted it back and stared at the ceiling.

Wonderful. In a couple of hours, he'd be meeting with a man who spoke little English and a woman who only wanted to get her hands inside his fly. He had no translator, and now his private life was the topic of discussion among his employees.

Why wouldn't it be?

Elin had made one hell of a scene, storming in, demanding to know about "that blonde bimbo" as she tossed a photo on his desk. It had appeared online, on some gossip site, she said. One look and Lucas knew it was a Photoshopped miracle but done so carelessly that the "bimbo"—an actress, the text said—seemed to hover next to him, her feet a few inches off the ground.

He'd looked up, already smiling, a second away from telling Elin exactly that. Then he'd looked at her icy eyes, the grim set of her mouth, and inconsequential annoyances suddenly began to add up.

Elin's little makeup bag, left in a vanity drawer. The jeans, shirt, and sneakers left in his closet. So she could get out of a cab at her place at seven in the morning, she'd purred, without raising eyebrows.

Stupid, he'd thought, *worse than stupid!* Elin didn't care about raising eyebrows. Besides, half the women in Manhattan got out of cabs in the early morning, still dressed as they'd been the prior night.

And maybe the most obvious part of that lie was that he could count on one hand the number of times Elin, or any other woman, had slept in his bed the entire night.

He wasn't into that. Sex was sex; sleep was sleep. You did one with a woman. You did the other alone.

"You think it's funny that you sneaked around? That you cheated on me?" Elin had slapped her hands on her hips. "I'm waiting for an explanation."

That did it.

Lucas had risen to his feet. Elin was tall but at six-three, he towered over her.

"I do not cheat," he'd said coldly. "I do not sneak. And I do not explain myself. To you or anyone else."

She had grown very still. Progress, he'd thought, and he'd gone on, calmly, to remind her of how things were between them. That they were having an affair and it was enjoyable, but—

She'd screamed something at him. In Finnish, but still, he could tell what she'd said was not complimentary.

A second later, she was gone.

No big thing. That was what he'd thought. In fact, it was long past time they said goodbye to each other...

And then, reality had come rushing in.

The dinner. Leonid Rostov. His wife. For one wild second, Lucas had imagined going after Elin and asking if this meant she wasn't going to go with him tonight...

He stalked to the built-in rosewood cabinet across the room, bypassed Denise-Elise's witch's brew, opened a sliding door and took out a thin Baccarat highball glass and a bottle of Macallan single malt Scotch.

It was all his fault. He should have known better than to mix business with pleasure but it had seemed perfect. A beautiful, sophisticated woman who would know which fork to use even as she translated Russian into English and English into Russian. Where in hell could a man find a woman like that at the eleventh hour, even in New—

"M-M-Mr. Vieira?"

"Damnit," Lucas snarled, and swung toward the door. His P.A. was trembling. Beside her stood, hell, Jack Gordon. Lucas had hired him a year ago. Gordon was bright and innovative. Still, there were times Lucas wondered if there was more to Gordon than met the eye.

Or maybe less.

Lucas jerked his head. Denise-Elise stepped back and closed the door, and Lucas turned an icy look on Gordon.

"This had better be good."

Gordon blanched but he held his ground. Lucas had to admire him for that.

"Sir. Lucas. I think, when you hear what I have to say—"

"Say it and then get out of here."

Gordon took a breath. "This isn't easy…" He took another breath. "I know what happened. You and the Jansson woman… Wait a minute, okay? I'm not here to talk about that."

"You damned well better not be."

"She was supposed to go with you tonight. To that meeting," Gordon said hurriedly. "You mentioned it Monday morning, how Rostov didn't want real translators, so he'd talk through his wife and you—"

"Get to the point."

"Sir. I know someone who's fluent in Russian."

"Perhaps you weren't listening to everything I said on Monday," Lucas said with icy precision. "Rostov refuses to have anyone he thinks of as a functionary present tonight. He says that's what official translators are, and perhaps they are, in his world, but what it comes down to is—"

"Dani can pretend to be your date."

Lucas's mouth twisted. "I don't think I can fool our Russian friend into thinking I've suddenly decided to go in for boys."

"Dani's a girl, sir. A gorgeous girl. She's smart, too. And she speaks Russian."

Lucas felt a flare of hope. Then he faced reality. A girl, sight unseen? For an evening as important as this? No way. For all he knew, he'd be compounding what was already a mess into a disaster.

"Forget it."

"Sir, it would work."

Lucas shook his head. "It's clever, Jack, but this is a twenty billion dollar deal. I can't run the risk of this woman screwing things."

Gordon laughed. Lucas's eyes narrowed to emerald slits.

"Did I say something amusing?"

"No, no, of course not. Look, I've know Dani for years. She's exactly what you need for a situation like this."

"And if I were foolish enough to say yes to your suggestion, she would do this because…?"

"Like I said. We're old friends. She'd do it as a favor to me."

A muscle flickered in Lucas's jaw. A twenty billion dollar deal, hinging on a man who drank too much vodka, a woman who had more limbs and libido than an octopus and a woman he'd never met?

Impossible.

And impossible to pass up.

"All right," he said sharply. "Call her."

Jack Gordon's eyebrows rose. "You mean it?"

"Isn't that what this conversation was all about? Call her. Tell her—"

"Dani. Dani Sinclair."

"Dani. Tell her I'll pick her up at seven-thirty. Where does she live?"

"She'll meet you," Jack said quickly.

"The lobby of the Palace. Eight o'clock sharp. No. Make it ten of the hour." That way, he'd have time to hand the Sinclair woman cab fare and get rid of her if she turned out to be totally wrong for the job. "Tell her to dress appropriately." He paused. "She can do that, can't she?"

"She'll dress appropriately, sir."

"And, of course, make it clear I'll pay her for her time. Say, one thousand dollars for the evening."

He could see Gordon all but swallowing another laugh. Yes, Lucas thought coldly, why wouldn't he find his employer's predicament amusing? If this worked, he could take credit for saving Lucas's corporate ass. But oh, if it didn't...

"That sounds fine, sir." Gordon held out his hand. "Good luck."

Lucas looked at the outstretched hand, fought back a sense of repugnance he knew was foolish and accepted the handshake.

Jack Gordon hurried back to his own office before he pulled out his cell and hit a speed dial digit.

"Dani. Baby, have I got a deal for you!"

He explained as quickly as possible; Dani Sinclair was not one for long conversations but then, that wasn't what men paid her for. When he'd finished, he heard the slow exhalation of her breath.

"So, let me get this straight. You told some guy—"

"Not just some guy, baby. Lucas Vieira. *The* Lucas Vieira. The guy with more money than God."

"You told him I'd give him a date?"

"Yeah. Only, not that kind of date. This is dinner with Vieira, a Russian guy and the guy's wife. You need to act like you and Vieira are a thing. And you need to translate." Jack laughed softly. "I guess taking a degree in Cyrillic languages was a good idea after all."

"I'm taking my Master's," Dani Sinclair said, "and a girl has to think about her future." She paused. "How much did you say he'll pay?"

"A thousand."

Dani laughed. "Did you forget my going rate, Jack? It's ten thousand for the evening."

"Baby, we go way back. Elementary school. Middle school. High school."

"Fine. I'll give you a special discount. Five thousand."

"Jeez. For a meal?"

"And, of course, my usual fee if your Mr. Vieira wants anything else."

Jack Gordon rubbed the top of his head. "If he wants more, you can negotiate the fee yourself."

Dani chuckled. "Jack, you wily fox. You haven't told him about me. What, you want him to be shocked?"

"I want him to owe me," Jack Gordon said, his tone suddenly cold. "And he will, no matter how this goes."

"Charming. Okay, so when does this happen?"

"I thought I told you. Tonight. The Palace lobby. Ten minutes of eight."

"Oh, but I…" Dani fell silent. Five K to eat a fancy meal, talk some Russian and in between, pretend she was the date of Lucas Vieira, the gorgeous, sexy, take-no-prisoners Wall Street tough guy. And a minimum of ten K if he ended up wanting to prolong the evening.

So tempting. If only she could do it. Trouble was, she already had a date for tonight, with a Texas oilman who came through the city once a month like clockwork.

There had to be a way…

"Dani?"

And there was. She could clear, say, forty-five hundred without doing a thing besides making a phone call.

"Yes," she said briskly. "Fine. The lobby, the Palace, ten of eight."

She disconnected, checked her cell's contact list and hit a button. A female voice answered on the third ring, sounding breathless and a little rushed.

"Caroline? It's Dani. Dani, from the Chekhov seminar? Listen, sweetie, I have a translating job that I don't have time to take and I thought, right away, of you."

Caroline Hamilton used a hip to shut the door of her Hell's Kitchen walk-up, then tucked her cell phone between her ear and her shoulder, shifted the grocery bags she held so she could free a hand and secure the door's three locks.

Dani from the Chekhov seminar? Caroline tried to picture her as she made her way across the six feet of floor space to what her landlord insisted was a kitchen. Yes, okay. Dani, a fellow Master of Arts student in Russian and Slavic Studies. Tall, stunning, dressed in the latest designer stuff. They'd never spoken except to say "hi" and "see you next time," and to exchange numbers in case one needed to check with the other about an assignment.

"Caroline? You still there?"

"I'm here." Caroline eased the grocery bags onto the counter, took a Lean Cuisine from one, worked at opening the little tear strip on the box while still keeping the phone at her ear. "A translating job, you said?"

"That's right. An unusual one. It involves dinner."

Caroline's belly rumbled. She had passed on lunch. No time, less money. The phone slipped as she finally got the container from the package. She grabbed it before it hit the Formica counter.

"...as the pretend G.F. of a rich guy."

"What?" Caroline said, reading the directions. Three

minutes on high, peel back the liner, stir, another minute and a half—

"I said, it's dinner. You meet this hotshot business guy at the Palace Hotel and you pretend you're his girlfriend. See, there's another couple and they speak Russian. Your guy doesn't, so you'll translate for him."

Caroline put the Lean Cuisine into the nuker, shrugged off her jacket, pushed her thick, straight-as-a-stick mane of no-real-color hair back from her face, blew strands of it out of her hazel eyes.

"Why would I pretend I'm his girlfriend?"

"You just would," Dani said, "that's all."

Caroline punched in the three minutes. "Thanks but I'll pass. I mean, it sounds, well, weird."

"One hundred bucks."

"Dani, look…"

"Two hundred. And that meal. Then the night's over, you go home with two hundred dollars in your jeans. Except," she added hurriedly, "except, of course, you can't wear jeans."

"Well, that's that, then. I definitely don't have—"

"I'm a size six. You?"

"A six. But—"

"Size seven shoes, right?"

Caroline sank onto the rickety wooden stool that graced the counter. "Right. But honestly—"

"Three hundred," Dani said briskly. "And I'm on my way. A dress. Shoes. Makeup. Think of what fun this will be."

All Caroline could think of was three hundred dollars. You didn't need to be a linguist to translate that into a piece of next month's rent.

"Caroline! I need your address. We're running out of time here."

Caroline gave it. Told herself to ignore the prickly feeling dancing down her spine, told herself that same thing again, two hours later, when Dani spun her toward the mirror and she saw…

"Cinderella," Dani said, laughing at Caroline's shocked expression. "Hey, one last thing, okay? Let this guy think you're me. See, the friend who set this up thinks I'm gonna do the date, I mean, be the date, and it's easier all around if we keep it that way."

Caroline looked at her reflection again. Dani's fifty-dollar-a-bottle conditioner had taken her hair from no-color to pale gold. Her hazel eyes glittered, thanks to the light sparkle of gold shadow on her lids. Her cheekbones and mouth were a delicate pink and her dress… Cobwebs. Slinky black cobwebs that showed more leg than she'd ever shown except in shorts or a swimsuit. And on her feet, gold sandals, their heels so high she wondered if she'd be able to walk.

She didn't look like herself anymore, and something about that terrified her.

"Dani. I don't—I can't—"

"You're meeting him in half an hour."

"No, really, it just feels wrong. To lie, to pretend I'm you, that I'm this Luke Vieira's girlfriend—"

"Lucas," Dani said impatiently. "Lucas Vieira. Okay. Five hundred."

Caroline stared at her. "Five hundred dollars?"

"We're running out of time. What's it gonna be? Yes or no?"

Caroline swallowed hard. And said the only thing she could.

She said, "Yes."

CHAPTER TWO

LUCAS went home, showered and changed clothes. White shirt, blue tie, gray suit. A little casual, a little businesslike. Now, all he had to do was calm down.

The hotel was fiftieth and Madison and he lived on Fifth Avenue, only a couple of blocks away. There was no need for his car; like any New Yorker, he knew the fastest way to cover that distance was to walk.

Besides, walking might give him time to tame his temper. He'd snapped at his driver on the way from the office to his condo; he'd barely responded to the doorman's pleasant "good evening, Mr. Vieira," he'd scowled at his housekeeper in response to a simple question.

He was breathing fire, and what for? Ultimately, he was the one responsible for this mess. Why turn his anger on everyone else?

He'd made a mistake, not recognizing that Elin was trying to make more of their affair than it ever could be, but the way to recover from a mistake was to learn from it and move on.

The Palace's elegant lobby was crowded. Lucas found a relatively clear space that gave him an unimpeded view of the entrance, then checked his watch. It was seven forty-five. On the chance Dani Sinclair might have arrived early, he scanned the room for a late-twenties, tall woman with light brown hair, blue eyes and what Jack Gordon had slyly described as "a body that just won't quit" when Lucas had phoned him for a description an hour ago.

"A total babe," he'd said, with a low laugh. "Built for action, if you get my drift."

Lucas's mouth twisted. He didn't like Gordon's increasingly smarmy tone, and he had no interest in knowing if he and the woman had been intimate. As long as she looked presentable, seemed credible as his date and spoke Russian, he'd be satisfied.

There were lots of women in the lobby, some that met Gordon's description, but none were alone as Dani Sinclair would be. If she ever showed up. Frowning, Lucas checked the time again. Four minutes had gone by.

Another slipped past.

Lucas folded his arms, felt a flicker of apprehension. She was late.

It was not a good start.

At five of eight, Lucas could feel the muscles in his jaw tense. Yes, Rostov had said he and his wife would be late but if the Sinclair woman didn't show up soon—

A woman entered the lobby. She was by herself. Lucas felt a surge of hope until he realized this couldn't be the woman he was waiting for. Nothing about her fit Jack Gordon's description.

Her hair was pale gold, not brown. He couldn't tell the color of her eyes from here, only that they were wide-set, like a cat's. Her face was oval, her mouth a soft pink.

Even at a distance, she was stunning.

Feminine. Delicate. Curves gently accented by an incredibly short, clinging silky black dress, long legs that lent sexiness to already-sexy gold sandals with stiletto heels. An erotic image flashed into his head. This woman, wearing only those heels and whatever wisp of silk she had on under that amazing dress…

He scowled.

What kind of nonsense was this? He was here on important business. Besides, it would be a while before he'd want to be with a woman again. The thing with Elin had left a bad taste.

Still, he lifted his gaze, took one last look at the woman's face...

And found her staring at him.

For a heartbeat, their eyes met and held. Lucas felt something knot, deep in his belly. He took a step forward—and then her gaze swept past him and the moment, whatever it had been, was over.

Hell.

He needed a break.

He'd finish the Rostov deal, clear up a couple of other things and then he'd go out to his house in the Hamptons for a long weekend. Alone. Just him and the sun and the sea. Three, four days like that and he'd be ready to get back to work, and to women.

All he had to do was wind things up tonight—except, how was he going to do that? His watch read five after eight.

No question about it.

Dani Sinclair had been a mistake.

Lucas ran his hand through his hair.

He could call the Rostov suite. Plead sudden illness. No. That was the easy way out. More to the point, he wanted things settled, tonight. His only real choice was to go through with the dinner plans, let Ilana Rostov do all the translating, try to ignore her fingers in his lap and if things got bad enough—

"Excuse me."

If things got bad enough, say to hell with it and tell Rostov that he needed to leash his barracuda of a wife...

"Sir? Excuse me."

A hand fell lightly on his arm. Damnit, what now?

"Yes?" he growled as he swung around… And saw the blonde with the cat's eyes looking up at him. This close, he could see that her eyes were hazel, that she was even lovelier than he'd thought.

A woman on the prowl. New York had more than its fair share of assertive women. Or she might be a high-priced call girl. New York had plenty of those, too, and though places like this did all it could to discourage them, they were around.

Either way, he wasn't interested. He liked assertive women but not tonight, with a deal like this on the agenda. And if she was a so-called working girl, even an expensive one…

Forget it. He'd never paid for sex in his life and he never would.

"I—ah, I wonder if you—if you—"

"No. I would not."

She flinched. Hell, she turned pale. Lucas felt a twinge of guilt. She wasn't a pro. And he was behaving like an ass. It had been a long day and it was going to be an even longer evening, but why let it out on her?

"Look," he said, "you're a beautiful woman. I'm flattered that you'd like to have a drink, dinner, whatever—"

"No," she said quickly, "that's not—"

"I'm meeting someone. On business. Your timing is off, okay?"

Those hazel eyes turned cold.

"You have an interesting opinion of yourself, mister."

Lucas raised his eyebrows. "Hey, I'm not the one who—"

"I'm not interested in a drink. Or dinner." The woman drew herself up, steel suddenly in her spine and in her voice. "Actually, I'd sooner have drinks with—with SpongeBob Squarepants than someone as rude and self-centered as you."

Lucas blinked. Then, despite himself, he laughed.

"Thank you."

"For what?" She tossed her head and strands of her hair fell against her cheek. He fought back the insane desire to take those strands between his fingers and tuck them back behind her ear. "And what's so amusing? Do you like having people tell you what you are to your face?"

"No one ever does," he said. "No one would dare."

Her smile was sweet enough to make his teeth ache. And to make him grin.

"What a pity."

"You're right. I owe you an apology. I'm in a bad mood but that's no reason to take it out on you."

He could see her trying to decide whether or not to accept his request for forgiveness. Suddenly, it seemed important that she would.

"Truce?" he said, holding out his hand.

She hesitated. Then her lips curved in a smile. She put her hand in his and he could have sworn he felt a jolt of electricity.

"Truce."

"Good." He smiled back at her. "Look, this really is a bad time. Why don't I give you my card? Call me tomorrow. Better still, give me your number and—"

The blonde tugged her hand free.

"You don't get it." The steel was back in her voice. "I'm not trying to—to pick you up. I'm supposed to meet someone here. On business, the same as you."

Lucas's eyes narrowed. "A man?" he said slowly. She nodded. "And what does he look like?"

"Well, that's just it. I don't know. I mean, I've never met him. But I'm pretty sure he's middle-aged. And probably, well, probably not very good-looking. And... Why are you looking at me like that?"

"What's this middle-aged, homely guy's name?"

The blonde's chin lifted. "I don't think that's any of your—"

"Is it, by any chance, Lucas Vieira?"

Her mouth fell open.

"Ohmygod," she said, "ohmygod!"

"Don't tell me," Lucas said slowly. "You can't be…Dani Sinclair?"

The woman looked as if she might faint.

"You're right," she said. "I can't be Dani Sinclair. But I am."

Impossible, Caroline thought.

No. Not impossible.

Insane. This entire thing, from the minute Dani had called her, right up until now.

This was Lucas Vieira? This tall, dark-haired, absolutely spectacular hunk? She'd noticed him instantly. And she wasn't the only one. The lobby was crowded. It was a Friday night, warm even for early June, and it seemed as if everybody was out for the evening.

There must have been a couple of dozen women milling around with their dates, their husbands and boyfriends, and from what she'd been able to see, every one of them managed to shoot little assessing looks at the gorgeous guy standing all by himself.

He'd been watching the door, as if he was waiting for someone.

Okay, she'd thought. He was alone, he *was* waiting for someone.

But he couldn't be Lucas Vieira.

A man who looked like that wouldn't need to hire a woman to pretend to be his date. True, there was more to it than that, Lucas Vieira needed a date who could translate Russian—even more bizarre, really—but whatever the situation, this was not her guy.

If only he was…

And, even as she'd thought the words, she'd realized his eyes were focused on her. Her heart had thumped; she'd felt a rush of heat in her breasts, in her belly, in her blood. It went with the way she'd been feeling since leaving her apartment, as if she had stepped into a different reality, assuming another woman's identity, wearing her clothes, about to meet a stranger and pretend she was his girlfriend…

The stranger's eyes had seemed to narrow. He'd taken a step forward.

Caroline had torn her gaze from his and set out blindly through the crowd, heading anywhere but in his direction. She had to concentrate on finding Lucas Vieira, but how to identify him? Dani hadn't described him beyond saying he'd be alone and that he was incredibly rich.

The "incredibly rich" tag could probably be hung on most of the men in the lobby, but none of them were alone—except for the one whose eyes had blazed with fire when he'd looked at her.

Could he be the guy she was supposed to meet? Unless she'd missed something, he was the only man by himself. And he'd been watching the door with such intensity…

There was only one way to find out.

She'd taken a deep breath. And another. Then she'd walked up to him, said "excuse me" as politely as possible… Someone had jostled her. She'd teetered on the ridiculous heels. The stranger's hand—Lucas Vieira's hand—had closed around her elbow, steadying her. She'd already teetered once tonight, getting into the cab that had brought her here.

Then, all she'd thought was how huge a sum she'd owe Dani if she fell and tore this dress.

Now, all she could think of was the burn of this man's fingers on her skin.

Her heart began to race. She tried to step back and he caught hold of her hand again.

"Careful," he said. "This mob is like a herd of wildebeest on the Serengeti. They'd trample you before they knew they'd done it."

It was such an accurate description that Caroline laughed.

"That's good. You have to relax. We won't be able to pull this off unless you're at ease with me."

Her smile faded. This was business. How could she have forgotten that, even for an instant?

"You were supposed to be here twenty minutes ago."

Business, for sure. The smile, the charm, the *I'm-male, you're-female* thing had vanished.

"I know. But the traffic—"

"I'd wanted a little time for us to get a feel for each other."

She already had a feel for him. Not just rich but disgustingly rich. Not just good-looking but fantastically good-looking. Charming when he wanted to be, bitingly cold when he thought that would work better.

Oh, yes, she had a feel for that kind of man.

Her mother's kind.

Not rich like this, of course. You grew up in a small town at the end of nowhere, the men with all the money and power owned the Chevy dealership. The gas station. The shops on what really was called Main Street. And none had been as handsome as Lucas Vieira but the basics were the same.

Too much money, too much power, too much arrogance. Mama had always fallen hard for men who were rich and good-looking and one hundred percent no-good.

Caroline had never understood it. Mama was bright. She was logical about everything else; you had to be, to raise a child without money or a husband. Still, she'd fallen for the same kind of guy over and over.

One good thing was that Caroline had learned from Mama's

mistakes. She'd avoided boys like that in high school, in college, here in New York.

So, what in hell was she doing tonight?

She could never pull this off. Pretend to be Lucas Vieira's date. His girlfriend. Anybody's girlfriend, in a setting like this.

"Mr. Vieira," she said, rushing the words together, "I think I've made a mistake."

"I agree. But the people we're meeting haven't shown up yet, so—"

"I shouldn't be here. I'm not—I'm not going to be very good at this."

"You'll be fine."

There was a grim quality to his voice. He was desperate, but how could a man like this be desperate? He could snap his fingers and damned near every female in the place would come running. Okay. He needed a translator. She could, she supposed, be that, but she could never pull off pretending to be involved with him.

"I can translate for you. But the rest—"

"The rest is the most important part."

Caroline frowned. "I don't get it. Why would me pretending to be your date be important?"

"Not just my date." His mouth thinned. "My lover. My mistress." His hand moved up her arm to her shoulder. She could feel the heat of his fingers on her bare skin. "We'll need to convey a sense of intimacy, Dani. Do you understand?"

She blinked. Dani? Right. Right. That was her name tonight. She was Dani. Oh, if only she were! She had no idea what Dani did when she wasn't in class but there was a sense of sophistication to her that suggested Dani would know how to deal with a man who looked like this. Who sounded like this, that faint, sexy accent, that husky tone of command. A man whose scent was clean and masculine and crisp, if you could call a scent "crisp."

And when had they moved closer to each other? She didn't recall that happening but, somehow, it had, close enough so she had to tilt her head back to look into his face.

"Dani. Do you follow what I'm saying?"

"Intimacy," she said, her voice trembling.

"Yes."

"But why? If this is a business dinner—"

He hesitated. To her surprise, faint stripes of color appeared on his cheeks. He shrugged his shoulders and she thought, *why, he's almost human!*

"The man I'm doing business with has a wife. She's—she's an unusual woman. Very assertive. Make that aggressive. When she wants something, she goes after it." The color in his face deepened. "No matter what that something is, no matter if that something reciprocates or not—"

"She's hitting on you?"

"You, ah, you might say she's…" He paused. "Damned right, she is. And I'm counting on your presence to stop it."

Caroline swallowed hard. "Mr. Vieira—"

"Lucas."

"Lucas. That just cinches it. I can't—there's no way I could—"

"Damnit!"

He was staring over her head. The expression on his face went from harsh to grave.

Caroline stiffened. "What?" she said, and tried to look back, but his hand tightened on her shoulder.

"No. Keep looking at me."

"But—"

"It's the Rostovs. The people we're meeting. They're coming toward us."

If he'd said Genghis Khan's army was thundering out of

the steppes at that moment, she couldn't have felt a greater
flash of terror.

"This is not good, Mr. Vieira."

"For God's sake, it's Lucas. Lucas! Mistresses do not call
their lovers by their surnames!"

"But I'm not your mistress. I don't want anyone to think
I'm your mistress." Caroline could hear the rising panic in
her voice and she took a steadying breath. "I don't believe in
women being mistresses. In them being property. In being
owned and supported and—and held as chattel by men,
and—"

"Luke-ahs!"

A meaty hand slapped Lucas on the shoulder. The man that
went with it was meaty, too. "Enormous" was a better word,
Caroline thought. He had small eyes, a big nose and a grin
that stretched from ear to ear.

"Leo," Lucas said. "It's good to see you again."

Leo Rostov's gaze slid to Caroline.

"Ah. This is your voman."

"No," Caroline said, "I'm—"

"Yes," Lucas said with a little chuckle that had no connection to the pressure of his fingers digging into her flesh as he
slipped his arm around her waist and brought her to his side.
"But she's one of the 'liberated' women, Leo, if you know
what I mean. She'll bristle if you call her 'my woman.'" He
looked down at Caroline. "Isn't that right, sweetheart?"

Was that a note of desperation in Lucas Vieira's voice?
A glint of it in his green eyes? Well, he'd got himself into
this mess. How he'd done it was anyone's guess but he could
damned well get himself out of—

"Luke-ahhhs!"

A woman slipped from behind Rostov's bulky figure. One
look, and Caroline understood everything. Ilana Rostov was
stunning. Big hair. Big breasts. Big diamonds.

And from the way she looked at Lucas, she was, without question, a cougar on the hunt.

"Luke-ahhhs, oh Luke-ahhhs, you darling man. How lovely to see you again."

"Ilana." Lucas's arm tightened around Caroline. "I'd like to introduce my—"

"Howdoyoudo?" Ilana said, without taking her eyes from Lucas. Smiling, batting her lashes, she stepped in front of him, her face upturned, her breasts touching his chest. "A kiss, darling. You know that is how we Russians greet old friends." Smiling, she rose on her toes and wound her arms around his neck. Lucas jerked back but it didn't matter. Nothing was going to stop her.

Not true, Caroline thought. Something could, and would. Her spiked gold heel, nailing Ilana Rostov's instep.

Ilana shrieked and stumbled back. Caroline threw her a look of abject innocence.

"My goodness, did I step on your foot? I am so sorry!" Swinging toward Lucas, taking the place Ilana Rostov had vacated, Caroline looked up at him. The expression on his face was priceless; it took all her effort not to burst into giggles, but why spoil things now? "Lucas? Sweetie? I'm thrilled to meet your friends but what about dinner?" Still smiling, she moved closer, until they were a breath apart. "I'm absolutely starved, darling."

She watched the swift play of emotions across his face as surprise gave way to sheer delight—and then to something darker, deeper, and far more dangerous. His arms went around her. She spread her hands flat against his chest, felt the strong, steady beat of his heart.

"Yes," he said. "So am I."

No way was he talking about a meal.

Caroline felt her heart thud. When had he seized control of the game?

"Mr. Vieira," she said, "I mean, Lucas—"

He laughed, bent his head to hers and took hot, exciting possession of her mouth.

CHAPTER THREE

THAT little slip, Dani calling him "Mr. Vieira," could have been Lucas's undoing.

That was the reason he kissed her. The sole reason. Anything to convince the Rostovs that he and the woman in his arms had an intimate relationship.

Why else would he kiss her? He didn't know her and she didn't know him. He didn't have any wish to know her; he was off women for a while.

Kissing the woman with the pale gold hair and hazel eyes was a matter of expediency. It was meant to establish intimacy, to take the sting out of the way she'd addressed him and that glimpse he'd had of Ilana's raised eyebrows.

And, while he was at it, the kiss was to remind her of her function here tonight.

For those reasons, no other, Lucas took his supposed mistress in his arms and kissed her. It wasn't even much of a kiss, just a light brush of his mouth over hers.

But her lips were warm. Silken. Her little "oh" of shocked breath was warm, too, and tasted of mint. Toothpaste, he thought in surprise, a taste that didn't quite go with the sexy dress, the do-me shoes, and…

And, he stopped thinking.

Everything around him faded. The crowd. The noise. The

Rostovs. It was as if each of his senses was solely concentrated on the woman in his arms.

Lucas drew her closer. Slid one hand to the base of her spine and lifted her slightly, just enough so that she fit the contours of his body while he cupped her face with his other hand.

He felt the soft pressure of her breasts against his chest. The tilt of her hips against his. The delicate arc of her cheekbone under his fingers.

Felt himself turn hard as granite.

His lips parted hers. She made a little whisper of sound and he thought, *Yes, that's it, kiss me back.*

She did. For a heartbeat. Then she stiffened. She was going to pull away.

He told himself, with admirable logic, that he couldn't permit that. If they were lovers, she would be eager for his kisses. Anytime. Anywhere. Not just in bed.

Which made him imagine her in his bed, her hair spilling in golden disarray over his pillows, her eyes hot with hunger as he entered her...

Dani sank her small, sharp teeth into his lip.

"Cristos!" Lucas jerked back. Touched the spot with his finger. No blood, nothing but a flash-fire rush of fury.

Rostov roared with laughter. Ilana's eyebrows sought refuge in her hairline. And Dani...Dani looked as if she might turn and run and, damnit, he could not let that happen!

Lucas's life had taught him many lessons. Quick recovery. Damage control. Self-control. He needed all those skills now. Somehow, he managed a smile as he wrapped his hand around the blonde's slender wrist. She'd have to wrestle herself free of his grasp and he was betting she wouldn't let that happen.

"Now, sweetheart," he said, his smile changing, going sexy and intimate, "you know we don't play those games in public."

Another laugh from Rostov. A pause, and then a little sigh from Ilana.

And the best reward of all, the cold pleasure of seeing crimson sweep into his defiant translator's beautiful face.

"No," she said, "we—you and I—we don't pl—"

"Exactly, darling. We don't." She looked as if she were torn between embarrassment and the desire to murder him, and that made it easier for him to tug her closer, curve his arm around her waist and hold her captive against his body. "If you want your reward, you have to wait until the evening ends. You know that, Dani."

He knew the second his message registered. If she wanted his thousand dollars, she'd have to play the role Jack Gordon had crafted for her.

"Understand, sweetheart?"

Her eyes flashed. No embarrassment now, no fear. "I understand completely—*sweetheart*."

Lucas laughed. The lady had guts. He had to admit, he liked that in her. He wasn't accustomed to it. Women rarely stood up to him. Well, not until he ended a relationship and then some of them balked, but flying into a rage wasn't the same thing as standing up to him.

Rostov elbowed him in the side. "Your lady is vildcat, Luke-ahs."

Yes. She was.

She was a great many things. Beautiful. Bright. Skilled in Russian—he had no proof of that yet but, somehow, he felt no reason to doubt it. Add the sweet taste of her mouth, the alluring scent of her skin, the lush feel of her against him and she was an intriguing package, the embodiment of sex and intellect rolled into one.

Except for her name.

It didn't fit her. It was flippant. Unfeminine. And she was neither. She'd be an interesting woman to get to know.

Too bad that wasn't on the agenda.

"You know," he said, glancing at his watch, "it's getting late. Why don't we go straight to the restaurant and have drinks there?"

"Ve vill haff champagne," Rostov said, clapping Lucas on the back, "once we walk over two tiny spots, *da*?"

Lucas cocked his head. Dani rattled off something in Russian, Rostov answered, and she looked at Lucas.

"He means that there are two small areas of concern in the deal you and he have made, and he wants to talk about them."

Lucas smiled.

His plan had worked. Rostov was ready to conclude things, Dani understood the nuances of translating. And seeing her now, cheeks still slightly flushed, hair a little disheveled, eyes glittering, not even Ilana would question their relationship.

He could relax.

All that remained was a final few hours of sociability. Then he and Rostov would shake hands and say goodbye, Ilana would become a bad memory, he'd give Dani Sinclair a check for a thousand dollars and they'd never see each other again.

He'd have to thank Jack Gordon.

This wasn't the disaster he'd anticipated. In fact, it was working out just fine.

Caroline sat across the restaurant table from The Woman With The Frozen Face and wondered how she could have got herself into such a situation.

Two rich men. A woman married to one of them but on the make for the other. And she, the buffer between them.

Actually, that part had worked out just fine.

She still couldn't believe how quickly Lucas Vieira had got

out of the quicksand after she'd bitten him. She still couldn't even believe she'd bitten him!

Hell, he was lucky she hadn't grabbed the nearest lethal object and brained him with it.

Kissing her that way. Pulling her against him. Letting her feel the beat of his heart, the warmth of his body. The swift hardening of his aroused flesh.

Biting him was better than he'd deserved and though she'd been furious at how easily he'd turned the bite into something sexy, she had to admire him for being fast on his feet.

Caroline reached for her champagne flute and brought it to her lips.

And for using the incident to convince the Botox Cougar that they were lovers.

Ilana had bought the entire act. She'd followed Caroline into the loo after they'd taxied to the restaurant and looked at her reflection in the mirror that hung above the elegant triple vanity.

"Congratulations, Miss Sinclair."

"Who?" Caroline had almost said, but she'd remembered just in time.

"Your lover is quite a man."

A blush had crept into Caroline's face. What did you say to that?

"Surely," the Cougar had purred, "he is remarkable in bed."

The mirror had shown Caroline the color in her face going from pink to red.

"He's all right," she'd blurted.

Ilana had laughed. Even the attendant, who'd come to the vanity to provide them with little hand towels, couldn't repress a smile.

"I think he must find your attitude a change from the usual, *da*? The careless way you treat him." The Cougar's eyes had met Caroline's in the glass. "You know, I did not at first be-lieve you were his mistress. You do not seem his type."

Truth time. Caroline had taken a breath.

"Of course I'm his mistress," she'd said calmly. "Why else would I be with him tonight?"

For five hundred dollars, the voice within her had whis-pered.

Because, no question about it, Ilana Rostov was right. She was, most assuredly, not Lucas's type.

She wasn't the type that belonged in this restaurant, either.

The place was small, intimate and elegant. The patrons were elegant, too. She recognized familiar faces from movies and television and magazine covers. The women were expen-sively dressed. The men exuded wealth and power.

And almost all of them, men and women, had noticed Lucas, the men with nods and smiles of recognition, the women with glances that could only be called covetous.

More than one woman had looked at her in a way that said she was amazingly lucky to have such a man's attention. And she was. Or she would have been, if any of this was real, but it wasn't. It wasn't, and she had to keep remembering that—and it was difficult because Lucas was so attentive.

And so dangerously, excitingly sexy, even when he and Rostov had dropped into intense conversation over drinks. Ilana had translated for her husband in a low voice. Caroline had done the same for Lucas.

It had gone very well—except for those times he'd posed a question to her, or leaned in, to hear what she had to say. Then he'd brought his dark head down to hers; she'd felt the whisper of his breath on her skin, found herself thinking that all she had to do was lift her head, just a little, and her cheek would brush his, she'd feel the faint abrasion of that sexy five o'clock stubble against her skin.

Even now, with the deal concluded, a second bottle of champagne opened and poured, the danger wasn't over.

Every now and then, Lucas would touch her.

Her hair. Her hand. Her shoulder, when he lay his arm along the back of her chair and brushed his fingers against her bare skin.

It was part of the masquerade, or maybe he wasn't even aware he was doing it. He was a man accustomed to being with women; everything about him made that clear. Either way, it meant nothing. But whenever he touched her—whenever he touched her…

A tremor shot through her. Lucas, who was talking with Rostov but had his hand on Caroline's, leaned in.

"Are you cold, sweetheart? Do you want my jacket?"

His jacket? Warm from his body, undoubtedly bearing his scent?

"Dani? If you like, I can warm you."

Her eyes flew to his. Something glowed in those deep green depths. Was he toying with her? Her heart was trying to claw its way out of her chest.

"Thank you," she said carefully, "I'm fine."

He smiled. Her heart took another leap.

He had the sexiest smile she'd ever seen.

He had the sexiest everything.

Eyes. Face. Hands. Body. And that kiss. That just-for-show kiss… She'd felt it straight down to her toes. The warmth of his mouth, the feel of his hands…

She made a little sound. Lucas raised an eyebrow. "Are you sure you're all right?"

"Yes," she said quickly. "I just—I just can't decide what to order."

"Let me order for you, darling."

She wanted to say "no" but that would have been foolish. Reading Chekhov was easier than reading the menu. Black truffle mayonnaise. Whipped dill. She doubted either had anything to do with what you put on a bacon, lettuce and tomato sandwich, or the kosher dill pickle you'd eat with it.

It was only that saying she'd let him do something personal for her made her feel uncomfortable—

"Dani?"

And that was ridiculous. There was nothing personal about ordering a meal.

"Yes," she said. "Thank you. I'd like that."

Lucas brought her hand to his lips. "Two thank-yous in a row. I must be doing something right."

The Rostovs smiled. That was good. After all, this performance was for them.

She had to keep remembering that.

Her toes curled.

Oh God, she thought again, as the waiter took their orders, she was as out of her element as a hummingbird in a blizzard. Not just here, in these surroundings.

She was out of her element with this man.

She could leave now. She could. She'd done her job. Ilana Rostov was behaving herself. Her translation duties were completed now that, metaphorically, twenty billion dollars had changed hands. Twenty billion! She couldn't even start to envision that amount of money but Lucas had mentioned it with less fuss than Dani had shown about the five hundred she'd pay her for tonight's masquerade.

It was a lie, all of it, and Caroline understood the reason for it. If she'd had the Botox Cougar after her, well, the male equivalent, she'd have done whatever it took to throw her off the trail.

It was just that—that there'd been moments tonight when she'd thought, when she'd wondered, when she'd imagined how it would feel if she really were Lucas Vieira's date, if she were his lover, if the evening would end in a softly lit room with him undressing her, baring her body to his hands, his mouth…

And thinking like that was wrong.

The waiter brought the first course. Just in time. She needed food. She hadn't eaten in hours and hours. No wonder her brain was in meltdown.

Unfortunately, she couldn't swallow much more than a mouthful. She couldn't eat the main course, either. She was sure it had to be delicious. It looked beautiful, nothing like food, but beautiful anyway.

Trouble was, her stomach had gone on strike. *No room for food here*, it said, *butterflies in residence*.

"Lucas." Was that breathless, desperate little voice hers? "Lucas," she said again, and he turned to her. "I—I—"

His eyes searched hers. A muscle knotted in his jaw. Then he took her hand, did that incredible-hand-kissing thing again and looked across the table at Leo Rostov, who was in the middle of telling an endless joke.

"Leo," he said politely, "Dani's exhausted. You're going to have to excuse us."

It was a request but it wasn't. There was a tone of command in his voice. She heard it and she knew Rostov did, too. His ruddy face grew ruddier. Leonid Rostov wasn't accustomed to having someone else call an end to the festivities.

"Lucas," Caroline whispered, "it's okay. If you have to—"

"What I have to do," he said quietly, "is see you home."

For the second time, she saw that her gorgeous, arrogant date was gorgeous and arrogant but that somewhere inside him, he was real.

There was a flurry of activity. Lucas took out his cell phone, arranged for his driver to meet him outside the restaurant. He waved off Rostov's attempt to pay the bill and ordered another bottle of Cristal.

"You and Ilana stay and enjoy yourselves," he said.

And then they were out of the restaurant, into the midnight streets. Lucas turned her toward him.

"Are you all right?"

"Yes. Thank you. I just— I've had a long day, and—"

His hands were warm and hard on her elbows. There was a look of concern on his face. They were standing so close that she could feel the heat coming off him, see that the emerald irises of his eyes were ringed with black.

Caroline shuddered.

"Damnit," he said gruffly, and he took off his suit jacket and draped it around her shoulders.

Just as she feared, as she'd longed, the fabric held his warmth. His scent.

"No," she said quickly, "really, I don't—"

"Let me warm you," he said, just as he'd said a while ago, but this time there was no questioning what she heard in his voice, what she saw in his eyes as she looked up at him.

The world seemed to stop.

"Hell," he said roughly.

She could have asked why he'd said that. Why his voice sounded as if it had been run through gravel. But asking would have been foolish and she had done enough foolish things tonight, starting with accepting Dani's proposal and ending with not walking out of the hotel lobby the second she'd laid eyes on Lucas Vieira.

"Dani," he said, the single word dark with warning, and she made a little sound, took a step toward him and he knotted his hands in the lapels of the jacket and pulled her into the heat, the power of his body.

And did what he'd wanted to do the entire night.

Bent his head. Took her mouth. Kissed her gently and when she whimpered, rose on her toes and wound her arms around his neck. When she opened her lips to his, his kiss deepened, burned hotter than a flame.

"Dani," he said, against her mouth, and Caroline caught Lucas's face between her palms and brought it to hers so the kiss could go on and on.

And on.

CHAPTER FOUR

A LONG, black Mercedes pulled to the curb.

Lucas got in, held his hand out to Caroline. She took it and he drew her into the limo's dark, leather-scented interior.

It was like stepping into their own world. No lights. No people.

"Take us home," he told his driver, and then the privacy screen went up and they were alone. "Come here," he said roughly, and without hesitation, she went into his arms.

The Mercedes moved swiftly through the dark city streets, a magical craft sailing the seas of a dream. A lover beyond imagining, his lips on hers, his body hard beneath hers as he drew her into his lap.

Wrong, Caroline thought, this was wrong…

"Open your mouth," he whispered. "Let me taste you."

A moan rose in her throat. Her lips parted against his as the limo sped toward Fifth Avenue.

"I've wanted this all night. You, in my arms. Kissing me."

Yes. Oh, yes. She'd wanted it, too, but—

"Dani. God, you're so beautiful.

"No. Lucas—"

"Do you want me to stop?" He drew back, just enough so he could look into her eyes.

Caroline stared at him. What she wanted was to tell him

that she was Caroline, that she was not a woman named Dani...

"If this isn't what you want, too," he said hoarsely, "tell me now."

She shook her head. "Don't stop. Don't stop. Don't—"

He kissed her, and the world went away.

He lived in the sky.

That was how it seemed, with moonlight pouring in through the windows, as if she and he were surrounded by stars that burned in a private universe.

He kissed her in the private elevator that rose to his penthouse, kissed her as he swept her into his arms and carried her to his bedroom, kissed her as he set her on her feet.

He cupped her breast, moved his fingers over the silk-covered nipple that leaped to his touch. A cry rose in her throat; he captured it with his mouth.

She was on fire for him.

"Dani," he said, and together, they fell back against the wall. His mouth ravaged hers; he pushed up her skirt, his hands big and urgent on her skin. She trembled, clasped his face with her hands, offered him her lips, her tongue, her hunger.

He said something in Spanish. Portuguese. She didn't know, didn't care, didn't care about anything but the feel of his hands, his mouth.

Caroline reached for the buttons on his shirt. He tore aside her thong. His hands clasped her bottom; he lifted her and she gasped at the shock of his erection against her.

"Wrap your legs around me," he said gruffly.

She did, and gasped again as he freed one hand, fumbled between them and then...

And then, God, then he was driving into her, hot and hard, silk over steel, stretching her, filling her and it was wonderful, it was terrifying, it was nothing like the one time she'd been with a man, nothing like she'd ever imagined.

The world began to tilt.

"Lucas," she sobbed. "Oh God, Lucas!"

It was too much, too much, too much…

Caroline screamed in ecstasy.

And felt herself fly with him into the molten heat of the stars.

Lucas had no idea how long they'd been standing like this, Dani still in his arms, her legs around his hips, him holding her up, both of them breathing hard while sweat sheened their skin.

Hours might have gone by. Or minutes. He'd lost the ability to think straight.

Hell, that was painfully apparent. A thinking man didn't do what he'd just done. Made love to a woman with all the finesse of a bull moose in rut.

And without protection.

He couldn't believe it.

The twin demons of a bachelor's life. Disease. Pregnancy. Always out there, waiting for some damned fool. Had he been the fool tonight? Even at sixteen, his first time with a woman, he'd been smarter than this.

How could he have let passion override logic?

"—please."

Dani was speaking to him. Whispering, was more like it. She'd buried her face in the crook of his neck, as if she didn't want to look at him. Between that and the sound of that tremulous whisper, he was willing to bet she was upset.

Merda, why wouldn't she be?

"Dani," he said softly, "look at me."

She shook her head. Her hair, all that spun gold silk, flew around her face, brushed against his nose and mouth. Even now, he shut his eyes, let the scent and soft feel of it tease his senses.

"Sweetheart. I know this wasn't—"

"Please. Put me down."

There was a faint note of panic in her words. He nodded, lowered her to her feet, gritting his teeth against the swift rush of desire he felt as her body brushed his.

"Dani—"

"You don't understand." She lifted her head; his throat constricted at what he saw in her eyes. "Listen to me, Lucas. What—what I just did. I don't—I don't ever—"

"I *do* understand." He cupped her face, lowered his head until their eyes were level. "This was too quick. My fault. I'm sorry. I meant to do this right." His voice roughened. "But, I wanted you so badly…"

"No." She clasped his wrists. "That's not it. I meant that I—that I—"

"I didn't give you enough time."

Caroline have a helpless little laugh. "Lucas. We aren't talking about the same—"

"We are," he said. "It's my fault."

They were talking about different things, but what did it matter? What was the sense in explaining now? And—and the truth was, after what she'd just done, having sex with a stranger, going wild in his arms…

All things considered, she was willing to go on pretending to be a woman who could do those things without recrimination. He'd never know she was really Caroline Hamilton, not Dani Sinclair. There was no way she and Lucas Vieira would ever see each other again. Their worlds had intersected by accident and accidents didn't happen twice.

"You have the right to know that I'm healthy," he said softly, taking a strand of her hair between his fingers.

She blinked. "What?"

"I'm healthy, sweetheart." He dipped his head, brushed his lips over hers. "Still, I should have used a condom."

The word made her blush, and wasn't that pathetic?

"Are you—" He hesitated.

She felt her color deepen.

"Yes," she said quickly, "I am. I'm perfectly healthy." No lie there. When the last time you'd had sex was three years ago, you could be sure you didn't have an STD.

Lucas shifted his weight, put his hands flat against the wall on either side of her.

"I didn't mean that. I meant, are you on the pill?"

Stupid, she thought, so stupid! She was. She took it to regulate her period, but he didn't have to know that.

"Yes," she said, and wasn't it ridiculous to blush even harder? She'd had sex with a stranger, sex so out of control she'd thought she might die from the incredible pleasure of it, and talking about condoms and birth control embarrassed her.

Pathetic.

"Good. But if anything should go wrong…"

"Nothing will," she said quickly. One more second of this conversation and she was either going to burst into tears or hysterical laughter.

How could she have done this?

And what did she do now?

Lucas had her caged against the wall. One of her shoes was missing. Her thong was a bit of torn silk, caught around one ankle. What was the protocol? Did she search for the lost shoe? Kick off what remained of the thong? Did she say, *Goodbye, Mr. Vieira, and thank you for a pleasant evening*?

A muffled sound caught in her throat. Laughter or sobs? Either would only add to her humiliation and she thought, without any logical reason, that the woman she was pretending to be would probably know how to deal with all those questions.

"Dani?"

"Don't—don't call me that." Caroline swallowed hard. "I mean—I mean, I've never liked that name."

Lucas flashed a smile. "Actually, I don't think it suits you."

"No. I mean, yes. I mean…" Damn. Her overworked emotions made their own choice. Tears rose in her eyes and rolled down her cheeks. "I have to leave," she said, but when she tried to get by him, Lucas caught her shoulders and held her still.

"Sweetheart." His mouth twisted. "Damnit, I've made you cry."

"No." She shook her head. "No, it isn't your fault."

The hell it wasn't. She was crying. Silently, which somehow only made it worse. He put his hand under her chin, raised her face to his. Her mascara was running, her eyeliner, whatever women called that stuff, had smudged into black streaks. She was a mess.

A beautiful, heartbreaking mess, he thought, and he gathered her into his arms.

"I hurt you," he said gruffly.

She shook her head again but he knew better.

"I did. I was too rough, too fast."

"You weren't." Her voice was soft, as was the hand she lay against his cheek. "It's me. It's what I've done, coming up here with you, behaving like—like—"

"Hush." Lucas gathered her against him, rocked her gently in his arms. It took a long time until he felt the rigidity in her start to ease but he went on holding her close. "What happened is nothing to regret. It was—" What? Unplanned. Unexpected. Being with a woman was the last thing he'd imagined he'd want tonight, but he had no regrets. If anything, instinct told

him what they'd just shared would be something he would
not soon forget. "It was wonderful," he said softly, tipping up
her chin. "Incredible. And it's my fault it wasn't like that for
you."

"But it was. Wonderful, I mean."

She was blushing. It was— The only word that worked was
"charming," especially when the blush was from a woman
who'd given herself with nothing held back.

"I'm glad. Still..." He brushed his lips over hers. "Still, I'll
bet I can make it even better."

He heard the little intake of her breath. "It's late. And—"

"I want to undress you."

His voice was rough. Just the sound of it made her knees
go weak.

"Undress you. Kiss you. Touch you everywhere. Slowly this
time. Very slowly." He drew her to her toes, took her mouth
in a kiss that sent her pulse soaring. "We can spend the rest
of the night getting to know each other."

She met his eyes, lifted a tentative hand to his face again.
Which was stronger, the desire to run...or the desire to let
what she knew, she *knew* she wanted, happen? He turned his
head, captured her hand, kissed her palm, her wrist, her arm,
and Caroline had her answer.

"Lucas," she whispered, and she put her hand behind his
head, rose to him and kissed him back.

Slowly, he began to undress her, doing this as he should
have the first time, drawing out each caress, each whisper of
skin against skin, turning her so her back was to him, nuzzling
aside her hair, kissing the column of her spine as he undid her
zipper.

The dress fell open. She started to catch it but he slipped
his arms around her, cupped her breasts, felt the shudder go
through her as he did.

He held her that way, his hands on her, until she moaned

his name and leaned back against him. Her bra had a front closure and he released it, let the bit of silk fall away, bit back a groan when her naked breasts tumbled into his hands.

He heard her breath catch. Felt a tremor go through her. He moved his thumbs over her nipples and she made the kind of little sound that left him wanting to turn her to him and bury himself inside her.

But not yet.

He slid one hand over her ribs. Her belly. Put his mouth to the nape of her neck and kissed the fragrant skin. He moved his hand lower. Lower still. She gasped his name, tried to turn but he wouldn't let her, not now, not when his hand was between her thighs, when her heat filled his palm, when he was harder than a man could possibly be and survive.

Concentrate, he told himself fiercely, concentrate on Dani. On the woman in your arms.

Gently, he parted her with his fingers.

Stroked her.

Heard the hiss of her breath. Felt her try to clamp her thighs together to stop him.

Felt her stop fighting him, fighting herself, and, instead, move against his hand.

"No," she said, "no, don't. Lucas. Don't. I'm going to—I'm going to—"

She gave a long, keening cry. The sound filled him with pleasure and he swung her toward him, swept her into his arms and brought her to his bed.

Moonlight from the big skylight overhead bathed her in ivory.

Her hair streamed over his pillow, burnished gold against cream. He had imagined her like this but the reality was more perfect than the mental image. She was lovely. All of her.

And she was his.

He made love to her slowly, as he'd promised, watching

her face as he did, loving the way her eyes widened, her lips parted as he caressed her. When his hand reached her breast, she caught it in hers.

"Let me touch you," he said in a husky whisper, and she released his hand, held her breath, cried out as he feathered his thumb over a dusky-pink nipple, then lowered his head and drew one tightly furled tip into the heat of his mouth.

The taste of her was almost his undoing. Honey. Cream. Vanilla. He sucked her nipples, licked them until her moans told him she was crazy with wanting him...

As he was crazy with wanting her.

"Lucas."

Her whisper was a plea.

He took her in his arms. Lifted her to him and kissed her with slow, thorough deliberation. He couldn't get enough of her; as much as he wanted to sheathe himself within her silken heat, he wanted the kiss to go on and on. She trembled against him and he trembled, too, aching to possess her.

It was sweet torture.

She sighed his name again, this time with growing urgency. Her arms went around his neck. She lifted herself to him, pressed herself to him. He knew what she longed for; he longed for it, too, that hot, exciting release but he told himself he could wait, he could wait...

"Lucas," she whispered, "Lucas, please."

It was the "please" that almost finished him, something in the softness of how she said it, the innocence with which she said it, that nearly sent him over the edge.

He stood, stripped off his clothes, saw her eyes widen when she saw his erection. He was big; he knew that. Big, and proud of it because he was male, but there was a flash of fear in her eyes.

"It's all right," he said hoarsely. "We fit, remember? Just a little while ago."

He took her hand, brought it to him.

Bad move.

Her hand closed around him. He groaned. Her hand moved again and he caught it, held it in his as he opened a drawer in the table beside the bed and fumbled for a condom. Seconds later, he knelt between her thighs.

Slowly, his gaze linked to hers, he entered her.

"Is this good for you?" he whispered. "Tell me it is. Tell me—"

She reached for him. Brought his face to hers. Kissed him, sighed his name, and he lost himself in the kiss, in the rhythm they set, in possession of her.

The world went up in flame.

After a long, long time, Lucas rolled onto his side with her curled like a satisfied kitten in his arms. He liked the feel of her, soft and warm against him.

"Sweetheart? Are you okay?"

She made a sound that was so close to a purr, it made him smile. It was as fine a recommendation as a man could want, he thought as he drew the duvet over them.

"Close your eyes, then," he said softly.

"Mmmm."

Her lashes drifted to her cheeks. He kissed her temple, drew her closer, felt her breathing slow.

Amazing.

He'd ended the day wanting nothing to do with women, and ended the night with a woman in his arms. He couldn't make sense of it—unless wanting her so badly, taking her so slowly was the sexual equivalent of downing a drink in the morning when you woke with a hangover. He hadn't ever had a hangover—getting drunk was a weakness—and he hadn't ever needed sex to forget an affair that had just ended, but anything was possible.

Lucas yawned.

And he was too tired to try to make sense of anything right now.

The illuminated clock beside the bed read three-thirty. They had three hours to sleep until his alarm went off, unless he woke a little earlier and woke her, too, so he could make love with her one more time.

Maybe that wasn't such a hot idea.

Maybe he should have taken her to her apartment, instead of to his.

Maybe he'd regret her spending the night. Look at what had just happened with Elin. She'd spent a handful of nights here and decided it meant their relationship, if you could call it that, had turned serious.

Maybe…

Maybe what he needed was some sleep.

Lucas drew his beautiful translator closer. His eyelids drooped. He smiled a little, remembering that she didn't like being called "Dani," but she'd never told him what she preferred. Danielle? Was that her full name? Somehow, it didn't suit her, either.

He'd find out in the morning.

He'd find out a lot of things in the morning.

The name she preferred. Her address. Her phone number. Because he wanted to see her again. *See* her, not turn this into anything exclusive, of course, although he wouldn't want her seeing other men. He would not tolerate it. He needed his space. He needed his freedom. But—but—

But, he'd work it all out tomorrow. The only possible problem would be if she misinterpreted spending the night in his bed. Women did…

Lucas tumbled into sleep.

And when the alarm rang at six-thirty, there were no problems to work out because Dani Sinclair was gone.

CHAPTER FIVE

CAROLINE came awake with a start.

In a movie, the heroine would have opened her eyes and come to a slow realization that she was not in her own bed. But this wasn't a movie, it was real life and she knew instantly that she was in a stranger's bed.

There was the enormous size of the bed itself. The faint predawn light, streaming through the arched floor-to-ceiling windows. The skylight overhead. The silk comforter.

Caroline shuddered.

Most of all, there was that hard, warm male body lying against hers, that tanned, muscular arm draped possessively around her waist.

Her heart bumped into her throat.

Scenes of the night flashed through her mind. Throwing herself into Lucas's arms in his limo. Kissing him in the elevator.

Making love against the wall and then in this bed.

Except, it hadn't been love, it had been sex. Trying to turn last night into something soft and romantic was like—like trying to pretend that Madame Bovary was Cinderella.

Useless, pointless, and that she had never done anything like this before, that she looked down on women who went in for hooking up—and that was what this had been, a hook-up, plain and simple—only made it more humiliating.

She'd gone to bed with a man she didn't know and the only good part of it was that he was still asleep.

Sound asleep.

He lay sprawled on his belly, his head turned toward her on the pillow. The duvet had slipped to his waist. Caroline's gaze moved over him.

Even in sleep, he was a magnificent sight.

All that dark, tousled hair. The thick, black lashes that curved against his cheek. The straight nose, sculpted mouth, the tiny dimple in that strong, assertive chin, even the morning stubble on his jaw, was beautiful and sexy.

The comforter was caught just at the base of his spine; she couldn't see the rest of him but she knew, oh how well she knew, that his backside was tight, his legs long, just as she knew that if he rolled over, the rest of him was perfect.

Heat started at the tips of her toes, spread low in her belly, made her nipples tighten.

That's it, Caroline. That's just great. Lie here and turn yourself on, admiring your seducer instead of getting your butt out the door...

Except, he hadn't seduced her.

He had taken her in his arms and kissed her. That was all he'd done. The choices afterward had been hers. She could have pushed him away. Slapped his face. She could even have let the kiss happen and then ended it and walked away. Nobody had forced her into his car, against that wall, into his bed...

Enough.

She breathed in, then slowly out. Inch by careful inch, she moved from beneath his arm. Waking him, having to face him again, was the last thing in the world she wanted.

If there was a morning protocol for what she was supposed to do now, she didn't know it, didn't want to know it.

"Mmmf."

Caroline froze. Waited. After what seemed forever, Lucas rolled onto his side, away from her.

She went into action, located her scattered clothes—shoes, dress, bra, little evening purse. She couldn't find her thong panties—her torn panties—and after a couple of minutes, she gave up looking.

Time to get out while she still could.

The gray light of dawn lit the rooms of the penthouse as she made her way downstairs. She had no memory of the place; all her attention had been on Lucas. Now, she saw that it was huge and handsome, furnished in light woods and glass. The elevator, small and elegant, stood at the end of the foyer.

Precious seconds flew while she figured out how to operate it. At last, she got it moving and as it dropped toward the lobby, she tried not to think about what had happened in this car a few hours ago.

Lucas, lifting her into him. His mouth, hungry on hers. Desire, welling hot and sweet within her.

The elevator gave a delicate bounce when it reached the lobby. The door slid open but not before Caroline got a clear look at herself in its mirrored surface.

What she saw made her cringe.

Smudged makeup. Tangled hair. Skinny gold heels and a dress that might as well have had *Guess What I Did Last Night* printed across it.

In a better world, the lobby would have been empty but this was the same world in which she'd already humiliated herself once. Now, it was time for Round Two.

A man in a blue blazer sat behind a desk. He looked up, saw her, smiled pleasantly and said, "Good morning, miss," as if women in her state stepped out of Lucas's private elevator all the time, which they undoubtedly did.

"Morning," she mumbled, but the embarrassment wasn't over, not yet, because—of course—there was a doorman and he said the same thing, just as pleasantly, and all Caroline could do was wish the marble floor would open and swallow her whole.

"Shall I hail a cab for you, miss?" the doorman said as he opened the door.

She said, "Yes, please," because even imagining getting into a subway car looking as she did at this hour of the morning made her feel sick.

"Thank you," she said, when a cab pulled to the curb. Was she supposed to tip the doorman or wasn't she? she wondered, and then she almost laughed because what did a question about tipping matter now? The fact was, she was in way over her head.

She gave the doorman a five-dollar bill, gave the cabbie her address and told herself that saying *I know how this looks but really, I'm not the kind of woman you think I am* would accomplish nothing. Either the cabbie wouldn't care or, if he did, then she was exactly the kind of woman he thought she was.

At least, she was that kind of woman, now.

She made it into her flat without bumping into anybody and then she locked the door, peeled off her dress—Dani's dress—kicked off her shoes—Dani's shoes—and went straight into the shower where not all the hot water nor all the soap in the world would have been enough to make her forget what she'd done.

If only she could forget the sex, the incredible sex, because it had been that. Incredible. Amazing. Fantastic. Or if she could remember it without feeling the awful guilt of having gone to bed with a man she didn't know.

But she couldn't. And, after a while, she just stopped trying.

Lucas awoke to a sound.

Faint. Distant. What…? The elevator. The purr of the motor.

He rolled over. Sat up. Saw that the space beside him was empty, that Dani's clothes were no longer scattered around the room.

She was gone.

He sank back against the pillows, folded his arms beneath his head. Well, that was a good thing. A very good thing. No need for forced early-morning conversation. No need to fend off offers to make coffee. No pretending that he loved having it with someone when he much preferred having it alone. No long, drawn-out goodbye.

He sat up again and swung his feet to the floor.

The only thing he ever wanted in the morning, besides black coffee and a shower, was sex. Wake-up sex, no frills, and women weren't into basics. None he'd ever encountered, anyway.

Besides, he thought as he headed for the bathroom, he had the feeling Dani Sinclair would have a bundle of morning-after recriminations. Not that she'd said "no" to anything last night—if she had, that would have been the end of it. But there'd been that innocence to her...

Ridiculous, of course. She had responded to him with un-believable hunger, and that was another good thing. He wasn't into innocence or lack of experience—although he could see advantages to it.

To being the man who taught a woman what passion was all about.

He stepped into the shower, set the multiple sprays to pro-duce a hot, needle-fine mist, bowed his head as the water sluiced on him and over him.

There'd been that moment when he'd teased Dani's dusty-pink nipples into tight little buds and she'd cried out as if something so simple was new. And later, when he'd parted her thighs, kissed her most intimate flesh, tasted her against his mouth...

Hell.

Lucas switched the water from hot to cold. Enough thinking about last night.

He had a long day ahead of him.

The day was not going well.

Lucas had sat through a morning meeting without hearing most of what was said. He'd canceled his lunch appointment. Now, he was at his desk, trying to answer a question that was as unanswerable as it was unimportant.

Why had Dani Sinclair run away?

What else could you call it when a woman spent the night in your bed and then disappeared without saying goodbye, without leaving a note, without leaving her phone number? Never mind seeing her again. Perhaps it was best that he not. But he had to get in touch with her. He hadn't paid her the thousand dollars for the work she'd done.

Hell. That wasn't going to come across well. Handing Dani money after they'd made love all night had an unpleasant connotation. Never mind. Business was business. He owed her money for the Rostov portion of the evening. What had happened after was not business; it had nothing to do with the fact that she'd translated for him.

And all of that brought him back to the initial question. Why had she vanished? He didn't like it. Women didn't walk out on him as Dani Sinclair had…and why did he keep thinking of her as if the name were one word instead of two? Because it didn't suit her? Ridiculous. Still, she'd said she didn't like the name, either. If she didn't, what name did she prefer?

Not that it mattered.

He had spent the night with her. Nothing more. So what if the name didn't suit her? So what if she'd walked out while he slept?

So what if he couldn't stop thinking about her, remembering the feel of her skin, the sweetness of her mouth…

"Mr. Vieira?"

Lucas rolled his eyes. Denise-Elise sounded pathetic even over the intercom.

"Yes?"

"Mr. Gordon's here to see you, sir."

Jack Gordon. Lucas's mouth thinned. He had no wish to see the man now but Gordon had done him a favor last night. Besides, Gordon would have Dani's address so that he could mail her the check he'd forgotten to give her.

"Tell him to come in."

Gordon smiled as he strolled through the door.

"Lucas. Well? How did things go?"

"Very well. In fact, I was going to call you to thank you and to ask for—"

"Was I right or was I right? I knew Dani would be perfect."

"Yes. She was. And I need her—"

"She's one amazing babe. Hot as well as smart. Some package, huh?"

Lucas wanted to get up from his chair, grab Gordon by the collar and toss him out. Instead, he mustered a polite smile.

"I'm busy this morning, Jack. So, thanks for recommending Ms. Sinclair. And please leave her address with my P.A."

"Dani's address? Why would you—" Jack Gordon smiled slyly. "Aha. The evening went that well, did it?"

Lucas narrowed his eyes. "I forgot to pay her."

Gordon raised his eyebrows. "Pay her?"

"The thousand I mentioned, although she deserves a bonus."

"A bonus?"

"What's her regular rate, do you know? I should have asked her but I—"

"But you got sidetracked." Gordon grinned and hitched a hip on the edge of Lucas's desk. "Yeah. Understandable. Her regular rate? Well, it ain't cheap."

"Just tell me what it is."

"For an evening? Ten K."

"Fine. Ten thou—" Lucas blinked. "What?"

"She's expensive. But you gotta know for yourself, she's worth every—"

A coldness seeped into Lucas's bones. "Nobody makes that kind of money translating."

"Translating?" Gordon laughed. "Sure, but Dani—"

"But Dani what?" Lucas's eyes flashed as he rose to his feet. "What does she do to earn that kind of money?"

Gordon stared at his boss. "She—she does—she does what she did for you last night. I mean, she did do something, uh, special for you, right?"

Lucas felt a stillness come over him. "Answer the question, Jack. What does Dani Sinclair do that earns her ten thousand dollars an evening?"

Jack Gordon's Adam's apple moved up and down in his throat. "She's—she's… You know. She's—she's an escort."

"An escort."

"Yeah. She, ah, she goes on dates with—with men. Like she did with you. And you have to admit, she's worth every—"

Lucas hit him. Hard. A right uppercut to the jaw. Gordon staggered, went down on one knee, his hand to his mouth. Lucas went around the desk, reached for him again…

And stopped.

An escort. A prostitute. He'd had sex with a woman who sold herself to any man who could afford her services.

A whore had spent the night in his bed.

His heart was beating hard and fast. His vision was blurred; he blinked to clear it. Gordon was still on one knee, face white, eyes wide with fear. Lucas felt his gut twist. Jack was a pig, but he'd let out his rage on the wrong person.

"Get up."

"Don't hit me again."

"Get up, damnit!"

"Lucas. Mr. Vieira. I should have told you."

"But you didn't."

"No. I thought—I thought maybe you wouldn't go for it, if you knew—"

"You thought, maybe it would be satisfying to make a fool of me."

Gordon winced, and Lucas knew he'd hit on the truth. He reached into a desk drawer, tossed Gordon a handful of tissues. Then he thrust a pad and pen across the desk. "Write down her address."

"Yeah, Sure. Look, I made a mistake, okay? I'm sorry. Really. I'm—

"You're finished here, Gordon."

Jack Gordon's expression turned ugly.

"You think so? If I tell this story around—"

"Do it, and so help me God, you won't live long enough to enjoy it."

"You wouldn't…"

Lucas laughed. And Jack Gordon, hearing that laugh, looking into Lucas's eyes, knew that the game was lost.

Fridays were always the easiest day of Caroline's week.

During the school semester, she had a morning seminar. After that, she could go home and collapse. Now, with school over for the summer, the entire day was hers. Normally, that would have been great.

Not today.

Without something to do, memories of the night kept intruding. So when one of the waitresses at Dilly's Deli, where

Caroline had recently started working, called to ask if she could cover for her for a couple of hours, she said yes even though she already hated the place for its painfully clever menu, its spoiled but famous show business clientele, its ogling tourists.

By two o'clock, she regretted her decision. A family of tourists, five of them, had run up a bill of $120.00 and left her a two-dollar tip. A woman in booth four was still considering what to order after reading the menu for the past fifteen minutes. And the man in booth six, a puffed-up talk show host, had sent back his hamburger three different times.

"Your burger's up."

Caroline nodded to the middle-aged waitress who'd breezed by her, went through the swinging doors into the kitchen, retrieved the burger and took it to booth six.

At least you could take back a food order.

You couldn't take back behavior that made you want to die just thinking about it. Or, even worse, made you remember what it had felt like to be kissed and caressed as if nothing in the world mattered half as much as—

"Miss? Miss!"

Booth six. Caroline pasted a smile on her lips.

"Yes, sir?"

"Does the chef not understand the meaning of the word, 'rare'?"

Caroline looked at the burger. It was bleeding into its plate like an extra in a slasher movie. She picked up the plate, forced a smile, marched through the swinging doors into the kitchen and set the plate on the counter beside the grill.

"Not rare enough."

Caroline echoed the fry cook's sigh before she hurried back onto the serving floor just in time for the woman in booth three to make "check, please" motions with her fingers.

Caroline nodded, took her order pad from her pocket and

tallied the bill. It came to a lot but then, everything in this place was costly.

Not as costly as what she'd done last night.

Sex with a stranger. A sexy, gorgeous stranger.

Thinking about it made her cringe…except, except there was this tiny part of her that kept whispering, *Don't regret it. It was everything you ever dreamed and more.*

"Miss!"

Oh God. "Yes, sir?"

"Where is my hamburger?"

"Sir. You sent it back. The cook is—"

"I want it now, miss."

"But, sir—"

"Are you arguing with me, miss?"

"No. Certainly not. But—"

"Get the manager. Get him now! I am not going to be insulted by—"

It was the final straw. The job, the patrons… Enough. There were other restaurants, other jobs, and she had five hundred dollars coming to her. Last night, she'd thought how awful it would be to take that money but that was ridiculous. She had done what Dani had asked her to do, and that was what Dani would pay her for doing it.

Caroline tossed her order pad on the counter. Undid the tie of the frilly white apron all the waitresses wore and tossed it at the idiot in booth six.

"I beg your pardon," he sputtered.

Caroline flashed a smile. A real one, the first one since she'd awakened this morning.

"And well you should," she said sweetly.

And she left.

Should she call Dani, or just show up at her door? She'd never been to Dani's but she remembered the address. Just show up, she decided. Get the money Dani owed her and that would be that.

Dani's address turned out to be a brownstone on a trendy street in the sixties. Caroline raised her eyebrows. Maybe she only thought she'd remembered the address; maybe she had it wrong.

But when she rang the bell, it was Dani who opened the door.

"Caroline? What are you doing here?"

Caroline felt foolish. She was wearing jeans, a T-shirt and sneakers. Dani was wearing a scarlet dress cut to midthigh and knee-high, stiletto-heeled black leather boots. Her perfect face was perfectly made up; her brown hair seemed sexily windblown but any woman who'd ever spent two minutes struggling with hair that really was windblown would know a hairstylist had probably taken an hour to get it to look that way.

Caroline swallowed dryly. "I came to—to… You owe me money," she blurted.

"Oh. Oh, that's right, I do." Dani stepped back. "Well, don't just stand there. Come in. You can't stay long—I'm getting ready to go out."

"Go out where?" Caroline said, just to have something to say.

"Just out," Dani said briskly, heels tapping as she made her way across the clearly expensive floor of a designer-expensive living room. "Five hundred, right?" she said, opening her handbag.

Caroline nodded as she looked around her. She'd been in the apartments of a couple of other grad students. They all looked like hers: thrift shop furniture, dingy walls.

Dani's place was a palace.

"Wow," Caroline said softly.

Dani swung toward her, followed Caroline's gaze and smiled. "Like it?"

"It's beautiful."

Dani cocked her head. "You know," she said slowly, "you could have a place like this, if you wanted."

"Me?" Caroline laughed. "Right. By hitting the lottery."

Dani smiled again. "By working."

"Oh, sure."

"I'm serious, Caroline. I could, you know, get you started. Introduce you to some people, help you buy some clothes."

Caroline shook her head. "I don't understand. You mean, model?"

"Model?" Dani laughed. "Well, that's one way of considering it."

"Thanks, but I don't think—"

The doorbell pealed. Dani made a face. "I was *so* not expecting company this afternoon! Here." She held out five hundred-dollar bills. "Well, go on, take the money."

Caroline did. Hesitantly. Suddenly, accepting it seemed dead wrong. Her stomach gave a little jump.

"May I—may I use the bathroom?"

"Down the hall, on the right." Dani rolled her eyes as she *click-clicked* her way to the door. "Just be quick, okay? I told you, I have a date."

Caroline locked the bathroom door behind her. She felt hot and cold all at once. The money, the damned money had reminded her of everything all over again. Why had she come here? Why had she accepted the five hundred dollars? Well, she wouldn't. She'd give it back. She'd—

Ohmygod!

She could hear voices. Dani's. And a man's. Not just any man. The voice belonged to Lucas Vieira.

Quickly, she undid the lock. Stepped into the hall. Saw

Lucas, his tall, powerful body so familiar to her now. And Dani, facing him, hands on her hips, face tilted up.

"Of course I'm Dani Sinclair," she was saying. "And who the hell are you?"

"I am Lucas Vieira," Lucas growled. "And you are not Dani Sinclair."

"Don't be ridiculous! I should know who I—"

"Lucas?"

Caroline moved slowly down the hall. Lucas looked up. She saw the confusion in his eyes. "Dani?"

"Dani?" the real Dani said, and then she laughed. "I get it! You're the guy from last night. And you think that she, that Caroline, is me!"

Lucas's expression went from perplexed to confused. "What the hell is going on here?"

Caroline licked her lips. "I can explain. I'm really Caroline. Caroline Hamilton. See, Dani was supposed to—to be your translator—"

Lucas's mouth twisted. "My date, you mean," he said tonelessly. "The one Jack Gordon arranged."

"I don't know anybody named Jack Gordon. Dani arranged it. And yes, I was supposed to be your date."

"And you agreed."

"Well, yes. I didn't want to do it. I really, really didn't want to do it. But you have to understand, I needed the money."

"You needed the money." Lucas's gaze fell to the bills Caroline clutched in her hand, then rose to her face. *"Cristos,"* he growled, the word thick with disgust, "you needed the money."

Caroline drew herself up. "Five hundred dollars might not mean anything to you, but to me—"

Lucas swung toward Dani. "That's it? Gordon paid you your usual fee and all you gave her was five hundred dollars?"

"No one's paid me a dime yet," Dani said coolly. "All I've had out of this so far is more trouble than I really want."

"What usual fee? Who's Jack Gordon? What trouble?" Caroline came quickly forward, stopped inches from Lucas, whose anger was all but palpable. "Lucas." Her voice trembled. "Five hundred dollars is a lot of money. I needed it. And, for whatever it's worth, I've never done anything like that before."

She saw a stillness come over him, a coolness replace the rage.

"Haven't you?"

She shook her head. Pretend to be someone she wasn't? Of course not.

"No," she said emphatically, "never!"

"You want me to believe last night was your first time."

Caroline stiffened. "You act as if this was all my fault, but what about you? You were part of the game. You paid me to play a role."

The muscle in Lucas's jaw flickered. She was right. He'd paid her to pretend to be his lover. As for what had happened afterward...

That had been a role, too.

Going to bed with strangers was her profession. She was a call girl. A prostitute. A woman who sold herself to men. And he—he had thought, if only for a moment, that something special had happened between them.

Rage sent a flood of heat through his blood. He wanted to put his fist through the wall, to grab Caroline Hamilton and shake her like a rag doll.

Instead, he took out his checkbook and a gold pen, wrote two checks, tore both out and gave one to Dani Sinclair. She looked at it, then at him.

"Paid in full," he said coldly.

"Indeed, Mr. Vieira." She smiled. "Lucas."

"Stick with Mr. Vieira," he said, even more coldly, and held out the second check, to Caroline.

"What's that?" she asked in bewilderment.

"It's what I owe you for last night."

Heat shot into her face. "You don't owe me anything."

"Of course I do," he said impatiently. "I told Gordon I'd pay you a thousand dollars."

"No." Caroline shook her head; she took a quick step back, her eyes never leaving the check in his outstretched hand. "You don't owe me anything."

"Take the damned check!"

"I don't want it."

"I never renege on a deal." He shoved the check at her. "Take it."

"Lucas." Her voice trembled. "Whatever you're thinking—"

"You need the money," he said coldly, "remember? And I sure as hell had everything I needed from you."

She didn't move. All the color had drained from her face. Tears glittered in her eyes. Something inside him seemed to crack. He wanted to take her in his arms, kiss her until she stopped weeping.

Cristos, she was a damned fine actress.

But she would never make a fool of him again.

His hand closed around her wrist and he hauled her against him. He bent his head, took her mouth, kissed her hard enough to make her gasp. She raised her hand, balled it, hit his shoulder—and then her fist loosened, her fingers sought his cheek, spread over it and her lips softened under his, parted...

Lucas cursed.

Then he flung Caroline from him, let the check flutter to the floor and walked out.

CHAPTER SIX

LUCAS knew he was in a dangerous frame of mind.

Caroline Hamilton had lied to him, not just about who she was but *what* she was. The knowledge that he had taken her to his bed made him furious.

He knew there was no point going back to his office. Making decisions, even dealing with people, would be a mistake when he was fighting to keep his temper under control.

He had to work off some of his energy, find a physical focal point for the adrenaline raging through him. Going to the gym would surely do it.

An hour later, he was sweaty, breathing hard—but his mood was still the same.

Okay, he thought grimly as he showered, okay, there was only one other way to deal with this. To hell with permitting one deceitful woman to take up residence in his head. If a horse threw you, you climbed right back on.

He had numbers in his BlackBerry, women he'd met, women who'd made it clear they were eager for him to call. Within minutes, he'd filled his weekend with enough variety to erase the memory of Caroline Hamilton forever.

He went home, shaved, changed, phoned a restaurant where it took a month to get a table and, of course, got one for eight o'clock and prepared to enjoy the hell out of a brunette who greeted him with a big smile.

Two hours later, he pleaded an early appointment the next morning, took her home and left her at her door.

"I had a wonderful time," she gushed, and he knew damned well it was a lie. He'd been the worst kind of company: silent, unsmiling, rushing her through a meal that normally would have taken three hours and then pretending he had no idea what she hinted at when she stepped close and turned her pretty face up to his.

"So did I," he said.

Liar, he thought...but not a liar anywhere near the equal of Caroline Hamilton.

He went back to his gym Saturday, played a couple of games of racquetball, lifted weights, traded the workout room for a run through Central Park. At night, instead of simply sending a check to a charity auction, he attended it with a redhead with an infectious smile and legs that went on forever. Afterward, he took her for a light supper because he knew it was the right thing to do but when she took his hand and said she lived nearby and the night was really young and it would be lovely if he came up for drinks, he pleaded another early appointment, delivered her to her door and left her there with a handshake.

Merda, a handshake!

He made himself a vow. He would do much better tomorrow, when he had a date to take a stunning Broadway actress to lunch.

If anything, he did worse.

"It isn't you," he said, when she asked him what was wrong, and before he could say, "it's me," she was on her feet and gone.

Enough.

He went home, packed, phoned his pilot, flew to Martha's Vineyard. A banker he knew had a weekend home on the beach; the guy and his wife were having a big party. They'd invited him but he'd declined.

"Turn up if you change your mind," the banker had said.

Well, he had definitely changed his mind.

He drank some excellent wine, ate a grilled-to-perfection lobster, got hit on by two women…and excused himself and went, alone, for a walk along the sand.

The day was not the kind chambers of commerce hope for. The sea was the color of pewter, the waves were high, the sky was bleak. All of that was fine.

It suited his mood.

Why in hell couldn't he stop thinking about Caroline? He despised her, despised what she was. So what if she was beautiful? He'd had the chance to get involved with several women equally beautiful in the past couple of days and he'd walked away from each one. He hadn't wanted to pretend interest in their conversations or smile at their jokes, and he sure as hell had not wanted to take one of them to bed.

And yet, he knew that if Caroline materialized in front of him at this moment, as willing and eager as she'd been the other night, he'd strip her of her clothes, take her in his arms, draw her down to the sand and bury himself inside her.

And she'd respond. No subterfuge, no games, no coy teasing.

"Damnit," he snarled, because it had *all* been subterfuge. She, and everything she'd done, had been an endless, ugly, practiced lie.

Turning him on, making all those little sounds, those whispers, driving him out of his mind with want and need…

They were the cornerstones of her profession. She traded sex for money.

And if there were moments it had seemed as if she'd never let a man do half the things he'd done to her that night, maybe that was her specialty. What had he heard it called, that blend of sex and innocence? The Madonna-whore thing. He'd never wanted those traits in a woman himself but then, he'd never been with a woman like Caroline before.

God knew, he would never be with one again.

The Elins of this world were more honest. They traded sex with powerful men for the tokens of that power. He wasn't a fool; he understood that. He'd always understood it. Jewels. Gifts. Being seen in the right places at the right times. It was what such women wanted and absolutely, that was more honest, wasn't it?

Wasn't it?

The sky went from gray to charcoal. Lightning flashed out over the Atlantic; rain beat down with a swift ferocity. He jogged back to the party, laughed along with everyone else at his soaked condition, took a taxi to the airport and got the hell out of Dodge.

Monday morning, things looked better.

He woke up feeling more like himself. His P.A. was back at her desk. His coffee tasted the way it was supposed to. Jack Gordon was history. Six months severance pay, no letter of recommendation.

Goodbye to the old, hello to the new. No question about it. Caroline Hamilton had become a meaningless memory.

He had meetings until noon, then a quick lunch at his desk. At one o'clock, in the middle of a complex telephone conversation with his attorney to tie up the final legalities of the Rostov deal, it all fell apart.

Nothing had changed. Why tell himself it had? That he'd filled the day with enough crap to keep six men busy was the sole reason he hadn't spent it staring out the window.

Gordon was a sneaky, ingratiating little worm. He'd deserved to be fired, but what penalty had Caroline paid? She had lied to him. The scene at Dani Sinclair's apartment, his show of anger, tossing that check at her, hadn't even come close to settling things.

And he had to do that. Settle things. Erase the memory of her lies. The only question was, how?

"Lucas?" his attorney was saying, "Lucas? Man, are you still there?"

Lucas took a breath. "Sorry. Yes, I'm here but something's come up." He paused. "Ted. If I needed an investigator..."

"I can recommend one." The lawyer rattled off a name and phone number, and then it was he who paused. "Can I help in any way?"

Lucas forced a chuckle. "No, no, it's nothing special."

The hell it wasn't.

He hung up the phone and got to his feet. The only way to put this behind him was to confront Caroline, tell her what he thought of her, tell her...

How should he know what he'd tell her? The right words would come when he saw her.

A couple of hours later, he had more information than he needed. All he'd wanted was Caroline's address. Now, he had her age: twenty-four. Her place of birth: some little town in upstate New York. Her education: an undergraduate degree in French. Now she was working toward a Master's degree in Russian and Slavic Studies.

The P.I. didn't come up with the rest of it, that she had an income on the side, but Lucas hadn't expected that he would. Caroline was clever. Her occupation, if you could call it that, would be carefully hidden.

Her address was no surprise at all.

She lived in one of those Manhattan neighborhoods that had gone from providing shelter for those who sweated to make enough to live on to providing it to those who had more money than they could ever need. It was home to hotshot young Wall Street traders who thought selling overvalued stocks entitled them to seven figure bonuses, and spoiled little rich girls whose parents funded their extravagant lifestyles while they played at working in the fashion business.

He'd been to a couple of dinner parties in Hell's Kitchen, so he knew what Caroline's place would be like.

An airy duplex in what had once been a tenement. A converted loft in what had once been a factory. Lots of pale wood, exposed brick, uncomfortable furniture and indecipherable art.

Expensive, but not a problem for a woman who was a student by day but had a source of income from an old but infinitely profitable profession.

Lucas almost laughed as he left his office.

Student by Day.

It sounded like the title of a bad movie. Only problem? It was real. And he, who had never paid for sex in his life, who had never been with a woman for any reason but mutual desire...

He had bought her services.

His laughter died.

"Goddamnit," he muttered, and a guy walking by on the street, even here in Manhattan where people never looked at each other, never showed a reaction, even here, the guy glanced at his face and detoured around him.

Traffic was a mess. Forget hailing a taxi. Walking was faster. And it kept him moving, which was what he needed right now.

Gradually, the streets changed, went from commercial to residential until, finally, he was in Caroline's neighborhood, then on her street.

It wasn't what he'd expected.

A handful of streets had not been converted from careworn to chic. This was one of them.

Overflowing trash cans lined the curb. Gang names and symbols adorned graffiti-filled walls. A fetid breeze sent bits of debris scattering along the sidewalk. All the buildings looked tired, Caroline's, in particular. It was a five-story pile of age-darkened red brick that seemed held together by a century's worth of grime.

A police car was parked in front of it.

Lucas felt his heart thump.

He knew some cops. They were, for the most part, good people. Still, thanks to his childhood in Rio, there were times when the sight of a police uniform or police car still made him uneasy.

This was one of those times.

And that was ridiculous. The cops were here. So what? It was not his problem.

The building's front door was not locked. His mouth thinned. Unlocked front doors were never a good idea but on streets like these, they were an invitation to trouble.

Not his problem, either.

The vestibule smelled bad. Dirt, cooking and something more pungent that was probably better not identified, hung thick in the air.

Again, not his concern.

There was another door ahead and, to his left, a panel of labeled call buttons. The one for apartment 3G read *C. Hamilton*.

At least Caroline had the good sense not to use her first name. Not that it mattered all that much. Using only a first initial was pretty much a giveaway that the name belonged to a woman.

He thought of the women he'd taken out over the weekend.

They all lived in buildings with security cameras, locks and what looked like retired wrestlers as doormen.

So what? Caroline's security—or the lack of it—came under that same not-my-problem heading, as did the fact that the interior door yawned onto a dim hall.

How she lived meant nothing to him.

It just ticked him off that an intelligent woman—and she was smart, he had to give her that—would live in a place like this. It certainly couldn't be because of money, not when she made her living as she did.

Lucas frowned.

Then, why had she let him pay her only a thousand dollars for that night in his bed? God only knew what being with her should have cost him. He'd never put a price on such things but if he had—if he had…

Lucas spat out a word that was as ugly in Portuguese as it would have been in English. Who gave a damn? Not him.

He took the sagging stairs and paused on the third-floor landing. Apartment 3G was directly ahead. That feeling of unease, an icy clenching in his gut, swept through him again.

Something was definitely wrong.

The police car at the curb. The unnatural quiet of the old building, broken now by the barely imperceptible *snick* of the door to the apartment adjoining Caroline's opening an inch, then quickly closing again.

He moved forward fast, pressed his hand, flat, against her buzzer, then hammered his fist against the door.

"Caroline?" He grasped the knob, rattled it. "Damnit, Caroline—"

The door swung open. Caroline stood before him, wearing sweats, no makeup, her face pale, eyes reddened, her hair damp and wild on her shoulders.

"Mother of God," he said hoarsely, "*querida*, what is it?"

"Lucas," she said, "Lucas…"

Every logical thought, all the rage, all the bitter desire for payback, flew out of his head. He opened his arms and she flew into them.

He gathered her to his heart, held her close, whispered soothing words to her in Portuguese. She was trembling; he thought of a puppy he'd once found in an alley in Rio, how it had whimpered and trembled, how he had held it in his arms until it was silent and still…

"Caroline. Sweetheart. *Que aconteceu?* What happened?"

"A man," she said. "A man…"

"Excuse me, sir."

Lucas swept her behind him at the sound of the male voice. Every muscle in his body went on alert—but the source of the voice was a uniformed police officer, emerging from a doorway to the left. A second, shorter officer stood just behind him.

The cops from the patrol car.

His blood became a river of ice.

"What happened here?" he demanded.

The first officer took a step forward.

"Sir? Please identify yourself."

What he wanted to do was sweep Caroline into his arms and take her from this place, to turn back the clock so that it was still Thursday night and she was safe in his bed.

"Sir?"

Lucas nodded as he curved his arm around Caroline and drew her to his side.

"I am Lucas Vieira. And I asked you a question."

"Are you a friend of Ms. Hamilton's, Mr. Vieira?"

Caroline turned against him and buried her face in his shoulder. Lucas nodded again.

"I am a very good friend of Ms. Hamilton's, Officer."

"And you're here because…?"

"I've answered all the questions I intend to answer until you tell me what happened."

"Someone broke into Ms. Hamilton's apartment."

The other policeman stepped aside, revealing what had been a window and was now an empty frame for the rusted iron fire escape that clung to the building's exterior wall.

Glass littered the linoleum floor.

Lucas's vision reddened, narrowed until he could see only the broken window. He felt rage like none he had ever known before.

"Caroline." He clasped her shoulders and looked at her pale face. "Tell me who did this."

She shook her head. "I never saw the man before."

"What did he do to you?" She didn't answer and he knew he was nearer the total loss of the civilized man he was supposed to have become than he had ever been in his entire life. "Sweetheart. *Querida*, did he hurt you?"

She drew a long, tremulous breath.

"No."

"Are you sure? Because if he did—"

"He didn't—he didn't touch me. I screamed and—and—"

Her breath hitched. Her face was turned up to his; her lips were parted. He fought back the desire to gather her against him and kiss away the terror in her eyes.

"I was—I was just coming out of the shower. I thought I heard something break. Glass, I thought. In the kitchen."

She nodded toward a wall where a refrigerator that would have looked at home in one of the better Rio *favelas* leaned drunkenly against an ancient stove.

"So—so I came out of the bathroom. I wasn't expecting to see anything but broken glass on the floor, you know, something the cat knocked over, and—"

"The cat," Lucas said, because he had to grab on to

something simple or the fury inside him inside him would surely explode.

"Yes. My cat. Well, he's my cat now. I mean, I found him yesterday. Sunday, when I went down to get the paper, just sitting huddled by the stoop, and—"

"Caroline." Lucas cleared his throat. "What happened?"

"I saw the broken glass on the floor. And—and I saw the man. He was coming through the window. I screamed. And it must have been a really loud scream because Mr. Witkin, who lives next door, he banged on the wall the way he does if I play my CDs too loud except I don't, I don't ever play them loud at all—"

She began to weep. Soundlessly, shoulders shaking, which somehow turned Lucas's hot rage to icy fear. He gathered her into his arms again and held her close.

"The intruder took off. Ms. Hamilton phoned 911," the taller cop said.

"The police came right away," Caroline whispered.

Lucas looked at the two officers. "Thank you," he said, and meant it. "Thank you for everything."

Both of them nodded.

"Yeah. We just wish we could have caught the bas—the guy."

Lucas would have preferred catching the bastard himself, but he thought it best not to say so.

"There's been a rash of break-ins on this street the last couple of weeks," the smaller policeman said. "Same M.O. Guy breaks a window, comes in, takes whatever isn't nailed down…"

"Lately," the other cop said, "he's upped the ante." His eyes darted to Caroline, who was trembling in Lucas's arms. "He's been targeting apartments where women live alone, you know…" He paused; clearly, there was more, but he wasn't about to say it.

"The lady better get that window fixed," the smaller officer said. "Have a grill put in. Should have had one there all along. Windows that lead out to fire escapes are bad news."

"Yes," Lucas said, half-amazed he could say anything at all. He cleared his throat. "Are you finished speaking with Ms. Hamilton?"

The cops nodded. "We might need to get in touch with her again, but for now—"

Lucas let go of Caroline, got out his black leather business card holder and a pen, scrawled his home address on the back of a card and handed it over.

"You can reach Ms. Hamilton at that address," he said, putting his arm around her again, "should you need her."

"No," Caroline said quickly. "You can reach me right here. I'll get the window fixed and—"

"That is incorrect. Ms Hamilton will be staying with me."

"Lucas." Caroline looked up at him, calmer now, her voice steadier though she was still trembling. "I couldn't possibly—"

"Let me see you out, Officers," Lucas said politely, as if there were a formal hallway before them rather than a door.

He held out his hand; both men shook it. He watched them start down the stairs. Then he closed the door, took a breath and swung toward Caroline, all the while telling himself to be calm. He knew she was going to argue about going with him and that he would tolerate no argument, and he knew, too, that the last thing she needed was to have him snap at her…

Or have him take her in his arms and kiss her until color returned to her face.

And what kind of nonsense was that? He'd come here for closure. Just because he'd found not a brittle, defiant Caroline but a fragile one, just because some faceless monster had come within inches of doing God only knew what to her…

None of that changed anything.

Of course, it didn't.

He didn't feel any differently toward her. He was just doing what any decent man would when he saw a woman in a difficult situation.

There was nothing like regaining perspective.

"All right," he said evenly. "Here's what is going to happen. You'll pack a few things, only what you think you'll need immediately."

"Thank you for your concern. It's very kind, but—"

"My driver will pick up the rest later."

Caroline stood a little straighter. "You're not listening. I appreciate your offer, but—"

"It isn't an offer. It's what you're going to do."

She looked at him. The color was coming back into her face. It hadn't taken his kisses to get it there, after all.

"If I decide to leave here," she said carefully, "I'll stay with a friend."

A muscle knotted in his jaw. "What friend?"

"I don't know. Someone. It isn't your problem."

She was right. Nothing about her was his problem. Wasn't that what he'd been telling himself for the past hour?

"What friend?" he heard himself say again.

"I just told you—"

"Jack Gordon?"

"I already told you, I don't know any Jack Gordon."

Lucas looked at her. "Dani Sinclair, then. Will you stay with her?"

Caroline's eyes flashed. "Dani and I are in the same graduate program. She's not a friend."

No, he thought coldly. The Sinclair woman was a business associate… But this wasn't the time for that.

"So, what friend will you stay with?"

"Goodbye, Lucas."

"Goodbye?" He moved toward her even as he asked himself what in hell he was doing. "A few minutes ago, you were so glad to see me that you threw yourself into my arms."

"A few minutes ago, the only people I'd seen today were a burglar and two cops." She stood even straighter, as if her spine had turned into steel. "I'd have thrown myself at Bozo the Clown, if he'd walked through that door."

"Such a compliment, *querida*. I am flattered."

She folded her arms; he folded his. It occurred to him that they probably resembled a pair of fighters, squaring off at a weigh-in.

"Once again," she said, "thank you. But—"

"You are coming with me, Caroline." He smiled grimly. "One way or another."

"Oh, for heaven's sake!" She stalked toward him, chin lifted, eyes defiant, more beautiful than any woman had a right to be, and jabbed a finger into the center of his chest. "Listen to me, Mr. Vieira. I make my own decisions. Understand? And I am not going anywhere with you!"

"Your choice," he said calmly. "On your own two feet, or slung over my shoulder."

She stared at him, her breasts rising and falling in the quick measure of her breath. Good, he thought. At least he had chased her fear away.

"You," she said coldly, "have not heard anything until you've heard me scream."

"And you," he said, just as coldly, "have not heard anything until you've heard me explain to your Mr. Sitkin—"

"Witkin," she said, through her teeth.

"Until you've heard me explain to Mr. Witkin why I, as your *nuivo*, cannot possibly—"

"My what?"

"Your fiancé, *querida*," Lucas purred. "I'm sure Mr. Witkin will be most sympathetic after I explain that what happened to you a little while ago has left you somewhat unstable and that I can use his help opening doors for us as I carry you downstairs so I can put you in my car and take you to my physician's office."

"He'd never fall for that!"

Lucas flashed a smile. "Want to bet?"

"Damn you, Lucas Vieira!"

"Damn me, indeed. But that's how it's going to be. You're coming with me, Caroline. Your only choice is how."

She glared at him. Despite everything, he wanted to laugh. Such fire in her. Such defiance.

"Very well," she said through gritted teeth. "I'll do this. For one night. But I warn you, I am not interested in having you—in letting you—"

"In letting me what?" he said, and he reached for her, took her in his arms and kissed her the way he'd wanted to kiss her ever since he'd come through the door.

She stiffened. Then she gave a little sigh, leaned into him, kissed him back...

"Yeow!"

Sharp, hot knives dug into Lucas's leg. He jumped back, looked down, saw an emaciated thing the size of a Cocker Spaniel attached to his leg.

Caroline looked down, too... And laughed.

"Oh my goodness! Oliver!"

She bent, snatched the creature into her arms and stood up. An enormous, bony, painfully ugly cat glared wildly at him through malevolent yellow eyes.

"Merda," he said, "what is that?"

"It's Oliver," Caroline crooned, burying her face in the animal's fur. "My cat." The cat turned its big head toward her, purred and butted its jaw against hers. "Poor baby. He's terrified."

Rabid, seemed more like it. No blood, Lucas thought,

dragging up his cuff and checking, but what did that matter when what had to be the most mangy creature in cat-dom attacked you?

"Oliver," he said flatly, as it all fell into place. "The cat you found yesterday?"

"In the street. Yes. Dirty. Half-starved. Scared to death of everything."

"It's still dirty," Lucas said, narrowing his eyes.

"He. Oliver is a he. And he's not dirty anymore. I gave him a bath last night." Caroline nuzzled the animal again. "He just has a splotchy coat, that's all."

"He doesn't look scared, either. Not scared enough to want to let me live."

Carolyn giggled. It was so unexpected, all things considered, and such a lovely sound that he had a difficult time not smiling.

"He's wary around people, that's all." The cat made a delicate sound, a meow that should have come from a purebred kitten instead of the bedraggled beast in Caroline's arms. "But not me, because I saved him."

"How fortunate for you both."

"You may find this amusing but I promise you, it isn't. I'm Oliver's person. The one he's always going to love. He must have thought you were trying to hurt me."

Lucas nodded. "And, of course, you're not going to want to leave him here." The look on Caroline's face was all the answer he needed. "Okay," he said briskly, and took out his cell phone. "I'll make a couple of calls. The first to my driver, so he can pick us up. The second to a guy I know on the board at the ASPCA—"

"What?"

"The American Society for the Protection of An—"

"I know what the initials mean but if you think I'm going

to give Oliver to a place that will put him in a cage and—and destroy him—"

"They'll put him in a foster home," Lucas said, though he couldn't imagine anyone insane enough to give shelter to the creature. "And he won't be destroyed."

Caroline narrowed her eyes. "Oliver goes with me."

"Caroline. Be sensible. That cat—"

"He goes with me or I stay put."

"Damnit, woman—"

"And why did you come here today, anyway?" Her chin rose. "That last time I saw you, in Dani's apartment, was more than enough for me."

"That has nothing to do with this."

"It has everything to do with it! You acted as if—as if I were dirt under your feet and now, here you are, playing at being a knight come to rescue a damsel in distress."

"Look, maybe I overreacted that last time, okay?" Hell, maybe he had. He'd hired Caroline to do a job. And she'd done it well. If anyone were to blame for what had happened, it was Jack Gordon for not telling him, up-front, that Caroline was—that she was more than a translator.

And why was he letting her take this conversation off-track?

"Very well," he said brusquely. "You can bring the cat. Go on, pack what you need. I'm tired of wasting time."

"Good. So am I. And just so you know, if you'd tried to drag me out of here, if you'd lied to Mr. Witkin, I'd have screamed so loud the cops would have come back!"

They glared at each other. Then Caroline thrust the cat at him.

"Here. Well, go on. Take him. I can't pack and hold Oliver at the same time!"

The skinny, writhing denizen of hell landed on his chest and inserted all its claws into his suit jacket. Lucas looked at the cat. The cat looked at him. A demonic sound vibrated in its throat.

One last attempt at sanity, Lucas thought, and made a wild grab at anything that seemed reasonable.

"I'm not sure pets are permitted in my building."

Caroline laughed.

He couldn't blame her.

She knew, as well as he, that whether pets were permitted or not would never matter to him. If he wanted to house a Martian with two heads and six tentacles and Martians were not allowed in his building, he would simply get himself a Martian and march it straight through the lobby.

The thing was, he didn't understand why people had pets. Get attached to something, it dies on you. Or walks away. Even if it didn't, anything you developed affection for demanded a lot of time and care and he could not imagine what it would give in return.

Still, this wasn't the time to explain his philosophy. Besides, why would he have to explain anything about himself to anyone?

"Just get on with it," he snapped.

Caroline tossed her head and walked into the bedroom. Lucas held the cat in one arm. That sound emerged from its throat again.

"Do not push your luck, cat," he said in a low voice.

Then he called his driver, arranged for him to meet them at the curb. As he concluded the call, Caroline emerged from the bedroom clutching an overflowing tote bag in the curve of one arm and a potted plant in the other.

"It's a fern," she said coldly, before he could say anything. "And, yes, I found it on the street, too, and yes, it's coming with me. It needs care."

What it needed, Lucas thought, was a vial of bleach and a quick burial.

She strode past him, arms overflowing, and somehow managed to free a hand and open the door.

"I know it's hard for you to understand," she said over her shoulder, "but I don't believe in letting living things suffer."

Lucas, following after her as the cat tried to claw its way to freedom through his suit jacket, through his shirt and, *Deus*, through his flesh, could only wonder if that philosophy might yet apply to him.

CHAPTER SEVEN

A THIRTY-TWO million dollar penthouse. A place that could have made the pages of *Architectural Digest*, if Lucas had not been so protective of his privacy.

On the walls, an eclectic mix of Japanese woodcuts, Mark Rothko paintings and Lucas's latest find, a moody and magnificent Edward Hopper oil.

On the floors, antique Tabriz carpets over Brazilian rosewood.

In the twelve light-filled rooms, soaring ceilings, pale cherry furniture, low white silk sofas and fresh flowers massed in beautiful Steuben vases and bowls.

Now, two new pieces had been added. The fern that looked like a Pleistocene leftover was—well, it was somewhere in the guest suite. Caroline had lugged it up the stairs after she had Oliver settled in. Lucas had offered to carry it but she'd refused him.

"I'm perfectly capable of doing it myself," she'd said coolly.

Now, she and the fern were out of sight.

A bright red cat litter pan was not. It stood in the elegant downstairs lavatory. It was a hooded pan, for sure, but there was no disguising its purpose, especially now, Lucas thought grimly, as he made the mistake of glancing toward the lavatory just in time to see the somewhat battered head of the cat poke out the hole in the pan's domed cover.

The cat and Lucas made eye contact.

The cat hissed. Its ears, what there were of them, folded back.

"The same to you, pal," Lucas muttered, and kept going.

That there was a dying fern in his home seemed improbable. That there was a litter pan seemed impossible. That he was the person who'd purchased it seemed beyond logic, but it had been that or have Caroline hand him the cat again after they'd settled in the backseat of his limo, the fern on the floor, the cat once again in her arms.

"We'll have to make a stop," she'd said. "Oliver will need some things."

Lucas had decided there was nothing to be gained by pointing out that what Oliver needed was a personality transplant.

"A pet shop. Or a drugstore will do."

Lucas had leaned forward. "Stop at the Duane Reade on the next block, please, James," he'd said.

His driver had complied, pulling to the curb in front of the all-purpose pharmacy.

And Caroline had held out the cat.

The cat had looked at Lucas and hummed. Lucas narrowed his eyes, hoped the cat was half as good at reading minds as it was at drawing blood and reached for the door handle instead.

"I'll go in," he'd said coldly. "Just tell me what you need."

It was the first time he'd ever gone up and down the aisles of a Duane Reed. Of any store, other than Saks or Tiffany's or Barney's, for that matter, in a very, very long time.

It was also the first time he'd stood in a queue of people waiting to pay for their purchases. It was not an experience he was eager to repeat, especially not while he balanced two litter pans, two covers, half a dozen cans of something called Daintee Deelites, a bag of Kitty Krunchies, and two plastic things euphemistically called litter scoops.

When he'd finally emerged from the store, his driver sprang from the car, went to the rear and opened the trunk. Caroline, who'd watched him as he approached, put down her window.

"Where's the litter?"

The litter.

His driver had coughed. Lucas had glared. And if The Cat from Hell could have flashed a feline smile, he was sure that it would have done so.

"Shall I go, sir?" his driver had asked.

But Lucas had already turned away and marched back to the store. This time, at least, he knew the correct aisle but the wait to pay was just as long.

He'd been tempted to ask Caroline if the cat would like to make a stop at Zabar's for smoked salmon, but he had the uneasy feeling she might have said yes.

Now, a handful of hours later, he stood at the wall of glass in his living room, watching the lights come on in Central Park and wondering how he, a man who had set out to confront a woman who had lied to him, could have ended up in this situation.

His orderly, well-planned life was in total disarray. How else to describe it?

There was a cat peeing, or worse, in his bathroom. A dead plant sucking up oxygen in his guest suite. The second litter pan was also there, which explained why Caroline had ordered him to purchase two.

I'd confine Oliver to my rooms with me, she'd said, *but he's accustomed to the streets. He might not take well to confinement behind a closed door.*

Evidently not.

There was also a pair of Mikasa stoneware soup bowls on the Italian tile kitchen floor, one filled with the contents of a can of Daintee Deelites—which, it turned out, looked like tuna and smelled like nothing Lucas ever wanted to smell again—and the other filled with water.

"Soup bowls?" Lucas had said, and Caroline had given him a look he was coming to know and said yes, soup bowls, because he had neglected to buy dishes for Oliver.

He'd opened his mouth to tell her she had neglected to request them, but what was the point? Then she'd stroked her hand slowly, slowly down the cat's back but the cat had ignored her in favor of burying its face in the bowl of Daintee Deelites, and Lucas had thought what a damned fool the animal was, choosing food over the soft touch of Caroline's hand.

That was when she'd asked him where she was to stay.

He'd looked at the cat, looked at her and come within a heartbeat of saying, *Where do you think you're going to stay? In my bed, damnit, and get yourself there right now.*

But he hadn't. Why would he? The last place he'd ever want her again was in his bed.

She was a liar and a cheat. She was more than that, and just because she lived on the edge of poverty, just because she'd taken in a dying plant and a starving cat when dozens, maybe hundreds of New Yorkers had walked by and probably never even noticed the animal, didn't change a thing.

It couldn't.

She was what she was, who she was, and he could never accept that. Not that he had to, any more than he had to like the fact that she was here, plant, cat and all, messing up his life.

Lucas turned from the window, walked mindlessly through the living room, turning on lamps and chandeliers until the huge space seemed to blaze with man-made fire. Then he stood still, tilted back his head and stared at the ceiling.

"Hell," he muttered, and he went into his study, closed the door and sank into a leather armchair.

In the dark.

The truth was—and truth mattered, if he was going to be such a damned stickler about honesty—the truth was that he was the only one to blame for this mess.

Caroline was in his life because he'd hired her to play a part. She was in his home because he'd insisted on it. What kind of man would leave a woman, any woman, in a place with doors that you couldn't lock and an intruder who might decide to pay another visit?

Sure, he'd gone to her apartment to confront her but could he have done that after she'd flown into his arms, trembling, saying his name as if it were all that could keep her safe?

Lucas rose to his feet, tucked his hands into his trouser pockets and paced the room.

He had done the right thing. The only thing. But he had his feet on the ground. He wasn't going to get drawn in any deeper. He knew exactly how to handle things when life threatened to turn you inside out. Take a logical approach. Determine the problem, find the solution.

He was good at that.

Better than good.

It was why he had come so far.

Even these few moments of rational thought had been enough to clarify the situation.

He knew half a dozen top Realtors. One phone call, and his problem would be solved. Caroline would probably claim she couldn't afford whatever a Realtor found and he wouldn't argue, wouldn't ask what a woman who earned her living selling herself did with all her money…

Five hundred dollars is a lot of money. I needed it. And, for whatever it's worth, I've never done anything like that before.

He could hear her saying those words in his head. Maybe it was true. Maybe that night she'd spent with him really had been the first time she'd put a price on sex...

Lucas scowled. What did it matter? Her finances were her business. He didn't want to know anything about them, or her. He would simply pay a couple of months rent in advance, hell, he'd pay for the year, and that would be that.

And if he never managed that confrontation, so what? Someday, he'd look back on this entire thing and laugh. Lucas Vieira, taken in by an innocent girl who'd turned out not to be innocent at all.

Sure he would. He'd laugh.

His mouth twisted.

And if he didn't laugh, that was okay, too. He would get past this. He was a man, not a boy. He would move on.

Lucas took his telephone directory from his desk, leafed through it, chose a Realtor he'd dealt with in the past. It was late, but so what?. Being able to call someone at virtually any hour was one of the perks of having power and money.

The call was brief. He wanted an apartment for a friend. In the fifties. On Madison or Park, or just off those streets. One bedroom. A building with a doorman, of course, as if there were any other kind in this neighborhood. And a security system. Yes. Cameras, video, whatever was current. Price didn't matter.

He hung up and felt relieved.

Why mention it to Caroline until it was a done deal? he decided, and after a few minutes, he stood up and paced the room some more.

Time dragged by.

He listened for any sounds from upstairs. Nothing. There was a woman in his home and he might as well have been alone.

Which was fine.

He liked it that way.

Still, Caroline was here. Didn't she intend to come down and say something? Say anything? What about eating? He was hungry; he hadn't had a thing except coffee and that was hours ago. She had to be hungry, too.

Was she waiting for an invitation?

Maybe so. Maybe she expected him to knock on her door and invite her to join him for dinner.

He could take her out to dinner, instead.

There was a quiet little restaurant a couple of blocks away. It was small. Intimate. Candles on the tables. The kind of place where the owner came by and told you what was on the night's menu. He'd only been there once. With Elin, but Elin hadn't liked it.

"I never heard of this place," she'd said with faint but perceptible disdain. "And I don't see a person I know."

He suspected Caroline wouldn't say anything remotely like that. If her lover took her to a dimly lit restaurant, her lover's face would be the only one that interested her…

Lucas snorted. Who cared what she would say or do? Besides, he thought coldly, the word "lover" didn't have much meaning in her life. She would say or do whatever a man wanted her to say or do. That was what she'd done the other night, wasn't it? Starting in the hotel lobby, going right through dinner…

And ending in his bed.

"Hell!"

How many times was he going to go over this nonsense? Enough was enough, he thought, and strode toward the kitchen. Whether she ate or not, what she did or didn't do, wasn't his business. Right now, his business was to put food in his empty belly.

This was his housekeeper's regular day off. No problem.

There were always neatly marked packets of ready-to-heat things in the freezer, eggs and bacon in the refrigerator and, better still, take-out menus in the kitchen desk drawer.

Lucas reached the kitchen, opened the fridge, took out a bottle of Corona…

The cat came barreling out of the darkness and shot between his legs. There was no telling which of them was the more startled—but Lucas was the only one holding a glass bottle. It slid from his grasp and shattered against the tile floor.

He jumped back.

Too late.

The cold beer splashed over his shoes and trouser cuffs, splattered the stainless steel door of the refrigerator and the pristine ivory walls. Lucas stared at the mess and then he raised his arms, hands knotted into fists and wagged them at the ceiling.

"That's it," he shouted. "I've had enough. More than enough!"

"What happened?"

The kitchen lights came on. He swung around and saw Caroline in the doorway. She was still wearing the baggy sweats, her hair was flattened on one side, her eyes were bleary. One look, and he knew she'd been asleep.

Asleep while his life got turned upside down. While he tiptoed around his own home like a stranger, while he dealt with a psychotic cat, while he wasted time trying to figure out how an ordinary, perfectly normal man could have got himself into a situation like this.

She didn't look beautiful anymore, she looked like a woman who needed to comb her hair and put on makeup and some decent clothes, and how could that make him want to haul her into his arms and kiss her until she was breathless?

Her gaze flew to the broken glass, then to his face.

"Oh. Did Oliver…?" She swallowed. "Lucas. It isn't his fault. I told you, he's terrified of—"

"Is that the only living creature you give a damn about? Oliver?"

She was pale. Frightened. He could see it in her eyes but he didn't care. He was frightened, too. Of going crazy, because that was what was surely happening to him, he was going freaking crazy, trying to make sense out of what was happening to his carefully organized life.

"Please. Tell me what happ—"

"I'll tell you what happened," he snarled, because anger was an emotion he understood and he sure as hell didn't understand much else, not anymore. He walked quickly toward her, shoes crunching over glass, and stopped an inch away. "I hired you to translate for me and instead, you—you—"

"I what?" she said in bewilderment.

"Instead, you—you…" Lucas clasped her shoulders. "Damnit, Caroline," he growled, and he pulled her into his arms and kissed her.

Kissed her hard. Deep. Kissed her again and again, clasping her face between his big hands, thrusting his tongue between her lips, forcing his kisses on her…

Until he realized that he wasn't.

She was kissing him back.

Her lips were parted to his. Her hands were knotted in his shirt. She was standing on tiptoe, soft, exciting little moans coming from her throat.

"Lucas," she whispered against his mouth, "Lucas…"

Lucas groaned, cupped her bottom, lifted her into the hard urgency of his body. She gasped and moved against him.

"We can't do this," she whispered.

"We can. We have to."

"We can't. It's wrong…"

"Then tell me to stop, *querida*. Say it, and I'll let you go."

"Stop," she said, but her body was pressed to his, her mouth was warm and open against his mouth.

Lucas caught her wrists.

"I want you. I want you more than I've ever wanted a woman. And it has to be the same for you, do you understand? You have to want me. Me. Lucas Vieira. No games. No masquerade. No pretense. Because if that isn't how it is for you—"

"That's exactly how it is," she said, and he swung her into his arms, and carried her up the stairs, to his bedroom. To his bed.

His hands, his body, were shaking.

He wanted to take her as he should have taken her that very first time they'd been together.

But he couldn't wait. He couldn't, and there was no sense in wondering why he was so out of control because it wouldn't change anything. His need, his hunger, were almost unbearable.

Still, he used the last of that control to try to make her understand what was going to happen.

"Listen to me," he said roughly. "I want to make slow love to you. I want to touch you until you beg me for release." His hand slid under her sweatshirt; he cupped her breast, stroked her nipple and she cried out and arched toward him. "But I can't. Not now. Do you understand? I need you too badly. This time. This way. No holding back, no finesse, no—"

"Damnit," Caroline said, "damnit, Lucas…"

She pushed his hand away. Sat up. Yanked her sweatshirt over her head. Pulled off her sweatpants.

She was wearing a white cotton bra. White cotton panties. Nothing exotic, nothing silk, nothing lace, just her, just Caroline, and it was all he'd ever wanted.

He told her, in Portuguese, how beautiful she was. How he

hungered for her, and as he did, he stripped off his clothes, then the last of hers.

She lay back. Gave herself up to him. His mouth. His hands. His body. Her eyes grew dark, her breathing quickened, his name sighed from her lips as his sweat-slicked skin met hers and the broad head of his swollen penis brushed against her.

"Caroline," he said, the one word hot and urgent, and he thrust into her.

Caroline cried out. Not with pain, though he was deep inside her, so deep that, for a heart-stopping moment, she wondered if she could take all of him in.

Her cry was one of ecstasy. Of fulfillment. Of knowing that this, only this, was what she had been created for. Of knowing that she wanted him, wanted him, wanted him. Her muscles quivered, her body accepted the exquisite intrusion.

"Lucas," she sobbed, "oh, Lucas…"

Tears slipped down her cheeks.

He kissed them away. Kissed her mouth. And then he began to possess her, to drive her toward that place he, only he, had taken her before.

His strokes were hard. Demanding. Possessive. She loved it, loved the sense of being his, of belonging to him, of being claimed by him.

And then she stopped thinking.

The world spun. Her vision dimmed. Caroline cried out, Lucas threw back his head and groaned, and they flew over the edge of the universe, together.

CHAPTER EIGHT

THEY lay sprawled across the big bed, breathing hard, skin salt-slicked, Lucas's powerful body over Caroline's.

Slowly, the world righted itself.

She sighed, turned her head, kissed his shoulder. He murmured something she couldn't understand but that was all right because it was enough to understand this. That she was with him, lying with him, feeling the race of his heart against hers, the weight of his muscled strength bearing her down into the softness of the cool linen sheets.

He kissed her temple. Stroked one big hand the length of her side, his thumb sliding over her nipple, then over the curve of her hip.

"I'm too heavy for you," he murmured, and she responded by putting her hand at the base of his spine. The feel of him against her, warm and hard and male, was too wonderful. She didn't want him to move, didn't want either of them to move, not in this lifetime or any other.

Still, after another couple of minutes, he lifted his head, brushed his lips over hers and rolled onto his side.

"No," she whispered, and he slid his arm under her shoulders and drew her close against him.

"I'm not going anywhere," he said softly, and she turned toward him and pressed her face against him, her nose at the junction of his shoulder and his arm. She loved the smell of him there, earthy and masculine.

"That was," he said, "that was—"

"Yes," she said. "It certainly was."

He laughed softly and pressed a kiss to her tangled hair.

"I'm just sorry I was so fast, but—"

"You were perfect."

"We were perfect," he said. "Perfect together."

Her heart did a little dance step. She tilted her head and looked into his face. Such a beautiful, sexy face. She wanted to tell him that but she had the feeling he was not a man who'd want to be referred to as "beautiful."

She smiled. He smiled back at her, and kissed her with such tenderness that her throat constricted.

"Querida?" His tone softened. "Seriously. Are you sure you're all right?"

"Yes."

"Because…I know, truly, it was fast—"

"Lucas. It was wonderful. It was everything I—I—"

He rolled again so that now he was on his belly, one arm lying across her, his eyes intent on hers.

"It was everything you what?"

Caroline felt her face heat. "It was everything I've dreamed of since—since—"

"Since that night."

She nodded. "Yes."

He said nothing for a long minute. Then he traced the outline of her mouth with the tip of his index finger.

"Then why did you run away from me?"

"I didn't run. I left."

"You ran, Caroline. In the middle of the night. Without leaving me your phone number. Without leaving me anything but memories I couldn't erase."

She put her hand to his cheek, felt the roughness of the end-of-day stubble. He turned his face and kissed her palm.

"I took my memories with me," she said softly.

That made him smile. "Yeah?"

She loved that simple "yeah," filled with arrogance though it was. She didn't like arrogant men; her mother might have been a fool for the type, but she wasn't.

But Lucas was different.

His arrogance was part of him. It wasn't an act meant to impress others, it was raw self-confidence, very male, very appealing.

Incredibly sexy.

"You're not going to run away this time."

She looked into his eyes. They were as dark as she'd ever seen them, and hot with something that made her breath quicken. His body was stirring against hers.

Heat slithered through her veins.

"No?" she whispered.

"No," he said.

He was right. She wasn't going anywhere. Not tonight. Tomorrow would come soon enough and reason would come with it but for now—for now, there was this. Lucas's mouth on hers. His taste on her tongue. His hand on her breast, his leg between her thighs…

Caroline smiled.

"And how are you going to stop me?" she murmured.

He laughed, low in his throat. Lifted her leg, brought it high over his hip. Teased her with the fullness of his newly aroused flesh rubbing against her sudden wetness until she moaned.

"Lucas."

"Caroline."

Despite this, what he was doing to her, the exquisite torture of it, she was determined to repay his teasing with her own.

"Lucas," she said, "do you really think what you're doing is enough to—is enough to—"

She gasped as he rocked into her.

"I don't know," he said, the roughness of his voice denying the innocence of his words. "Is it?"

"No," she said, and caught her breath as he rocked into her again. Not deeply enough. God, nowhere near deeply enough. "No," she repeated, but the word was a moan.

"Because if it isn't…"

He thrust harder. Deeper. Caroline arched like a bow at the pleasure of it.

"Do you like this?" he said thickly.

"Yes." She framed his face between her hands. "Yes, oh yes!"

"Good. Because I like it, too. I love it. The feel of you all around me. Opening for me. Stretching for me."

"Please," she whispered. "Lucas, please…"

He groaned, drove deep, sank into her until there was no him, no her, no beginning and no end.

And took her with him, to paradise.

The cat woke her.

"Mrrow," it said, in a voice surprisingly delicate for such an arrogant winner of a thousand back-alley fights—but maybe she knew less than she'd assumed about arrogance and tough guys.

Maybe some of them wore those qualities like a shield and only let a handful of people get past it.

"Mrrow," the cat said again, and Caroline sighed.

Oliver—she'd named him for the half-starved, brutalized little boy in Dickens' sad tale—Oliver was right. Middle of the night philosophizing wasn't helpful when there was an immediate problem to solve, and Oliver's problem was probably an empty dinner bowl.

She reached down, felt a ragged ear and caressed it.

"Okay," she whispered, "I'm coming."

Lucas lay sleeping beside her, his arm looped around her shoulders. Slowly, carefully, she eased away from him. He stirred in his sleep, muttered something in Portuguese—she'd finally figured out that what he occasionally spoke was not Spanish but something close to it—and she froze, not wanting to wake him.

That was what she'd done that first night. Awakened suddenly in the dark, stayed absolutely still for fear of waking him, but this was different. She wasn't worried about waking him this time, she simply wanted him to get some sleep. Neither was she shocked at finding herself in his bed…

Okay.

She was. A little. Sleeping with him again—not that they'd done much sleeping—was the last thing she'd ever imagined she would do. Not that she hadn't thought about it. About him. About what he'd made her feel, what being with him had been like.

But she and he came from different worlds. That those worlds had intersected had been a quirk of fate. And then, when fate had brought them together again, at Dani's, Lucas has been so angry, so cold to her, treating her as if she had done something unspeakably wrong. Yes, she'd slipped from his bed that first night but surely that wasn't enough to…

"Mrrow, rorrow, mrrow," the cat said with obvious impatience, and Caroline rose, reached for a silk throw at the foot of the bed, improvised a sarong and padded, barefoot, from the room.

The cat wound around her ankles as she made her way down the stairs. There was just enough light to see where she was going and she remembered the broken glass in the kitchen in time to avoid it.

Oliver avoided it, too, all but tiptoeing his way through

the little minefield of shards. He jumped onto a wicker stool and from there to the white stone counter where he sat, tail curled around his feet, watching Caroline with almond-eyed interest.

First things first, she thought, and she searched for a utility closet, found one, found a dustpan and broom, carefully swept up the glass and dumped it in the trash.

"Now you won't cut yourself," she told the cat, who answered by lifting a paw and licking it.

She checked Oliver's dishes. The water bowl was still full but she emptied it, rinsed it, then refilled it. Just as she'd figured, his food bowl was empty.

"I'm sorry, sweetheart," she said guiltily.

She washed that, too, dried it and filled it with Kitty Krunchies.

"Meow," the cat said politely, and yawned.

Caroline smiled and scooped him into her arms.

"Were you lonely, baby? Is that why you woke me?"

The cat purred and closed his eyes. Caroline kissed the top of his head, wandered out of the kitchen, into the living room and sank down in the corner of a white sofa that surely had cost more than everything she owned.

"It's okay," she said softly. "You have me now. You won't feel lonely ever again."

The cat seemed to grow heavier. His purrs slowed. He was falling asleep, safe in her arms.

Caroline lay her head back.

That was how she'd fallen asleep in Lucas's arms that very first night. They'd made love that second time and he'd held her close and she'd felt an emotion, a state of being, whatever you could call it, that she had never felt before.

She'd felt safe.

Such a strange thing for a grown woman to feel, but there was no other way to describe it. That was why she'd fallen asleep in a strange bed, in a strange man's arms...until she'd awakened and realized that she'd had sex with a stranger...

Caroline's lashes drooped.

Lucas was right. She *had* run away. The reality of what she'd done had been too shameful to bear.

Now, she had done it again, gone to his bed even though he was still little more than a stranger, a stranger who confused her beyond words, talking to her with such tamped-down rage at Dani's, then coming to her rescue, soothing her terror...

Coldness seeped into her bones.

Was she her mother's daughter after all?

It was years since she'd let in those buried memories but they flooded through her now. Mama in their little house just outside town, a new man with her. Mama, bright and happy and excited, certain he was the one.

And, weeks or sometimes months later, the inevitable signs that the affair was running its course. For the man, never for her mother. Mama's Prince Charming would drop by less often. He would call less frequently. He had excuses when Mama invited him to supper.

The only good thing about those times was that, for a little while, Caroline would have her mother to herself; she wouldn't have to pretend she wanted to watch stuff on TV when Mama and the current love of her life went out or, even worse, disappeared into Mama's bedroom.

It happened over and over. Still, when each affair played out to its predictable end, her mother was always devastated. Shocked, to find herself discarded. Not Caroline. She'd been able to read the signs by the time she was eight or nine.

If nothing else, growing up that way, she'd learned something valuable.

You didn't let yourself get involved with a man who thought he owned the world. You didn't treat sex casually. And you certainly didn't give a man all of yourself. Not ever. Bad enough if you gave a man your body, but you never gave away your heart and your soul.

She took a long breath.

Okay. One out of three wasn't so bad.

She was involved with an arrogant man. Some might say she'd treated sex casually. But she absolutely had not, absolutely never would give Lucas anything but her body.

Her heart, her soul, were safe. Completely safe—

"Caroline?"

A light came on. Caroline's eyes flew open. The cat hissed, jumped off her lap and ran.

"*Querida?* What are you doing, sitting alone in the dark?"

Lucas stood in the center of the living room, naked except for a pair of sweatpants, his dark hair tousled, his face shadowed by that sexy end-of-day stubble she'd felt beneath her fingers.

Her heart thudded.

He was so beautiful. So much more than beautiful. Just seeing him scattered her doubts, made her think only of what it was like to be in his arms.

"I thought you'd left me again," he said, as he came toward her. He bent and kissed her, his lips taking hers with possessive hunger.

"This time," he said in a rough voice, "this time, I would have come after you."

She looked up at him. She wanted to say something clever and sophisticated. Instead, what she was thinking tumbled from her mouth.

"Then—then, why didn't you last time?"

He nodded, as if she'd asked him to explain some complex mathematical formula.

"Lucas? Why didn't you look for me?"

He nodded again and ran his hand through his hair.

It was an excellent question. Why hadn't he sought her out the morning she'd left his bed?

Ego, at first. Women did not walk out on him. Going after her would have damaged his pride. Stupid, but there it was.

Then, after Jack Gordon told him more about Dani Sinclair, after he'd put two and two together and figured out what Caroline was…

If that was what she was. Only if…but still, how could he tell her that?

How could he say, *I couldn't go after you because it kills me to think of you with other men. Because I am too proud to have ever imagined myself in such a situation. Because, even now, a part of me wonders if you are acting, if sex is a performance for you, if what you said was true, that the night you were with me was truly the first time you had sold yourself…*

It must have been, he thought fiercely. A woman whose profession was sex would not cry out with shock when he parted her thighs, sought the delicate bud between them, teased it with his tongue. She would not blush under the intensity of his gaze when he drew back and said he wanted to watch her face as he made love to her…

"Lucas? You didn't look for me and yet, today, you insisted I come home with you." Caroline swallowed dryly; he saw the muscles in her throat constrict. "It doesn't make sense."

No. It did not. None of it did. He only knew that she belonged with him. That he wanted her with him. That he had told himself he'd gone to her apartment for closure when the truth was, he'd gone there for her.

"Perhaps we're looking for logic where there is none," he said softly. He took her hands in his, drew her to her feet. "All that matters is that I did come after you this time. And now, we are together." He smiled as he drew her to him, hoping to ease the darkness from her eyes. "You, and me, and a cat that is sitting in a corner, plotting how to get rid of me."

Caroline laughed, as he'd hoped she would.

"He'll come around, you'll see. It won't take more than a couple of days. By the time I leave here—"

"You're not leaving."

"Not tonight, no. I meant, when I find an apartment…"

Lucas sat down on the sofa and drew her into his lap. "Let's not talk about that now," he said softly.

No. She didn't want to talk about it, either.

"All right." She smiled. "Let's talk about you."

He looked startled. "Me?"

"I don't know anything about you." She smiled again. "Well, I know that you can read a menu written in hyperbole."

Lucas laughed. "Harder to read than Russian, huh?"

"Definitely." She lowered her lashes, batted them at him. *"Mais, monsieur, je peux lire un menu en français très bien."*

"Very nice." He smiled, brushed his lips over hers. "I'm impressed."

Caroline sighed. "Me, too. Not so much that I can speak and read French and Russian, that I ever had the chance to learn them at all."

"Meaning?"

She gave a little shrug.

"Well, I grew up in a small town."

Yes, he almost said, I know. He stopped himself just in time.

"It was the kind of place where your life was, I don't know, I guess it was sort of planned for you." She lay her head against his shoulder. "The banker's son was going to go to college, come home and be a banker. The baker's daughter was going to go to a two-year college, study nutrition and—"

"And, come home and be a baker."

Caroline gave a soft laugh.

"Exactly." She touched a finger to his jaw, rubbed it over the dark stubble. "There was a plant in town that made garden tractors. My mother worked there, on the assembly line." Her smile tilted. "In high school, I signed up to take French. And my guidance counselor called me down to his office and said I'd be better off taking cosmetology or shop because what good would French do me after I graduated and my mother got me a job working beside her?"

Lucas nodded calmly while he envisioned going to Caroline's hometown, finding the counselor and beating the crap out of him.

"But you had no intention of working in that factory," he said.

"Not for a second. I wanted something—something—"

"Better?"

"Something more."

He nodded. "So you told the counselor what he could do with his advice and signed up for French."

She grinned. It was the kind of grin that gave him a glimpse of the kid she must have been: beautiful, defiant, determined.

"I was tactful but basically, I guess that's just what I told him." Her face grew serious. "One thing I learned, growing up, was that you have to take care of yourself in this world."

They had that in common, he thought, and wished, for her sake, that they didn't.

"And," he said, keeping things light, "you turned out to be a genius at French."

"I turned out to be a good student. I won a scholarship, came to New York—"

"But New York wasn't quite what you'd expected."

"It was more than I'd expected. Big. Wonderful. Exciting."

"And expensive."

Was that a subtle change in his tone?

"Well, yes. Very. Back home—"

"Back home, that scholarship money had seemed enormous but when you got to the city, you had to supplement it."

"Of course."

"And so you did," he said, and now, there was no mistaking the change in his voice.

Did he know she waited tables? Did he think less of her for that?

"People do what they have to do," she said quietly. "A man like you might not understand that, but—"

Lucas cursed, cupped one big hand behind her head and brought her mouth to his. At first, all she did was accept his kiss. Then her lips softened and parted; he tasted the sweetness of her and after he ended the kiss, he gathered her against his heart.

He was no one to sit in judgment. His childhood had been one of doing what he had to do to survive. Petty thefts. Food snatched from market stands. Wallets lifted from the pockets of fat tourists. Who knew what more he might have done, as the years went by?

She was right.

People did what they had to do to survive.

Besides, all that was in the past. He'd never let her return to her former life, not even after—after their time together had run its course. He couldn't know when that day would come but it always did. And when that happened, he'd see that she was safe. An apartment. A job. He knew people everywhere who could surely offer solid employment to such a bright young woman.

He sensed it wouldn't be easy to convince her to accept his help but he'd find a way to do it. She would see that his wanting to help her was a good thing.

For now, they would be together. That was all that was important.

"See?" he said lightly. "I've learned something about you, and you've learned something about me."

"No," she said, her eyes on his, "I haven't."

"Sure you have. You've learned that I'm a bear before I have my morning coffee."

His tone was carefree but Caroline knew it was a cover-up. He didn't want to talk about himself. She wanted to know more, to know him, but for now, just being with him was enough. So she smiled and gave him a quick kiss.

"In that case, let's go make coffee."

She rose to her feet. The silk sarong she'd improvised slipped, exposing her breasts. She grabbed for it but Lucas caught her wrists, drew them to her sides.

In a heartbeat, the mood of the moment changed.

"Coffee. *Sim.* But first, just a taste of you."

He drew a rose-pink nipple into his mouth. Carolyn caught her breath.

"Do you like that?" he whispered.

"I love it. The feel of your mouth—"

With deft fingers, he undid the knot in the silk throw. It slipped to her feet, leaving her naked.

"Caroline. *Meu amor.* You are so beautiful. So beautiful…"

He stood and gathered her against him. She felt the swift hardening of his flesh.

That she could do this to him thrilled her.

That he would soon be inside her, moving inside her, thrilled her even more.

She put her hand between them. He made a rough sound in the back of his throat. Her fingers danced the length of his penis. She could feel his flesh pulse beneath the soft cotton sweats.

"Caroline." His voice carried a warming. "If you keep doing that—"

She put her hands at his hips, slowly eased the sweatpants down. She watched his face, loved the darkening of his eyes, the narrowing of his mouth.

"Caroline," he said hoarsely. "Do you have any idea what—"

Her hand closed around him. He groaned. He was silk and steel, incredible softness laid over all that raw masculine hardness.

She had never touched a man this way before, had never even imagined wanting to. But she wanted to know everything about her lover. If he wouldn't talk about himself, she would find other ways to explore him.

Like this.

Caroline dropped to her knees. Held him in her hands. Licked his length. Touched the tip of her tongue to his swollen sex.

Lucas shuddered. His hands threaded into her hair. He rocked back on his heels, groaning, and then he reached for her, drew her to her feet, tumbled her back on the white silk sofa and plunged into her.

She came instantly.

So did he.

He thought, as he held her, that what she had just done for him, to him, was wonderful.

And then he thought, *How many times has she done it before?*

His gut twisted.

He rose to his feet, plucked the silk throw from the carpet and covered her with it.

"Lucas?" she said, and sat up.

He smiled, and it was one of the most difficult things he'd ever done.

"Let me bring you a robe," he said brightly. "Then we'll have breakfast."

He thought he sounded cheerful but when he came back with a robe, he saw that she had wrapped the discarded silk throw around herself. That, and the look on her face, told him he hadn't pulled it off.

"Caroline. Sweetheart—"

"What is it? What's the matter? Did I—did I do something—what I just did, was it—"

Her eyes glittered with unshed tears, her mouth trembled. How could he have thought, even for a second, that she had done this with other men? Cursing himself, he reached for her, took her in his arms and kissed her.

"What did I tell you, *querida*? A bear before coffee, *sim*?" He kissed her again, kept kissing her until her body softened against his and the doubt had left her eyes. "I'm going to make you the best breakfast you ever had. It's the national dish of Brazil. Bacon and waffles, with maple syrup."

The foolish joke worked. A smile curved her lips.

"Waffles are not the national dish of anywhere!"

"But they should be, because I make the best waffles in the world."

Her eyebrows rose. "Really."

"Really. And the best coffee."

"If you're going to make the coffee and the waffles, what's left for me to do?"

"You'll have a very important job."

"Which is?"

"You're going to make my kitchen look beautiful."

She laughed. "That certainly does sound important."

"Very important," he said solemnly. "And I'm sure you're going to be very good at it."

Just as he was going to be very good at forgetting what he

knew about her past. Or wondering about it. Hadn't he learned that as a boy?

Who you were at the beginning of your life meant nothing.

It was who you ultimately became that mattered.

CHAPTER NINE

THEY showered. Put on robes.

And had breakfast.

Breakfast took a long time.

It had to, when every mouthful was interspersed with soft, teasing kisses that tasted of maple syrup.

Lucas made the waffles and coffee. Caroline found a real job to do, after all. She made the bacon. She said his waffles were heavenly. He said he had never tasted bacon so delicious.

"Thank you, sir," she said demurely. "That compliment almost justifies the time I've spent in greasy-spoon kitchens." She smiled. "Notice, I said 'almost.'"

"Greasy-spoon kitchens?" Lucas drank some coffee. "What kind are those?"

Caroline laughed.

"Not the kind you'd know, I'm sure."

"You mean," he said with wide-eyed innocence, "not one that would be found in that restaurant the night we met?"

It was the first reference either of them had made to the start of that evening, and he'd made it with as much grace as if they'd been on a real date, not a pretend one.

"No," she said softly, "not like that place at all."

"Ah." He grinned. "I didn't think so."

Caroline ate a bit of waffle. A drop of syrup glittered in

the very center of her bottom lip. Lucas leaned toward her and licked it away, loving the way she caught her breath as he did, loving it enough to cover her mouth with his and turn the moment of contact into a real kiss.

"Maple syrup," he said softly. "I wanted to make sure it didn't drip."

She smiled. "That's very kind of you," she said, just as softly. "Let me return the compliment."

She cupped her hand around the back of his head, brought his face to hers again and kissed him, her mouth soft beneath his. He cupped her face, his fingers threading into her hair, and took the kiss deep. After endless seconds, she drew back.

Deus, he loved it when she looked like this, cheeks rosy, mouth delicately swollen, eyes filled with him.

"The waffles will get cold," she whispered.

Lucas was on the verge of saying he didn't give a damn if they turned to ice. From the look on her face, he doubted if she did, either…

"Good morning, Mr. Vieira."

Startled, Caroline jumped. Lucas bit back a curse. He'd forgotten his housekeeper would be coming in this morning.

He turned toward her and thought, with amusement, that Mrs. Kennelly would make an excellent poker player. Nothing showed in her placid face even though she'd never before found him at breakfast with a woman.

And then he thought, *Deus*, he was at breakfast. With a woman. Here, in his own kitchen.

It was a first.

Women sometimes spent the night, sure. And, early in the morning, they left. Oh, on Sundays he might take a woman who'd spent the night to brunch but this, sitting in his own kitchen, sharing a meal they'd prepared together…

Caroline was getting ready to bolt. He could feel it. Calmly, as if nothing unusual had happened, he reached for her hand.

"Good morning, Mrs. Kennelly. Caroline, this is Mrs. Kennelly. My housekeeper."

He looked at Caroline. She was pink with embarrassment. That made him want to kiss her, which made no sense. Besides, that would only add to her embarrassment so he clasped her hand more tightly and wove his fingers through hers.

Mrs. Kennelly smiled politely. "How do you do, miss?"

He heard Caroline's deep intake of breath, saw the proud lift of her chin.

"It's nice to meet you, Mrs. Kennelly."

"Miss Hamilton is going to be staying with us for a while."

Caroline shot him a look.

"No," she said in a low voice, "really, I'm—"

Lucas rose to his feet, his hand still holding hers, and drew her up beside him.

"We'll get out of your way, Mrs. Kennelly," he said pleasantly. "Isn't that right, sweetheart?"

Only if getting out of the way meant the floor would open and swallow her, Caroline thought frantically.

How did a woman deal with a scene like this?

Lucas was composed. So was his housekeeper. She was the only one who wanted to die, and wasn't that ridiculous? She had spent the night in bed with him, doing things. Wonderful, exciting things.

And now what horrified her was his housekeeper finding her in his robe, in his kitchen?

But then, why would Lucas or Mrs. Kennelly be horrified? This scene had to be fairly commonplace for a man like him.

Trouble was, it was anything but for a woman like her. She

had never even spent the night with a man before, much less faced his housekeeper the next morning.

"Caroline?"

She blinked. Lucas smiled at her.

"Let's let Mrs. Kennelly get started, *sim*?"

That "sim" was meaningful. Lucas rarely used Portuguese. He spoke it when he was angry. When he made love to her. And that "sim," a word she figured meant "yes," crept in every once in a while but only when he was determined to make a point and right now, the point was that he wanted her to behave like a grown-up. So she did. She let him draw her from the stool while she forced what she hoped was a smile.

"Of course. Just let me clean up before—"

"Nonsense, miss," the housekeeper said briskly. "You go on. I'll take care of this."

Well, of course. If she didn't know how to behave by being found all but naked in a man's kitchen, she surely didn't know how to behave around a housekeeper.

The best thing was to keep smiling, to keep holding Lucas's hand or, rather, to let him hold hers, to follow him through the sunny penthouse, to the steps, up the steps, down the hall, to his bedroom…

And to remember, all too quickly, what she was doing here, that she didn't belong here, that she'd made one mistake after another where Lucas Vieira was concerned.

Actually, his housekeeper's appearance was a very good thing.

Lucas shut the door. Let go of her hand. Folded his arms and looked at her. What was he going to say? She couldn't imagine. And it wouldn't matter. She was going to speak first.

"Lucas."

He raised an eyebrow. She hated when he did that. Actually, she loved it. It made him look dangerous and sexy, although he looked dangerous and sexy enough without doing anything at all.

"Lucas," she said again, "I—"

"My housekeeper is a better poker player than you are."

"Excuse me?"

"She saw you and showed no reaction. You saw her and looked as if you wished the floor would open and swallow you."

Did he read minds? Caroline mimicked his action, folded her arms and looked straight at him.

"I was—surprised."

Lucas's mouth twitched. "I'd never have known."

Her eyes narrowed. "You might find this amusing. I don't."

"I find it—interesting."

That tiny muscle flickered in his jaw. Whenever it did, she had an almost overwhelming desire to run up to him and press her lips to his skin.

Which was the last thing she should be thinking right now.

"To hell with interesting," she said briskly. "I had it right the first time. You find this amusing."

"Wrong, *querida*. A man who has never shared breakfast with a woman in his very own kitchen and who suddenly realizes it when his housekeeper discovers him doing so, does not find the situation amusing."

Caroline blinked. "Never?"

"Never what?"

"Never both things. I mean— You've never had breakfast here with a—with a woman before?"

Lucas shrugged. "No."

"But—"

"I am not a man who does such things."

"But—"

"You already said that."

"I know I did. I just don't understand why you—"

"No." His voice was suddenly low and rough. "I don't understand it, either." His arms fell to his sides. Slowly, he came toward her, his eyes hot. "I don't understand any of it."

Caroline's heart began to race.

"What don't you understand?" she whispered.

Lucas gathered her into his arms. She sighed as he drew her against him and when she did, he thought it was the most perfect sound he'd ever heard a woman make.

"You," he said. "Me. This."

He groaned, brought her to her toes and claimed her mouth with his.

What he'd offered was not an answer and yet it was the only answer he had, the only one he could give, the only one that made sense.

"Lucas," she said unsteadily, "Lucas…"

Slowly, he opened the sash of her robe. His robe, he thought. His. The robe slid from her shoulders and he looked at her, the lovely face and body that were without artifice.

He told her she was beautiful. That she was perfect. He told it to her in Portuguese, told her, too, how much he wanted her.

He could see the pulse beating in the hollow of her throat.

"What about—what about Mrs. Kennelly?"

Despite everything—his desire, his passion, the almost painful hardening of his flesh—he laughed.

"We won't tell her," he said softly, and Caroline stared at him and then, to his delight, she giggled.

"Such a good idea," she said.

And then her smile changed, her hazel eyes darkened and

she reached for him, lay her hand over him where his aroused flesh swelled and throbbed.

"Make love to me," she whispered, and he lifted her in his arms. Carried her to his bed. Lay her down so that her hair was a halo of gold against the pillows and then he pulled off his sweatpants, kicked them aside, came down over her and made love to her with such care, such tenderness that when it was over, Caroline wept.

And Lucas—

He held her close, felt her heart beating against his, her breath on his throat, and he stroked her and kissed her and wondered what in hell was happening to him.

He had to go to work.

People, appointments, emails and phone calls and paperwork were waiting for him.

He told it to himself. He told it to Caroline.

"Of course," she said.

"Of course," he said solemnly. Then he reached past her for the bedside phone, called his P.A., told her he would not be in and that she could reach him on his cell if something important came up.

"Something vital," he said, just to clarify things. He paused. "On second thought, don't call me at all."

He hung up, laughing at what he knew had to be the look on his P.A.'s face.

"What's funny?" Caroline asked, and Lucas kissed her, kissed her again and blew bubbles against her belly button and she laughed and he looked up and suddenly knew that he had never been happier in his entire life.

The thought stilled his laughter.

"What?" Caroline said, but there was nothing he could say that would not be dangerous so he scooped her up. "Where are you taking me? Lucas. Lucas! Where...?"

She shrieked as he stepped into the shower stall with her in his arms, turned on all the sprays until they were cocooned in a warm, delicious waterfall, and her pretended protests faded as he kissed her, set her on her feet, kissed her breasts and slid his hand between her thighs.

"Lucas," she whispered.

"What, sweetheart?" he said, against her mouth, but she had no answer, none she could afford to give him, because she was happy, so happy, and she knew happiness like this couldn't last…

"Put your arms around me," he said. And he stepped back against the wall, lifted her and she wrapped her legs around him and then there were no questions, no answers, none were needed because they were lost in each other's arms.

Caroline fed Oliver. Changed the water in his bowl. Opened a Daintee Deelites. Scooped out his litter pan.

The cat purred and wove around her ankles.

"I'll see you soon, baby," she cooed as she picked him up and kissed his head while the cat and Lucas eyed each other in silent communication.

His driver took them to Caroline's apartment.

Lucas wasn't happy about it.

"I don't like the thought of you being here," he said, "even for a little while."

Caroline didn't answer. What would she say? Yesterday, she'd agreed she couldn't go on living in this place. Today, she was calmer. She knew she had little choice. It had taken forever to find her apartment; affordable rents were tough enough in Manhattan but when "affordable" referred to the stipend she received as a teaching assistant and her earnings as a waitress—and she'd have to find another job, and quickly— when that was the meaning of "affordable," the miserable rooms she already had were better than most others.

She'd thought about the problem on the way and she'd come up with a simple plan. She'd accept Lucas's hospitality for a couple of days. Three, at the most. And she'd look for an apartment. If she didn't find one—and she was willing to bet that she wouldn't—she'd move back here.

She already knew better than to tell that to Lucas.

Instead, she offered a noncommittal "Mmm," and obeyed his command to give him her keys and stand in back of him when he opened the door to her apartment.

"Command" was the only way to describe that macho arrogance.

That oh-so-sexy macho arrogance.

The door opened. Lucas stepped into the living room, then motioned her forward.

The room was as she'd left it. No, not quite. The super had installed a new window as well as a locking window gate. That, at least, made her feel better.

It didn't do a thing for Lucas, who shut the door, strode to the window, clamped his hand around the top of the iron gate and shook it.

"Too little, too late," he growled.

"It seems sturdy enough."

"Maybe. But the locks on the door wouldn't stop an amateur."

Okay. This wasn't going to be a fruitful discussion. Besides, there was no point to it. Lucas lived on a different planet. He could never understand her life, and she didn't expect him to.

Instead of answering, she went into the tiny bedroom and opened the closet, began pulling things from hangers, the few garments she'd need for the next few apartment-hunting days.

Lucas cleared his throat.

"You know," he said, "you could leave all that here and, ah, and start fresh."

Caroline looked at him. "No," she said, "I could not."

He opened his mouth, then shut it. A good thing, too. Did he actually think she could afford to toss these things out and buy new ones? He was not just from another planet, he was from another galaxy.

She turned back to the closet, added two pairs of shoes and a purse to the small stack of items she'd put on the bed.

What else?

Some of her textbooks. Her laptop computer. A stack of printed notes. She put them all into a backpack, stuffed the clothes, shoes and purse into a canvas messenger bag, took a last look around and swung toward Lucas.

"There," she said, "that'll…" The look on his face silenced her. He was looking around him as if he'd never seen a place so small, so pitiful before. And, yes, it was both those things, but it was honest, it was hers, she had paid for it all, and she wasn't in anyone's debt.

"Is there a problem?"

She'd meant to sound coolly amused. Instead, she sounded just plain cool.

He looked at her.

"You should not have to live like this," he said gruffly.

Caroline folded her arms. "Not everyone can live in the sky."

"In the…? My condo, you mean."

"Yes. I know it must come as a terrible surprise but in the real world—"

"Don't take that tone with me!"

"I'll take any tone I like! As I said, in the real world—"

"I know all about the real world, damnit!" He was on her in two strides, clasping her elbows, lifting her to her toes, his head lowered so their eyes were on the same level. "Do you think I was born, as you put it, in the sky?"

"Let go of me."

"Answer the question. Do you think I was always rich?" His mouth twisted. "Do you know what a *favela* is?"

She stared at him. "I've heard the word. It's a—a Brazilian slum."

Lucas gave a bitter laugh. "A slum is much higher on the socio-economic ladder, *querida*."

He was upset. Very upset. Caroline's anger faded.

"Lucas. I didn't mean to pry."

"I was born in a shack with a tin roof. A couple of years later, things got really bad and we traded that for what was, basically, a cardboard box in an alley."

Her eyebrows rose. Was it in shock at what he was saying, or because his tone was curt? And why was he telling her this? No one knew his story. It wasn't that he was ashamed of it.

Not exactly.

It was just that it wasn't pretty. The poverty. The abandonment by his mother. The foster homes.

The thefts. The pockets he'd picked. Ugly and, yes, he was ashamed. Besides, his personal life was his; he saw no reason to share it with anyone else.

And yet—and yet—

For the first time ever, he felt the temptation to tell someone who he was. Who he really was. People knew him as he presented himself, a man rich almost beyond comprehension, in full command of his own life and, though it was a daunting realization, in command of the lives of others, as well.

But sometimes, in the deepest part of the night, he wondered how people would view him if they knew that he had become that man after a beginning a caseworker in the first shelter that had taken him in had called "humble" when the truth was, his beginnings had not been humble but squalid.

How would Caroline see him if she knew all the details? What would she think of him? Was the Lucas Vieira she cared for rich and powerful, or was he simply a man?

And what in hell was he doing, thinking any of this? What was he doing, thinking Caroline cared for him? She liked him, yes. She was grateful to him for what he had done yesterday. And she liked having sex with him, or she seemed to, unless that was all an act, unless it was yet another part of the game they'd played from that first night...

"Lucas?"

He blinked and looked at her.

"You don't know me, Caroline. You don't know a damned thing about me."

"No." Her voice was low. She reached up, lay her palm against his jaw. "I don't. The truth is, we don't know anything about each other."

For an instant, the tension in him had eased. Now, she felt it return.

"You're right," he said. "For instance, I don't understand why you live in a place like this."

Caroline snatched back her hand. "Because it's what I can afford on a TA's salary. On a waitress's tips. For a man who claims he grew up in poverty, you don't understand much."

Lucas's hands tightened on her.

"Is that all you do? Teach? Wait on tables?"

"What's that supposed to mean?"

"I gave you a thousand dollars."

A flush rose in her face. "You mean, you paid me a thousand dollars for a night's work."

His jaw tightened. "Indeed."

"And, what? That gives you the right to ask what I did with it?"

It didn't. He knew that. He knew he was on the verge of saying something he would regret but he had questions, endless questions. Yesterday, he'd been so fixed on the danger of where Caroline lived, on what had almost happened to her, that he hadn't thought of anything else.

Now, he saw the real poverty of her furnishings. The drabness of her clothes.

What did she do with the money she earned selling herself? *If* she sold herself. He had to keep that "if" in mind.

"Lucas."

Dani Sinclair's fee for a night was many times what he had paid Caroline. Caroline's should have been twenty times more than that.

She was everything a man could want, in bed and out. Warm and sweet and funny. Giving and loving and exciting.

The way she laughed at his jokes. Complimented his cooking. Sighed in his arms and gave herself so completely when they made love. Even her devotion to The Cat from Hell, to that pathetic fern...

How could she be a woman who sold herself? How could she give herself to anyone but him? And that was what this was all about. That he wanted her to give herself only to him...

"Lucas. You're hurting me!"

He looked at his hands, gripping her shoulders so hard that he could feel each finger digging into her flesh.

Deus, he was losing his mind!

Carefully, he let go of her. She started to step back and he shook his head, lightly clasped her wrists and drew her to him.

"Caroline." His voice was low. "*Querida*. Forgive me."

He could see the shine of tears in her eyes.

"I don't understand," she said in a shaky voice. "What is it you want from me?"

He held her gaze for a long minute as he searched for an answer, not only for her but for himself. Then, gently, he ran his thumb over the curve of her lower lip, bent his head and pressed a kiss to it.

"I want you," he said softly. "Only you."

He kissed her. She didn't respond. He kissed her again, whispered her name. And, finally, Caroline kissed him back.

That was all she wanted. Lucas's kisses. His arms, holding her to him. Those simple things, and the dizzying realization that something as exhilarating as it was terrifying was happening to her.

That it was happening to—there was no other word for it—to her heart.

CHAPTER TEN

WEDNESDAY morning, Lucas phoned his office again and told his P.A. that he wouldn't be coming in.

"Cancel all my appointments, please."

Was there a split second of hesitancy before she said, "Yes, Mr. Vieira."

No. Why would there be? They had a pleasant relationship but he was her employer; she never questioned anything he said or did.

But he had never stayed out of the office two days in a row unless it was because he was away on business.

Never, he thought. His behavior was...unusual.

But necessary.

He had things to do. Caroline had mentioned that the semester was over; she had an office at the university.

"Half a closet, actually," she'd said with a quick smile.

She had to pack her books and files, move them out. She didn't ask but, of course, he had to help her. He also had to convince her that she couldn't transport them to her apartment. That was out of the question. He didn't want her in that place for a second, or taking endless subway trips, her arms loaded with boxes, or climbing the dark stairs to those miserable rooms in that building she had called home.

And he had to find a way to keep her from looking for a place to live.

She talked about that, too. Whenever she did, he changed the subject.

He knew she'd have to go out on her own sooner or later. He wanted that, too. At least, he *didn't* want the alternative, a woman living with him, sharing his meals, his quiet mornings, his evenings.

His life.

But it was surprisingly pleasant. For now. Pleasant, surely only because it was a new experience, having her clothes in the guest room closet, her makeup, her hairbrush, all her things in the guest bath. Silly, really, because she spent the nights with him.

In his bed. In his arms.

But it couldn't be a long-term solution.

Of course, it couldn't.

Not a problem.

He had the Realtor looking for that apartment. Someplace bright and safe. Someplace nearby. And he'd called Saks Fifth Avenue, asked to speak to a personal shopper and been put through to someone who sounded efficient.

"I'll need clothes for a, uh, a young woman," he'd said, speaking briskly because he'd suddenly felt foolish.

"Certainly, sir," the personal shopper replied, as if this kind of thing happened all the time. Maybe it did, but the experience was brand-new for Lucas.

"The lady's size?"

"She's a six," he'd said, because he'd anticipated the question and he'd taken a quick look at the labels in some of Caroline's things.

"Her height?"

Height. A difficult question. *Tall enough to come up to my heart when she's barefoot*, he'd almost said, and caught himself just in time.

"Average," was his answer, even though there was nothing

"average" about his Caroline, but the answer seemed to satisfy the personal shopper.

"And her style, sir."

"Her style?"

"Yes. Is she into current fashion? Does she like a glamorous look? Has she any favorite designers?"

His Caroline's style was strictly her own. Easy. Simple. As for designers, from what he could tell, she chose them by price tag.

"She, ah, she prefers a casual look."

And then he thought of the spectacular outfit she'd worn the night they met—and he thought, too, that of everything he'd seen in the guest room closet when he'd checked her clothing for size, he had not seen anything remotely close to that short, leg-baring dress or the sky-high stilettos.

"But she looks amazing in other things, too," he'd added. "Silk dresses. Skinny heels. Soft, feminine stuff..."

Deus, he'd thought, almost groaning with embarrassment.

The shopper had come to his rescue.

"You've given me an excellent portrait to work with," she'd said pleasantly.

Lucas certainly hoped so. Going through this again would be hell.

He told her to charge everything to his black Amex card and to wait for delivery until he called with an address. So that was taken care of. Clothes and, soon, an apartment. He thought about how pleased Caroline would be with those surprises.

She would be pleased, wouldn't she?

Of course, she would.

But he couldn't surprise her when it came to packing up her office stuff. Only she'd know what she wanted to take and what she wanted to leave.

He'd considered having his driver take her uptown to the university campus.

Then he thought how much simpler it would be if he did it instead.

He kept a red Ferrari 599 in a garage a few blocks away. He loved the car's elegant lines and incredible power but he hadn't had much chance to drive it. Business took up more and more of his life.

This would be a good opportunity to put some mileage on the Ferrari.

All in all, it made sense to take the day off.

They made breakfast together again. He'd decided to give Mrs. Kennelly the week off, with a month's pay. She deserved it and, yes, if it meant he had his penthouse all to himself, he and Caroline, that he could make love to her wherever, whenever they both wanted, well, that was simply a coincidental benefit.

It was the kind of morning that made June in New York close to perfect, and they took their coffee out to the terrace. Lucas told Caroline the plans he'd made for the day.

She smiled. "It's a very sweet offer."

And while he was still wondering when anyone had ever called anything he'd done "sweet," she added that she didn't want him to turn his schedule inside out for her.

"I'm not," he said, with calm self-assurance. "And you'll be doing me a favor."

Caroline raised her eyebrows. "I will?"

"The car really needs to be driven. My mechanic says so."

She looked dubious. No wonder. It was a lie but how could he tell her that turning his schedule inside out seemed far less important than being separated for her, even for a day?

Where had that thought come from? Although, *sim*, it made a kind of sense. Their relationship was so new…

No. It wasn't a relationship. He didn't have "relationships." It was simply—it was just—it was something but he couldn't manage to call it an "affair," not with the cool sophistication the term implied.

Caroline lay her hand over his.

"Then, thank you," she said softly, and he heard himself say, with a roughness that caught him off-guard, that if she really wanted to thank him she could offer him a kiss, just a little kiss, and she laughed and leaned over the table and pressed her lips gently to his and then it was a good thing, a very good thing that Mrs. Kennelly wasn't there because Lucas got to his feet, swept Caroline into his arms, carried her to a chaise longue and took her under the soft June sky with a ferocity that turned to tenderness with such breathtaking speed that when she reached orgasm, tears glittered in her eyes. And he—

He felt something happen, deep in his heart.

When she began to rise, he shook his head.

"Don't go," he said softly, and he held her cradled against him, the warmth of her skin kissing his, the delicate scent of her in his nostrils, and he thought how amazing it was that he was a grown man, that sex—great sex—had been part of his life for years…

But it had never been like this.

They showered and dressed, both of them in jeans and T-shirts, Lucas with a cashmere sweater over his shirt, Caroline with a hoodie over hers.

She looked beautiful and he told her so, and though he knew that nothing could ever improve her beauty because it was already perfect, the silks and cashmeres the personal shopper would provide would be the right touch for her lovely face and feminine curves.

He phoned his garage. The car was ready when they arrived, long and sleek and red, as high-spirited as a race horse.

"Oh," Caroline said softly, "oh, my! It's beautiful!"

He grinned. "And fast."

"I'll bet. It looks like it's moving, even standing still. What did you say it was?"

"A Ferrari. A Ferrari 599."

She wrinkled her brow. "What's that mean, exactly?"

So he explained. Exactly. The engine specs. The paint. The customization. He explained his car in detail even though he knew, from past experience, that what women wanted to know was if whatever he drove was as expensive as it looked.

But Caroline listened. Asked questions. And once they were moving through the Manhattan streets—slowly, because of traffic, though he could almost feel the car trying to break free—once they were moving, he found himself describing the first car he'd ever owned.

"It was a clunker."

She laughed. "A clunker, huh?"

"Absolutely. It was older than I was."

She laughed again. "It's hard to imagine you driving something like that."

"Hey, I loved that car. It took me wherever I wanted to go—as long as I pulled over every fifty miles and added a can of oil."

They both laughed, and Lucas thought how amazing it was that he'd remembered that old car, much less told her the story. He never shared anything from his past with anyone, it just wasn't what he did, and yet, in a few short days, he'd revealed more about himself to Caroline than he ever had before.

What would she think if she knew his entire story? That his mother had abandoned him. That he'd survived by being a thief and a con artist. That he'd run from the cops. That he'd grown up in foster homes where sometimes, same as in the streets, nothing mattered but survival.

When he'd first come to the States, tough and street-hardened, unwilling to let anybody or anything get past the barriers he'd built, a well-meaning counselor who treated kids like him told him that he had to accept his past before he could address his future, that pretending bad things had never happened to him was like living a lie…

"But you lied to me, Lucas."

Shocked, he looked at Caroline. "No," he said quickly, "never."

Then the look on her face registered. She was teasing him. The breath eased from his lungs.

"You said you'd help me move my stuff."

"And I will."

"Not in this beautiful beast. It's far too handsome to be filled with boxes. Besides, even if we wanted to, there's no room."

Lucas tried for a look of wounded innocence.

"It's more spacious than you think, *querida*."

She craned her neck and looked at the nonexistent space behind them.

"Uh-huh."

"It is. You'll see."

It wasn't, but what else could he say? Could he tell her he wanted to share his pleasure in the car with her? That being with her, sharing with her, was what mattered?

"And how are you going to park? Where? You can't leave this car on the street."

She was being practical, which was more than he could say of himself. Of course he couldn't leave the Ferrari on the street.

Well, actually, he could.

He loved the car. Its lines, its grace, its speed. He had

worked long and hard for it. But loving an inanimate object wasn't the same as loving a woman.

Not that he knew what loving a woman was like, he thought quickly. Not that he ever wanted to know. Love was a fake word, invented by frauds. It was a concept at best, nothing more. He understood that. He had always understood that, at least since his mother had taught it to him that day she'd left him on a street in Copacabana…

"Lucas." Caroline laughed and poked him with her elbow. "You just drove right past campus."

He had, indeed. Where was his head? Not on his work, or the appointments he'd canceled, or anything useful.

He frowned.

What in hell was he doing? Behaving like a kid with a crush when he was a man with a multibillion dollar empire to run.

His hands flexed on the steering wheel.

It was still early. Plenty of time to head back downtown, garage the car, arrange for James to shuttle Caroline and her cartons while he changed into a suit, went to his office, got some work done.

"You're right," he said. "The car's too small, and where would I park it in this area?"

She nodded. "That's what I thought," she said, in a very soft voice. "This was a lovely idea, but—"

"But completely impractical." Ahead, the light changed, went from red to green. He'd make a left at the intersection, head back toward Fifth Avenue.

He reached the intersection—and said something under his breath as he wrenched the wheel right, not left, and headed for the Long Island Expressway.

He reached for Caroline's hand. Her fingers curled tightly with his.

"Forget about packing your things," he said gruffly. "It's too nice a day for that."

"Then, where are we going?"

"I have a house…"

He fell silent. He'd bought his house in the Hamptons a couple of years ago. The towns on the southeastern end of Long Island were charming, the beaches magnificent, and they were within a couple of hours of the city.

The rich and famous kept summer homes there.

That had influenced him, not because he wanted any part of that world but because he'd heard that people in the Hamptons understood the value of privacy.

If you wanted to be left alone, you were. Lucas wanted exactly that. For him, the place would be a retreat. Sand. Sea. The vastness of the blue sky.

It had turned out to be all that.

It was also lonely.

The house was big. The ocean was endless. Without his work to keep him busy, he'd felt unsettled. Maybe that was the reason he'd spent a couple of weekends there with women he'd been seeing at the time.

Two women. Two weekends. And that had been enough.

He'd been foolish to expect that sand and sea and sky were things women would see as entertainment.

Was he about to make the same mistake again? It had been annoying those other times but if Caroline wasn't happy in his house by the sea…

"A house?" she said. "Where?"

He looked at her. The windows were all open; sunlight glinted on her face and her hair. The moment was so perfect that he wanted to pull to the curb and take her in his arms but in New York traffic, he'd have needed an armored truck, not a Ferrari, to make that happen.

"I have a place on the beach. In the Hamptons. The caretaker keeps it open for me year-round."

"What's it like? Your house?"

He shrugged. The truth was, he loved the house the way he loved the Ferrari.

"It's okay," he said. "Just, you know, a beach house. Lots of glass. A deck. A pool. And the sea."

Caroline sighed. "That's it?"

His heart fell just a little.

"That's it." He cleared his throat. "You know, it's probably not a great idea. Going out there, I mean. It's still early in the season and the weather's kind of cool. Plus, it's midweek. Lots of the clubs will be closed, and—"

"You don't go there for the clubs, do you?"

"Well, no. But there won't be much to do."

"Can you see the stars? You can't see them in the city."

Lucas thought of the big telescope in the great room. He'd bought it even before he'd bought furniture.

"Yeah. You can."

"And crickets. Can you hear them at night?"

Her tone was wistful. He looked at her and cleared his throat again.

"After sundown, it's a cricket symphony."

She turned her face to him. "I grew up in the country."

He felt a twinge of guilt because he already knew that.

"And I love the city. The energy, the endless wonderful places to explore… But there are some things about the country I'll always miss. The quiet." She smiled. "The stars. And the sound of crickets." She gave a little laugh. "Sounds silly, I suppose, but—"

To hell with traffic.

Lucas checked the mirrors, shot across a lane of traffic

to the blare of angry horns and pulled to the curb. He undid his seat belt, undid Caroline's, gathered her in his arms and kissed her.

They were almost at his beach house when Caroline gasped and said, "Oh my gosh. Oliver!"

Lucas nodded. Oliver, indeed. The cat had food, water and the attitude of a lion. He suspected Oliver could take care of himself for a day, but he didn't say that. Instead, he called Mrs. Kennelly on his cell, apologized for the intrusion and asked if she could stop by to deal with Oliver.

"I know I told you to take the week off and this is lot to ask…"

"I'll do better than that, sir," his housekeeper said. "I'll stay with him."

"Oh, you don't have to do—"

"I'm happy to do it. Oliver's such a fine, sweet-natured cat!"

Sweet-natured? Lucas said that was good to hear.

"Okay," he said, when he ended the call. "Mrs. Kennelly will stay with Oliver."

"Thank you."

Lucas reached for Caroline's hand. And felt a tightness in his chest. The house was down the next lane. Would she like it?

"We're here," he said.

Caroline sat up straight. Ahead, she saw massive stone walls and impressive iron gates. Lucas pressed a button, the gates swung open and she caught her breath.

She wasn't naive. She'd lived in New York long enough to know that property in the Hamptons was expensive but the sight of Lucas's so-called beach house took her breath away.

Glass, he'd said. And a deck, and a pool. What he hadn't

mentioned was that there were what looked like acres of glass, or that the deck seemed to hang over a beach that stretched over the dunes to the sea, or that a waterfall tumbled into the pool, or that the pool was the kind that seemed to have no boundaries around it.

"It's called an infinity pool," Lucas said as he took her on a slow walk around the place.

"It's wonderful. All of it. Wonderful," Caroline said, beaming up at him.

He nodded. "Yes," he said, as if it didn't matter, because it mattered too much, "it's nice."

"Nice?" She laughed, let go of his hand and danced out in front of him. "It's incredible!"

What was incredible, he thought, was the color in Caroline's face, the glow in her eyes. Watching her brought back the excitement he'd felt helping design the house, explaining what he wanted to the architect and builders.

When they stepped through the front door, she gave a soft, breathless "oooh" of delight.

High ceilings. Skylights. White walls. Italian tile floors in some rooms, bamboo in others.

"It's like a dream," she said softly. "It's perfect!"

"Perfect," Lucas said, and he drew her into his arms.

"What's the rest of it like?"

He smiled. "I'll show you." Slowly, he eased the hoodie from her shoulders. "I'll show you all of it. But now—" He swung her into his arms. "Let me show you the master bedroom," he said softly.

Caroline looped her arms around his neck and buried her face against his throat.

"That's an excellent idea," she said, and thought, *if this is a dream, may it never end.*

* * *

They did all the things he'd imagined doing here but had somehow never done.

They made love. Went skinny-dipping in the heated pool after he assured Caroline there were no neighbors; his property extended for more than five acres around and behind the house. He found an old shirt for her to wear; he put on shorts and they poked around in the kitchen cupboards and the freezer to find stuff for lunch.

At sunset, they strolled along the beach, just at the surfline, the cool Atlantic nipping at their toes. Drove into town, to a quiet little café for a candlelit dinner. When they returned to the house, the sky was deepest black and the stars blazed fiercely overhead.

"The stars," Caroline said in a hushed voice.

They watched the heavens from the deck, her leaning back against Lucas, his arms hard around her.

Lucas could feel her heart beating. He could hear the soft whisper of her breath.

Something inside him seemed to rise and take flight.

He was happy.

"Caroline," he whispered.

He turned her in his arms. She looked up at him, her face pale and lovely in the light of a full moon.

"Caroline," he said again, and because he knew there was more to say and that he was afraid to say it, he bent his head and kissed her.

Then he undressed her.

Eased her out of her clothing with the moon and the stars looking on. Stripped her bare and shuddered when she reached to him and began undressing him, too.

When they were naked, he led her inside, to his bedroom, to an enormous bed on a platform under a huge skylight that let in the burning light of the sky.

Lucas worshipped her mouth. Her breasts. Her dusty-rose

nipples. He kissed her belly, her thighs, moved between them and stroked her hot, ready flesh with the tips of his fingers.

"Watch me as I make love to you," he said thickly, and Caroline wanted to tell him she would watch him forever, that she adored him, that she loved him, loved him, loved him...

And then he was deep inside her and the world went away.

They drove into town the next day, to a little shop on Jobs Lane so simple on the outside that Caroline knew, instinctively, she could never afford anything it sold, but she needed a change of clothes.

Lucas wanted to buy her everything he saw. She said an emphatic "no," selected a bra, panties, a cotton sweater and a pair of cropped pants.

"I'll pay you back," she whispered after the clerk had gone in back to wrap them.

He laughed, twiddled an imaginary mustache, bent her back over his arm, gave her a dramatic kiss and said yes, she surely would.

She laughed, too. She knew he was joking, that he would never let her give him the hundreds of dollars the handful of items had cost and it was a sudden jolt of reality, a reminder that there was very little money left in her bank account, that she had to find a job, and quickly.

And she had to find a place to live.

The realization made her unusually quiet on the trip back to the beach house. How had she let herself become so dependent on this man? She thought of her mother and shuddered.

"*Querida?* Shall I put on the heat?"

"No," she said quickly, forcing a smile as she turned toward him. "I'm fine. Just—maybe too much sun this afternoon, hmm? What do you think?"

"I think," he said solemnly, reaching for her hand and

lifting it to his lips, "I think that there is only one way to deal with a chill."

How could she not laugh? She did, and Lucas looked at her and grinned. He loved that laugh of hers. It was sexy, earthy, and yet, somehow, innocent.

"You do, huh?"

"Sim," he said, and proved it to her as soon as they reached the house.

They stayed at the beach for two days.

Lucas would have stayed for the rest of the week but his P.A. called on his cell phone, filled with apologies, to tell him that the owner and CEO of a French bank he'd been looking at for months had phoned and asked for a meeting.

"I wouldn't have bothered you, Mr. Vieira, but—"

Lucas assured her she'd been right to call. Still, when he told Caroline it was time to return to the city, he couldn't help feeling that something irreplaceable was coming to an end.

She seemed to sense the same thing. She stepped into his arms and cuddled against him while he stroked her hair.

"Ah," she said with a sad little smile, "what's that old saying? All good things must come to an end."

She spoke the words lightly but Lucas felt a chill.

"We'll come back on the weekend," he said. "I promise."

But they didn't come back on the weekend. He should have known they wouldn't.

He should have known that she'd gotten it right.

All good things always did come to an end.

CHAPTER ELEVEN

THERE came a time when a person could no longer evade reality.

It had happened to Lucas as a boy, the day his mother abandoned him.

Now, it was happening again. Returning to the city was like taking an icy plunge into the real world. No more starry nights, no more crickets, no more lingering over a bottle of wine before dinner on the deck overlooking the sea.

They drove to New York early the next morning. By noon, life had returned to what Lucas had, for many years, thought of as normal.

He was in his office, dressed in banker's gray Armani, meeting with his staff and planning the strategy of the next three days, which was how long the French banker would be in the city.

Someone had done a quick PowerPoint presentation. Someone else had run pages and pages of numbers. His team was sharp, intelligent, hand-picked.

But he found it difficult to concentrate.

His thoughts kept circling back to the days and nights in the Hamptons and to the perfect little world he and Caroline had created.

Leaving her this morning had been one of the hardest things he'd ever done.

"I'll call you when I can," he'd said, as he held her in his arms.

She'd fussed with his tie, smoothed back his dark hair and smiled up at him.

"I'll miss you," she'd said softly.

"No," he'd said with a quick smile, "you won't. You have all those boxes from your office to go through."

"I'll miss you," Caroline had said again, and Lucas's smile had faded. He would miss her, too. Terribly. How could a woman have won his—have won his interest so completely in only a handful of days?

"I'll get rid of the Frenchman in no time."

"You can't do that, Lucas. I don't want you to do that. I'm not going to keep you from your responsibilities."

You're my responsibility, he thought…and the realization that he wanted her to be his responsibility had stunned him.

"What?" Caroline had said, reading something in his eyes.

"Nothing." *Everything.* But he wasn't ready to think about what that meant. Not yet. Instead, he'd raised her face to his and kissed her. "We'll go somewhere special for dinner. How's that sound?"

"Anyplace would be special with you," she'd replied, and his heart felt as if it might take wing.

Now, with the hours passing, he knew he wouldn't get rid of the French banker all that quickly. He probably wouldn't even make it home for dinner, let alone in time to take Caroline somewhere special.

The Frenchman was eager to conclude a deal he'd been sitting on for months and Lucas was, too. The quicker, the better.

Then he could get back to more important things.

To Caroline.

He phoned her a few times during the day. The phone rang

and rang and then, with Mrs. Kennelly gone again, went to voice mail.

"Hi," he said whenever it did, "it's me."

He said that he missed her. That he was sorry but he wouldn't be home in time for dinner. He said he'd only just realized he had never taken her cell number and would she call him when she had the chance and give it to him.

She didn't call.

And he began to worry.

Foolish, he knew. She was capable of taking care of herself and she was not new to the city, but he worried anyway. Had she gone back to her apartment? Was she there even now, in that run-down building, that dangerous street with a dangerous burglar on the loose? He couldn't think of a reason she would be, but he knew how stubbornly independent she was.

So he worried, and it was a new experience. Worrying about someone. About a woman. Thinking about her, all the time.

It made him edgy.

He felt as if he were at some kind of turning point. Caroline dominated his thoughts. He had—he had feelings for her that transcended even what he felt for her in bed.

In midafternoon, after an endless lunch with the Frenchman, Lucas went back to his office, checked his cell phone for messages on the way, his desk phone for voice mail when he got there. He ran his hand through his hair, told himself to stop being an idiot...

And went out of his office, to his P.A.'s desk.

"Has a Ms. Hamilton phoned?"

"No, sir," she said politely, but he saw the curiosity in her eyes. Her phone rang while he was standing there. "Lucas Vieira's office," she said, listened, looked at Lucas who was already reaching for the receiver. She muted the call and shook her head. "It's a Realtor for you, sir."

A Realtor? Lucas nodded, went into his office and took the call. He'd damned near forgotten asking the guy to find an apartment for Caroline.

"Vieira here," he said briskly.

The Realtor's voice bubbled with good news. He'd found the perfect place. On Park Avenue. A building with a doorman, of course. Concierge service. Within an easy walk of Lucas's penthouse on Fifth. Three big rooms. A fireplace. A terrace. The keys were with the doorman, if Lucas wanted to take a look.

Lucas swiveled his chair around, massaged his forehead with the tips of his fingers.

"Yes," he said, "it sounds fine. But—"

But what?

But, he didn't want to think about Caroline living apart from him. Didn't want to imagine waking in the morning without her in his arms, or going to sleep at night without her head on his shoulder.

He told the Realtor he'd get back to him.

Told himself that he needed to think.

Caroline couldn't stay with him indefinitely. Of course, she couldn't. He didn't do that. He never had. He'd never had a woman living with him before. Not that a handful of days qualified as someone living with him but it was a serious change in the pattern he'd always maintained.

His mistresses always had their own places; he'd paid the rent for more than a few of them. And he'd never given any thought to doing things another way.

Live with a woman under his roof? Be with her 24/7? Wake up with her. Go to sleep with her. Start the entire thing over again the following morning?

The idea had always seemed impossible.

Now, it seemed—it seemed not just possible but, but interesting. Even enticing.

He reached for the phone, tried his penthouse again. *Ring. Ring. Ring.* And then, Caroline, sounding breathless, said, "Hello?"

"Querida." Lucas expelled a sigh of relief. "I was worried about you."

Caroline smiled. It was lovely to hear those words from her lover. It made her feel cherished.

"Why would you worry? I'm fine."

"I know. I was just being—just overly cautious, I guess." He wanted to ask if she'd gone to her apartment but decided against it. He had no right to check up on her. "Did you have a good day?"

Caroline looked at the little gaily wrapped package in her hand. It was from Barnes and Noble. Inside the wrapping was a book about the stars and the planets. They'd used Lucas's telescope one night at his beach house and argued over which group of stars was the constellation Cassiopeia and which wasn't.

The argument had ended in the way all arguments should, she thought now, loving the memory of Lucas sweeping her off her feet and into his arms.

"There's only one way to settle this," he'd said with a mock growl, and she'd squealed in equally fake indignation as he took her to his bed.

The book was to be a surprise.

She wanted badly to give him something, a gift from her that would have meaning, but the gorgeous Steuben glass sculptures, the Winslow Homer prints of ships and the sea that she'd spent the afternoon looking at were thousands of times beyond her means.

The book would be just right.

It wasn't an expensive gift, especially not for a man like him, but she'd learned enough about Lucas to know that what she'd paid for it wouldn't matter. He'd love the book because he loved looking at the stars.

And maybe he'd love it even more because it was from her.

Not that she was foolish enough to think he'd fallen in love with her but he did care for her, she was certain of that.

He'd even stopped looking at her as he had every once in a while at the beginning, an expression on his face that she couldn't read but that had frightened her just the same. It was as if he didn't approve of her, as if he were judging her, and whenever it had happened, she'd come close to asking him what he was thinking. But then that look would vanish, and why would she ask questions that might bring it back?

"Sweetheart? Are you still there?"

"Yes," Caroline said, "I'm here."

"I know I said I'd be home for dinner, but—"

"That's all right," she said, even though it wasn't. She missed him terribly. "I understand."

"Good." Not good. He'd wanted her to tell him she was devastated by the news.

"I'm liable to be very late, so if you get tired, don't wait up for me. *Sim*?"

"Sim," Caroline said softly.

But when he came home just before midnight, she was waiting in the living room, Oliver in her lap, and the minute he stepped from the elevator she put the cat aside and ran straight into Lucas's arms.

"I missed you," she said, and as he held her to his heart, he knew he wasn't going to sign the lease on that apartment for her.

He wasn't ready to let her go.

And in the very back of his mind, he began to wonder if he ever would be.

* * *

He rose at six the next morning, showered, dressed, dropped a light kiss on Caroline's hair as she slept and headed to the kitchen for a cup of coffee.

He'd told his staff to be prepared to work through the weekend. They understood. The deal was important. What they couldn't possibly know was that Lucas wanted to conclude it so he could clear his agenda for the next couple of weeks. He hadn't been to his Caribbean island since he'd bought it. He wanted to go there with Caroline. She'd love it. The privacy, the sea…

"Good morning."

He turned and saw her in the doorway, yawning, her hair in her eyes, barefoot, wearing one of his T-shirts and he thought, *No way in the world am I going to work today.*

He told her that as he poured coffee for them both and sat down beside her at the white stone counter. She shook her head.

"Of course you are," she said.

"Hey," he said, flashing her a supposedly indignant smile, "I'm the boss, remember?"

"Exactly. You're the boss. People depend on you." She fluttered her lashes and leaned toward him. "I should have known I'd be too ravishing a sight for you to deal with at this hour of the day."

She laughed but he didn't. She *was* ravishing, uncombed hair, no makeup, the tiniest fold in her cheek from sleeping with her head on his shoulder.

I love you, he thought, and the realization swept through him with the unbridled force of a tidal wave.

"Caroline," he said, "Caroline…"

No. This wasn't the moment. He'd wait until tonight, when he wasn't about to rush out the door. He'd take her someplace romantic and quiet. Candles, music, the whole sentimental thing he'd always thought foolish, and he'd put his heart in her hands.

It was a terrifying prospect but—but she cared for him. He could tell. Hell, she loved him. She had to love him...

"Lucas?" She put her hand over his. "What's the matter?"

"Nothing. I, uh, I just—I just— You know, you never gave me your cell number."

She held out her hand. He was baffled for a moment. Then he dug his cell from his pocket and gave it to her. She punched in numbers, made the entry and handed it back.

"Just don't worry if you can't reach me," she said. "I'm going job-hunting. And apartment hunting. Well, I won't try to do both today, but—"

"You don't need to do either."

Her heart skipped a beat. What did that mean? What was he thinking? About her? About their situation? Anything was possible, she thought, anything.

Even a miracle.

"You have a place to live," he said gruffly. "And if you need money..."

He took our his wallet, pulled out a sheaf of bills.

So much for miracles.

"Do not," Caroline said with sudden coldness, "do not do that."

"But if you need money—"

"I know how to earn it."

He looked at her. The uptilted chin. The defiant set to her mouth. The determined glint in her hazel eyes.

And for one awful instant, he thought, *How?*

He hated himself for it.

He had been wrong about her from Day One. She'd never taken money for sex. He'd finally come to believe it. She was incredible in bed but that was only because there was something special between them. She was innately passionate; he'd just been the man lucky enough to find that passion in her and set it free.

Why should such an ugly thought even cross his mind now?

"I almost forgot," he said, trying to lighten the moment. "The Queen of the Greasy Spoon."

She didn't move. Didn't change that look on her face. Then, finally, she nodded.

"That's me," she said, but he could still hear the tension in her voice. He wanted to tell her she wouldn't need a job or a place to live, not after tonight when he told her he wanted her to stay with him. To be with him. To be—to be—

His head was swimming. There was too much going on. The French deal. And now this.

Tonight. There'd be time to talk tonight. To figure things out. For now, he murmured her name and took her in his arms. After a minute, the tension went out of her; she leaned into him, sighed and put her arms around his neck.

"Sweetheart. *Querida*, I just want you to be happy."

"I am happy," she said softly.

She walked him to the elevator. He tilted her face to his and kissed her. But as the elevator took him away from her, Caroline wrapped her arms around herself to ward off a sudden chill.

I am not my mother, she thought fiercely. And Lucas was not like any of the men who'd used her mother so badly.

But the ugly image—Lucas, pulling that money from his pocket—lingered. And, without warning, she thought again of the way he'd looked at her every once in a while, at the start of their relationship.

She almost pressed the elevator button and went after him. But she wasn't dressed. Besides, she was being foolish.

Something soft pressed against her ankle. It was Oliver, purring like a small engine.

"Foolish," Caroline said softly, and she lifted the cat into her arms.

It was a typical New York-in-June day. Cool in the morning, warm in the afternoon, hot by the time Caroline had trudged from restaurant to diner to deli.

With zero success.

Nobody needed a waitress.

College and high school kids seemed to have snapped up all the openings. There was one possibility, in a deli near Union Square, but the manager had put his hand on her butt as she was leaving and she knew it would not stop with that, so she'd scratched the place off her list.

This time of year, the odds on a translating job were slim to none. Still, she stopped on campus anyway on the odd chance something might be available. There was, not translating, just some research on Pushkin, but the prof who needed it wouldn't be in until the next day.

Her cell phone buzzed a couple of times. Lucas, saying he just wanted to hear her voice, which went a long way toward making her feel better.

Still, she returned home—to Lucas's home—sweaty and weary. The doorman greeted her by name; the concierge, too. It felt nice, having them know her.

But she could not, must not, get used to it.

Oliver gave her his usual big greeting. Caroline picked him up, kissed his scarred head and told him what a good boy he was. She put him down, went into the kitchen, put ice in a glass, filled it with water…

Her cell phone rang.

Not Lucas. It was Dani Sinclair. Surprised, Caroline took the call.

Dani cut right to the chase.

"I have a translating job I can't do," she said briskly. "Tomorrow, four in the afternoon at the Roosevelt Hotel. It shouldn't take you more than a couple of hours. Interested?"

Caroline sat at the counter.

"I won't do anything like what I did last time, Dani. No pretending to be someone I'm not."

Dani chuckled. "Relax, sweetie. This is a straight deal. A Russian bigwig has a suite there, he's meeting with a guy representing the mayor's office. The mayor's rep will have his own translator. The Russian wants one, too. He called me because I've worked for him before but, you know, I have another engagement. What do you say?"

Despite Dani's assurances, Caroline still hesitated. The night she'd spent standing in for the other woman had left her with mixed feelings. It had led her to meeting Lucas, and that was wonderful, but the evening had had a strangeness to it she couldn't get past.

"Listen, you can't tell me you don't need the work. There's nothing much out there. You know how it is when the university's on summer session."

"You're right," Caroline said slowly. Oliver meowed and jumped into her lap. "But I might have something tomorrow."

"At school?"

"Yes. With Ethan Brustein."

"Yuck."

Caroline laughed. Professor Brustein was not well-liked. He was brilliant, but he had a nasty temper and a short fuse.

"I know. Brustein's not my idea of a good time, either, but he only wants an hour or two with me."

"The job at the hotel is three hours, minimum. Might run to four."

"Four hours," Caroline said slowly. "And I'll only have to handle the one guy?"

"Didn't I just say that?" Dani said impatiently.

"Well… Okay. Give me his name and his suite number. Oh, and how much is he supposed to pay me, and—"

"Mrroww!"

Oliver jumped to the floor, using Caroline's thigh as a springboard. Tail bushed, back arched, he stood at her feet, hissing. Caroline swung around and saw Lucas, standing in the doorway.

All her weariness vanished. She got to her feet, her lips curving in a smile.

"Lucas. What a nice sur—"

She stopped in midsentence. Lucas's face was dark. Stony. His green eyes were the color of the winter sea.

Her heart gave a resounding thump.

"Dani," she said into the phone, "I have to go."

"No, wait. I didn't give you the guy's name and—"

"I'll call you back," Caroline said, and flipped her phone shut. "Lucas? What's wrong?"

His lips drew back from his teeth in a chilling parody of a smile.

"Why should anything be wrong?"

"I don't know. That's why I asked the question." Her eyes swept over him. There it was again, that cold, accusative expression. No. This was worse. His posture was rigid, his hands were knotted at his sides. "Sweetheart. Please. What's happened?"

Lucas felt as if he were drowning in rage.

It was the first time she'd used a term of endearment instead of his name. It should have filled him with happiness. Instead, it added to his fury. How could she call him "sweetheart" after what he'd just heard? That brisk business chat with Dani Sinclair. About Caroline's return to—to work.

Bile rose in his throat.

She was standing in front of him now, staring at him through enormous eyes. She wore sandals, a pink cotton tank top and a white cotton skirt; there was a little white purse still slung across her body.

She'd obviously just come home. The doorman had told him so and he'd ridden the elevator filled with a hot combination of joy and terror at what he was about to do, to say, stepped out of it and heard her voice, followed it here, saw her looking beautiful and sweetly innocent…

Maybe that was her particular forté. That look of girlish innocence. That supposed naiveté. It had worked on him before.

But it would never work on him again.

"Lucas?"

She put her hand on his arm. He shook it off.

"I told you, nothing happened. Nothing's wrong. I came back early, that's all."

Caroline stared at him. Of course, something was wrong. Very wrong, and whatever it was, it had to do with her. She swallowed, moistened her lips with the tip of her tongue.

"I'm—I'm happy that you did."

More words to torment him. He thought of how he'd suddenly lost all interest in the contract he and the Frenchman had been discussing, how he'd shot to his feet during drinks with the man.

The banker had looked as surprised as Lucas had felt.

And then, maybe because the banker was French and the French were supposed to know about affairs of the heart, or maybe because he just couldn't keep from doing what he knew he had to do, he'd said that there was a woman, that he was sorry, that he had to leave.

The banker had smiled, risen from his chair and held out his hand.

"What is it you Americans say? Go for it, dude!"

Lucas had laughed, rushed out the door, snared a taxi, told the driver there was an extra fifty in the tip if he got him home in record time…

"Lucas. Please. Talk to me. What are you thinking? Why are you looking at me that way?"

His jaw tightened. *Slow down*, a voice within him said, *damnit, man, slow down and think.*

But he couldn't.

He felt as if he were dying and the only way to stop that from happening was to keep moving and do what he should have done right from the beginning.

Get Caroline Hamilton out of his life.

Or put her into it, but in the only way they'd both understand.

He told her to follow him.

"Follow him" turned out to be exactly what he meant.

His pace was breakneck. Into the elevator. Down to the lobby. Through it, without pause. No *hello, how are you, nice day* formalities to the concierge or the doorman, no lessening of his stride as he went out the door and started briskly toward the corner.

Caroline had to trot to keep up.

"Where are we going?" she said, but he didn't answer and finally she gave up, concentrated on trying to stay with him as they crossed Madison Avenue and approached Park where Lucas made his way to a tall apartment building. A few words to the doorman, then a key changed hands.

"Shall I send someone up with you, sir?" the doorman said.

Lucas didn't bother answering. He put his hand in the small of Caroline's back and damned near pushed her into the lobby, then into the elevator.

Her heart wasn't just thumping, it was threatening to burst from her chest.

"Lucas." Her voice shook. "Lucas, what is this about?"

Still no answer.

The elevator stopped. The doors opened. Lucas got out. Caroline told herself to stand her ground. Why should she follow him when he wouldn't tell her where they were going? When he wouldn't speak a single word? But curiosity and a simmering anger got the better of her, and she did.

Down the hall. Past two doors. Three. He came to a halt. She watched as he took a deep breath, then stabbed the key into the lock. The door swung open on a tiled foyer that opened onto a handsome living room. She saw a terrace. A fireplace. A view of Park Avenue.

Lucas's eyes were cold and flat as he motioned her forward and let the door swing shut behind her. She turned and looked at him. She could hear the beat of her heart throbbing in her ears.

"What is this place?"

"It's your new home, *querida*. Three rooms, complete with a view."

"I don't—I don't understand—"

"You can select your own furnishings. Or call ABC. Or Bloomingdale's. Let a designer handle things."

"I don't understand," she said again, but in a voice so small, so pathetic it didn't sound like her own because, of course, all at once, she did.

"I've already ordered some clothes for you. From Saks. They'll deliver whenever you—"

"I don't want any of this. Why would you even think I would?"

"The apartment is in my name. You'll charge the furniture to me, as well. I'll open accounts for you at whatever shops you like."

"Lucas!" She stepped in front of him, looked up at his stony face. She was shaking; her legs felt as if the muscles were turning to water. "Don't do this. I beg you. Don't—"

"In addition, I'll deposit forty thousand a month into whatever bank you choose."

Caroline's hand flew to her mouth. Her head was spinning. She was going to faint. Or be sick.

"Not enough? Fifty, then." Lucas reached for her hand, folded her lifeless fingers around the key. "With only one stipulation."

She gasped as he caught her wrists, hoisted her to her toes. His mouth came down on hers, hard and hurtful.

"You'll belong to me," he growled, "for as long as I want you. Nobody else. No other men. No arrangements through Dani Sinclair or some other procurer." His mouth twisted. "I don't want the smell, the taste of anyone else on you. Just me, you understand? Only me, until I'm tired of—"

Caroline wrenched away, tears streaming down her face.

"I hate you," she said, "I hate you, I hate you, I hate—"

An agonized cry broke from her throat. She whirled toward the door. Flung it open. Lucas reached out for her, then let his hand fall to his side.

The elevator swallowed her up. He was alone.

Nothing new in that. He had always been alone.

But never as much as in that last, terrible moment.

CHAPTER TWELVE

DUSK had finally faded to the cheerless dark of night.

A black, impenetrable night.

No moon. No stars. Nothing but the mournful sigh of the wind, swooping through the maze of Manhattan's concrete canyons in advance of a predicted rainstorm.

Lucas sat in his living room, a glass of Scotch between his palms. The room was dark. Not even the glow of the street lamps in Central Park, the distant lights of the city skyline, could penetrate the massing clouds.

Any minute now, he'd turn on the lamps, head into the kitchen and heat something for his dinner. He just wasn't hungry yet. Wasn't in the mood for lights, either.

The cry of the wind, the advancing storm, the all-encompassing darkness, suited his mood.

It was hard to accept you'd been played for a fool by a pretty face and a soft voice. And, damnit, it had happened to him twice in as many weeks. First Elin, now Caroline.

Lucas lifted the glass to his lips, took a long swallow.

No.

This was a night for honesty. What had happened with Elin had been little more than a petty annoyance. What had happened with Caroline was...

It was different.

For a little while, he'd thought she was—that she might

be—that there was something more than sex between them. He gave a bitter laugh.

And there had been.

There'd been her, reeling him in like a trout on a line.

"Stupid," he growled, "damned stupid fool!"

How had he let it happen? He, of all men. He'd grown up knowing what the world was like. No teddy bears and fairy tales for him. The world took. It never gave. You survived only by never forgetting that hard-won wisdom.

As for women— Another lesson learned in childhood. At his mother's knee, you might say. Women lied. They cheated. They said they loved you and then—

"Hell," he said, and drank more of the Scotch. No point in going overboard. Caroline had never said she loved him. And he, thank God, had never said he loved her.

A damned good thing, because he hadn't. He'd let himself toy with the idea, that was all.

Amazing, what a few days and nights of particularly good sex could do to a man's mind but then, a woman like Caroline would be good at sex. She'd make it an art.

And he couldn't even place all the blame on her. After all, he'd known what she was from the start. He'd just convinced himself that he had it wrong. The sighs. The whispers. The incredibly innocent, incredibly arousing ways she'd touched him, explored his body as if sex, as if men, as it everything they did when she was in his arms was new…

"Back to square one," he muttered.

She hadn't been naive. He was the one. He'd been more than naive. He'd been a fool.

Lucas drained the last of the whisky, rose to his feet and went to the sideboard where he'd left the bottle of Macallan. He poured another generous couple of inches, then drank.

Now he was compounding his stupid actions by feeling sorry for himself. Well, no way was he going to continue with that. It was unproductive. Unmanly. The thing to do was get past his anger, put what had happened in perspective.

And if that meant getting the memory of Caroline out of his head, the taste of her off his lips, so be it. When a man lived with a woman, memories of her were bound to linger.

Except, he hadn't lived with Caroline. A week didn't constitute "living with" anyone.

But he'd come painfully close to asking her to do just that. Live with him. Stay with him. Be his—his mistress. Only his mistress; he'd never have wanted her to be more than that...

And wasn't that a laugh? What was it she'd said, back when they'd met? Something about not believing in women being mistresses? Oh, yeah, she'd been good at games.

Another long drink of whisky. Maybe enough of it would thaw the lump of ice that seemed lodged in his heart.

If he'd come home five minutes sooner. Or five minutes later. Or if he hadn't been so quiet as he stepped out of the elevator, he'd never have heard that conversation.

But he'd wanted to surprise her with a declaration of—of what? Not love. *Caralho*, not that! The most he'd have said was *Caroline, will you live with me? Will you stay here with me because I—because I—*

Lucas shuddered.

Why in hell had she been making that—that appointment through the Sinclair woman? Money? He'd tried to give her some only this morning and look how that had turned out. And that time in Southampton, when he'd taken her shopping on Jobs Lane... He'd have bought out the boutique but she'd refused to let him buy anything but the simple things she absolutely needed.

It just didn't make sense.

Unless she'd been scheming for the bigger prize. Waiting and hoping he'd actually ask her to become his wife.

No. She must have known he'd never have done that.

His mistress, then. That would have been a coup. Trouble with that theory was that, basically, he'd made that offer at the Park Avenue apartment. He hadn't done it romantically but surely he'd offered her everything a woman like her could want. An expensive flat. Charge cards. A monthly stipend. Wasn't all that a fair enough substitute for hearts and flowers?

Apparently not—which left only one other possibility.

What she'd wanted from the deal she'd been making through Dani Sinclair was sex.

Sex with somebody else. With a different man. A different man than him.

A new face. A new body. Someone else's hands on her. Someone else's mouth. Rougher sex, maybe, but, goddamnit, if she wanted it rough...

Lucas hurled the glass of Scotch at the wall. The amber liquid darkened the ivory surface; shards of glass rained down on the floor.

Who gave a damn?

The cat would. If it walked on the bits of glass. Not that he gave a damn about the cat but the animal was his responsibility. For now, anyway. Tomorrow, he'd call the ASPCA.

His mouth twisted as he went to the utility closet.

Caroline had walked out on the cat, same as she'd walked out on him. And she *had* walked out on him, never mind the part he'd played.

Glass swept, wall sponged, he put everything away, glanced at the illuminated dial of his watch.

Tomorrow was Sunday but he had meetings scheduled throughout the day. His staff at eight. His attorneys at nine, his CFO and his accountants at ten. And, finally, the French banker at noon. He needed to be sharp. Alert. All this nonsense gone and forgotten. And it would be.

Damned right, it would be.

One last glass of whisky before bed...

Lightning slashed the sky; thunder roared. The storm was finally here. Good, he thought as he settled into a corner of the living room sofa. Storms, summer storms especially, always left the city seeming fresh and new.

That was how he would feel in the morning. As if he were starting over. No more thoughts of Caroline, or trying to figure out what he'd felt for her. What he'd *imagined* he'd felt for her. No more wondering how he could have fallen for that sweet and innocent act, for believing she'd cared for him.

Lucas snorted. What she'd cared about was delivering a stellar performance, starting with the masquerade that first night with the Rostovs.

Lightning lit the room again. Thunder rolled overhead, loud enough, near enough to make the whisky in the glass shiver.

Something brushed against his ankle. Lucas jerked back.

"Meow?"

It was the cat. The big, ugly, vile-tempered cat Caroline had professed to love.

Lucas glared at the creature. "What the hell do you want?"

"Mrrorw," the cat said, and this time, when lightning flashed through the room, Lucas saw that the animal was shaking.

"Don't tell me you're scared. A take-no-prisoners tough guy like you?"

The cat leaned against Lucas's leg. He could feel it trembling.

He watched the cat for a long minute. Then he put his glass on the coffee table and offered his hand, fingers outstretched, for sniffing.

"Bite me," he said, "and you'll never see a bowl of Daintee Deelites again."

The cat made a small, questioning sound. Carefully, in

what looked like slow motion, it leaned forward and pressed its battered head, face first, into Lucas's palm.

This was not fair.

Lucas was not a cat person.

The cat was not a Lucas-person.

Over the last week, they'd developed a gentleman's understanding. Lucas had tolerated the cat's presence. The cat had tolerated his. Caroline had been their go-between and yes, she was gone but the cat still had food, water and shelter.

What more could a street cat possibly want?

"Mrrow, mrrow, mrrow," the cat said in a voice that would better have suited a purebred Persian.

Lucas scowled.

"Damnit," he said, and lifted the cat into his arms. "I'm not her, okay? I don't do cuddling. And soothing. You want any of that, you've got the wrong guy."

The cat settled like a warm pillow against his chest, looked into his face, gave a meow so soft and sweet it had no business coming from The Cat from Hell.

A muscle knotted in Lucas's jaw.

"Sim," he said gruffly, "I know. She's gone. And you miss her."

He swallowed hard. Stroked his big hand over the cat's— over Oliver's—beat-up ears.

"Damnit," he whispered, "so do I."

Oliver offered another plaintive little *meow*, raised his head and rubbed it against Lucas's jaw.

Lucas closed his eyes. He felt moisture on his cheeks, tasted salt on his lips.

Did cats cry?

They must, for surely these tears could not be his.

Caroline had spent the past hours hot with rage.

She knew that her anger was all but written across her face.

She probably looked like a deranged street person. New Yorkers, inured to the odd, the unusual and, therefore, the dangerous, kept their distance, edging away from her on the subway, giving her a wide berth on the walk from the station to her old apartment house. A drunk or a doper, whatever he was, said "whoa" and scurried away as she ran up the stairs to the front door.

Good. Excellent.

Nobody was going to screw around with her and get away with it.

Caroline unlocked her apartment door, set the locks, threw her purse on the sagging sofa and began pacing from one end of the shoebox-size living room to the other.

That rat! That no-good, cold-blooded, arrogant, self-centered, self-aggrandizing… And if she was repeating herself, so be it.

"How could you?" she said. "Damn you to hell, Lucas Vieira, how *could* you?"

That awful, horrible, ugly thing he'd said. About her. About not wanting to—to smell other men on her, to taste them on her, the brutal, obvious implication being that she—that she would ever—that she was a woman who would—

"Bastard," she snarled, and kicked the sofa as she marched by.

And that look on his face. That look she'd seen on it before. That look she'd never understood. She understood it now. He'd always thought of her as—as a whore. Because that was what it came down to, didn't it? That a man who'd say such things to a woman thought that woman was—that she was little better than—than—

A sob rose in her throat. But she would not cry. She would not! Lucas didn't deserve her tears.

He was cold. He was evil. He was insane. How else to explain that after all he'd said, he'd added that he wanted her to be his mistress? He'd all but commanded it. She was to live in a place he'd paid for, wear clothes he bought her, spend money he deposited in a bank account for her so that he could have her near enough to—to use when the mood was on him.

This time, she couldn't keep a low, agonized sob from bursting from her lips.

"Stop that," she said fiercely.

What was there to cry about? She was angry, not sorrowful. She was better off without him. A thousand times better off. She just could not understand how a man who'd seemed so tender and caring could have turned into a monster right before her eyes.

Caroline flung herself down on the sofa. Snatched a throw pillow and wrapped her arms around it.

"I hate you, Lucas!"

Her voice shook but it was only with anger. Anger was what she felt, she reminded herself. It was all she felt. Why would she feel anything else, ever, for him?

What made it even worse was that she knew, in her heart, that she had to shoulder some of the blame.

She'd slept with him the first night they met. What kind of woman did that? Lots, she knew, but not someone like her.

Then, a couple of days later, she'd moved into his home. Into his bed. Let him pay for the roof over her head, the food that went into her belly. Let him take her away for what she'd thought of as a magical, impromptu weekend when he'd probably had it all planned.

He'd figured he was buying her. That she was a woman a man *could* buy…

The years she'd spent, condemning her mother's behavior, thinking of Mama as stupid for trusting men, for giving away her heart. The years she'd spent, telling herself she'd never, ever be as foolish as that.

Caroline swallowed hard.

And here she was—surprise, surprise—a proverbial chip off the old block, a foolish woman walking right in her mother's footsteps.

Caroline jumped to her feet. Enough. No way was she succumbing to self-pity!

God, the apartment was stifling! The only window in the living room was the one at the fire escape and now there was an iron gate across it. She could still open the window but the thought of it being open, gate or no gate, made her feel sick.

Water, splashed on her face and wrists would cool her off. An old trick, but sometimes it worked.

She went into the tiny bathroom, switched on the light and stared at herself in the mirror over the sink. A creature with disheveled hair and a red, blotchy face stared back.

"Pitiful," Caroline said, "absolutely pitiful, thinking that man cared for you. Thinking you cared for him. Because you didn't. You didn't. You—"

Her voice broke.

Quickly, she turned on the cold water, scooped some up and splashed it over her burning cheeks.

Lucas meant nothing to her.

Oliver did.

Tomorrow was Sunday, but Lucas would be going to his office. He'd told her so, even sounded apologetic about it. Well, as soon as she knew he'd left, she'd go collect the cat. She hated leaving him alone at Lucas's tonight…

Lucas wouldn't turn him out, would he?

No. The man obviously had a block of ice where he was supposed to have a heart but even he wouldn't do a thing like that.

Caroline reached for a towel, dried her face and hands.

It was time to make plans.

She'd get Oliver. And her things. Well, not all of them. Managing to carry a cat home on the subway would be difficult enough, assuming you could take a cat on the subway. But a cat and a suitcase—a cat, a suitcase, her laptop computer, half a dozen boxes of files and books, and the fern, she wouldn't abandon the fern…

But Oliver came first. He needed her. And she needed him. She loved him. She always would.

"You hear that, Oliver?" she said, as fiercely, as if he could hear her. "I love you. And I'll always love you. Always, Lucas, no matter what, and—"

And, she meant Oliver, of course. The cat. Not Lucas. Not him. What was there to love? Why would she waste her tears on Lucas Vieira?

"Oh, God," Caroline whispered.

She sank to the linoleum floor, brought her knees up to her chest, buried her face in her hands.

And wept.

Sunday morning dawned gray, rainy and ugly.

Mrs. Kennelly, who had Saturdays and Mondays off, arrived at her usual time. Lucas was waiting impatiently to be told his car had arrived.

"Morning, sir," she said.

Lucas grunted a reply. She looked at him, raised an eyebrow.

"Would you like me to put on some coffee?"

Another grunt.

"Perhaps Ms. Hamilton would care for—"

"Ms. Hamilton no longer lives here," Lucas said coldly. "And where in hell is my driver?"

The house phone rang. His car had arrived.

"About time," Lucas growled, and went down to the lobby.

His driver took one glance at him and didn't even venture a

"good morning." When he reached his office, his P.A. looked up from her computer, saw his face and averted her eyes.

What the hell was wrong with everybody? Lucas thought angrily, and strode past her.

Word went around. The big man had a look to him that said, *Screw with me and heads will roll.*

Nobody was that dumb. They figured something had gone wrong with the French deal. Except, they'd seen things go wrong on other occasions and he'd never looked so—so...

"So closed off," one of his assistants whispered.

Closed off. Yes. They all agreed that was the perfect description.

The good news was that nothing had gone wrong with the French deal because when Lucas met with his people, he told them the contract would be finalized today.

One of his men, younger and newer than the others, cleared his throat.

"Then, uh, then nothing's wrong, sir?"

The look Lucas flashed made them all pull their necks lower into their shirts and shrink back in their seats around the big conference room table.

"Why would you think something was wrong?" he snarled.

No one was foolish enough to answer.

He made it through the meetings.

Made it through lunch with the Frenchman.

"Did everything work out with your lady yesterday?" the Frenchman said, over a glass of red wine.

The muscle in Lucas's jaw flexed.

"Yes."

That was all he said, but a look passed between the two men.

"Sometimes," the Frenchman said quietly, "life is not quite what we expect."

Gallic wisdom? Or the Bordeaux? Lucas wasn't sure which. He simply nodded in agreement. They finished lunch, shook hands and that was that.

He got home after seven, tired, fighting a headache that had already defeated four aspirin tablets, and trying hard to concentrate on the deal he'd concluded. The Rostov contract had been important. This one would move Vieira Financial to a level all its own, something he'd been working to achieve for years.

And he thought, *So what?*

There was a note from Mrs. Kennelly on the kitchen counter. She'd had to leave a bit early, she hoped he didn't mind. And the phone was out, some sort of problem the storm had left behind. The phone company promised things would be back to normal within the next several hours.

Lucas showered. Put on jeans, a T-shirt, mocs. Started for the stairs and, instead, walked slowly down the hall, to the guest suite.

Caroline's things were still there. Her scent, that soft vanilla fragrance, was in the air.

The ridiculous fern stood on a table near the window, but it didn't look as pathetic anymore. The fronds were green, lacy, healthy. A little TLC had revived it.

That was the thing about tender, loving care. It could work wonders.

Lucas scowled, went downstairs to the kitchen, checked to be sure Oliver had food and water. He did. So did Lucas. There were a couple of bottles of Corona in the refrigerator and a pan of something on the counter.

Lucas opened a beer, heated the pan, dumped the contents on a plate and poked at it with his fork. Oliver came into the kitchen, tail up and crooked, looked at him and said, *"Meow?"*

"Yeah," Lucas said, "hello to you, too." He stabbed at his dinner again. Looked at Oliver. "Wanna try some?"

The cat approached. Accepted a tidbit from Lucas's fingers. Chewed, swallowed, but Lucas could see the cat was just being polite.

"Me, too," he said, and dumped the rest into the trash. When he sat down again, the cat jumped into his lap.

"So," Lucas said, "how was your day?"

"Mrrow."

"Good. I'm glad to hear it. My day was fine, too."

"Meow?"

"I concluded a deal. I'm excited about it."

About as excited as the cat had been over that mouthful of food. Lucas sighed, scooped Oliver into his arms and walked into his study, sank down on a burgundy leather love seat, the cat in his lap.

"About this deal…"

The cat shut its eyes. Lucas nodded.

"To tell you the truth, I don't much give a damn, either. Crazy, isn't it? Last month, last week, I'd have been doing handstands…"

Last month, last week, he had not yet met Caroline.

And he had not yet lost her.

He cleared his throat. "The thing is," he said, "I know I should feel pleased about this French thing, but—"

But, he didn't feel much of anything.

Except alone. And lost. And painfully, brutally lonely. For Caroline, and wasn't that pathetic? Amazing, how good her masquerade had been, that he should think he missed her now.

He thought of those couple of days in the Hamptons. The joy she'd taken—the joy she'd seemed to take in the simple things they'd done. Walking the beach. Swimming in the pool. Strolling the streets of the village, hand in hand with him.

Watching the stars burn against the black silk of the night sky.

"Oh, how beautiful," she'd said.

"Beautiful," he'd agreed, but he'd been talking about her. Not just her face but her sweetness, that special quality that made her the woman she was.

The woman he'd thought she was.

Could he... Was there any possibility he'd been wrong? Heard what she'd said wrong? Misunderstood it? His throat constricted. Maybe. Maybe...

No. He'd heard the conversation. Her end of it, anyway, heard her say those things to Dani...

He gave himself a couple of seconds. Then he put Oliver on the love seat and went to his desk. He had to keep busy. That was what he always did, what he had done all his life. He'd make some notes about an investment that had caught his eye, some details he wanted researched...

What was that?

A small package sat on the edge of his desk, half-hidden by his appointment calendar. It was brightly wrapped, tied with a ribbon, festooned with a bow.

Puzzled, he tore open the wrapping paper. There was a small book inside.

A Guide To The Stars.

He felt a sudden tightness in his throat.

Slowly, carefully, he opened the book to the title page. And saw an inscription done in a delicate, feminine hand.

For Lucas, in memory of a starry, starry night.
Your Caroline

Lucas didn't move. Didn't blink. He just stared at the page. At what she'd written, what she'd said, how she'd signed her name. Not just "Caroline" but "Your Caroline."

How many times had he thought of her just that way? As his. His Caroline. His loving, giving, innocent Caroline. Because she was all those things.

She was.

"God," he whispered, "oh, God!"

What had he done?

To hell with what he'd overheard in that phone call. Everything he'd accused her of being, of doing, was a lie. His Caroline had never sold herself, never given herself to anyone or anything except with honesty and honor. He knew that as surely as he knew that the world was round.

Whatever he'd overheard in the phone conversation surely had a simple explanation.

Why hadn't he asked? Better still, why had he let himself leap to such an ugly conclusion?

Because he was a coward. Because he'd been terrified of putting his heart in Caroline's hands. Because he'd been afraid she'd break it.

Because it had been safer to drive her away.

He loved her.

He'd loved her from that first night when she'd dealt with him, with Leo Rostov, with Ilana Rostov, with all the unexpected nonsense he'd dumped on her, and never once flinched.

He'd loved her as soon as she'd gone into his arms, kissed him, responded to his passion with all the honesty in her heart, just as if they'd been waiting for each other all their lives.

And he had been. Waiting. For her. For his Caroline. For a love that was fearless and deep and true.

A love he had pushed away.

Could he get her back? Would she ever speak to him again, much less love him? Because she had loved him. She had loved him as he loved her until he'd said those terrible things…

"Mrrrow," Oliver said from the depths of the leather love seat.

He had to get her back, but he needed a plan. He never acted on anything without a plan.

"Mrrow," the cat said again.

Well, that wasn't exactly true. He hadn't planned any of what had happened with Caroline. That was how he'd won her. And how he'd lost her.

Lucas shot to his feet. Got a jacket. Five seconds later, he was gone.

Caroline stood on Fifth Avenue, Central Park behind her, Lucas's condominium building directly opposite her on the other side of the street.

It was raining. Drizzling, really, but the stuff was cold and she'd left her apartment in such a mad rush that she'd neglected to take an umbrella or a rain jacket.

What now? she kept thinking, but she couldn't come up with an answer.

She had come to get Oliver after a day of trying to reach Mrs. Kennelly with no success. She'd phoned first thing this morning but nobody answered. Voice mail didn't pick up, either.

She'd tried again. And again. And again. The phone just kept ringing. Either nobody was home or nobody was answering the phone, and that left her with a problem.

The last thing she wanted was to go to Lucas's building, take the elevator to his penthouse and have the bad luck of finding him there. Not that he meant anything to her. That was over. She just didn't want any unpleasant run-ins, that was all.

And then there was another possibility. It was even worse.

Suppose she walked into the lobby and the doorman who'd

been so friendly, the concierge who'd been so nice, told her that Mr. Vieira had left instructions to deny her entrance to his apartment?

To his life.

She wasn't sure she could have survived that.

So she'd kept phoning, pausing only long enough to take a call from Dani, who'd wanted to know if she was going to do the translating job or not.

"Not," Caroline had said, and then she'd taken a long, deep breath because, by now, it was all coming together, Lucas's fury when he found her accepting money from Dani, his fury when he'd overheard that phone call. Little things had finally added up, and she was entitled to some answers. "Dani?" she'd said. "How can you afford that townhouse? Those clothes? What, exactly, do you do for a living?"

Dani had given a low, delighted laugh.

"You're such a country mouse, Caroline! I thought you'd never figure it out. What I do for a living is just what you think I do." The laughter had left her voice. "And don't you dare sit in judgment on me!"

No, Caroline thought, she wouldn't. Who was she to sit in judgment on anyone after these last few days?

Judging Lucas, though... That was different. That he could have thought she was—she was what Dani was. Or that she was with him for his money...

Never mind.

Right now, Oliver was her sole concern. She was sure he must be scared half to death, alone and lonely as he tried to stay out of Lucas's way. She had to go and get the cat, no matter what happened in the process.

"You are not a coward," she'd told herself grimly, only a couple of hours ago.

Wrong, she thought now. She *was* a coward. Standing here, in the cold drizzle, instead of going to get her cat, proved it.

That she'd let herself think she still loved Lucas proved it, too. She didn't love him, of course. She knew that, now. She was a romantic fool, was all, and—

The light changed. Caroline took a deep breath, stepped off the curb and ran across the street. The lobby door opened.

"Ms. Hamilton," the night doorman said, "what are you doing out on an evening like—"

A sudden gust of wind all but tore the heavy door from his hand. Caroline staggered forward. Her hair whipped across her face, obscuring her vision, and she stumbled against something hard and big and unyielding...

Not "something."

Lucas.

She knew it even before he said, in a tones of disbelief, "Caroline?" She knew it because she knew the feel of him, the scent of him, and her heart began to thud.

She was a coward, after all. And a liar, because just the sound of his voice made her eyes fill with tears.

She spun away, ready to run, but his arms closed around her and he said her name again and she gave a little sob and he swung her toward him, lifted her off her feet and kissed her. For a heartbeat, she yielded to the kiss. Then, she pulled back.

"Don't," she said. "Don't you dare touch me, Lucas Vieira!"

"Caroline. Sweetheart—"

"How could you think such a thing? That I was—that I would—"

"Because I'm an idiot. That's how."

"You're worse than that." Her voice broke. "You're—you're a horrid, terrible man, and I—"

"I love you, *querida*."

"Do not *'querida'* me," she said fiercely, and slammed her fist against his shoulder.

"Caroline. I love you with all my heart. With my soul. I've loved you from the minute we met."

"Too bad, because I don't feel anything for you."

Lucas drew her to him. "Kiss me," he said, "and then tell me you don't feel anything for me."

"No. Why would I kiss you? Why would I—"

He kissed her.

"I hate you," she said, against his mouth. "I hate you, Lucas, I hate—"

He kissed her again, tasted her tears and his own.

"I despise you," she whispered, and he kissed her a third time and said he understood that she despised him, she had every right to despise him, but that didn't have to mean she didn't love him, too.

Caroline laughed. She was still crying, but she laughed anyway. How could she not? Had there ever been a man as arrogant, as impossible as her Lucas?

"I love you," he said. "I adore you."

"But you said—you believed—"

"No. I didn't. What I believed was that you were sweet and good, that you were everything I had ever dreamed of finding." Gently, he kissed her tear-dampened eyes. "I was afraid of how you made me feel, *querida*. I thought that loving you was a weakness. If I gave you my heart and you broke it…"

Caroline looked into the dark, pleading eyes of the man she loved.

"That apartment…"

Lucas nodded. "I wanted it for you." She tensed, and he shook his head. "Wait. Hear me out. It wasn't the way I made it sound." He cleared his throat. "I started out just wanting you to have a safe place to live. When we first met."

"A week ago," Caroline said with a watery laugh.

Lucas lowered his head, rested his forehead against hers.

"A lifetime ago," he said. "But then I decided against it because—because I came up with a better idea."

"What better idea?"

"I decided that the best way to keep you safe was to ask you to stay with me. To live with me." He took a steadying breath. *Deus*, he had not felt this vulnerable since the day he'd walked into his first foster home. "To become my wife."

Her heart skipped a beat but she kept her eyes on his.

"That's going a long way, just to keep a woman safe."

He smiled. "Yes," he said softly, "it is. But that's what a man does, when he loves a woman. He asks her to marry him." He tucked strands of wet hair behind her ear. "I could hardly wait to get home." He paused. This was the bad part. "I got out of the elevator and you were talking to Dani Sinclair about a job."

"She offered me a translating job. But you thought—you thought—" Her voice shook. "How could you have believed that of me?"

"What I believed was that everything I'd always known was true. That love is ephemeral. That happiness is fleeting. That what a man most loves, he loses."

Caroline took a deep breath. "You haven't lost me," she whispered, and Lucas kissed her. It was a long, sweet kiss but when it ended, he knew there was more to tell her.

"You need to know that I—that I have not led what you might call an exemplary life."

"You have. You're a good man," she said with fierce conviction.

"I was not a good child, *querida*. I told you I was poor. I didn't tell you that I was a thief. A pickpocket. That I robbed, stole money, clothing, food, anything I could. That I fought with others like savages over scraps of food. I did whatever I had to do to survive. And I learned not to trust anyone." He paused. "Sometimes, those instincts are still with me."

Tears rose in Caroline's eyes.

"It breaks my heart to think of you living like that," she whispered.

"Caroline. *Querida*, I'm not asking for your pity."

"You don't understand. Same as you, I know how the past can affect the present." Her eyes searched his. "I promised myself I'd never be like my mother. That I'd never believe in a man, trust him, only to learn that he'd deceived me."

"You can trust me. You can believe in me. I swear it." Lucas gathered Caroline close against him. "I love you. I'll always love you. All I ask is that you love me. And Oliver. He wants you back," he said solemnly. "And so do I. Marry me, sweetheart. Love me forever, as I will love you."

It wasn't a question, it was a statement. Caroline smiled through her tears. Her arrogant, assured, wonderful Brazilian lover was back.

"I love you, Lucas," she said softly. "I adore you. And I will be your wife, forever."

Lucas kissed her, to a smattering of applause.

"Congratulations," the doorman and the concierge said.

Caroline blushed. Lucas grinned. Then he swept his bride-to-be into his arms and took her home.

HIRED FOR THE
BOSS'S BEDROOM

CATHY WILLIAMS

CHAPTER ONE

OF COURSE, Leo had known what his mother was thinking when she had said, without any hint of inflection in her voice, that they had hoped he might have arrived a little earlier—several hours earlier, she could have said, were she to have been absolutely precise. Instead, she had held back her obvious disappointment and had listened to his excuses without comment.

Meetings had overrun. An urgent call had come through just as he had been leaving the office. Inevitable Friday traffic. Leo had kept the excuses brief, knowing that his mother would never actually tell him exactly what she was thinking, would never express disapproval or condemnation. In fact, he doubted whether there had been any need at all to make excuses, but politeness had driven him to apologise just as politeness had driven his mother to respond as she had, without any hint of censure.

'Daniel,' she had said eventually, 'has popped out to see Heather. Just next door. The quickest way is to walk across the fields to her house, but I expect you would rather drive. Or, of course, you could wait here. I told Heather that he was to be back no later than seven.'

'I'll walk.' He would not take the car because, as a city gent, a billionaire who had no time for country walks, he would never choose to wait.

So now here he was, sampling at first hand the extensive acreage that surrounded the exquisite country house which he had bought for his mother over six years ago following his father's death.

Leo had never stepped foot beyond the neatly manicured gardens surrounding the house. Naturally, he had known that the grounds stretched as far as the eye could see, encompassing fields and a thickly wooded area which became lush with lilac lavender during the warm summer-months. Hadn't he, after all, carefully read the reports sent to him by the people he had commissioned to find the property in the first place? Hadn't he duly noted the practicality of his mother living in a house which would not, in due course, find itself surrounded by housing estates due to greedy building contractors having no respect for open space?

But only now, as he tramped across the endless fields, inappropriately clad in handmade leather shoes and a pale-grey suit which had cost the earth, did he appreciate the true size of his investment. Surely his mother, now edging towards her seventies, didn't ever explore the furthest reaches of the estate?

It occurred to him that in truth he had no real inkling as to what his mother did from one day to the next. He dutifully telephoned three times a week—or considerably more now that Daniel had landed on the scene—and was told that she was fine, Daniel was fine, the house was fine, *life* was fine. Then he would attempt to have a conversation with Daniel, which elicited much the same response but in a rather more hostile tone of voice. The details of this *fine* life were never painted in, so he was at a loss to know whether his mother actually realised just how much walking this hike to 'the house next door' entailed.

He cursed himself for thinking that he would enjoy the

fresh air and exercise. Fresh air, he acknowledged—swatting past some brambles, while the summer sunshine reminded him of the folly of venturing out in the countryside wearing a jacket—was best confined to those brief mini-breaks called holidays which he took a couple of times a year—usually combining them with work, women or, more often than not, both. As for exercise, he got ample amounts of that at his London gym where he thrashed out the stress of his high-powered job on a punching bag and then cooled down with fifty-odd laps in the Olympic-sized swimming pool. No one could accuse him of being unfit. This, however, seemed to require a different sort of stamina. He found himself wishing that he had had the foresight to bring his mobile phone with him, because he could have usefully used the time to make a couple of calls, which he would now have to do when he returned to the house.

Heather's house, his mother had assured him, couldn't be missed—it was a small, white, cosy cottage and the garden was spilling over with flowers of every description. Her face had softened when she had said this, and he had wondered whether Heather was one of her pals from the village, someone with whom she shared gossip once a week over pots of tea.

Or something along those lines, at any rate.

It was a heartening thought. Somehow he felt less of the guilty older-son, knowing that his mother had someone virtually on her doorstep with whom she could pass the time of day. And less of the guilty absentee-father, knowing that this kindly neighbour had also bonded with his son.

The cottage in question leapt out at him without warning, and his mother was right; there was no danger of him missing it. 'Strike out west and head for the house that looks as though it belongs in the pages of a fairy tale'. Leo hadn't realised that so many types of flora existed, and he surprised himself by pausing for a couple of seconds to admire the profusion of colour.

Then he circled the cottage, noting the white picket-fence, the clambering roses, all those tell-tale signs of someone who was seriously into clichés. He almost expected to spot a couple of garden gnomes peering out from between the riot of flowers that bordered the little stone path to the front door, but fortunately he was spared that particular horror.

Leo himself was minimalist to the bone. His London pent-house apartment paid homage to the axiom 'less is more': black leather, chrome and glass. On the white walls, outra-geously expensive, abstract paintings were splashes of colour that slowly appreciated in value even as they adorned his walls; it was why he had bought them in the first place.

The door knocker appeared to be some quirky, mythical creature. Leo banged on it twice, just in case he was dealing with someone hard of hearing.

He heard the sound of quickly approaching footsteps, and something that sounded like muffled laughter. Then the door was opened and he found himself staring down into the bluest eyes he had ever seen. A tangle of pure gold, curly hair framed a heart-shaped face, and as his eyes involuntarily travelled further downwards they took in the small, curvaceous figure that, in a society that prized the stick-thin figure, would be labelled 'overweight'.

'Who are you?' he demanded without preamble, lounging against the door frame.

'You must be Daniel's dad.' Heather stood aside to let him enter. She couldn't help herself. Disapproval had seeped into her voice, and he must have noticed it, because his ebony brows pleated into a frown.

'And you must be Heather. I was expecting someone... older.'

Heather could have told him that he was exactly what *she* had been expecting. Her neighbour Katherine had talked about him, of course, had told her all about his meteoric career in the city. And Heather had heard between the lines a description of a workaholic, someone who was driven to succeed, someone who had precious little time for the things that mattered most in life. A lousy son and an even lousier father.

Up close and personal, he was every inch the successful businessman she had expected.

He was also incredibly good-looking; this bit was doing its best to nudge a hole in her disapproval. A lot better looking than those grainy pictures she had been shown in the scrap book Katherine kept of all his achievements, in fact. Indeed, the man was drop-dead gorgeous. Raven-black hair framed a face whose perfect, chiselled symmetry was harshly, coolly sensational. His eyes were grey and watchful, eyes that chose to give nothing away. She felt a shockingly potent quiver of awareness, then thankfully the moment was gone, lost under the weight of her disapproval.

Charitable by nature, Heather knew that it was crazy to judge a book by its cover, but she had had more than a passing brush with arrogance and success. Some women might find all that power and wealth an incredible turn on, but she knew from first-hand experience the price that had to be paid for being attracted to such dazzling light: too high.

'I have come for my son.' Having cursorily inspected the tiny hall, with its cosy flag-stoned floor and bowls of flowers on the window ledges by the door, Leo swung back round to face the woman who appeared to be dithering by the front door.

It had been a hot day, and she was wearing what looked

like a loose, flowing gypsy-style affair, the sort of outfit that had been fashionable once upon a time. She was also looking at him with the sort of expression that promised a lecture, given half a chance. Leo sincerely hoped she would keep whatever was on her mind to herself, and he had an inkling of an idea what it was. He had no time for lectures, well-intentioned or otherwise.

'He's just finishing his tea.'

'His *tea*?'

'Dinner, if you prefer.'

'Why is he eating here? I told my mother that I would take them both out for something to eat.'

'I guess he just got hungry.' Heather refrained from adding to that statement. The fact was, Daniel had refused point-blank to have dinner with his father.

'Well, thank you very much, but it might have been worth finding out first whether plans had been made.'

This was just too much. Heather slipped past Leo to the kitchen, where she told Daniel that his father was here, and registered his expression of scowling indifference. Then she quietly shut the kitchen door and folded her arms.

'On the subject of *plans*…' she delivered coldly, ignoring the forbidding expression on his face.

'Before you go any further, I'm in no mood to listen to someone I don't know from Adam climbing on a podium and giving me a lecture.'

Faced with such a blunt, arrogant dismissal of what she had been about to say, Heather's mouth dropped open, and Leo took that as immediate and obedient closure on a subject about which he had little interest. He walked past her towards the kitchen but she caught his wrist. It was like being zapped with a very powerful electric charge, and it took all her will power to stand her ground and not cower. She suspected that this was a man who specialised in inspiring fear.

'I think we should talk before you get your son, Mr West.'

'The name's Leo; I think we can dispense with the formalities, considering you're apparently an honorary member of the family.' He looked at her small hand circling his wrist and then back to her face. 'And I guarantee that whatever you have to say is going to be of little interest to me. So why not spare yourself the sermon?'

'I don't intend to give you a sermon.'

'Wonderful! Then what exactly is it you want to talk about?' He glanced at his watch. 'But you'll have to make it short, I'm afraid. It's been a hellish trip up here, and I have work to do when I get back to the house.'

Heather took a deep breath. 'Okay. I *am* a little annoyed.'

Leo made no effort to conceal his impatience. In that rarefied world in which he lived, people didn't get *annoyed* with him—least of all women—but this one was practically pulsating, so he shrugged. He would let her have her say, and then he would clear off with his son. 'Okay. Spit it out.'

'In the sitting room. I don't want Daniel to hear us.'

She led the way, acutely conscious of him behind her. Once they were both in the room, staring at each other like combatants in an arena, she said in a controlled voice, 'I don't think you realise how disappointed Daniel was that you didn't make it to his Sports Day. It's a big deal at the school, and he'd been practising for weeks.'

Leo flushed guiltily. Of course he had known that this would be flung at him but it still irked him, that this perfect stranger had the brazenness to stand there, staring at him with wide, accusing, critical eyes.

'That, as I explained to my mother, was unavoidable—

and, now you've got that off your chest, I think I'll leave with my son.'

'Why was it unavoidable?' Heather persisted. 'Don't tell me that there was something more important than seeing your son come first in the hundred-metre sprint?'

'Actually, I don't have to tell you anything,' Leo informed her coolly. 'I don't make a habit of explaining myself to anyone, least of all someone I've known for—what?—roughly fifteen minutes. I don't recall my mother even mentioning your name in any of the conversations I've had with her.'

That came as no surprise to Heather. Daniel went to the local private school. He stayed in the house with Katherine, and occasionally, over the past eight months his father had deigned to visit, usually on a Sunday; a full weekend presumably was just too much for him. More often than not, he imported both Katherine and Daniel to London, sending his driver to collect them on the Saturday morning, and delivering them back to the country promptly on the Sunday afternoon.

Anyone would think that a man who had lost his son for years, when his ex-wife had disappeared off to Australia, would have wanted to spend as much time as possible making up for the wasted time!

Clearly not the man standing in front of her.

Katherine would not have mentioned Heather because her son would have had zero interest in finding out about the people who figured in his mother's life. From what Heather had gleaned, Leo West was an utterly selfish money-making machine.

'I realise I don't have any right to tell you how to lead your life,' Heather said, doing her best to be fair, 'but Daniel needs you. He would never say so because he's probably scared of you.'

'Has he told you that he's scared of me?' This conversation was now becoming bizarre. He had expected to be greeted by a motherly lady, maybe to be offered a cup of tea, which he would, naturally, have refused; to leave with his son in tow, any sullenness over his absence at the wretched Sports Day to be forgotten when he presented him with the present he had bought. It was the very latest mobile phone, capable of doing pretty much anything bar washing the dishes and cooking the meals.

Instead, he was being held to account by a twenty-something girl with a challenged sense of dress who had probably never set foot out of the village.

'He doesn't have to. I can tell. He doesn't see enough of you. I know it's none of my business, but relationships have to be worked on. Daniel's a very vulnerable little boy, and he needs his father. Especially now. He's suffered the loss of his mother. He needs the security of his dad to see him through.'

'You're right—it's none of your business.'

'You're not much into listening to what other people have to say, are you?' Heather flared angrily.

'On the contrary, I spend a good deal of my time listening to what other people have to say. I just have no interest in an interfering neighbour regaling me with amateur psychobabble—unless, of course, you have some kind of degree in child psychology. Do you?'

'No, I don't, but—'

'Well, maybe you're his teacher, hmm…?'

'No, I'm not. But that's not the—'

'And you're not exactly a lifelong friend of my mother's, are you? I'm sure, if you were, I might just have a passing idea of who you are.'

'No, but—'

'In fact, when and how did you exactly come into contact with my mother?'

'We met a while back, at a gardening convention at the

village hall. A television celebrity was giving a talk about orchids, and we both just—'

'Fascinating, but here's what I'm wondering—what's a young girl like you doing at *gardening conventions*? Isn't that the luxury of retired people who have endless time on their hands to potter around in their gardens? Don't you have more exciting things to do? You know, if you did, maybe you wouldn't find yourself drawn to nosing into other people's lives.'

Leo was in equal measure outraged that she'd dared to voice opinions that breached his personal boundaries, and borderline distracted by the rising tide of colour that was colouring her cheeks. The woman blushed like a virgin, and it struck him that he wasn't very often in the company of a woman whose face was so transparent. He favoured the career woman, and it had to be said that career women weren't given to blushing.

'How *dare* you?'

'Pretty easily, as a matter of fact,' Leo commented smoothly. 'Don't go on the attack unless you're ready for a fight—first law of success.'

Heather looked at the impossibly handsome man staring coolly at her, and wanted to fly across the room and punch him in his arrogant face. That reaction was so out of character for her that she closed her eyes briefly and blinked it away. She was placid by nature, not given to screeching hysterics. So who was this wild creature that had taken over her body?

'Okay,' she said tightly. 'You're right. Your relationship with your son is no business of mine. I'll go and get him right now.' She walked towards the door and only looked at him to say quietly, 'And, for your information, I have a job and I don't *nose* into other people's private lives because I have nothing better to do with my life. I wanted to be helpful. I'm very sorry you misread my intentions.'

Instead of feeling like the victor in what had always promised to be a pointless exchange from where he was standing, Leo now felt like the villain. How had that happened? He had said what needed to be said, had told her to keep out of his business, she had agreed—so why did he now feel as though he had won the battle but lost the war?

Always the winner in any verbal showdown, Leo was unaccustomed to being caught on the back foot, and for the first time he was rendered temporarily speechless. He found that he was staring into space and hurried out, almost bumping into Daniel, who greeted him with a sulky glower.

'I… I apologise for missing your Sports Day, Daniel,' Leo began, very much aware of Heather standing in the background—probably committing this awkward little scene to memory so that she could bring it out at a later date and use it against him should the opportunity ever again arise.

'Whatever.'

'I hear you came first in the hundred-metre sprint,' Leo said, trying to bring the tension down a notch or two. 'Well done!'

He looked at Heather, and as their eyes tangled she felt a wave of sympathy for the man. Of course, he didn't deserve her sympathy. From all accounts, he threw money at his son but rarely gave him the time that was so essential. But, her naturally warm nature reluctantly seeing the situation from both points of view, how hard it must be, she thought, for him to incorporate a young child into his life? Up until eight months ago, he had been completely unaware of his son's existence, and had been accustomed to doing everything his own way, with no need to consider the welfare of another human being.

'He's a star,' she interjected into the silence, moving forward and pulling Daniel towards her in a natural embrace. She wondered how his father couldn't be charmed by his gorgeous, dark-haired seven-year-old son with those big brown eyes and skinny, vulnerable legs sticking out from his school shorts, which he had yet to change out of. 'Aren't you, Dan?' She ruffled his hair affectionately and then said brightly, 'You have a wonderful weekend, and don't forget you can pop over any time if you want help with your English homework!'

Relegated to the sidelines, Leo saw that rarest of things, a shy smile of warmth and affection from his son. Naturally not directed at *him*, but a smile nevertheless. He looked at his watch and said briskly, 'I think we should be heading back to the house now, Daniel; leave Heather to get on with…whatever she has to get on with.'

'Can't you come across on the weekend?' Daniel suddenly turned to Heather with a pleading look, which of course immediately made Leo frown impatiently. Was his own company so dire that his son needed rescuing from any possibility of prolonged, unwanted bonding at all costs? Leo was uncomfortably reminded of Heather's little talk, the first little talk he had had on the subject of his son since he had met him on that plane at Heathrow all those months ago.

'We could go see that Disney movie,' Daniel was now saying with a touch of desperation in his voice. 'You know, you told me that you wanted to see it but you would have to rent a child to take along…'

'I'm sorry, Daniel. I've got heaps of things to do, and I was just teasing when I said that I wanted to see that movie. I don't actually *like* Disney movies.'

'You've got lots of them in that cabinet in your sitting room,' Daniel was quick to point out, with the unerring talent of a child to say precisely the wrong thing at the wrong time.

Heather reddened, cleared her throat, could think of nothing to say, reddened a bit more and eventually broke the expectant silence. 'I'll think about it.'

Of course, she had no intention of going to a movie with them, or going anywhere else for that matter.

She had spoken her mind, for better or for worse, and had met with a resounding lack of success. Leo West was egotistical, driven to the point of obsession and would never take advice from anyone, least of all from a woman like her. Hadn't he assumed that she busied herself meddling in other people's lives because she had no life of her own?

She had a life. A very good one!

In the stillness of the cottage, which seemed unnaturally quiet when her warring visitors had disappeared, she considered the excellent life she had.

Wonderful job, doing the one thing she couldn't have been happier doing, illustrating children's books, getting inspiration from her garden which she translated into pictures that were slowly achieving notoriety as works of art in themselves. She worked from home, travelling into London once a month so that she could go through her graphics with her art editor. It was a real luxury.

She also owned her cottage outright. No mortgage; no debt owing, in fact, to anyone. Which made her as free as a bird.

True, there was no man in her life, but that, she told herself, was exactly how she wanted it.

Little snippets of her past intruded into her peaceful cottage: Brian, as she had first known him when she had still been a young girl of eighteen and he had been on the brink of his glittering career. Blonde hair, straight, thick and always falling across his face, until he had had it cut because, he had told her seriously, in his profession men all wore their hair short.

Heather blinked and shoved that little nest of bitter memories back into their Pandora's box. She had learnt years ago that dwelling on things that couldn't be changed was a waste of time.

Instead, she shifted her attention to the kitchen which still bore the remnants of Daniel's hastily eaten meal of spaghetti Bolognese. His father, he had told her, had planned on taking them out to dinner but he hadn't wanted to go. He hated those fancy restaurants they went to. He hated the food. As a postscript, he had added that he hated his father.

Which made her start thinking of Leo and, once she started, she found that she couldn't seem to stop. That cold, ruthless face swam into her head until she was forced to retreat to her little office and try and lose herself in the illustration she was currently working on. She was peering at the detail of a fairy wing, every pore in her being focused on the minute detail of painting, when the bang on her front door sent her jerking back, knocking over the jar of water, which shattered into a thousand pieces on the wooden floor.

A second bang, more demanding this time, had her running to the front door before she had time to clean up the slowly spreading mess on the ground.

She pulled open the door before a third bang brought down the roof.

'*You!* What are you doing here?' He was no longer in his suit. Instead, he was wearing a pair of cream trousers and a navy-blue polo shirt. Behind him was a gleaming silver Bentley.

At nearly nine in the evening, the sun had faded to a dull, mellow, grey light.

Leo dealt Heather a grim nod. 'Believe me, I don't want to be here any more than you want me to be here, but I have been put in the difficult position of having to ask you to accompany us to the cinema tomorrow. Daniel has dug his heels in and refused to budge. I'm being blackmailed by someone who hasn't even graduated to books without pictures. It's ridiculous, but it's true, hence the reason I'm here when I should be reading over a due-diligence report that can't wait.'

'I don't know what you're talking about.'

'Why don't you let me in and I can explain?'

'I'm sorry, but can't this wait until tomorrow? It's late, and I have stuff to do.'

'Late?' Leo made a show of consulting his watch. 'It's ten past nine. On a Friday night. Since when is that *late*?'

Heather heard the amused incredulity in his voice and felt her hackles rise.

'I was *working*,' she said stiffly.

'Of course. You never got around to telling me exactly what you do for a living.'

'You aren't interested in what I do for a living.'

Leo thought that she was spot on with that, but circumstances had forced his hand. He had returned to the house with Daniel in frozen silence and had endured what could only be called silent warfare.

The mobile phone had been looked at and then refused, on the grounds of, 'Thank you very much, but the teacher doesn't allow mobile phones at school.'

And, 'It's a kind thought, but young children don't need mobile telephones,' from his mother.

Frustration had almost driven him to ask his mother what the hell was going on because surely, *surely*, this complete lack of co operation couldn't just be caused by the fact that he had missed a Sports Day! But Katherine had taken herself off to bed at a ridiculously early hour, and so here he was, compelled to try and do a patch-up job with the amateur psychologist in the hope that the weekend might not end up a complete write-off.

'You seem to have something on your face…' He rubbed his finger along the blue streak adorning her chin and gazed in bemusement at his finger. 'What is it? Paint? Is that how you spend your Friday evenings—painting your house?'

Heather pushed the door, but Leo wasn't having any of that. He wedged his foot neatly into the open space and met her hostile stare with a grimly determined expression.

'You can't just come here and disturb me at this hour,' she said through gritted teeth.

'Needs must. Now, are you going to let me in?' He stood back and raked his hands impatiently through his hair. 'I don't suppose,' he said heavily, 'that I was the only father who didn't make it to the Sports Day.' It was a concession of sorts and as close to an olive branch that Leo was going to offer.

Situation defused.

'Yes.'

'You're kidding, right?'

'No, I'm not. Every single parent was there, taking pictures. Daniel had asked me to come along to watch, pretended that he didn't care whether you came or not, but I watched him, and he kept looking around for you, wondering if you were somewhere in the crowd.'

'Are you going to let me in?' Leo asked brusquely, not liking this image of himself as some kind of heartless monster.

Heather reluctantly opened the door and allowed him to stride past her. She hadn't noticed earlier, but he dominated the space—not just because he was tall, but because of that aura he exuded, an aura of supreme power. He owned the air around him in a way that Brian never had, even though it had seemed so at the time. She shivered.

'So, where were you painting?' Leo asked, looking around him. He had quizzed his mother about Heather, ignoring her look of surprise at his interest, and had gleaned that she and Daniel trotted over to the cottage whenever they had a chance. Heather had, it would seem, become quite a fixture in the household. Little wonder that she had been polishing her soapbox in anticipation of his arrival.

He followed her into a room at the back of the house, and was confronted by walls on which hung every manner of artwork. Yet more were housed in an antique architect's chest against the wall.

'I broke my glass,' Heather said, kneeling down so that she could begin carefully picking up the shards. 'When you banged on the door. I wasn't expecting anyone.'

'You...paint?'

Heather looked briefly at him and blushed, suddenly feeling vulnerable as those flint-grey eyes roved over the artwork on her walls. 'I told you that I had a job,' she said, before resuming her glass-collecting task. It would take a heck of a lot more elbow grease to fully clean the ground, but the biggest bits had been collected; the elbow grease would have to wait until the morning, because right now she was finding it hard to think properly. She just wanted him out of her cottage so that she could get her scattered wits back into order.

Leo dragged his eyes away from the paintings and focused entirely on the woman standing in front of him. When she had told him that she had a job, he had assumed something along the lines of a secretary, maybe a receptionist somewhere, perhaps. But she was an artist, and it explained a lot. Her apparent lack of any recognisable fashion sense, her woolly-headed assumption that she could say whatever she wanted to say without thinking, her earnest belief that she could somehow solve a situation over a cup of tea and a good chat.

Artists occupied a different world to most normal people. It was common knowledge they lived in a world of their own.

He refocused on the matter at hand. 'I don't know how you've managed to form such a strong bond with my son,' he said, not beating about the bush. 'But after the Sports Day…situation…it seems that the only way this weekend isn't going to descend into a nightmare is if you…' Leo searched around to find the right words. It wasn't in his nature to ask favours of anyone, and having to do so now left a sour taste in his mouth. He especially didn't like asking favours from a woman who got on his nerves. Moreover, he would have to be pleasant towards her.

Leo had tried his damnedest to form a bond with his son, but there was murky water under the bridge, and he had had time to reflect that it wasn't Daniel's fault. Without a great deal of difficulty, he could see any relationship he might have with his son sink without trace beneath a tide of remembered bitterness.

'If I…what?'

'Movies…lunch…dinner. I leave on Sunday afternoon,' he felt compelled to tack on because he could see the dawning dismay spreading across her face.

'You mean you want me to sacrifice my entire weekend to bail you out of a situation you can't handle?'

'*Sacrifice?*' Leo laughed drily. 'I don't think there's a woman alive who has ever seen a weekend spent in my company as a *sacrifice*.'

'That's the problem,' Heather said. 'Men like you never do.'

CHAPTER TWO

LEO decided to leave that half-muttered remark alone. Why get embroiled in a lengthy question-and-answer session with a woman who was an irrelevance in his life? On a more practical note, he needed her for the weekend, because he couldn't face a day and a half of his son's withdrawn sadness. If she could smooth things over, then far be it from him to invite further hostility from her. As far as he was concerned, though, all this interest in a kid who happened to live a couple of fields away from her spoke of an unhealthy lack of social life, but each to their own.

By lunchtime the following day—having spent the morning at the zoo, where his son had displayed an amazing knowledge of animals, rattling off facts to Heather and his mother while studiously ignoring him—Leo was beginning to feel his curiosity piqued.

She exuded warmth, and when she laughed, which she seemed to do often, it was a rich, infectious laughter.

Of course the laughter, like his son's encyclopaediac knowledge of every animal, was not directed at him.

Over a cup of tea in the canteen at the zoo—which Leo could only describe as a marginally more savoury experience than if he had actually pulled his chair into one of the animal enclosures—he noticed that the woman was not strictly limited to conversations about dinosaurs, reptiles and computer games. When his mother asked him about work, in an attempt to include him in the conversation, Leo was taken aback to be quizzed about the politics of mergers and acquisitions in so far as they affected the lives of countless hapless victims of 'marauding conglomerates'.

While his mother tried to hide her amusement, Leo stared at Heather as though she had mutated into one of the animals they had just been feeding.

Marauding conglomerates? Since when did country bumpkins use expressions like that?

He also didn't like the way her mouth curled with scorn when she addressed him, but in front of his mother and Daniel there was nothing he could do but smile coldly at her and change the subject.

Now, with the animals out of the way, he was taking them all to lunch; that nasty little remark she had flung at him the evening before, the remark which he had generously chosen to overlook, was beginning to prey on his mind.

Just who the hell did the woman think she was? Did she imagine that because she was doing him a favour she could indulge in whatever cheap shot she wanted at his expense?

People rarely got under Leo's skin. This particularly applied to women. He was astute when it came to reading their feminine wiles, and could see through any minor sulk to exactly what lay underneath. In short, they were a predictable entity.

As they headed for the Italian on the main street, he stuck his hands in his pockets and murmured, bending so that his words were for her ears only,

'Artist and financial expert, hmm? A woman of many talents. I had no idea you had such a keen interest in the business world.'

Heather pulled back. Something about his warm breath against her face had made the hairs on the back of her neck tingle.

It had been a mistake to let him rattle her, and she had been unable to resist wiping that lazy, condescending expression off his face by parrying with him about finance. Against her will, she had once known those money markets until they were coming out of her ears—and, once learnt, always remembered. It had been worth it just to see the shocked look on his face when she'd thrown in a few technical terms that surely a country hick like her should never have known.

Now, with his gleaming eyes fixed on her, Heather was belatedly realising that she might have been better off keeping her mouth shut and letting him get on with thinking whatever he wanted to think of her.

'I read the newspapers,' she muttered stiffly.

'You'd have to be a very avid reader of the *Financial Times* to know as much as you do about the global trading-market. So what's going on here?'

'Nothing's going on, and can I just remind you that I don't actually have to be here? I only agreed to come because I knew that Daniel would have been disappointed if I hadn't—and he's already had enough disappointment with you missing his Sports Day because of "unavoidable work commitments".'

'It's not going to work, so you can forget it.'

'What's not going to work?'

'Your attempt to change the subject. Who the hell are you *really*? That's the question I can't stop asking myself.'

Ahead of them, Daniel and Katherine were putting a bit of distance between them; when Katherine turned round and gesticulated that she and Daniel were going to pop into his favourite sports shop, Heather could have groaned with despair.

Leo was intrigued by her reaction to his remark. From not

really caring one way or another who she was, he now seriously began to wonder about her provenance.

'Are you always so suspicious?'

'Comes with the territory.'

'And what territory would that be? No, don't bother answering that—I already know.'

'Care to explain?'

'No, not really. If you don't mind, I think I'll just go and see what Katherine and Daniel are up to in there.'

'Oh, I'm sure they won't mind if we go ahead to the restaurant and wait there for them. It's a beautiful day. Why rush?'

'Because I have things to do at the house.'

'What things?'

'None of your business!'

'I'm getting the impression that you don't like me very much. Would I be right in that assumption?' He went into the sports shop to tell his mother that he would wait for them at the restaurant with Heather. No rush; take as long as they wanted. 'But don't buy anything.' He looked at his son, who stared back at him with grudging curiosity. 'I want to see whatever you buy—an athlete like you needs the best equipment.' He was rewarded with something approaching a smile.

The sports shop was an Aladdin's den. Leo reckoned his son could spend a satisfyingly long time browsing with his mother and that, he decided, would give him sufficient time to put his sudden curiosity to bed.

He had no doubt that she would be waiting for him outside. If there was one thing Leo knew with absolute certainty, it was that no one ever walked out on him until he was finished with them.

Sure enough, there she was, peering through the window of the shoe shop, and he took a little time to look at her. The strange gypsy-skirt of the night before had been replaced by something equally shapeless, but it was a hot day and her tee shirt outlined the contours of breasts that would be more than a handful. What would they look like? What would she feel like?

That sudden thought seemed to spring from nowhere and Leo shoved it aside, disconcerted.

The woman was most definitely not his type. After his short-lived and disastrous marriage to Sophia, he had exorcised pretty little airheads from his repertoire of beddable women, and he hadn't looked back.

Although…

The girl next door wasn't exactly quite the airhead he had assumed. Nor was she exactly pretty, although he supposed that there were a fair few men who might look twice at her, with her unruly gold hair and her lush curves.

She turned to find him staring, and he watched that tell-tale colour bloom into her cheeks.

'They'll be a little while,' Leo said. 'I told them to take their time.'

Heather fell into step with him. Without the presence of Daniel and Katherine, she was suddenly conscious of how intimidating she found him. Even when he was at his most casual, as he was now, in a pair of faded jeans and a white polo-shirt that emphasised his olive complexion.

Five minutes later, which was about long enough for Heather to really feel her nerves go into over drive, they were at the restaurant. It was tucked away up one of the smaller streets in the trendy part of the little town, with wine bars and little boutiques that specialised in selling designer clothes and designer kitchenware. Tables were laid outside, but Leo ignored them, choosing to stroll into the restaurant and net them the quietest table at the very back.

'So,' he said, relaxing his long body into the chair and giving her the benefit of all his undivided attention. 'You never explained your in-depth knowledge of the business markets. And I have to admit I'm curious. Were you a banker before you decided to throw it all aside and devote your life to painting little fairies?'

'I don't paint *little fairies*. I illustrate children's books,' Heather said mutinously. 'And I don't like the way you've manoeuvred me into being here alone with you.'

'Why? You have a suspicious mind. What do you think I'm going to get up to?'

'You have no right to question me about my private life.'

'Of course I have. Until yesterday, I didn't even know you existed. Now I'm to assume that you've become an integral part of my family.'

'I'm not an integral part of your family,' Heather protested. She looked at Leo's dark, clever, shockingly good-looking face with dislike. He was like a shark, patrolling his waters and ready to pounce on anything that might possibly be construed as prey. In this case, her. Wasn't it enough that she was helping him out? Obviously not.

Leo ignored that interruption. Without bothering to glance around, he summoned a waiter, who appeared as if by magic even though the restaurant was busy, and he ordered some wine, his eyes still focused on Heather's face.

'You've known my mother for a year or two, my son for considerably less time, and yet here you are—a vital part of this weekend's activities because you've managed to ingratiate yourself. Furthermore, you dabble in pretty little pictures yet seem to have an astute business mind, and I know when someone's lifting other people's opinions from the business section of a tabloid newspaper. You appear to have some kind of inside knowledge about how stock markets operate. A little unusual for someone who paints fairies, wouldn't you say?'

With a few bits and pieces of information, he had somehow managed to make her sound like a secret-service agent.

'I don't know where you're going with this.'

'Put it this way,' he drawled, taking his time to taste some of the wine that had been brought to their table and keeping those fabulous grey eyes fixed on her. 'In my position, it's always a good idea to be wary of anyone who doesn't fit their brief.'

'And I guess,' she said acidly, 'that my *brief* is the unattractive country girl without a brain cell in her head?'

'Do you think of yourself as unattractive?' Leo pounced on that small, unthinking slip of the tongue, and she flushed with embarrassment.

She could have told him that she never used to. Sure, she had always known that she didn't have the stick-insect glamour of some of the girls she had grown up with, but she had never had an inferiority complex about her looks. Not until she had moved to London with Brian.

However, the last thing Heather intended to do was bare her soul to the man sitting opposite her.

'Do you think I'm after…what? Your mother's money— do you think I might try to con her out of her fortune?'

'Stranger things have been known to happen.' He really couldn't credit that, though. If the woman had a taste for high living, then she was doing a good job of keeping it under wraps. So far he had yet to see her in something that didn't look as though its last home was a charity shop.

Heather didn't say anything. She could have scoffed at his cynicism, but she understood it. Brian had gone from the good-looking boy who had stolen her heart with his floppy blonde hair and sweats to a cold-eyed stranger in expensive clothes. He had made his money and, as the money had rolled in, so too had the gold diggers, the people who'd always been there, wanting something from him.

She sighed and tried to appreciate his suspicions even though they were directed at her.

'I guess so,' she said with a shrug. 'But not in this case. I think your mother's a really sweet lady. We share a passion for plants and flowers, that's all.'

'Is there no one else on whom you could lavish your passion?' Leo asked lazily. 'For all things…horticultural?'

For a second there Heather could feel her skin prickling at what she had imagined he was asking her.

'We get along, and I met Daniel quite by accident. He was exploring the fields; I guess he must have been lonely.' This was the perfect time to turn the tables and do a little accusing of her own, but his presence was stifling, clogging up her brain, turning it to mush. 'Anyway, I think he got lost. I asked him a few questions and he must have felt at ease because he came visiting again; I enjoy having him around.'

'I guess you might,' Leo mused thoughtfully. 'You must get very lonely in that cottage of yours. Working from home is an isolated way of earning an income. I'm surprised someone as young as you is content to stay indoors all day. Don't you crave to see what life in the fast lane is all about?'

'No. I don't.' She lowered her eyes.

'Really?' What was she hiding? Leo thought. And didn't she know that trying to keep secrets from a man was the one sure-fire way to fuel his curiosity? *His* curiosity was certainly on the move now…and he was beginning to enjoy the novelty. In fact, the weekend which had started on such an unfortunate note was definitely beginning to look up. Daniel had cracked one of those rare smiles of his, and even his mother seemed a little more relaxed than she normally did. The day so far had meandered in a more casual fashion than usual, and he had spent no time in front of his computer downloading his emails or generally continuing with business. It was proving to be all the more satisfying by the sudden challenge of ferreting out whatever Heather was keeping from him.

'You never answered my question,' he said, changing the subject so abruptly that she raised her startled blue gaze to him. 'The one about your banking knowledge. And here's another thing…' Leo leaned forward, noticing the way she flinched back warily a couple of inches in her chair. 'Last night you said that men like me take it for granted that women will want to spend time with them. What did you mean by that?'

'I didn't mean anything by it. In fact, I'm struggling to remember whether I made that remark or not.' She looked at him resentfully.

'If you deliver an insult, then you have to be prepared to back it up. What is a man like me?'

'Self-assured,' Heather told him bitterly. 'Arrogant…accustomed to giving orders and having them obeyed. Ruthless, dismissive; the sort of man who doesn't think it's wrong to use other people.'

Leo would have taken offence, but for the fact that this was more than just a casual dismissal; this was personal experience speaking. Ferociously controlled as he was, he felt a flare of sexual curiosity which took him by surprise, but he didn't fight it. He had a rich diet of very biddable women. Even women who could afford to pick and choose, women with both brains and beauty, had never been able to resist him. But he was without a woman at the moment, having parted company three months previously from the very delectable and very, very ambitious Eloise. Eloise had removed herself to New York, taking up a position with a hedge-fund company when it became obvious that their love affair wouldn't be travelling down the altar any time soon.

And there was something refreshing about this woman's candour as she glared at him with her cornflower-blue eyes, fully expecting him to hit the roof and duly confirm every scathing insult she had just listed.

'To get to the top requires a certain amount of ruthlessness.' Leo shrugged, sipped his wine and watched her over the rim of his glass.

'Maybe so, but that still doesn't make it acceptable. If you weren't so busy being ruthless, you might find that you had the time to spend with your family.'

'I will choose to overlook that,' Leo said, his expression still impassive and mildly interested, but with a hint of steel in his voice. 'Because what I really want to find out is why you're hiding here, in the middle of nowhere. What are you running from?'

'I'm not running from anything,' Heather stammered. 'And I'm not hiding. I happen to love living in the country! I don't enjoy being trapped in a building surrounded by pavements and street lights that never go off.' Behind him, Heather could see Katherine and Daniel finally making their long-overdue appearance. 'They're here,' she said, resisting the urge to groan with relief.

'Saved by the proverbial bell,' Leo murmured, but he was enjoying himself in ways he had never expected to. It occurred to him, and not for the first time, that the pursuit of money was always more rewarding than the possession of it. Eleven years ago he had made financial success his one driving ambition in life. It had eluded his parents. It had certainly eluded his brother, the mere thought of whom brought a twisted scowl of displeasure to Leo's mouth.

He had determined to prove to himself and to his parents that he could escape the cramped, stiflingly claustrophobic clutter of his lower middle-class background. Now, rich beyond his wildest dreams, he sometimes wondered whether he had managed to prove anything at all. Certainly not to his mother, even though he had been the one to bail her out of the massive debts which his father had incurred when he had chosen unwisely to invest his life savings on Alex and his ridiculous money-making ventures. He had provided her with enough financial security to last several lifetimes, and of course she was grateful—but years spent amassing his private fortune had left him with a jaded palate and a deep-rooted cynicism. Master of everything and everyone he surveyed, he had practically forgotten what it felt like to have someone ruffle his feathers.

Especially a woman—and, furthermore, a woman who could light up for seemingly everyone bar him. Right now, she was half-turned away from him, enthusing over a pair of football trainers, the must-have footwear for any aspiring footballer.

Leo leaned forward, invading her space. 'I used to play football when I was your age.'

'And you were a brilliant little footballer.' Katherine looked at her son and half-smiled. 'I remember your father taking you to your football game every Saturday morning. Do you remember that? I would stay at home with your little brother Alexander and you would trot off with your boots slung over your shoulder and a little packed lunch.'

'I remember,' Leo said gruffly. He did, now that the subject had been raised, but in truth that was a memory which had been well and truly buried.

He wasn't given to reminiscing, but he had to admit that it certainly helped to carry the conversation along. Long-forgotten football stories were brought out for the benefit of his son. Every so often as the food was brought to them Heather chipped in, although never with a personal anecdote of her own.

'You must have been to a football match or two,' Leo said lazily, pushing his empty plate away and settling his body into the chair, feet extended at an angle and lightly crossed at the ankles. 'Where did you grow up? Around here?'

'Not a million miles away,' Heather told him cautiously.

'Which would be where, exactly?'

'Reading. Near Reading, as a matter of fact.'

'Good football team there.' He looked to Daniel, including him in the conversation, making it impossible for her not to respond. 'And your family…do they still live there?'

'No. They don't. My father died years ago, and my mother remarried and moved to Portugal. She lives there now. Has a little hairdressing business.' No state secrets there, but Heather still didn't like exposing her private life to him, and she didn't know why.

'Brothers? Sisters?'

'Just me.'

'So let me get this straight…' Leo's smile made her heart beat with sickening force. 'You lived in Reading, no siblings, mother in Portugal with stepfather… What made you decide to move out here? Reading might not be one of the biggest cities in the UK, but it's still a city—still has nightclubs, restaurants, theatres, all the things that would appeal to a person of your age. In other words, you must find life pretty dead out here.'

'Stop interrogating the poor child!' Katherine said sharply, and Leo looked at his mother in amazement. When was the last time she had ever snapped at him? Normally she tiptoed around him, treating him as though he inhabited a different plane. 'You might have lots of money and power, Leonardo West, but that doesn't give you the right to do as you please with other people. You must be able to see that Heather feels uncomfortable about your probing!'

Duly chastised, Leo flushed. He noticed that his son was smirking at him.

'Which just goes to show—' he took advantage of the temporary ceasefire to draw Daniel into a conspiracy of male bonding '—that no man is safe from a nagging woman. You'll discover that for yourself in due course.'

One Disney movie and three bags of popcorn later, Heather was more than ready to make her excuses and get back to the safety of her cottage.

Her head was in a whirl. Before she had even met him, she had had some very strong, preconceived notions of Leo West: he was a selfish, egotistic workaholic who virtually ignored his mother and paid lip service to the fact that he had found himself in possession of a son, having been an absentee father for the majority of Daniel's life.

When she had finally set eyes on him, she was honest enough to admit she had been a little taken aback by the force of his personality and good looks. Having likened him to Brian in her head, she had very quickly realised that Brian was a minnow next to a man like Leo West.

After a few hours in his company, watching as some of that ferocious, icy discipline began to thaw, she was confused to find herself actually beginning to see him as more than just a comforting cardboard cutout. He was a complex, three-dimensional human being, and she didn't know whether she wanted to deal with that. Fortunately, she wouldn't have to.

Once there had been less of a necessity for her to be roped in as mediator, she had no trouble in wriggling out of the remainder of the planned evening. Daniel might not have been transformed into the loving son, but at least he seemed to have forgotten the debacle of the missed Sports Day. And Katherine…

That little show of backbone, when she had soundly ticked off Leo and spared Heather the embarrassment of being cross examined like a criminal in the dock, had been a telling reminder that she was still a mother and Leo still a son.

All told, she'd been able to leave with a pretty clear conscience.

By seven-thirty she was back in her studio. Painting had never before let her down. In the aftermath of Brian, she had retreated back to her art, and it had been a soothing balm.

Its soothing, balm-like qualities were proving more elusive now. In fact, as she peered at the fairy she had just spent forty-five minutes painting meticulously, she could swear that he bore a striking resemblance to Leo. How had that happened? And what role could a cruel, money-obsessed, self-centred workaholic fairy have in a children's book?

Having downgraded to the television—which was having a similarly non-remedial effect on her chaotic thoughts—she was startled when she heard a bang on the door.

Heather didn't think for a moment that it would be anyone but Leo, and she was shocked and frightened to discover that her heart was doing all sorts of weird things. Her head was behaving pretty badly as well, forcing her to recall the way his mouth curved in that smile that was always not very far away from cynical; the way he tilted his head to one side when he was listening to something, giving the impression that he was listening intently with every fibre of his being.

Faced with the unpalatable truth that the man had somehow managed to spark something in her that she had convinced herself was long dead and buried, Heather yanked open the door, bristling for attack.

'You've been painting again,' was the remark that greeted her. 'How are the fairies? All work and no play; you know what they say about that.'

'You keep showing up on my doorstep!'

'There's a lot to be said for predictability. Hope I'm not interrupting anything—aside from a painting jag, that is?'

'Why are you here?'

'I come bearing gifts.'

She hadn't noticed, but now he lifted both hands and she could see that he was carrying several carrier-bags.

'What's that?' Heather asked suspiciously.

'Food—Chinese. And a bottle of wine, of course. Today has worn Daniel out, and my mother has retreated to watch something on television. A historical romance; I didn't think I'd be able to stomach it.'

'And you didn't decide to work?'

'This seemed a more interesting option.' Besides, he felt in holiday mode. The day had gone well, and more than that... Leo had found himself watching her, watching the way she laughed, closing her eyes and throwing her head back, giving it everything. He watched the way she related to his mother and his son, gentle and compassionate. He had also found himself watching the way her body had shifted under her clothes, the bounce of her breasts when she had reached across to get the salt on the table...

After that illuminating little chat about the stock market, there had been no more work-related discussions, although he was pretty sure that she would rise to the challenge given half a chance. No, the conversation had been light and amusing, and he had enjoyed himself.

He had a chequered love life behind him, which was just the way he liked it. But lately he had become bored with the relentlessly intellectual conversations provided by the women he dated; bored with trying to arrange dates, with each of the women consulting their BlackBerries, endeavouring to find a suitable gap in hectic timetables, bored with leggy brunettes.

A change was as good as a rest, he had decided, and that change came in the small, curvy figure of the woman looking at him as though he might very well be something infectious.

She was a challenge, and Leo was in a mood to take on a challenge.

Furthermore, it had crossed his mind that seeing his son, and his mother for that matter, had been a considerably less stilted business with Heather in the mix. They relaxed with her in a way that they never relaxed around him. Taking on this challenge might have more than just the expected rewards.

He surfaced to the tail end of something she had been saying, and when he frowned she said very slowly, as if she were talking to someone mentally challenged, 'There was no need for you to come over here with food. You probably feel that this is a suitable thank-you gesture, but I don't need thanking.'

'Stop being so bad tempered and let me in. The food's going cold. Cold Chinese food is never a good sight— congeals.' He gave her a crooked smile. 'Besides, what's wrong with accepting a little thanks?'

It was the smile. Heather's mouth went dry and she stared at him. The sight of him took her breath away. She was aware that she was gaping, and she snapped her mouth shut and reminded herself that being deprived of breath was not a good place to be. In fact, it was terminal.

'It was a good day.' He was still smiling, his shrewd eyes taking in her response to him and banking it. She fought like a wild cat, but he got to her and, considering she got to him as well, it seemed only fitting. 'And you deserve credit for it.'

'Why are you being nice?'

'Maybe I want to show you that I'm not the self-centred, arrogant monster you seem to think I am.'

'I never said you were a monster.' She was struck by the thought that to turn him away would be to admit that her past still had a hold over her; that Brian—three years gone—still had a hold over her and could still influence the way she related to other people, other men.

'Okay.' She stood aside, making up her mind, realising that she had nothing to fear but herself and her stupid overreactions. Besides, he'd be gone in a few hours. 'But I really have to get back to my painting some time tonight.'

Leo stepped inside, brushing her protestations aside, and headed for the kitchen. Unerringly he knew where it would be, and felt her walking behind him; he liked the anticipation of what the evening might bring. Sure there was a lot to be said for predictability, but there was a great deal more to be said for the thrill of the unknown, and her obvious reluctance to be anywhere near him had roused his hunting instincts.

He dumped the bags on the table. The wine was still cold from the fridge.

'If you point to the plates…'

'Don't tell me that you're Mr Domestic?'

'You mean you wouldn't believe me?' He perched against the counter, arms folded, and laughed softly under his breath.

'I mean—' Heather had to take a deep breath to steady her sudden giddiness '—I'd quicker believe that there were lots of little green people dashing about on planet Mars.'

'Okay. You win.' He gave a mock gesture of defeat. 'Domesticity doesn't agree with me.' He watched as she opened the bottle of wine and poured them both a glass. The ubiquitous flowing skirt was gone. She was wearing some grey jogging-bottoms and an off-white vest bearing the tell-tale signs of her painting. For the first time, he could really see something of her figure, and his eyes roved appreciatively over the full breasts, the flat stomach, the womanly curve of her hips. She was by no means thin, but her body was toned and surprisingly tanned. He wondered whether she had been taking advantage of the hot weather, tanning in her garden—tanning nude in her garden…?

When she swung round to give him a glass, he surprised himself by flushing.

'And why is that?' Heather asked. 'Could it be that, the more money a person has, the more temptation there is to buy the services of other people who are a lot more handy at doing all those inconvenient chores like cooking?'

Instead of bringing down his shutters, that little undercurrent of belligerence sent a jolt of red-hot lust running through him.

'Ah…' He strolled towards her and took a sip of wine. 'But just think, my little economist, of how many people I keep employed…'

Looking up at him, she could feel that breathing thing happening again. She forced herself to get a grip, to bring the conversation back down to a level she could handle.

'Or maybe you're just scared at the thought of putting down roots,' she said wryly. 'And if you never treat your house like a home then you never put down roots, do you?'

CHAPTER THREE

HUGE inroads had been made into the Chinese food, which was spread on the table between them. Noodles and other assorted bits of food had managed to escape the chopsticks and were hardening on the pine table-top. The bottle of wine was nearing its end, but Heather was barely aware of having drunk anything at all. It had taken a little while, but she had lowered her defences and was proud of how normal she was behaving. As far as exercises went, this was a pretty good result. Yes, she could talk to the man without pigeon-holing him. She knew him for what he was, but was not letting that get in the way of responding to him like an adult. She was smugly aware of a sense of personal achievement.

Of course, it had to be said that Leo was making things easy for her. He was no longer on the attack, no longer looking at her with narrow-eyed suspicion which made her hackles rise. The conversation was light, skimming the surface, avoiding any pitfalls.

And the wine was helping. Heather rested her elbow on the table, cupped her face in her hand and looked at Leo sleepily.

'Don't tell me that you're going to doze off in the middle of my conversation?' he said, sipping his wine and looking at her over the rim of his glass. 'My ego would never recover.'

'And we both know that you've got a very healthy one of those,' Heather murmured. His eyes were hypnotic. She could stare into them for ever.

'I'm going to say thank you, even though I have a sneaking suspicion that there wasn't anything complimentary behind the observation.'

'My head feels a little woolly.'

'In which case, we'd better get you to the sitting room. Leave all this debris. I'll tidy it up.'

'You will? You're domestically challenged—you said that yourself. Do you even know what a dishwasher looks like?'

Leo gave a low laugh and looked at her. She was as soft and full as a peach. Her hair was a riot of gold ringlets framing her face, giving her a look that was impossibly feminine. No hard edges there. Sitting across from her as they had eaten had required a lot of restraint. He had watched her as she tipped her head back, her eyes half-closed, so that she could savour the noodles on her chopsticks, and he had had to shift his body because it had been so damned uncomfortable dealing with his aching erection.

'You seem to forget that I had a childhood,' he told her drily. 'And there was no one around then to do my bidding. My brother and I had our list of chores every day, and some of them included clearing the table after meals.' Another memory that had not surfaced for a very long time.

'I can't imagine you doing chores. I bet you paid your brother to do yours for you.' Heather had never met Alex. She knew that he was away somewhere distant and exotic and had been for a while.

'Come on. I'm going to get you into the sitting room.' The shutters had come down with the mention of his brother, and he stood up. But as she pushed herself away from the table he moved quickly around, and was sweeping her off her feet, taking her by surprise and therefore finding little resistance.

After a few startled seconds, Heather wriggled against him.

'What are you *doing*?'

'I'm carrying you into your sitting room. You look a little wobbly on your feet.'

'I'm perfectly capable of walking three inches!'

'Stop struggling.'

'You'll pull a muscle in your back, lifting me up!' After all her smug satisfaction at how amazingly adult she had been— chatting to Leo as though he was just another perfectly normal guy who didn't rattle her cage—she could now feel every nerve ending in her body screaming in response to this physical contact. His chest was hard and muscular and the hands supporting her were strong and sinewy; all those stir-rings, of whatever the heck they were that she didn't want, were flooding through her in a tidal wave.

The more she wriggled, the more the stirring magnified, so she stopped wriggling and told herself to get a grip.

'There.' Leo deposited her gently on the squashy sofa in the sitting room and stood back, looking down at her. 'Ordeal over.' He wasn't sure whether to be amused or disgruntled at her frantic efforts to bolt.

'It wasn't an *ordeal*,' Heather told him, gathering herself into a sitting position. 'I was— I was just *concerned* for you…' Her heartbeat should have been returning to normal, but it wasn't.

'Concerned?'

'I'm not the lightest person in the world.' She spelled it out for him, willing herself to get back into sensible, pro-tective mode.

Leo sat on the sofa and she immediately squirmed into a cross-legged position, her hands resting lightly on her knees.

'I have no idea what you're talking about.'

'It doesn't matter.'

'You do that.'

'What?'

'Introduce a topic and then suddenly decide to back off before you can explain what you're talking about.'

'There's nothing to explain.' She gave a careless shrug and linked her fingers together. 'I just think that caveman gestures like that are probably better done with someone skinnier than me. Probably with one of those women who fall over themselves to be in your company.'

Leo, well skilled in the ways of women, could recognise a fishing expedition from a mile away. She was curious about him, wanted to know more, but was reluctant to frame her questions directly. Good sign.

'I thought women liked the caveman approach.'

'Not when it can lead to personal injury.'

'Who on earth ever told you that you were…?'

'Fat?' Heather supplied for him. 'Overweight?' She stared at her fingers. 'In need of losing a few pounds? No one.'

'No one. Well, you can tell *no one* that he was way off-target. You are neither fat nor are you overweight. And as for all those women who fall over themselves to be in my company…' He noticed the way she inclined her head very slightly, as if stilling to hear some distant sound. This, he thought with satisfaction, was the sound of a woman who was sexually interested in a man. 'They do tend to be on the skinny side,' he admitted. He relaxed back on the sofa and crossed his legs.

'I knew it.'

'One more of those monstrously predictable things about me?'

'Why is it that men with lots of money are always attracted

to women who look as though they would have difficulty keeping upright in a strong wind? I mean, really, is there something *attractive* about a human being who doesn't eat?'

Leo laughed, and when he was finished laughing he looked at her and shook his head, as if a little dazed by the woman sitting opposite him on the sofa.

'No, there's absolutely nothing attractive about a woman who doesn't eat, and I have to admit that I've dated a lot of those.'

'Brainless bimbos?' She wanted to pull information out of him, and was guiltily aware that she was being as intrusive with him as he had been with her.

'Brainless bimbos? No, definitely not that.'

Now, that *did* surprise her, and Leo laughed again, amused. 'Why would I be attracted to a brainless bimbo?' he asked.

'Because she looks good on your arm?'

'And what about when there's no one around to see her looking good on my arm? What conversation could there possibly be with a brainless bimbo?'

'So what sort of women *do* you go out with?'

'Why do you ask?'

Why, Heather thought, do *I ask?* This wasn't the sort of casual, skimming-the-surface conversation which was safe and unthreatening. There was an edge to this conversation, but like someone standing on the edge of a precipice, peering down, she found that it was irresistible.

'No reason. Just making conversation. Really, though, you should go. I'm awfully tired. There's honestly no need for you to tidy the kitchen. I can do that later, or better still in the morning.'

Leo had no intention of leaving, but it dawned on him that Heather was not like any other woman he had known. That bristly, belligerent spark wasn't an act to get his attention. If she told him that he should go, then she meant it, and since Leo wasn't going anywhere—at least not yet—he stood up and shook his head in his best bedside manner, something of which he'd had precious little practice.

'You need some coffee.' Before she could launch into another goodbye speech, he left the room, only throwing over his shoulder that maybe she should doze for a bit. The occasional catnap could work wonders, he told her. Not that he knew, but it was all part of the bedside manner.

In truth, Leo had forgotten the art of seduction, or at least the art of persuasion.

With women, the outcome was usually apparent within a matter of minutes: conversation of the intelligent variety, a certain type of eye contact and then the unspoken assumption that they would end up as lovers.

With Heather, he realised that one false move and she would run a mile—and of course, given that he was no more than a highly competitive red-blooded male, what more of a turn on could there be than an uncertain outcome?

Not for a minute did it occur to Leo that a deliberate seduction was anything less than perfectly reasonable. He took his time in the kitchen. Dishes were washed and precariously balanced on the draining board, because drying and putting them away seemed a senseless waste of time when they would be used again at some point in the future—and she had been right with the 'dishwasher' accusation. There was some sort of coffee-making machine with nozzles and a vaguely threatening glass jug, which he ignored. Instead, he made them both a cup of instant coffee and was gratified to find that she wasn't dozing, as he'd suspected she might be, when he returned to the sitting room.

'Instant,' he said, handing her the cup and then sitting on

one of the big, comfortable chairs by the fireplace. 'There was a machine there, but…'

'But you didn't have a clue how to use it?' She cupped the mug between her hands and watched him as he sat back, relaxed, in the chair.

'I could have figured it out in time.' He shot her a wicked grin that made her toes curl. 'But life's too short to waste any of it trying to come to grips with a complicated machine that just ends up making stuff you can get out of a jar.'

'It tastes much better than the stuff you can get out of a jar.' After their very civilised evening, Heather knew that she should really be getting rid of him. He had made a nice gesture; she had not been churlish and thrown it back at him, and now she could close the evening on a satisfactory note. But didn't it make her feel alive, having him here? Looking at him? It was, in equal measure, exciting and disturbing.

'That's open to debate.' But he laughed again. 'Tell me about your work. Do you work freelance, or are you commissioned to a publisher?'

Since this was nice, safe conversation, Heather felt herself relax as she began explaining to him what she did, telling him about some of the books she had illustrated, then finding that they were talking about art in general. Working freelance as she did, she had relatively little contact with members of the opposite sex, and for the past three years that had suited her. After Brian, she had retreated to lick her wounds, only meeting the occasional guy through some of the women she had befriended in the town, mums from the school where she gave art lessons to their kids once a week. She had accepted no dates, and indeed had made sure to give off all the right 'hands off' signals to anyone who had looked even mildly interested.

It made a change to have male company. That, she told

herself, was why she was now talking to Leo. She had allowed him in to prove to herself that she was capable of rising above her past. Also, it made sense for them to be, if not friends, then at least on speaking terms, because she would bump into him now and again, and the less awkwardness between them the better.

She resolutely slammed the door on the little voice telling her that she was enjoying that weird, tingly, excited flutter inside her; that she was turned on by his charisma, mesmerised by the raw power of his sex appeal.

Heather was not in the market for being turned on or mesmerised by anyone. In due course, she would emerge from the protective walls she had built around herself and would get back into the dating scene. If she wasn't too old by then. And, when she did, she would be very careful about the type of men she went out with. In fact, she might get them to fill out a questionnaire before the first date—nothing too complicated, just a few sheets of questions so that she could make sure that only the right kind of guy got through the net.

Since Leo was the complete opposite of the right kind of guy, she felt herself fully protected. Yes, she could appreciate all that alpha-male sex appeal; yes, she could admit that he was ferociously intelligent. But there was no way that she could ever physically be attracted to him, not when her head told her that it made no sense—and she was always careful to be guided by her head now.

So why shouldn't she enjoy talking to someone who seemed interested in her art? In fact, she even found herself showing him some of her past illustrations, ones she had done for a trilogy about a ballerina.

'So you don't just do the fairies,' Leo murmured, impressed

by what he saw, but not liking the way the evening was descending ever increasingly into friendly chit-chat. 'Tell me something, do you make a living from this?'

'Depends on what you call "a living".' Heather stashed her portfolio to the side of the sofa and sat back down. 'Compared to what you probably earn, I don't even begin to make a living, but then again I realised a long time ago that money's way overrated.'

'Yes?' Leo's ears pricked up. 'Tell me about it.' He stood up and began pacing the small room, pausing to look at pictures in frames, eventually settling on the sofa with her. Sitting on the opposite side of the room was not working for him. In a minute she would be gearing up to remind him of how tired she was before she sent him on his way.

His frustration levels were growing by the second.

'There's nothing to tell,' Heather said casually. 'You just have to read about all those super-rich, super-privileged people who end up in rehab all the time. I mean, have you ever thought that *you* might end up in rehab one day?'

Distracted from his intention to go beyond the harmless conversation about art and culture and steer them into edgier waters, Leo raised his eyebrows, amused.

'I'll admit, that that's one thing I've never worried about.'

'Why not?' Heather looked at him thoughtfully. She could feel every nerve in her body on red alert. It wasn't a massive sofa, and, now that he had plonked himself on it, it seemed to have shrunk to the size of a pin cushion. If she stretched her foot out just a tiny bit it would make contact with his thigh, so she was making very sure to huddle into herself. Her knees were drawn up to her chest and her arms were firmly clasped around them.

'Why should I? In case you hadn't noticed, I'm not a loser. People end up in rehab when they've lost control of their lives.'

'Or when they're lonely, maybe. Then they take refuge in all sorts of things.'

'But I'm not lonely, and the concept of taking refuge in anything is abhorrent to me. I have no time for people who waste their lives in drugs or alcohol. And how did we get onto this anyway?'

'Because I said that money can buy a lot of things, but it doesn't buy happiness.' She looked at him and her breath caught in her throat. The sun had dipped, and the long shadows in the room accentuated the angles of his face, the beautiful, harsh set of his features. Their easy banter had lulled her into a false sense of security, she realised. She had silenced those nagging little voices at the back of her mind, but they had re-surfaced with double their vigour, telling her that she could pretend to feel in control, but underneath the pretence was the reality that she was attracted to him. Staring at him like a dumbstruck teenager was just one of the things she wanted to do. The rest brought her out in a cold sweat.

'I mean,' she said, poised to redress the balance, 'you're rich, and yet can you honestly say that you're completely happy?'

Leo raked restless fingers through his dark hair and wondered how he had managed to get caught on the back foot. 'Yes, I can, but I expect you're going to tell me that actually I'm not.'

'You can't be completely satisfied with your relationship with Katherine and Daniel,' Heather said flatly. She regretted her outburst the minute it left her lips, but it was too late, and she conceded that it might be the only way to fight the dawning realisation that she was attracted to the worst possible man for her.

'I'm working on that,' Leo grated. 'And enough said on that subject.'

'I think it's time you went, Leo.' Heather stood up and

made a pretence of yawning. 'I'm shattered. I'm not accustomed to drinking, and it's made me feel really sleepy. Thank you for coming over and for bringing a meal for me, and I'm glad that we've managed to…get over our initial differences.' She took up a defensive position by the door, standing to one side and watching in silence as Leo finally took the hint and stood up, although it had to be said that he didn't look in a frantic rush to leave. His eyes tangled with hers and she looked away nervously.

'I think we've done more than just *get over our initial differences*,' he murmured, walking towards her.

'Um…' Heather felt the words dry up in her throat with each step closer to her that he took.

'I think that we got over our initial differences some time earlier today, in fact. It might have been in the cinema, when you absent-mindedly helped yourself to some of my popcorn.'

Heather flushed. His voice was low, sexy and coaxing, and there was a lazy, speculative look in his eyes that made her feel hot and self-conscious—although she wasn't sure why, because all he was talking about, for goodness' sake, was a bag of popcorn!

'I didn't think you'd noticed,' she mumbled, glancing away, because his eyes seemed to be boring holes in her. Hadn't anyone ever told him that it was rude to stare? 'I have a problem with popcorn. I always feel that I can do without it, but the minute the movie starts I realise I can't.'

She could feel his eyes still on her, making her even more horribly aware of her inadequate dress-code. Her shameless probing had not managed to elicit a huge amount about his love life, but she had managed to glean that he appreciated women who were slim and brainy. Slim, brainy women would not be caught dead in a pair of old jogging-bottoms and a tee shirt, even if they were comfortable. Slim, brainy women relaxed in designer jeans and super-expensive blouses with pearl buttons, maybe a silk scarf casually draped around their necks. She had met a fair few slim, brainy women in her time and they had all spoken with cut-glass accents and looked like beautiful, porcelain mannequins.

She realised that she wanted to find out more about these women. Was there one on the scene now, waiting back in London for Leo to return from doing his paternal duties?

She slammed the door shut on her curiosity and adopted a bright smile.

'What time do you leave tomorrow?' she asked. 'Have you got any plans for Daniel? I know he really enjoyed today; I could tell. He's not the most talkative child on the face of the earth, but you can always see when he's in a good mood and he was in a very good mood, today. I'm very proud of you. You made a big effort after having missed his Sports Day and he appreciated it. Kids are like that. They don't harbour grudges or have long memories…' He was looking less and less impressed the longer her eulogy continued, until she finally faltered into an uncertain silence.

'You're very *proud* of me?'

'Well, yes…'

'I'm not ten years old, Heather. Obviously it's heart warming to know that you're *proud* of me, but…' This time he did more than just allow his eyes to linger on her face, to travel the length of her small, voluptuous body. He reached out and placed his hand behind her neck. There was nothing passionate about the gesture. He remained where he was, leaning against the wall, feet lightly crossed at the ankles. With anyone else, it would have felt almost fraternal. With Leo, it felt as though he had stripped her of her clothes and ordered her to do an erotic dance. The wobbly legs which she had earlier put down to a glass too much of wine now felt like jelly, and every shameful, idiotic, indecent tug of attraction which she had managed to airbrush away surfaced with red-hot ferocity through her veins. She felt weak and dizzy from the force of it all, and she half-closed her eyes as she drew in her breath unevenly.

Leo could feel reluctance mixed with desire in those few seconds as he detailed her reaction to his touch with an expert eye.

She had thoroughly disapproved of him at their first meeting and hadn't been able to resist the opportunity to lecture. Now, he had succeeded in becoming the star pupil. Add to that the fact that she was probably very innocent in her experiences with men, cooped up as she was in the middle of nowhere, and he really wasn't that surprised that she was now licking her lips nervously. If he wasn't mistaken, she was trembling a little, like the fragile petal of a flower being blown by a very slight breeze.

He brushed the pad of his thumb against the soft, sensitive skin of her neck and then tangled his fingers in her hair, which was as soft as silk.

'But…' He was finding it hard to remember what he was saying. He was finding it hard, in fact, to think coherently, which was a novelty for him and gave him a certain buzz. 'There are far more satisfying ways you could use to reward my Brownie points.' The hand which had been plunged into her glorious golden curls now moved to trace the contours of her neckline, which was pretty frustrating for him, because, whilst her close-fitting tee shirt proudly advertised the bounty it shielded, the round neckline made damn sure that his wandering fingers couldn't get anywhere near it.

Heather stared at him, her lips parted. Her brain was having trouble keeping pace with the bizarre turn of events. In a series of rapid, thumbnail clips, she mentally went over the evening, starting with his unexpected arrival, Chinese food in hand, and travelling down the enjoyable few hours they had spent—him being ultra-nice and ultra-interested in everything she had to say while she watched him surreptitiously from under her lashes and told herself that everything was normal, that it made perfect sense to be friendly, because that was how good neighbours should be.

She knew he was going to kiss her. For a few seconds, all rational thought went into free fall as he dipped her head back, and then his mouth was on hers, urgent, hungry, demanding, pressing her back against the wall.

As the walls of her resistance such as there had been came tumbling down, Leo felt a surge of lust and triumph. Against his, her body was as soft as he had imagined. Her breasts were squashed against his chest, and with a groan he pushed his hands under the tee shirt, sliding them effortlessly out of her stretchy bra and then losing himself in their abundance.

It was enough to galvanise Heather into horrified action. In the space of a few reckless minutes, she had succumbed to a need that was so powerful it overwhelmed all her ability to think rationally.

The touch of his hands on her breasts was like an urgent wake-up call and she pushed him back, scrambling in her desperation to regain her composure.

She was no match for him in the strength stakes, but she had the element of surprise on her side. The very last thing Leo had expected was to find himself repelled at the very height of his excitement.

'Go. Now.' She had awkwardly pulled the tee shirt back

into some semblance of order, and her arms were folded protectively across her breasts. On any other occasion, his look of disbelief would have had her laughing.

'*Go? Now?* If this is your version of playing hard to get, then it won't work.'

'I'm not playing hard to get. I'm asking you to leave. I shouldn't have…'

'Led me on?'

'I did *not* lead you on!'

'Don't play the outraged virgin with me. I've seen the way you've stolen looks at me, the way you've reacted when I've been within touching distance of you!'

Heather, guilty and appalled, stared at him mutely. 'I'm sorry,' she mumbled, unable to deny the charge, but likewise refusing to admit it. 'If you thought that I was leading you on, then you've got hold of the wrong end of the stick. That's the last thing I intended to do.'

'What was your intention, in that case?'

'I…'

'Because I don't hear you denying that what I felt here was a case of mutual attraction.' Leo was half-stunned to hear himself demanding an explanation from her, demanding to know why she hadn't immediately and without question fallen into bed with him. He hadn't been mistaken about the way she felt about him, the attraction that sizzled below the surface of their amicable exchanges. He was never wrong about things like that. When it came to second guessing female vibes, he could have written a book on the subject.

What he was inexperienced at was having to deal with a woman who felt the attraction and then came up short on the follow-through.

'Not all of us treat sex as a casual indulgence,' Heather told him shakily, backing away to escape the stranglehold of his powerful personality.

'You have no idea how I treat sex.'

'I can risk a guess—no strings, no commitments, something that hits the spot and then, when it stops hitting the spot, becomes disposable—like a Chinese takeaway, in other words. You're not domestic because you don't have to be, and I'll damn sure bet you're never even remotely domestic in the presence of a woman just in case she gets nesting ideas. Am I right?'

'And maybe there's a damn good reason for that,' Leo heard himself say grittily. 'Maybe I've learnt a couple of things about the joys of commitment. Maybe I've learnt that it's just not what it's cracked up to be, and I'm the kind of guy who learns lessons very fast. Some might say at the speed of light.'

He stared down at her and was as surprised at this admission as she appeared to be, judging from the wide-eyed look on her face. It was one of the rare moments when mention of his wife had been uttered on his lips, the last time being when she had died in the car crash in Australia, thereby catapulting his life into another lane. Even then, when the past had resurged into his present, he had conducted affairs with a businesslike approach, spurning all invitations from his mother to open up. On that swift and relentless rise to the top, Leo had discarded all possible weaknesses, and that included any maudlin tendencies to confide. Not that he had ever really had any. The sensitive role had been his brother's domain.

Maybe it was the silence that greeted his unexpected admission that encouraged him to continue. Or maybe it was the fact that she was reaching to play the moral trump-card again and he refused to allow himself to be boxed in.

He couldn't quite put his finger on it, but he said with

cutting cynicism, 'My ex-wife taught me some very valuable lessons, one of which was that life can get messy, complicated and downright ugly the minute a person makes the mistake of thinking that sex is better, more worthwhile, when a little love or infatuation is thrown into the mix.'

'What are you trying to say?'

'I'm trying to say that there's no virtue in self-denial because the happy-ever-after scenario isn't waiting just around the corner.'

Heather couldn't disagree with that. She couldn't, however, see the only alternative as throwing herself into whatever passing attraction she might happen to feel for any man.

'Well?' Leo prompted harshly, angry with himself for sinking so low as to explain his motivations, and angry with her because he had expected her to launch into a diatribe about love, romance and all that other rubbish which seemed to propel couples up the aisle only to find themselves racing for the divorce courts three years later.

'Well, what?' They stared at each other. Heather could hardly breathe, and she was holding her body so still that she could very well have grown roots. Eventually, she said quietly, 'Would you like another cup of coffee?'

For a split second, Leo hesitated. He had done more than was acceptable to him. Unbelievably, he had been rejected in his advances, and worse than that had not turned and walked away. It was what he should have done and what he would have expected himself to do. It wasn't as though there weren't other women around. In fact, he had files of them. But this one... Something about her turned him on so massively that he gave a curt nod and followed her into the kitchen, watching as she fiddled with the ridiculous coffee-making gadget so that she could produce two cups of superior coffee in a matter of seconds. It tasted nothing like the dishwater he had produced for her.

The fact that she had offered him the cup of coffee, which even now he was accepting with a slight inclination of his head, led him to believe that his words had struck a chord with her.

As they ought to! he considered.

'What did your wife do to leave you so bitter?'

'Details are unimportant.'

'Do you really think so?' Heather said sadly. 'Sometimes I think they're the most important things.'

'In that case, I'll tell you. My dearest wife enjoyed the fruits of my labours, but not the work entailed in providing them. She needed more than just a limitless bank account. She needed constant, round-the-clock flattery, and when I wasn't around to provide it she found others who could. She was beautiful. She was rich. She had a great deal of choice. Hence my scepticism about the wonders of love and marriage.'

'I'm sorry. It must have been awful for you. But when Daniel was born didn't you both try to…stitch things together? Give it a go?'

But Leo was done with answering questions and dwelling on his miserable, short-lived marriage. Instead he turned his mind to the glorious, contrary woman sitting opposite him, her brow knitted in a compassionate frown.

This sordid story, one which he had never told a soul, would have fractured her rosy picture of human relationships. It also would have made her see that what he had offered her—a satisfying relationship based on the one thing that made any sense—was not to be discarded. In fact, he was pretty sure that she had come to that conclusion herself even before his unprecedented confession.

The option of having her step down from her high horse and come to him, only to taste the same rejection that she had dished out to him, wasn't even considered.

He wanted her and he wasn't going to play any games. But the sound of her acquiescence would be truly sweet indeed.

CHAPTER FOUR

LEO relaxed. When it came to relationships, things had a disturbing tendency to become mundane once that brief pursuit was over, but he had a feeling that Heather would be different. Maybe it was because she was unwittingly involved in a side of his life to which none of his other women had been introduced. He had always made sure to keep London and the country very far apart. He bedded and entertained his women in the city. The country was for the family side of him, which had been hugely sidelined over the years, but which would always be there, more so now that Daniel had arrived on the scene. It was the first time he had ever considered the possibility of dating someone who knew his family. Frankly, he had never been in the country long enough to meet anyone, but even if he had he would have run a mile. He had never seen that, all things considered, there were certain advantages to the situation, especially now that Daniel was around.

High on the plus side would be the fact that dates wouldn't have to be made with the precision timing of a military campaign. Investment bankers and barristers were all well and good, but trying to arrange dates was usually a hellish business. He was busy, so were they and there had been more than one occasion when, having met and invariably spent the evening discussing aspects of work, he'd just been so damned tired that he could hardly be bothered to enjoy what should have been the highlight of the evening.

With Heather, it would be different. She was anchored in the country. He had a rosy image of her waiting there for him, waiting for her man. The idea of a roast in the oven was taking things a little too far, but it would really make a pleasant change to down-pedal a bit. He didn't know how much experience she had of city life but he would bet that the closest she had ever come to it would have been on television. The simplicity of what she had to offer would be a breath of fresh air. Heck, he might even bring her up to London now and again, take her to a play or some such thing, open her eyes to the big, bad world out there.

The more Leo thought about it, the more he figured that he needed a restful relationship, at least for the time being. What could be more restful than an artist, someone in tune with Nature? And yet wrapped up in such a sexy package that just thinking of her sent his mind further south.

Add to that the fact that time spent with his mother and Daniel was infinitely easier when she was in the mix, and Leo was satisfied that he had done the right thing in accepting the cup of coffee that was even now going slightly tepid. He took a sip and made some inconsequential remark about her being right, that the complicated coffee-making machine really did live up to its spec.

At the same time, his eyes lingered over her flushed face tinged with pink, the full breasts... God, when he thought about touching them again—not just a schoolboy grope under a tee shirt, but stripping her of her clothes and lavishing them with his full, undivided attention—spending time, taking those rosebud nipples into his mouth and hearing her moan as he suckled on them...

'I'm surprised we didn't meet sooner.' He tore himself away from his erotic, meandering thoughts.

'Are you? Why?'

'You live just round the corner, so to speak. I would have expected Katherine to have invited you up to the house for a meal.'

'You mean on a weekend? When you happened to be down?'

Leo didn't much care for the way she said that—*when you happened to be down*—but he let it go. He was in an extremely good mood now and he wasn't going to jeopardise it over a dodgy tone of voice.

'You weren't down very often, though, were you? I mean, how often did you visit your mother before Daniel arrived?'

'I have a lot of work commitments, as I think I've mentioned to you before,' Leo said, standing up to pour himself another mug of coffee and then returning to the chair, angling it to one side so that he could stretch out his legs. He could think of better things to do than talking, now that their differences were settled, but since talking seemed to be on the agenda he might just as well make himself as comfortable as he could. 'It's always very difficult finding time. I'm abroad a lot. I've never been a nine to five kind of guy. Sure, some are content with that, but there's no gain without pain.' He shrugged. 'That's just the way it is.'

Heather knew that all too well. That kiss, that mistake that she had allowed to happen, had caught her off-balance, but she was back in control now. She had to be. She also had to explain to him why she had pushed him away, and not so much because she was a fair-minded creature who felt some deep need to justify her actions. Heck, she doubted Leo West had ever justified his actions to anybody on the face of the earth! If there was one man to whom she need never justify herself, it was him. No, she had to explain because she had to hear herself verbalise all the reasons why she would never, ever have anything to do with a man like him. She had started seeing little sides to him, and every small glimpse had lowered her defences, and that just wasn't going to do.

It surprised her that he had taken rejection so well. In fact, she was astounded that he had actually agreed to come into the kitchen, have a cup of coffee and hear her out. She could only think that he must have the attitude of 'win a few, lose a few'. Or maybe he was so unaccustomed to any form of rejection from a woman that he felt compelled to hear her explain her behaviour.

Heather had no real idea why he had made a pass at her in the first place. She wasn't his type. She could only conclude that it was because he was a highly sexed male and he had tuned in to her unconscious fascination with him and interpreted that as availability. Available women were the curse of the wealthy man. He probably hadn't even stopped to think that he might not be able to just reach out and take whatever he saw and happened to want at that particular point in time, like a kid in a sweet shop with too much pocket money to spend.

'Why did you decide to send Daniel to school here?' she asked, changing the subject, wanting him to confirm with every sentence why she had been crazy to allow him to creep between the chink in her armour. 'I mean, why didn't you keep him with you, in London? There must have been hundreds of schools you could have sent him to.'

Leo frowned. 'Where are we going with all this?'

'We're having a conversation. Is there something wrong with that? I'm just expressing curiosity about the choices you made.'

'I couldn't have Daniel in London with me,' Leo told her

abruptly. 'You have to understand that my life there is not tailored for the inclusion of a child.'

Heather was nodding. She could believe that one, all right.

'Even if there had been a permanent *au pair* on tap, there would still have remained the question of my working hours. I'm out of the country fifty percent of the time. Empires don't run themselves; they need a captain at the helm. I'm that captain, and I'm steering a vast ship. I have offices in New York, Madrid and China, to name but a few. There would have been no consistency and that wouldn't have been fair to Daniel. I felt it far better that he settle in the country where he could have the benefit of my mother being permanently there for him.'

'That sounds incredibly convenient for you.'

'It made sense at the time.' Leo fought down his impatience, which he knew would get him nowhere fast.

'Did it make sense to Daniel?'

Leo's eyes narrowed. 'Maybe we could leave the question-and-answer session for another day?'

'Is that because you just don't fancy answering my questions because they make you feel uncomfortable?'

'You've already shared your thoughts with me on my relationship with Daniel. Frankly, I don't see the point of going over old ground.' He sought to hang on to his good humour, to think of what lay ahead. 'Today was a good day. The best day I've had with him since he came to England, in fact. Why analyse and dissect the past when it's so much more worthwhile to build on the present?'

'Okay.'

Leo relaxed. This was more like it. Bit of a shame that they were separated by the width of the kitchen table. If they hadn't been, he would have translated his relaxation into something a little more tangible, would have drawn her into him, seduced her with his mouth and his hands and smothered all her nagging concerns with his lips. Of course, she would have her nagging concerns. She had made those perfectly obvious the first time they had met, and they wouldn't have evaporated just because it had been a successful day out. He strove to understand and make allowances for someone whose personality was so wildly different from his own.

She was an innocent, someone whose lack of life experiences had given her a childishly disingenuous outlook on life. It was both charming and disconcerting at the same time. Add to that the sort of bluntness that would send most men running a mile, and the combination was incendiary. Since he wasn't most men, though, he felt well equipped to deal with her. In fact, it was all part and parcel of the package that was so irresistibly attractive. Those first signs of irritability vanished before the pleasing prospect of harnessing all that fire and making it his; a change from cool, intellectual, sophisticated power women was long overdue.

'Good,' he said with satisfaction. 'So…where do we go from here? I suggest somewhere a bit more comfortable than the kitchen.'

Heather looked at him, at the lazy smile curving his lips, at the unspoken suggestion behind his fabulous eyes, and the vague questions she had asked herself were suddenly answered in an instant of comprehension.

Leo hadn't politely taken rejection because he was indifferent, and he hadn't accepted a cup of coffee because he was eaten up with curiosity to hear why she had pushed him away.

How could she have been foolish enough to think that? He just wasn't built that way. He had accepted a cup of coffee because he had assumed it heralded her acquiescence, and he wouldn't have been in the least surprised at that because he was so used to getting what he wanted.

'Where do you have in mind?' she asked with a shuttered expression.

'Well…we could start in the sitting room and progress to the bedroom. Although, if you're really stuck on staying here…' He shot her a wolfish smile that made her stomach do a back flip and reminded her powerfully of why, exactly, he was so dangerous for her.

'If we stay in here?' she prompted. 'What? A quick romp against the kitchen units?'

The smile dropped from Leo's face. 'Poor use of words.'

'It doesn't matter how you wrap it up, that's what you're suggesting, isn't it? Or we could go upstairs to the bedroom. Might last a bit longer there.' She thought of them together on her king-sized bed with its floral duvet; she thought of the floral duvet being kicked off in the heat of the moment and shakily closed the door on the image. It was way too easy for her imagination to break its reins and run rampant.

'Why don't you let me show you? You can tell me afterwards whether you have any complaints. I guarantee you won't.'

'Because you're so sure of yourself?'

'Correct.'

'Conceited, aren't you?'

'Not conceited. I just don't see the point of hiding behind false modesty.'

Two patches of bright colour had appeared on her cheeks, and the hand wrapped round the mug was trembling. She set the mug down and clasped her hands together on her lap out of sight. The atmosphere between them sizzled like a live wire. She had expected him to be enraged by her slurs on his skills as a lover, and was now disproportionately shaken by the fact that he hadn't been.

'And then, after we've made love, what happens next? You return to London, feeling refreshed? Just out of interest, do you return to London to share your fabulous love-making skills with another woman? Maybe more than one?'

'Do you want a fight, Heather? Is that it?'

'I'm just curious.'

'Well, to satisfy your curiosity, I don't happen to be involved with anyone else at the moment, and in case you're not getting the message loud and clear I don't spread myself thin when it comes to women. The idea of having a harem of women on the go is repugnant.'

'So what *does* happen, in that case—after today?'

'Is that what's worrying you? You think that you might be a one-night stand? Well, let me put your mind to rest on that score—I don't do one-night stands. I don't do flocks of women because they happen to be available. I have a libido but I also have self-control.'

'But you don't do permanence, either.'

'No. I don't.'

'And how have all those women you've dated felt about that? Have they all conveniently shared your aversion to taking the plunge?' Like a dog with a bone, she was finding it difficult to let it go. She wanted him gone, but she didn't. She wanted to tell him her point of view, but she couldn't curb her desire to hear his. She hated her curiosity, but it was like an itch that needed to be scratched. She was desperate to get her anger to boiling point, because she would really have liked to despise him, but little pieces of him that didn't fit in with the stereotype kept sabotaging all her efforts, and her body was betraying her mind and ambushing her good intentions.

'I make it clear from the outset that a wedding ring isn't part of the agenda. If some of them have nursed any hopes in that direction, then they haven't said. I don't go out with women who throw hissy fits if they think they've been let down, and I don't go out with women who think that marriage is the inevitable conclusion to a relationship. Does that answer your question?'

'So all's fair in love and war?'

'Get to the point, Heather.' The tepid coffee was now stone cold. Leo pushed it aside and looked at her. Having dived into the water, he was only now realising that there were icebergs under the surface. He'd never had to put this amount of effort into a woman before, he thought ill-temperedly.

'The point is…' There was a jumble of words in her head and she was temporarily silenced as she tried to sift through them, find the words that were important and discard the ones that weren't.

She could feel his cool, watchful eyes on her and she wished that she could read what he was thinking. Why did he have to be so damned complex? Why couldn't he have done her the favour of just fitting into the handy box in her head?

'The point is…' She stood up awkwardly. 'Look, I can't have this type of conversation here.'

'Oh, but I thought the kitchen was the best bet.'

'If you don't want to hear what I have to say, then that's fine. You know where the door is.'

'Oh, don't think you're going to get off that easily,' Leo grated. 'I can't wait to hear what you have to say.'

He followed her into the sitting room where she proceeded to stand by the window, hugging herself and keeping as far away from him as possible. Outbursts and melodrama were two things he had no time for, but for some reason wild horses wouldn't have dragged him away from whatever lame story was about to unfold. If this was some kind of ruse to inveigle him into making promises he would inevitably fail to keep, however sexy her body was, then she was barking up the wrong tree, and he would enjoy telling her so in no uncertain terms. He should have guessed that she was all about flowers, chocolate and romance. He should have guessed it from the home-spun furnishings and the picture-postcard garden. She didn't know how the real world worked, but how could she, caught up in her own imaginary world of illustration, living in the middle of the countryside where life evolved at such a slower pace?

'It doesn't matter,' Heather said, starting somewhere in the middle, 'whether you fancy me or I fancy you.'

'And why would that be? I'm all ears. Because there's a higher plane somewhere? Some spiritual nirvana we should all be aiming for?' He had sat down on the sofa, legs crossed. She had switched on a couple of lamps and the room was bathed in a warm, mellow glow. The shadows made her look all the softer, more vulnerable, more unbearably feminine. He looked past her to the mantelpiece, which was cluttered with pictures in various size of frame. A hallmark of the incurable romantic, he thought cynically. There was no mantelpiece in his penthouse apartment and, if there had been, it certainly wouldn't have been groaning under the weight of photos.

'Because I used to be married!' There. It was out in the open now, and the silence that greeted her revelation was deafening. She could almost sense Leo's brutally sharp mind trying and failing to take it in.

'You were *married*?' he asked. He didn't know why he found that so shocking, but he did.

'To a man called Brian.' Having intended to leave out all

extraneous detail, Heather was now overcome with the urge to divulge every miserable second of her disillusioning experience. 'I… We were… I suppose you could say that we were childhood sweethearts. Went to the same secondary school, started going out when I was seventeen and he was eighteen, although we'd known each other long before then. Grew up together, you might say.'

Leo had said, in a voice that had been thick with sarcasm, that he was going to be all ears, that he couldn't wait to hear what she had to say. He hadn't expected this.

'You were married,' he repeated slowly.

'Yes. Haven't I just told you that?'

'I'm finding it hard to take in.'

'Why?' Because, she thought, he didn't think she really had what it took to get a guy for keeps? 'No, scrap that.'

'Because a husband isn't usually something most women keep to themselves, even husbands who are no longer on the scene.' He didn't add that most divorced women were fond of getting the sympathy vote and complaining about husbands who had left them high and dry—or maybe that was just his cynicism speaking, having been out with a couple of divorcees in the past, neither of which had lasted longer than three months apiece. Who wanted to spend what little free time they had listening to a woman ranting about her ex? 'Where is he now?' Leo asked.

He was already envisaging the type of guy she might have married, working out why she was so keen on fighting him. Once bitten, twice shy.

'In Hong Kong, as a matter of fact.'

'Hong Kong? What the hell is your ex-husband doing in Hong Kong?'

'You're amazed that I was married. You're amazed that my

ex-husband lives in Hong Kong. You don't have a very high opinion of me, do you?' Heather asked coldly, although there were tears just below the surface. She was remembering how she had failed to fit in to city life. The higher Brian had climbed, the more she had been left behind. She just hadn't been the right sort of woman. Why on earth was she feeling hurt because Leo was finding it hard to believe that she might ever have had a life outside the country cottage and the gardening interests?

'It has nothing to do with whether or not I have a high opinion of you.' *Married? Hong Kong?* He had managed to swallow his stupefaction that the woman had an ex in tow; had rapidly concluded that the hapless guy, the teenage sweetheart, must have been a country lad, had done whatever country lads did for a living—sheep farming, possibly—Heather would have become bored with him, with the monotony of being a farmer's wife... The familiar story of two lives drifting apart.

Sheep farmers, however, did not usually emigrate to Hong Kong.

'You portrayed yourself in a certain light,' Leo told her evenly. 'I took you at face value. You never once mentioned that you were married. You don't wear a wedding ring. Believe it or not, my immediate conclusion wasn't that you were a divorcee. Get where I'm going with this? If you can find the insult there, then please point it out.'

'You think that this—' she spread her arms wide to encompass everything inside the cottage and outside it '—is the sum total of my life? Is that why you figured that I was a safe bet to entice into bed with you—because I was so *backward* that I would be grateful and excited that a man like you, a man of the world, might condescend to show some interest in me?

Interest of a passing nature, of course—because, as you've told me, you're not into permanence. Not that I wouldn't have guessed that.'

Leo recalled his ready expectations that the attraction between them would result in bed and had the grace to flush.

'No one could accuse you of being backward,' he muttered grimly.

Heather looked at him with fierce, angry eyes. It would have been helpful if she could have superimposed Brian's face onto his, but no such luck. All she could see was his stupendous beauty, the lithe muscularity of his body. It made her more determined to have her say, to make sure that he knew in no uncertain terms that she wasn't up for grabs. That way, he would avoid her as much as she was desperate for him to. She didn't want to constantly feel fearful that she might just bump into him. She didn't want to be tempted.

His expression was still and watchful. For a couple of seconds, her imagination took flight, and she wondered where they would be now if she had never said anything, if she had given in to that kiss completely and had let it take her to the step beyond. They would be upstairs in her king-sized bed. They would be naked and entwined, and she would be burning up with lust.

She closed her eyes briefly, feeling faint. She had to make a big effort to remind herself that a bit of pleasure would never be worth the loss of her self-esteem, which had taken such a long time to reconstruct.

'How long have you been divorced?'

Heather opened her eyes and inhaled deeply. 'A couple of years.'

'What happened?' Did this qualify as drama? Leo didn't know. He just knew that he wanted her to finish whatever it was she had to say. If only, he told himself, so that he could walk away and thank his lucky stars for his near escape. A woman with baggage was never worth the hassle.

Besides, he still hadn't found out what the sheep farmer was doing on the other side of the world.

'What happened was that I married a guy who ended up making money his god.'

'Not following you. What did you say he did?'

'He was an investment banker. In the city. So, you see? I'm not quite the rustic country-bumpkin you thought I was.'

Like a jigsaw puzzle, the pieces were now slotting together at mind-boggling speed. So that was why she had been so knowledgeable about financial matters; why she had been so wary and distrustful of him. Did she think that she could just stand there and make comparisons?

Leo didn't know the guy, but he was outraged that he should be compared to anyone.

'Investment banker. Hence your knowledge of the stock market.'

'Oh yes,' Heather said bitterly. 'There was a time when I knew everything there was to know about what was happening in the world of high finance.' Her eyes glazed over. She forgot that Leo was there. 'You see, I thought that if I took an interest in what he did, I mean *really* took an interest, then he might be able to see that I was more than just the teenager who came from his home town. So I read up on all that stuff, even though it bored me to death.'

Leo, listening intently, could pick up on the hurt lying just below the surface, and he felt an irrational desire to find this character and knock him into kingdom come.

''Course, it didn't work.' Heather refocused on Leo. If he had tried interrupting her, asking questions, then she might have abbreviated everything, but his silence was the equivalent of a key unlocking a box. She hadn't poured her heart out to anyone, and a part of her was stunned that she should choose to do so now with the most unlikely of candidates. But then it wasn't as though she risked seeing him again. People bared their souls to their hairdressers, didn't they? It was the same sort of thing, wasn't it?

'He was in less and less. How could I show off my knowledge of all things financial if he just wasn't around?'

'How old were you?'

'Nineteen. Too young and too impressionable to see what was staring me in the face.'

'He moved on,' Leo said flatly, and she gave an imperceptible nod.

'He was talented. A whizz kid. There was a whole list of "youngest ever" records which he'd broken, as he kept telling me. He had to work all hours, he also kept telling me, and fool that I was I accepted it. I busied myself with my art course and dashed back in the evenings to make meals that ended up in the bin most of the time.' She glanced quickly at Leo but she couldn't read what he was thinking. She had come so far with the sorry recital that there seemed little point in cutting it short now. And, besides, it was cathartic, spilling her guts.

'I guess I knew it was all coming to an end, but I still hung on like an idiot until I got a call from an anonymous woman telling me that she was having an affair with my husband. She'd just been ditched in favour of a newer model, and I guess she decided that telling me was the best revenge she could have. 'Course, I confronted Brian and, needless to say, he didn't deny it. I think he was relieved, in a way.'

Watching her face was like watching a slideshow of emotions.

He realised that he was clenching his fists and he slowly breathed out, unclenched them, and waited for her to continue.

'You see, he was ashamed of me.' Heather held her chin up and looked Leo squarely in the face. 'Wrong clothes, wrong hair, not polished enough. The more money he earned, and the richer he became, the more his tastes changed. He no longer wanted small and plump and curly haired, he wanted leggy and blonde. Models. He was sorry, of course. And guilty too. He offered me as much money as I wanted, but all I took was enough to buy this cottage so that I could have a safe roof over my head while I kick-started my career back here. I didn't know whether I'd find work or not, but it was a relief not to have to worry about meeting a mortgage while I looked. He got a transfer to Hong Kong, and good luck to him. As far as I'm concerned, he sold his soul to the Devil.'

'And you've decided that I'm cut from the same cloth as a man who turned out to be an irresponsible philanderer.'

Put like that, Heather was uncomfortably aware that she might have been a bit liberal with her comparisons. But, when you looked at the bigger picture, weren't they more or less the same—rich men who thought that they could buy whatever and whoever they wanted to? That their wealth entitled them to walk all over people without any regard to feelings? Leo and his 'here today, gone tomorrow' women were only a hop and a skip away from Brian and his 'out with the old, in with the new', weren't they? Okay, so there might be some inconsistencies in the detail, but if you got bogged down in the detail, then you were lost.

She shrugged.

'You were more than willing to use me,' Heather began, but she faltered when she saw the thunderous, enraged expression on his face.

'Use you? *Use you?*'

'You think you can have whatever you want.'

'You're an adult. I'm an adult. As far as I'm concerned, sex between two consenting adults doesn't involve exploitation of any kind, and believe me, I don't need to coerce a woman into my bed. Your ex-husband may not have turned out to be the man you thought he was, but don't even think of lumping me in the same category.'

'You can't deny that you're cocooned by your wealth.' Heather was angry that he was trying to trip her up, trying to use clever words to make her feel as though she had made a mistake about him. She hadn't!

'I don't use it as an excuse to get women,' he grated. 'And that's a despicable insinuation. Have I tried to buy you with gifts, in any way?'

'No, but—'

'But *what*? Are you going to eliminate every man from your life whose name begins with the letter B?' he asked, his mouth twisting cynically. 'Maybe it might just be safer to eliminate all men from your life. Then you can be guaranteed never to be hurt again.' He stood up and noticed the way she cringed back, as though he posed some kind of physical threat to her. That was even more of a red rag as far as he was concerned.

'Don't worry,' he said scathingly. 'I won't come near you.'

On his way to the door, Leo paused and turned to her. 'An empty bed is a lonely place,' he said coolly.

'Better empty than littered with all the wrong kind of guys,' Heather threw back at him. Her eyes were stinging. She knew that as soon as he left she was going to cry, because she could feel the tears pricking against her eyelids.

Leo swore softly under his breath. He should never have

given in to this attraction, should never have seen her as a challenge. Challenge? The woman was more than a challenge! Had he forgotten how many thorns a rose could have? Damn it, the woman would have a hell of a time finding any man who wouldn't run a mile in the face of that tongue of hers!

The fact that she was standing there, looking as though she would collapse like a rag doll the minute her strings were cut, was no concern of his. She had said what she wanted to say, wrapped up in the greatest insults possible, and he didn't have time for this.

'*You* had a bad marriage,' she said tightly. 'And the way you deal with it is by never getting close to anyone. You don't want any woman to penetrate your fortress, so you just have affairs—nothing permanent, nothing that could get too emotionally messy.'

'Spare me the analysis.'

'Because that's something else you're *not into*? There are quite a few things you're *not into*, aren't there?' Her skin felt hot and tight. She knew in some part of her that was still being rational that there was no need for her to start having a go at him, but she wanted to. She was just so angry that she had allowed herself to get in this situation in the first place.

'I may have that lonely bed for a while, but at least I won't be scarred for ever. At least I know that there's someone out there who's right for me, and I know that someone isn't going to be a workaholic who doesn't have time for the rest of the human race!'

'This conversation,' Leo drawled, stepping out of the door and reaching for his car keys in his pocket, 'is officially closed.'

Heather watched as he let himself out of the room, out of the front door, out of her orbit. Success; she had said her piece. He wouldn't try anything again.

She should have been sagging with relief.

Instead, she felt one tear dribble down her cheek, followed by another, as she contemplated the lonely bed waiting for her upstairs.

CHAPTER FIVE

At TEN past nine on a Wednesday evening, Leo finally allowed himself to scan through the last of his emails, and swivelled his chair round so that he could stare at the uninterrupted view of skyline from his London office.

Like his apartment, his office was cool, uncluttered and furnished in the kind of uber-modern style that only real money could buy. One white wall was dominated by an abstract painting, subject incomprehensible. The carpet was pale and thick, and the furniture was a light, solid wood, handmade to stand the test of time, with very clever drawers that opened and closed without the benefit of handles. Leo had left it all to his design team and was still pleased with the result after five years. He could have had it stripped and updated but what would have been the point? He would still have gone for something similar.

A working environment should not indulge in the luxury of distractions.

And his private life should likewise be uncomplicated.

He frowned, very much aware that, since Heather Of The Background Issues had burst into his life a month previously, his private life had been anything but uncomplicated.

And this despite the fact that he hadn't set eyes on her since their last encounter.

Twice he had visited his mother and Daniel, even staying for the whole weekend, which he seldom did, as time was a commodity rarely at his disposal. On both occasions, Heather had been conspicuous by her absence. She was clearly avoiding him at all costs. After some casual questioning he had discovered, via Daniel and his mother separately, that she had variously been away on an art course or visiting friends up north.

'Busy lady,' he had remarked, at which point he had been subjected to an enthusiastic account of her good work in the community by his mother—art classes for the little kids; volunteer work helping with the gardens once a month at the local retirement homes; cake baking, apparently, whenever there was a cake to be baked.

'But no guy in her life,' he had murmured encouragingly. 'All that domestic stuff probably makes them run a mile.' Having taken minimal interest in the doings of the various people in his mother's life, a habit born over time and cemented through the years, he had been amused to find himself assaulted with all the tittle tattle that seemed to comprise village life.

His mother had even tentatively suggested, without prompting, two visits to London, and had arrived with Daniel clutching a London guide with pages marked at various places they wanted to visit. Gone were the expensive meals out and in had come sightseeing on a major scale. Leo had found, close and personal, queues, cafés and tourist sights he had never clapped eyes on.

Now, staring out of his window, he cursed himself for the fact that he couldn't stop thinking about Heather. He had left her house weeks ago and had convinced himself that he had

had a lucky escape. If she wanted to nurse her bitterness and bury herself in a solitary existence pretending that she was happy, then that was her affair. He wasn't in the business of trying to persuade her otherwise. In fact, he wasn't in the business of trying to persuade *any* woman into bed with him. He never had been, and he wasn't about to start now.

It irked him, however, that she was still managing to fester away inside some corner of his brain, disrupting the smooth running of his life, causing him to lose concentration in the middle of meetings. Even when he had been out with one of his lawyer friends, a glamorous blonde whom he had dated off and on in the past, he had still been unable to shake off the uninvited image of another woman—one with curly, golden hair and soft, blue eyes—adorning his bed.

Never having dealt with a woman walking away from him, Leo could only think that his problem lay in the novelty of the situation in which he now found himself.

Why else would she still be on his mind, like a low-level virus he hadn't quite managed to clear out of his system?

Or maybe, having bought into the notion that he needed to have a change from clever, hard-nosed power babes, he was just frustrated at having his plans thwarted.

Leo was unaccustomed to analysing emotional situations. The women he had dated in the past had seldom brought their personal baggage to the table, and the ones who had had been the quickest to go. That was just the way he operated and he was unapologetic about it. Now he found himself spending far too much time thinking about what Heather had said, furious at her self-righteous assumption that she was somehow morally superior to him because she had decided on a life of self-imposed celibacy to deal with what ob-viously had been a grim marriage.

He was scowling, chewing over her accusations that he was little more than a ruthless womaniser, when he felt the vibration of his mobile phone in his pocket.

His first thought was that he hoped it wasn't the leggy, blonde lawyer. They had parted company without having made any arrangements to meet up again, but she had threatened to be 'in touch', and he had been too polite to tell her not to bother.

He therefore answered in the tone of voice of someone prepared to deliver a let down.

To hear Heather's voice down the line brought him to his feet in surprise, but he recovered fast and bypassed all the usual pleasantries to ask curtly what she wanted.

His response was pretty much what she had expected, but, hearing his dark, velvety voice at the other end of the line, still had Heather's nerves jangling.

She had steeled herself to make the call, had known that she had to. In her hand, she was still clutching Katherine's address book, which she had found in the little chest of drawers by the telephone in the kitchen as instructed.

'I'm sorry to disturb you,' she apologised. 'I tried your land line at your house, but you weren't in.'

'Repeat. What do you want?'

'There's no need to be so hostile.'

'You've interrupted me in the middle of…let's just say I'm busy.'

Busy doing what? Heather thought. *And with whom?* She swallowed back a dark, intrusive jealousy that sprang out at her from nowhere and left her shaken.

'It's about your mother.'

Leo tensed. 'What about my mother?'

'She's in hospital,' Heather told him bluntly.

'*Hospital?* That's impossible. I spoke to her last night and she was perfectly fine.'

'She's had a fall, Leo. She was using the ladder to change a light bulb and she fell. Apparently she hadn't secured it properly, and she must have landed in an awkward position. Daniel and I have just come back from the hospital. She's broken her leg, and I'm afraid she's going to be there for at least a couple of weeks. I'm sorry. I know you're all wrapped up with you whatever it is you're in the middle of doing, but you're going to have to come up.'

'I'm on my way.'

So this was how it felt to have someone hang up on you. She took a couple of seconds to regain her composure, then she turned to Daniel, who was exhausted and finishing the last of the meal which she had hurriedly prepared for him the minute they had set foot back into the house.

'Your dad's on his way here,' she said with a reassuring smile. Daniel hadn't reacted well to his grandmother's fall, and Heather suspected that it was because she had become the one stable person in his life, the adult on whom he had learnt to depend following his mother's death. The ambulance, that ride to the hospital, seeing Katherine's ashen face, must have taken him back in time. Heather had made sure to be very gentle with him and to assure him that everything was going to be just fine. She had brought him home, sat him down at the kitchen table and made him a fluffy cheese-omelette with potatoes and chatted comfortingly about inconsequential things that had happened to him at school.

'When you've finished eating I'll run you a nice, hot bath, and then it's sleep time for you, Dan.'

'Do I have to go to school tomorrow? I haven't done my homework.'

'Oh, I think Miss Porter will understand. I'll take you in and explain the situation myself, so there's no need for you to worry on that score.' She began clearing away his dishes, stacking them in the dishwasher.

'Will my father be here when I get up in the morning?'

'Of course he will!' Just the thought of Leo closing the gap between them in that big, silent car of his was enough to bring her out in a cold sweat. She had been careful to avoid being around on the occasions he had visited. Yes, avoidance was always the coward's way of dealing with a problem, but Heather hadn't cared. If thinking about the man had sent her nerves into crazy free fall, then how bad would it have been to actually see him? Worse, to have to *talk* to him and feel those fabulous eyes of his rake over her with pity and scorn? Because she knew without a shadow of a doubt that he would not have understood a word of what she had told him about learning from her past experience with Brian, about not jumping into bed with anyone just because she happened to fancy them. He had looked at her as if she had taken leave of her senses, and she had been left feeling like Miss Haversham on a bad day.

'He's your dad, Daniel,' Heather asserted with more optimism than confidence. 'He's going to be here when you need him.'

'He can't be here. He works in London. He showed me around his office the last time we went down. He says he's away a lot. What if he's away and Gran's still in hospital? What then?'

'He runs his own company, Dan. He can choose whether he goes away or not, and if he's needed here then he'll *choose* to stay put.'

That closed that particular line of enquiry, and Heather didn't show how anxious she was that Daniel's predictions did not materialise. Katherine had been thrilled with what she had described as her son 'making such a big effort', but as far as Heather was concerned Leo's 'big effort' was only *really* big in comparison to how extremely *small* it had been before. With Katherine in hospital, Leo would have to make more than just what he considered 'a big effort'. He would have to put great sections of his life on hold.

The little boy fell into sleep within minutes and, without the distraction of his worrying list of questions, Heather had time on her hands to get really wound up over Leo's impending arrival.

She felt crumpled and unprepared. Three hours previously, Katherine had called and calmly explained that she had taken a tumble from a step ladder and was in a little bit of pain. In fact, Heather had rushed over to find the older woman on the ground, unable to move and white as a sheet. There had only been time to phone for an ambulance, to try to comfort a wide-eyed, terrified Daniel, and then the mad, panicked hospital scenario of waiting and X-rays and doctors. Any question of having a bath had been out of the question, and so here she was, dishevelled and unable to leave the house, because Daniel was upstairs sleeping and couldn't be left on his own.

She calmed herself with a pot of tea, having phoned the hospital and spoken to Katherine, who was sorted out in a private room, and thankfully in considerably less pain, but anxious about Daniel and about having to go under the knife.

She must have fallen into a light doze because the sharp ring of the doorbell made her jump and she hurried out, giving herself no time to dwell on the prospect of seeing Leo again and thereby get herself into a tizzy.

She had managed to convince herself that he couldn't be as impossibly overwhelming as she remembered, that his impact had really only been so powerful because initially she had not expected him to be so good-looking; that she had had valuable time to put everything into perspective and so would be prepared to face him. Besides, none of that mattered, given the situation.

She was wrong on all counts.

She pulled open the door and momentarily froze. Her skin suddenly felt hot and tight and she had a moment of sheer, blind panic as she took in the stunningly beautiful lines of his lean, chiselled face; she was as much affected by his masculine beauty now as she had been the first time she had clapped eyes on him. Against her lacy bra, she could feel her nipples tingle and harden and respond to that unbidden memory that this was the man who had wanted to make love to her.

'Are you going to stand there gaping for much longer?' Leo asked. He placed the palm of his hand flat against the door and gave it a little push, which was Heather's cue to step back immediately and rein in her turbulent thoughts.

He had noticed her gaping at him like a teenager with a crush! She could have died of embarrassment.

'You made good time,' she said, clearing her throat.

'No traffic at this time of night.' Leo strode into the house and then turned around to look at her. 'Tell me what happened. In detail.'

'Of course. Would you like something to drink?' She watched in fascination as he impatiently began rolling up the sleeves of his white shirt. He had ditched the tie at some point during the journey, and her eyes were drawn to that slither of bronzed skin where the top two buttons of his shirt had been undone.

'Just tell me what happened, and then I intend to head straight to the hospital.'

'Now?'

'I'm not one to stand around waiting for the grass to grow under my feet.'

'But no one's going to be there! I mean of course, your mother will be there, but you won't be able to find a doctor or anything.'

'You'd be surprised what I'm capable of achieving,' Leo informed her with such bone-deep, casual conviction that Heather was left in no doubt that he would have a consultant dashing out to see him at the speed of light.

He was heading towards the kitchen and Heather followed in his wake, rather like an obedient dog waiting to take orders from its master. As he grabbed himself a bottle of water from the fridge and began to drink, he actually snapped his fingers, and she began telling him the sequence of events, concluding by assuring him that his mother was fine, all things considered.

Leo continued to drink until the water was completely gone, then he looked at her carefully.

He had been looking forward to seeing her again, having, with a sense of satisfaction, regained control over the situation by realising that her vanishing acts had been a direct consequence of the impact he had made on her—forget all that rubbish about never going near a man like him in a thousand years. If she had been so convinced of her rightness, she wouldn't have spent the two weekends he had been up on mysterious away-days.

Of course, he wouldn't touch her with a barge pole now, but it still made him feel good that he hadn't been off-target when he had tuned in to that high-voltage sexual awareness he had felt emanating from her.

Annoyingly, however, he was aware that his body was lagging behind his thoughts for once.

Not even the alarming dullness of her clothes—a pair of

baggy, grey jogging-bottoms, an equally baggy tee shirt and an even baggier cardigan thrown over it—could reduce the surge of adrenaline he had felt the minute she had opened the door to him.

The fact that she hadn't been able to conceal her reaction to seeing him was overshadowed by the realisation that he wasn't quite as much in control of things as he had anticipated.

'Why didn't you think to call me sooner?'

Heather counted to ten. 'Everything was frantic here. By the time things had calmed down and Katherine had been seen to, I called you at your house, but you weren't there and your mother couldn't remember your mobile number.'

'It's programmed into her phone.'

'Which she didn't think to take with her!' She took a deep breath.

'She must have asked you to bring it for her once she was at hospital?'

'Katherine doesn't see her mobile phone as some kind of indispensable appendage, Leo. *You* might, but she doesn't. In fact, she very rarely remembers to take it with her when she goes out so, no, it wasn't on her list of requests when I came back here to fetch her some clothes for the hospital. If I had seen it lying around, then I might have thought to take it in for her, but I didn't.'

'And I suppose it didn't occur to you to look for it because it's not a *necessary appendage* for you either?' He raked his fingers through his hair in frustration because he could feel himself getting away from the matter in hand, falling victim to an inexplicable surge of something, some uninvited emotion that he didn't want or have time for. 'I might have got here sooner if I had been contacted earlier. How's Daniel been?'

'How do you think?' Heather asked, and then she subdued

her aggression to add, in a more level voice, 'He's been pretty rotten, poor kid. I think he remembers… Well, it might help if you talk to him. He's asleep now, but in the morning. Just reassure him that everything's going to be okay.'

'Of course.' How the hell was he going to do that? Leo wondered. That kind of intimate conversation with his son did not come naturally to him. Maybe, if he'd been a father figure throughout his formative years, he might know how to handle things… But, no; he refused to think of the unpleasant circumstances surrounding that murky issue. In the past month or so, the boy had at least begun to look at him slightly less unforgivingly. He had opened up enough to occasionally mention his mother, but there had been no heart-to-heart chats about feelings and emotions. How was he supposed to handle that now? 'I expect this must bring back memories,' Leo said, annoyed to realise that he was looking for clues on how to deal with the situation.

'Yes. I think so.' Some of Heather's tension melted away. 'He might need a bit of reassurance that you aren't going to disappear with Katherine in hospital.'

'Disappear?'

'As in hot foot it back to London the minute you have a quick word with the consultant.'

In truth, the reality of the situation was really only now beginning to sink in. His mother would be off her feet for some weeks. He would have to make suitable arrangements for Daniel. He could hardly be expected to abandon work for an indefinite period of time; it had been years since he had taken more than a few days off!

'Right. Well, I'm going to head off to the hospital now. I take it you will be able to cover here until I return?'

The underlying assumption was that she would be. Here

was a man who took it as a given that other people would have no problem in falling in with whatever plans he had for them, even if it meant disrupting their lives.

'Yes, but then I'll need to be away.'

'Naturally. Art courses to attend, friends to visit.'

'How did you know about the art course?'

Leo decided that it was definitely time to go. 'My mother must have said something in passing.' He began walking away. It was late, and it would probably have been more sensible to wait until morning before going to the hospital, but something had changed between his mother and him over the past weeks. Having been emotionally independent of her for more years than he cared to remember, Leo had recently made tentative steps to bridge the invisible gap that separated them. He had stepped out of his cocoon and begun to see the considerable sacrifices which she had made for him with Daniel. He had also been treated to one or two trips down memory lane, which was a place he had seldom visited, and had begun piecing together a past that might not have been quite as clear cut as he remembered.

Now, he was reluctant to jeopardise that fragile relationship by showing up in his own sweet time, allowing his mother to assume, with that resigned air of hers, that yet again the pressing demands of work took precedence over everything else.

'What time do you think you'll be back?' Heather pressed him for an answer.

'Couple of hours. Why?'

'Look at me!' She drew his attention to her dishevelled state and then instantly regretted it when he paused to look at her. It was a thorough inspection that took in the very worst of her stay-at-home gear, the sort of clothes which would have had her instantly hanged, drawn and quartered by the Fashion Police. She hadn't glanced into a mirror recently, but she was willing to bet that her face was shiny and her hair was a mop. 'I need a bath,' she muttered.

'I don't remember telling you that you couldn't have one.' Leo shrugged, gritting his teeth as his imagination surged beyond her unsightly garb to the body underneath. 'I have a wardrobe of spare clothes upstairs. Feel free to take what you need.'

Heather could think of nothing she would rather do less, but she nodded, willing him on his way so that she could take advantage of his absence to shower, change and scramble into one of the five spare bedrooms before he returned.

Thanks to an interruption by Daniel, who had woken and had needed comforting and then a rambling story before he fell back to sleep, it was nearly midnight by the time Heather had her much-longed-for bath. She found one of Leo's pristine white work-shirts to use as a nightie. Although it was much shorter than anything she usually dared wear, at least it was clean.

Having had nothing to eat for the evening, she was aware of the growling pains in her stomach when she finally settled into bed and turned off the light. Her last meal had been hours previously, a snatched sandwich in between preparing some stuff for the art class which she did at the local school.

Now, with her stomach noisily reminding her of that fact, she tiptoed out of the bedroom, down the majestic winding staircase and into the kitchen.

The house was in darkness save for the light in the hall. Leo still hadn't returned, or if he had he had managed to make absolutely no noise. Since he didn't strike her as the kind of thoughtful guy who would tiptoe through the house in darkness rather than wake its sleeping occupants, Heather assumed that he had become caught up in the sluggish hospital system and was probably tearing his hair out while he waited for people to do his bidding.

She was inspecting the contents of the fridge, and indulging in a pleasant daydream of the great man undone by a hospital system which refused to do as it was told, when she was aware of a sound behind her.

She spun around, armed with nothing but a bar of chocolate, and her eyes widened at the sight of Leo lounging against the kitchen door, eyebrows raised in an amused question.

'You're back.'

'So it would seem.' His gaze was shuttered as he looked at her, standing in front of him like a rabbit caught in the headlights, and wearing one of his shirts, something which he found unaccountably appealing. It was buttoned tight across her fabulous body and her breasts spilled beyond the confines of the thin fabric, revealing a generous cleavage and an eyeful of her circular, pouting nipples pressed darkly against the cotton. He quickly refocused on her face, now tinged pink with embarrassment, although she seemed unaware that the nightdress left precious little to the imagination.

'I… I was just getting myself something to eat… I haven't had anything today, what with one thing and another…'

'And all you've found is a bar of chocolate?' Leo was finding it hard not to stare. The woman had the body of a sex siren, with the sort of generous curves that were the stuff of most teenage boys' fantasies. He strode into the kitchen and watched out of the corner of his eye as she fell back onto one of the kitchen chairs, chocolate still in hand. 'I'll make you something to eat. Chocolate's just going to send a sugar rush through you, and you'll have to kiss sweet goodbye to getting any sleep.' He pulled out some eggs and cracked them into a bowl.

'There's no need for you to do this.' Heather was now painfully aware that she was being a chore on top of everything else. 'I've lost my appetite anyway.'

'No, you haven't,' Leo informed her. 'You're just embarrassed at being caught red-handed in the kitchen. At any rate, you need to keep your strength up.'

'What are you talking about?' When that failed to get a response, she added nastily, 'I thought you didn't do Mr Domestic.'

'I think I'm on safe territory with you. Eggs—scrambled or fried?'

'Scrambled would be fine. Thank you.' Of course he was on safe territory! She was history, as far as he was concerned. There was now some other sucker in his life. No; Heather was definitely *not* going to think about that. 'How is Katherine? Did you get to see her? Talk to her? Or was she asleep?'

'Yes, to the first two. Surprisingly awake, considering the time, but she tells me that she has trouble falling asleep. First I knew of that.' He began stirring the eggs in the frying pan, and put bread in the toaster.

'She must have been really pleased to see you. And the doctor—did you manage to get hold of one?' She could feel herself rambling and made an effort to stop, to act normally.

'Of course I did,' he said, sounding surprised that she had ever doubted that he would. 'It's all straightforward, but the healing time might run into weeks.' He tipped the egg onto the slice of toast on a plate and placed it in front of her. And without missing a beat he added, 'Which is where you come in.'

It took a few seconds for that postscript to sink in because she was busy losing herself in the fluffy perfection of the plate of food in front of her. She had never been heavily into meal-skipping.

'What?' She glanced across the table to where he had taken up position on the chair facing her.

'How's the egg?'

'Delicious. What did you say just then?'

'Finish eating and then we'll discuss it.' He noticed she didn't fiddle with her food, shoving it around her plate as if trying to distance herself from what she was eating. She dug in. He found that he liked that, or at any rate it made a pleasant change. Even power babes, intelligent enough to know better, were usually trapped by their own vanity and desire not to put on weight. The slice of toast would have been avoided like the plague.

'Discuss what?' She could have eaten the lot all over again. She felt calmer now, protected by the comforting width of the kitchen table. Being surprised by him like that had threatened to turn her into a dithering wreck, but she had taken her cue from him. They were just a couple of people discussing an unexpected situation. The fact that his presence did something to her peace of mind was neither here nor there.

'Ah…' Leo stood up and cleared away the plate, now scraped clean. 'My mother is going to need someone around while she's in hospital, and quite possibly when she gets out.'

'Yes. She will.' Heather challenged him with her direct gaze. 'And so will Daniel.'

'And I will be here, as much as I can. But when I am not…'

'You want me to cover for you.' She bristled with anger and with a certain amount of weird disappointment. 'Is that why you told me that I needed to keep my strength up? Why you decided to spend five minutes pretending to be thoughtful, whipping me up some scrambled eggs on toast?' That hurt. 'Katherine in hospital, and me bed ridden with flu because I haven't eaten, just wouldn't do, would it? Because nothing can be allowed to get in the way of work, can it?' She stood up abruptly and began to walk towards the door, only to turn around and find him virtually on top of her.

'This argument is beginning to get a little tired, Heather.' He took hold of her arm, and when she tried to shake him off held her a little harder, then he sighed and released her with an impatient shake of his head. He said heavily, 'I'm going to try to be around as much as I possibly can, but inevitably there will be times when I physically can't be.'

Reluctantly, Heather conceded that he was being realistic. 'I just don't like being manipulated,' she told him tightly, at which he flung back his head and gave a roar of laughter.

'You? *Manipulated?* Not a word that I would associate with you. If you don't feel that you have the time or the inclination to help me out here, then I will get my personal assistant to house sit as necessary when I can't be around. Naturally, Joanna wouldn't be my first choice, because you are familiar with Daniel and I am reluctant to introduce him to a stranger, but the choice is yours.'

It was a choice in name only, she acknowledged, but she wasn't going to cave in to his demands without laying down a few conditions of her own.

Before she could open her mouth, he added, 'Naturally, I wouldn't expect you to do it for nothing. You will be compensated financially. However much you want.'

'In other words, you would become my employer, so to speak?'

Leo frowned, taken aback at having his generosity, as he saw it, thrown back in his face. And *this* was the woman who had caused him sleepless nights! Pay her a compliment, and she would fight like a wild cat to prove she had been insulted. Give her a bunch of flowers, and she would probably claw your eyes out! *Narrow escape*, he told himself again. *And, when you're busy fantasising about ripping off her clothes and losing yourself in that body of hers, just remember that the woman's a hell cat.* Nowhere was it written that having a relationship with a hell cat was the sort of calming experience a man needed.

'In *other words*, I would recognise that having your life disrupted might interfere with your work, ergo a lack of income. End of story.'

Deprived of that line of argument, Heather huffed and then said, 'Well, I wouldn't dream of charging you for being here with Daniel if you're not around—which isn't to say that you have carte blanche to pop in now and again whenever it happens to suit you. And another thing—no women.'

'Come again?'

'No women.'

'And why would that be?'

Heather's cheeks flamed. 'Because it would be disres—'

'Climb off your high horse! I wouldn't dream of bringing any women up here. But, as a matter of interest,' he added, 'would you be jealous? Because that's just the sort of condition a jealous woman might consider.' He laughed again, because now she looked fit to explode. Give her a second or two, and he would have to dodge some serious aerial bombardment from whatever heavy objects were to hand. He had been stressed out, but finally he was beginning to relax.

'You really need to sit down and have a chat with your ego, Leo. If you let me know when you're going to be away…'

'Let you know? My life isn't predictable like that. No, I have a much better idea. You move in, and that way we can both save ourselves a lot of trouble making phone calls or knocking on doors. That would seem the most sensible option, wouldn't you agree?'

CHAPTER SIX

LESS than thirty-six hours later, Heather was standing in the sprawling hall of Katherine's house, watching with her mouth open as Leo basically commandeered the place. The man hadn't been kidding when he had told her that he didn't let the grass grow under his feet. The house was teeming with people in uniforms who were efficiently doing all sorts of clever things to turn two of the downstairs rooms into offices. In the midst of this organised chaos, Leo was standing, mobile glued to his ear, giving hand commands to the men while he restlessly barked orders to some hapless soul on the other end of the line.

Heather had just come across to fetch some books for Katherine and a few changes of clothes, but she was transfixed by the scene unfolding in front of her.

Three men, bending under the weight of an enormous desk, jostled her from behind, and she let out a little yelp and side-stepped them.

Just then, Leo spotted her dithering by the front door and he snapped his mobile shut and headed in her direction.

Despite the cataclysmic changes to his routine, he was feeling pretty good. When he had told his mother that he would be moving into her house so that she need not worry about Daniel, he had been first surprised, then tickled pink by the exuberance of her gratitude. Daniel was his responsibility, after all, he had thought with a stab of guilt. How distant had he and his mother become that she would think that he might swoop in and out, leaving them all to muddle along the best they could? Notwithstanding, he had left the hospital feeling well disposed and in high spirits.

He had also, in an unprecedented U-turn, decided to change his plans. Instead of dipping in and out to the best of his ability, he would simply shift his working arena from London to his mother's house. He wouldn't be able to guarantee a one-hundred-percent attendance rate, but his movements would certainly be a little more predictable. He had felt good making that decision, and he felt good now, watching his stuff being shifted in, everything that would turn his mother's den and little snug into a working environment suitable for him.

Heather, he noticed, was gulping like a fish out of water and looking as though she had barged into a scene from a science fiction movie.

'What on earth is going on?' she gasped when he was virtually on top of her.

'What does it look like? I'm kitting out some work space for myself.'

And he wasn't above getting down and dirty in the process, she noted, taking in the low-slung, faded jeans and the tee shirt, likewise faded; he was displaying all the signs of a man sweating at some manual labour.

In fact, her nostrils quivered at his rough, masculine scent. Whoever said that aftershave was a turn on?

'You never said…' she stammered, and he raised his eyebrows sardonically.

'I didn't think I had to run it by you to get permission first.'

'That's not what I meant! I just hadn't expected that you would be moving in lock, stock and smoking barrel!' She watched in horror as he stripped off the tee shirt and tossed it across the oak banister. Sure, it was hot and sure, he was sweaty and looked as though he had been lifting a few heavy objects, but was that really necessary? She dragged her eyes away from the fascinating sight of his bare chest, bronzed and muscled, his nipples flat and brown. To look at him now, no one could ever accuse him of being a soft, desk-bound money maker. In fact, he looked like a man born into manual work, and extremely challenging manual work. There wasn't a spare ounce of flab on him. She cleared her throat nervously and pinned her eyes to his amused face.

'Does Katherine know that you're rearranging all her furniture?' she snapped in a high voice. Now she sounded like a school mistress—prim, proper, disapproving. *He* was supposed to be the buttoned-up businessman, and *she* was supposed to be the easygoing artist. When had this role reversal occurred? she wondered feverishly. 'I just thought that your presence here was going to be on a more casual basis, that's all.'

'I didn't think that *casual* would work, given the circumstances. Care to have a look at the furniture rearrangements while you're here? Then you can report back to my mother.'

'Of course I'm not going to report back to your mother!'

'No? It's just that you suddenly seemed ablaze with self-righteous zeal.'

Heather scowled as, amused, he turned his back on her and began walking towards what had been Katherine's snug and den. *Self-righteous zeal?* Not content with making her feel like Miss Haversham, he had now managed to reduce her to prissy schoolmarm with an overdeveloped streak of Puritanism.

And her body was still in a state of hyper-sensitivity at the sight of his semi-nudity.

Her legs unfroze from where they had been nailed to the floor and she tripped behind him, still scowling, to pull up short in front of a fully functioning office in progress. Ornaments, dainty bits of furniture, pot plants, all had been cleared away and replaced by modems, telephones, a fax machine and a small, flat-screen TV which constantly recorded the levels of the stock market. This was a male-dominated space now, and the dominating male was currently looking around him with an expression of satisfaction.

'What do you think?' Leo asked, spinning on his heels to face her. It was strange how much he enjoyed getting under her skin. Maybe it was pay back for her getting under *his* skin. And maybe there was an even bigger pay back to be had. Wouldn't it be nice, he thought as he watched her trying not to watch him, if her defences came crashing down even though she didn't want them to? Wouldn't it be satisfying if she found herself jumping from her moral high-ground even though her brain told her that she shouldn't?

The brain, after all, was a strange thing. You could go blue in the face telling it to do something and it would just head off at a tangent and go its own merry way. Wasn't that what had happened with him? He had sworn himself off her but, now that he was here, and that so was she, some inner devil he hadn't known he possessed was playing mind-games with him—and he liked these mind-games. Hadn't he always been big into sport, both of the intellectual and the physical variety?

Right now she was as stiff as a block of wood, and was making damned sure to look anywhere but at him.

'You're bristling.'

'I am *not* bristling.'

'My mother's stuff has been safely stored away in one of the other rooms. You can rest assured that I haven't started a bonfire with the lot. If you like, I can take you for an inspection, make sure I haven't broken anything in the moving process.'

'Ha, ha. Hilarious. Just out of interest, exactly how long are you planning to stay?' Heather asked, roaming round the room and inspecting all the new additions with a jaundiced eye. She could feel him behind her, all alpha-male temptation, which her disobedient fingers were longing to touch. She folded her arms just in case they developed a mind of their own.

'As long as it takes. Within reason, of course.'

'You've gone to all this expense for a few days?'

'*Days?* That's either a monumental understatement or a severe case of wishful thinking. I would think along the line of *weeks* rather than days.'

'All right, then. *Weeks.*'

'Time is money, and it pays for me to be able to work to a hundred-percent capacity while I'm here.'

'You've certainly done away with all the atmosphere,' Heather remarked, looking at the black ash-and-chrome desk festooned with high-tech equipment, so at odds with the faded, flowered wallpaper and the lonesome bowl of pot pourri on the bookcase which Leo had obviously missed by accident.

'It pays to have a working environment that's devoid of distractions.' No peculiar, baggy jogging-bottoms and oversized sweat shirt today. She was wearing a cotton dress with a pattern of very tiny flowers and a pair of sandals. He wondered, idly, exactly long it would take him to undo the innumerable little pearl buttons that hooked her in.

He was vaguely aware that she was doing it again, making him lose focus, encouraging his rebellious mind to take a stroll down a pleasurable, imaginary path. Whereas before this had infuriated the hell out of him, Leo was fast losing interest in the urge to question the fact that the woman confused and confounded him like no other woman had ever done before.

Having always been a great believer in the inescapable truth that 'fate' was the last fallback of people who were too weak to realise that they controlled events, rather than the other way around, he was quite happy to put a different spin on things now. Fate had seen fit to throw them together, and who was he to deny his primal, manly urge to hunt and capture? He had tried bringing all his formidable intelligence and powers of reasoning to bear on the matter and what good had it done him? He had still ended up thinking of the woman way too much for his own good.

Logically, he deduced that if he could have her then he would be able to get her out of his system. Naturally, he would not be putting himself out to that end. It was all very well to rise above rejection, but he had his limits. No; she would come to him. *She* would surrender into his arms of her own volition. It would be a truly sweet surrender.

He surfaced to find her looking at him, at the tail end of something that had clearly been sarcastic, judging from the curl of her pink mouth.

'Sorry. Miles away. What did you say?'

Prissy, Heather thought, *self-righteous, zealous in all the wrong ways.* And now, to top it all, so boring that he had completely switched off from what she had been saying about liking distractions in the working environment.

'I was saying that I should get the clothes that I came for and then head for the hospital.'

'Give me half an hour. I'll take you.'

'There's no need, Leo…'

'No need for me to visit my mother?'

'You know that's not what I mean! You just seem to be very busy here.'

'Why don't you let me decide whether I can take time out or not? As you can see, I'm a big boy, more than capable of making decisions without a helping hand.'

Heather blushed furiously at the rebuke, but he wasn't looking at her. He was walking towards the door, pausing to discuss something with the guy who appeared to be in charge, then he turned to her.

'Why don't you go and do whatever it is you came here to do and meet me back in the hall in thirty minutes?'

'And why don't you stop giving orders?'

Leo shrugged and began making for the staircase. Heather was behind him. He could hear the soft tread of her steps above the noise of banging coming from the direction of the office. It was amazing how easy it was to rile her, he thought; not that that had been his intention. She was like a cat on a hot tin roof when she was around him, jumping at everything he said, bristling at hidden meanings to throwaway remarks, generally acting as though she would go up in smoke if he came too close to her.

'It's in my nature to give orders,' he said, not turning around. 'Why do you think that's a bad thing?'

'I'm surprised the people who work for you don't want you strung up! Don't you know that telling people what to do gets their back up?'

'Some people need telling what to do.' He made a right at the top of the staircase and was by his bedroom door when he finally turned to look at her. 'Besides, how else is a company supposed to be run unless there's someone in charge telling other people what to do? As a matter of fact, though, if you ask any of the people who work for me they'll tell you that I'm a pretty fair employer. Big bonuses, generous mater-nity and paternity leave, fantastic pension scheme… Nothing to complain about.' He leaned against the doorframe and stared down at her. 'Anyway,' he drawled, 'don't you think that some people actually *like* being told what to do?'

'No.'

'Because your ex made it his habit to tell *you* what to do?'

Heather flushed and then laughed derisively. 'Brian didn't tell me what to do. He just left me in the dark as to what *he* was up to. Anyway, that's not the point.'

Leo pushed himself away from the door frame and turned his back on her. 'You should loosen up,' he threw provoca-tively over his shoulder. 'You might find that life's less hard work when you're not continually arguing the finer points. In other words,' he added for good measure, 'you might actually *enjoy* being subservient…'

Heather was transfixed by the sight of him as he strolled towards his dressing table, leaning to support himself, hands flat on the polished wooden surface as he idly glanced down at the open laptop computer, then standing up, massaging his shoulder with one hand as he walked back towards her. The sound of his murmured, lazy voice was like a drug, making her thoughts sluggish and not giving her time to get herself all worked up by what he was saying.

'Subservient? I—I can't think of anything worse…' she stammered. She was having difficulty remembering what the original topic of conversation had been.

'No? Funny. Every woman I have ever known has ended up enjoying being controlled. Not in the boardroom, of course.'

He was standing right in front of her, and Heather took a couple of little steps back.

'Good for them.'

'You are not like them, however. That much I'll concede. But I guarantee there's one order I can give you that you'll jump to obey.'

'What?' she flung at him defiantly, her nerves skittering as he produced a wicked grin and reached for the zip on his jeans.

'Leave now or else watch me undress. I'm going to have a quick shower.'

Heather was out in two seconds flat. And in half an hour, during which the majority of Leo's extreme makeover appeared to have been completed, all bar the detail, she was standing at the door, still unnerved by that grinning last word he had had before she had fled the bedroom.

When he finally appeared, his hair was still damp and the jeans and sweaty tee shirt had been replaced with a pair of cream trousers and a cream shirt which made him look infuriatingly healthy and full of beans.

'I wasn't sure whether you would wait for me,' he said once they were on their way to the hospital. 'And if I embarrassed you back then, please accept my humble apologies.'

Heather looked at him suspiciously out of the corner of her eye. 'Contrite' wasn't an adjective she would have associated with him.

'You seem very nervous when you're around me—and I just want you to know,' Leo continued with a remorselessly pious voice, while he watched with fascination the transparent play of emotions on her face, 'that you have nothing to be afraid of.'

'Afraid? I'm not afraid.'

'No, maybe that's the wrong word. *Tense.* There's no need to feel tense when you're around me. Let's not lose sight of the main thing here, which is my mother. I see you're taking her a few books.'

Heather relaxed. Her imagination had gone into overdrive a bit earlier on, but she was coming back down to earth as she stared straight ahead and chatted to him about Katherine's progress. The operation had been a success, but she was still immobile and beginning to get bored. She was an avid reader, Heather said, hence the selection of books.

'She's particularly fond of travel books,' Heather told him. 'I think it makes her think of your brother, which is something I've been meaning to talk to you about.' With the busy hospital car-park now in sight, she was pleased with herself that she had managed to sustain a running conversation with Leo about nothing much in particular. There seemed to be a great black hole of missing information when it came to his mother, and he was either a very good actor or else he was genuinely interested in filling in some of the gaps which had hitherto existed.

'What about my brother?' Leo's mouth tightened but he kept his voice neutral.

'Do you know how to get in touch with him?'

'I fail to see where you're going with this.'

Heather glanced at him, surprised at the unwelcoming response. 'Don't you think that he should know about Katherine's fall?' This innocent question was greeted with stunning silence as Leo began driving slowly through the cluttered car-park, looking for a free space and complaining about the incompetence of the council, which had closed off a section of the car-park for repair work which appeared to be at a complete standstill.

'Aren't you going to give me a lecture about the virtues of public transport at this point?' he asked, neatly backing his car into a space which left them just about enough room to wriggle out. 'Or at least the perils of being seduced into buying cars that are too big to be useful? Maybe a sermon about the curse of the workaholic and the amount of time they waste trying to make money to buy things that aren't essential?'

After what had been a fraught-free drive to the hospital, Heather was confused at the sudden cool mockery in Leo's voice. Where had that come from?

'I don't care what you choose to spend your money on. It can't buy happiness.'

'There are times when you are a walking, breathing cliché, do you know that?'

'Why can't you be nice for longer than five seconds?' Heather snapped, glaring at him over the hood of his sleek car before slamming the door shut. 'One minute you're apologising for embarrassing me, and the next minute you're trying to start an argument for no good reason! I was just asking…'

'There's no need to drag my brother into this,' Leo told her abruptly, raking his fingers through his hair. 'Not that anyone is that certain of his whereabouts.'

'Your mother must know where he is,' Heather persisted. 'And wouldn't it be only fair to fill him in? Of course, if he's halfway across the world there's no need for him to head back to England, but he deserves to know.'

'This is not a matter open to discussion.'

'Your mother might disagree with that.'

Leo, striding towards the hospital entrance, swung round to face her.

She was staring up at him, hands planted firmly on her hips, her mouth pursed in angry defiance.

This was what turned him on and drove him nuts in equal measure. Driven by a sense of frustration, Leo reached out and pulled her angrily towards him, catching her by surprise so that she tumbled into him, her body soft and unresistant because she had had no time to shove him away.

There was nothing tender about the savage assault of his mouth against hers. He curled his long fingers into her hair and, although she was too stunned to put up much of a fight, he still drew her fiercely against him.

In that moment of complete shock, Heather felt her whole body go up in flames. It was as if a match had been struck inside her and had found that her defences, instead of being iron clad, were made of tinder.

Her lips parted wordlessly to accept his questing, urgent tongue. She heard herself give a soft moan. They were standing to one side, but she was still vaguely aware of people walking past them. Frankly, she couldn't have cared less what sort of spectacle they were making.

Her breasts were tender, crushed against his chest, and the abrasive rub of her bra against her nipples was sending tingling sensations all through her body, down to where a honeyed dampness had her aching for more.

When he tore himself away, it was like being hit suddenly by a cold breeze. She had a few seconds of realising that she actually missed having his arms around her. The silence between them seemed to stretch into eternity, and he wasn't looking at her. It didn't take the IQ of a genius to realise that he had come to his senses—which was more than she had done—and was already regretting his lapse in judgement.

'How dare you?' Heather struggled to hang on to her dignity, but her belated outrage withered away under his look of incredulity.

'Spare me the protest,' Leo told her. A group of people weaved around them and he pulled her further to one side. No, this was definitely *not* how things were supposed to happen. 'I didn't notice you turning away in revulsion. In fact, just the opposite— but then we both know what's going on here, don't we?'

'Yes! We're on our way to pay a visit to your mother and we—we made a bit of a mistake along the way…' She had the grace to blush. 'You kissed me, and…'

'You're going to have to stop doing that, you know.'

'Doing what?'

'Pretending that you're the innocent victim. It just doesn't sit well with the truth. Fact is, if we hadn't been here then there's no telling where we would have ended up.'

'Nowhere! I've already told you how I feel about you, how I feel about *relationships*.'

'I know. At great length. But it seems to me that your body's telling a different story.'

'I never said that I didn't find you an attractive specimen.' She liked the use of that word. It distanced her from the living, breathing, sexy, red-blooded male staring at her.

Leo cocked his head to one side and continued to look at her. In an ideal world—the one in which he played the starring role as the man destined to get precisely what he wanted and exactly in the manner in which he wanted it— there would have been dimmed lighting, an atmosphere of crackling, electric tension, the kind of tension that precedes inevitable surrender. She would have come to him, unable to resist her urges, melted into him and maybe, just maybe, he would have asked her to tell him just how much she wanted him.

Unfortunately the situation was hardly ideal. They were standing outside the hospital. There were people all around them, and the overhead sun was just about as far away from dimmed lighting as it was possible to get.

She also, crucially, had not come to him. She might not have been able to resist those urges of hers, but the stark truth of it was that she was backing away now at a rate of knots.

Leo was left wondering how the hell he had lost control of the situation yet again.

He had wanted to shut her up. The subject of his brother was off limits, and the desire to put it to rest had resulted in…

'Oh, I know that much,' he said softly. 'The little pretence you're hiding behind is that you can turn your attraction on and off like a tap.'

'We should go inside. Put that little lapse behind us.'

'Again.'

Heather flushed uncomfortably. *Again.* The softly spoken word dropped like a toxic rock into a still lake. She could feel the consequences rippling out.

'Okay. *Again.*' It took a lot of will power to meet his eyes when actually she wanted to duck inside the building and pretend that kiss had never taken place. *Again.*

'So what are you trying to say?'

'Nothing.' Leo shrugged and squinted against the sun. Twice he had felt the vibration of his mobile inside his pocket, twice he had chosen to ignore it. Playing truant definitely had its upside.

Although he was not looking at her—in fact, making sure not to look at her—he knew the female species intimately enough to know that this was a woman in the process of questioning herself, a woman on the edge of surrender, and the thought of that gave him an unbelievable high.

'Shall we go in? It's pretty hot out here.'

That was it, the sum total of his response?

Katherine was very upbeat, but for the entire time they were there Heather was unable to relax. Her eyes kept drifting to Leo—the way he sat, the way he crossed his legs, walked towards the window—everything.

By the time they finally left, she felt shattered. She had

meant to talk to Katherine about Alex, about whether she wanted him to know about the fall—because whether her son was told about the accident was her decision, and not Leo's—but in any event it never crossed her mind, which was far too busy thinking about other things.

It seemed ironic that when Leo had made that pass at her, had invited her into his bed, she had stoutly refused to have anything to do with the idea, had climbed onto her podium and made her feelings known loud and clear, had dispatched him with the ringing assertion that she was far too sensible to indulge in something for the wrong reasons.

She had just about managed to hold on to the notion that that one kiss had been an aberration.

This time, she knew what she had felt, and she knew that she had wanted much more. There was no way that she could hide behind the guise of the blushing fair maiden taken advantage of by the devil in disguise.

And now, Leo was far from interested in talking about anything. He might have kissed her, but it hadn't been a kiss of encouragement. He had been angry and frustrated with her, and his kiss had reflected that, it had been hard and punishing, and she had still clung to him like a limpet. She believed that she had actually moaned at one point.

'So…' she began hesitantly, once inside his car. 'Do you want to talk about what happened back then?'

Leo's brow knitted into a frown. 'What happened back then…?'

'You know.' He obviously had no idea what she was on about. 'You kissed me.'

'I thought we'd covered that subject.' Leo glanced across at her. 'Made a mistake, didn't make a mistake… There's just so much conversation two people can have on the subject of a kiss. We're not talking a national catastrophe here, Heather.'

She pursed her lips and stared straight ahead. Leo, focused on the road, couldn't see her expression, but he didn't have to. She had been thrown off-balance and this time she was finding it a little more difficult to dismiss. She couldn't duck and dive behind some phoney rubbish about being the horrified victim, and she couldn't even pretend that she had been caught off-guard and had therefore been the reluctant participant before coming to her senses. The lady had been his for the taking. But he wasn't going to indulge her very female need to discuss it to death, possibly to the point where she decided that flight, yet again, was the preferred response.

'No,' she said stiffly.

'We need to sort out the practicalities of what happens now,' he told her smoothly.

For a few seconds, Heather thought that he was talking about *them*. She felt a sickening lurch inside her as she realised that she wanted to talk about them, that she *wanted* to be persuaded to abandon every principle she had held dear for all these years, because her attraction to the wretched, inappropriate, totally unsuitable man was just too overwhelming.

When Heather had met Brian as a teenager she had been attracted to him, but it had been a girlish crush which had morphed over time into a relationship. Yes, she had always known that he was an attractive man, but she had never felt physically out of control when she had been around him. Leo did that to her. She didn't like it, but she could no longer deny it.

'Practicalities?' she asked faintly and he spared her another sidelong glance.

'Daniel?'

'Oh, right. Yes. Sure.' Heather sternly marshalled her

thoughts. 'Well, what's there to discuss? I mean, of course I'll be around if you need me at all, but I guess now that you've decided to adopt a hands-on approach to the situation it's pretty much sorted. Daniel sometimes trots over so that I can help him with some of his homework, and I don't mind that, especially if you're busy…'

'No can do.'

'I beg your pardon?'

'I've shifted my base, that's true, but my lifestyle is still going to be a little…erratic, shall we say?' They had cleared the town, and the open spaces around them seemed in harmony with his upbeat mood. It was odd, but in all his time coming here he had never really noticed his surroundings. Having always considered St James's Park to be the equivalent of the countryside, he was waking up to the reality that it was little more than a confined patch of green in the middle of a concrete jungle. So it was a pleasant eye-opener to be cruising along the winding little lanes, appreciating the scenery flashing past, not to mention the woman glowering in the seat next to him. That, likewise, was rather pleasant.

When he returned to the house, he knew that everything would be in place for him to slot neatly into an office that would be better equipped than most.

'Why should it be erratic?'

'Emergencies occasionally occur that require my presence. This afternoon, for example, I'm going to have to go to London to sort out some last-minute concerns from a small IT company I'm in the process of buying. Also, I may have set up camp in my mother's house, but that isn't to say that I'll be available for comment one hundred percent of the time. I would still like you to collect Daniel from school and feed him, by which time I will have done my utmost to make sure that my work's wrapped up for the evening. I know none of this is ideal for either of us, but it's for a limited period of time. Once it's over, we can both return to normality.'

'So you want me to spend the night at Katherine's?'

'If you don't mind?'

'No, that's fine.' While her head was still in a crazy spin, he, she couldn't help but notice, was as cool as a cucumber, super-polite and the last word in courteous. Heather was dismayed to find that she preferred the passion and heat of his anger.

'In fact,' Leo thought aloud, 'it might be altogether more convenient if you do as I've done—move in, just for a week or so. My mother should be back home by then, and I will get my housekeeper in London to come up and take care of all the chores as soon as she's back in the house. She'll need full-time help, and whilst Katrina's here she can also take care of the chores. She's an excellent cook in addition to everything else.'

A week or so... Temptation which would have had her bolting for cover a few weeks ago now dangled in front of her eyes like a banquet placed in front of a starving man. That second kiss had been a revelation. That little preaching voice that should have emerged and given her a strong lecture about keeping away from the man had gone into hiding, and in its place was a much more seductive voice, telling her that there was nothing wrong in snatching a little excitement. Was there?

'Sure.'

'Good,' Leo murmured with soft satisfaction. 'It's nice to know that we finally agree on something.'

CHAPTER SEVEN

LEO wasn't sure what demon possessed him. He really hadn't meant to return to his mother's house that evening. Who in his right mind would get in his car in the dead of night to commence a laborious drive into the country, when he could stay in the comfort of his own place which was a stone's throw away from his office?

In fact, he actually returned to his apartment, poured himself a whisky which he didn't drink and then came to the conclusion that for reasons unknown, the cool, undemanding, clutter-free confines of his penthouse apartment, which had been his sanctuary for all these years, now felt inadequate.

At which point he abandoned the untouched drink, switched off the banks of overhead spotlights which cruelly contoured every line and angle of the pale leather-and-chrome furniture and headed for his car.

This was the first time in living memory that Leo had undertaken the trip to his mother's house without first clearing his diary. Under normal circumstances, the visit would be arranged beforehand and he would arrive, usually running late because of work commitments, to a well-ordered and pre-planned weekend. He would undertake his paternal duties, which would involve expensive dining, and the purchase of at least one super-watt gift which Daniel would accept without a great deal of relish. Goodbyes would be said and he would return, with some relief, to the sanity of what he knew best: his work. His apartment. London.

He felt curiously light hearted as the car ate up the miles between London and his mother's house. He was looking forward to the change of environment, he told himself. His makeshift office had worked out even better than he had imagined. It wasn't the clinical, distraction-free zone to which he was accustomed, but it still felt weirdly comfortable.

Then there was Daniel. He had eventually broken through the barrier of his own reluctance and had had the little heart-to-heart chat which Heather had recommended. It had lasted all of fifteen minutes. He had awkwardly reassured his son that Katherine would be back in no time at all, and also that he would be at hand, making sure that everything was all right. Then they had talked about football. In between there had been glimpses of boyish charm, which had made Leo uneasily aware of the truth that life was never as clear cut as you might expect. As he might expect.

Now, cutting through the night, he found himself looking forward to seeing Daniel in the morning. He had managed to get a couple of tickets to a football game in London; prime spot. He figured they might strike a note, which none of his previous presents had, and he was looking forward to seeing his son's face when he was presented with them. With that in mind, he could push back the poisonous surge of regret, which was in a place he knew he was ill advised to visit.

And then there was Heather.

Heather, who would be moving in while Katherine was still in hospital. Heather, who had been at such pains to avoid him, now deciding to set up camp under his roof. Two and two, in Leo's opinion, made four. Right now, he was playing with the pleasurable conclusion that, having fought to keep her attraction at bay to the point where she had knocked him back with a few snappy remarks about 'being disillusioned' and 'waiting for the right guy'—who, incidentally, would never be him—she had finally cracked under the weight of the inevitable. Namely, she wanted him, and she was now willing to compromise her principles.

As far as Leo was concerned, it made perfect sense. Her principles might be laudably high minded, but they were totally unrealistic. She had talked scathingly of his lack of interest in emotional involvement, thereby putting herself on a moral pedestal. Not only would it be satisfying personally to see her step off that pedestal, he was also doing her a favour, he reckoned.

She might have been hurt, but hell, what sort of life was she condemning herself to? Did she imagine that she could escape all hurt by withdrawing from the process of living? He was reintroducing her to the notion of involvement: you had to stick your hands in and get dirty or else what you would be living was a non-life.

His thoughts were pleasant company for the duration of the journey which flew past, because at such a late hour there was little traffic on the roads. By the time he finally arrived at the house it was very late, but the outside light was on and there was a welcoming air to the place which, he had to admit, was lacking in his apartment. There was something to be said for the crunch of gravel under the wheels of a car, and the soft murmur of a breeze that didn't carry the sounds of ambulances, police cars and fire engines.

Letting himself in and standing still for a few seconds so that his eyes could adjust to the darkness, Leo quietly placed his computer case on the ground and then silently moved towards the curving banister. There was no point turning on all the lights. Heather and Daniel would both be asleep. He might have the kind of constitution that needed very little sleep, but he could appreciate that most people were not built like him, especially children.

By any standards, his mother's house was big. The first floor housed myriad rooms, including a small sitting-room. It had struck Leo, when he had looked over the floor plans from the Estate agency, as very handy for an older person. His mother could watch television at night without having to trek upstairs to get to her bedroom. It was now shrouded in darkness. He was glancing absentmindedly through the half-open door when the blow to his shoulder blades caught him by surprise and had him reeling against the wall. He regained his control and swung round, fists clenched in anticipation of teaching whoever had hit him from behind a lesson they wouldn't forget any time soon.

He knew it was Heather by her height; nothing else could be made out because the corridor was in complete darkness. He reached out and grabbed her hand before the five-inch thick, hardback book could deliver another well-aimed blow.

'What the hell do you think you're doing?'

Between swinging her hand and the book making contact with the intruder—an encyclopaedia of the type now virtually extinct, thanks to the Internet, but still in plentiful supply in Katherine's library—it had clicked in Heather's head that the intruder in question was Leo.

She hadn't had time to pull back from hitting him with cracking accuracy between his shoulder blades, which he was now rubbing with one hand.

She couldn't make out the expression on his face, but she didn't think he would be smiling indulgently at her mistake.

'I'm sorry, but you shouldn't be here!'

'Why are you always so shocked when I show up in my own house?'

'It's not technically *your* house, and you told me that you were going to be away for the night. I…I heard a noise…'

'I tried to be as quiet as possible!'

Heather could feel her heart beating like a drum inside her. Having spent the entire evening thinking about him, to see him now, towering over her, made her feel as though the oxygen was being sucked out of her body. He was like an addiction, and when he was around every ounce of her felt alive. She wondered whether he was aware that she was trembling.

'That's just it…I'm a light sleeper. I heard something, and I assumed it was a burglar.'

'So you just rushed out here, armed with…what is it? One of my mother's books?' Leo felt a rising tide of anger rush through him as he contemplated the consequences of her stupidity, *had* he indeed been a burglar. 'A…let's have a look now.' He relieved her of the book and pushed the light switch on the wall. 'Oh yes; an encyclopaedia of plants. Just the thing you'd need to protect yourself and Daniel against someone who might have been carrying a gun. Or a knife.'

'I'm sorry. I didn't think.' And she wasn't doing too well in the thinking stakes now either. Leo looked neither tired nor crumpled after his long drive out of London. In fact, he looked infuriatingly wide awake and every inch the staggeringly sexy alpha-male that had haunted her thoughts. Realising that she was inappropriately clad in her dressing gown, which she had hurriedly shoved over her shortie pyjamas, Heather pulled the cord tightly around her middle. But even that gesture of modesty couldn't staunch the tingling feeling in her nipples or the dryness in her mouth. She was crazily conscious of his masculinity as he continued to look at her with frowning concentration.

'Well, you damn well should have!'

'Lower your voice! You're going to wake Daniel!'

'I'm not finished with you. We can carry on this conversation downstairs.'

'I'm not coming downstairs with you. I'm tired. I want to get back to my bed.'

'Tough. Follow me.' He spun round on his heels, and after a few seconds of agonised indecision Heather grudgingly followed him down the staircase, still clutching her robe tightly around her as if afraid that it might fly open of its own volition and expose her swollen, tender breasts and stiff, aroused nipples. Her thoughts were everywhere, but she knew that there was no way she would get any sleep that night if she didn't pursue the conversation to its natural conclusion.

Instead of heading to the kitchen, where she expected he might want to make himself a cup of coffee, he peeled away towards one of the three sitting-rooms on the ground floor, and the only one which was actually used.

'You could have been killed,' he told her abruptly, moving to switch on a lamp on one of the many coffee tables before taking up position on the squashy, flowered sofa.

'*You* could have been killed on the way here,' Heather immediately countered. 'You could have lost control of your car and wrapped yourself round a tree.'

'Impossible. Sit. Please.'

'So you *do* remember what I said about not liking being ordered around.' She perched on the side of the sofa, simply because she didn't care for the thought of arguing with him across the width of the room in the early hours of the morning. 'What do you think your mother would have done in my position, if she had heard a noise? And it's happened before, for your information. Okay, it might just have been the house creaking, but she's done exactly what I did.'

'She told you that? She never told me. When did this happen?'

'The last time was several months ago, shortly after Daniel had arrived. She probably would have hunkered down and ignored the creak, but when there's a child in the house hunkering down isn't an option—and, short of sleeping with a gun under the pillow, you just have to use what you've got to hand.'

'I will need to do something about this. Why didn't she mention anything to me? No, scrap that question.'

Heather saw the flash of painful realisation that Katherine had kept quiet because she hadn't wanted to bother her busy son who had no time for her or her life in the country which was so far removed from his.

'It's a big house, Leo,' she said awkwardly. 'And it's old. Big, old houses make noises, and they can be a little creepy at night.'

'I had the most sophisticated alarm-system installed when the house was bought,' Leo pointed out, frowning.

'Katherine doesn't like to switch it on at night. She thinks she might wake up in the middle of the night to get something to drink and set if off by mistake.'

'Right.'

'Also, Daniel might, as well, and he'd be terrified if he set it off.'

'So you prefer to make use of the encyclopaedia of plants instead?'

She knew that he would be having a hard time understanding, probably never having been scared of anything in his life. 'It's pretty heavy.'

'I can't see my mother having the strength to lift it.'

'She probably uses the concise version.'

Leo looked at her and then threw back his dark, arrogant head and laughed. When he stopped laughing, the atmosphere had subtly changed. There was a sudden, charged intimacy in the air between them, and Heather found that she was holding her breath, riveted by his proximity and unable to tear her shamefully hungry eyes away from his face.

'You make me laugh,' Leo admitted roughly. 'Not many people do. I like that.'

Heather felt disproportionately good at that confession. This was what he did to her. He made her feel like a woman and not just like a faceless, sexless person who helped out at charity fund-raisers, pursued her isolated career, tended her garden and helped out at the local school. He made her feel wanton and youthful, and she had forgotten how that felt. Even when she had been married to Brian she had not felt that.

'And you make me feel…' She ran out of steam, and her half-finished sentence hung tantalisingly in the air between them.

'How? How do I make you feel? I'll take a couple of guesses here—angry? Pissed off?'

'That as well.'

'As well as what?'

'I…I should go back to bed.'

'No, you don't. You're not doing a runner on me, Heather,' Leo growled, catching her arm and pulling her back before she could take flight.

Heather gave a little yelp of dismay as she lost her precarious balance and toppled back onto the sofa, half-falling against him, and then stumbling frantically to right herself, in the process coming into way too much contact with his body for her liking.

His body was warm and hard, and feeling it under her

hands sent her mind into a tailspin. She half-closed her eyes and drew in a deep, steadying breath.

No, he wasn't holding on to her. No, he wasn't trying to pin her down or take advantage of her vulnerable position in any way whatsoever. In fact, he was in the process of straightening up so that she could angle her body away from him, but the guilty pleasure she had tried so hard to deny before finally accepting it now exploded inside her like a bomb that had been waiting to detonate. She was shaking like a leaf as she turned her face up to him, and reached forward, closing her eyes and blindly searching out his mouth.

Leo stifled a groan and awkwardly shifted his weight under her, because the erection pressing tight against his zip was downright uncomfortable.

This was what he had wanted, what he had felt assured would be the eventual outcome between them—but now that the moment was here he was compelled to recognise that this wasn't just any woman who would happily hop into bed with him at the snap of his arrogant fingers.

For Heather, this was a very big deal and for once Leo was not inclined to accept what had been handed to him on a plate with the easy presumption of a man who always, but always, got what he wanted.

He gritted his teeth, fighting the savage urge to wrap himself around her soft, womanly body, and instead gently eased her away from him just far enough so that her eyes flickered open and she looked at him in drowsy confusion.

'What's wrong?' Having come this far, Heather was appalled to realise just how much of herself she was willing to commit, and just how ready she was to take the plunge and hang the consequences.

'Nothing's wrong for *me*. I just want to make sure that this is what you want to do. I want to make sure that you're not going to pull away at the last minute and then accuse me of taking advantage of you.'

Heather settled fully against him. She could feel his erection stirring under her. Having long ago come to the conclusion that Leo was not a man who ever flirted with self-denial, she was disconcerted by the way he was looking at her now, his fabulous eyes lazy and questioning.

'Are you…are you trying to tell me that you've had second thoughts?' she asked in a light, shaky voice, and he pulled her down towards him in a kiss of shattering intensity. Heather clung to him, shuddering as his tongue plundered her mouth, tasting the wetness of his tongue and melting faster than an ice cube in a desert.

'I think you can feel what kind of second thoughts I might be having.' Leo pressed himself against her and she groaned when she felt his arousal.

'I think it's safe to say that you've just crossed the point of no return.' He shoved the dressing gown, now tangled around her, off her shoulders while she feverishly untied it from the front, still kissing him and wriggling in her efforts to loose the barrier of clothes between them.

There was something sweetly girlish about her eagerness to touch him, like a kid going wild in a candy shop, and he couldn't get enough of her in this mood. Her soft, full breasts were squashed against his chest, and he pushed up the small vest she was wearing to circle her back with his hands. It was mind-blowingly erotic to know that she was naked against him, that there was no bra working as a potential chastity-belt, in position to save her from herself in the nick of time.

'We should… A bedroom…'

'Is Daniel likely to wander down here at this hour of the

night?' Leo swirled his thumbs against the sensitive sides of her breasts, tickling her with the feathery caress which made it even more difficult for her to think straight.

'No, but it feels odd to be…doing this…*here*.'

'You mean with the family photos looking down at us?' Leo asked drily as he kissed her very slowly and very tenderly on her mouth, breaking off to punctuate his sentence, and then trailed his tongue against her swollen lips; Heather felt that she could have throttled him until he gave her just a little bit more.

'Now that's really done it.' She giggled and looked up to where his father appeared to be benevolently surveying the scene.

'My bedroom, in that case, although it's going to take a hell of a lot for me not to yank you down somewhere on the stairs and have my wicked way.'

'You want me *that* much?'

'Too damn much for my own good. Definitely too damn much to lie here discussing it with you when I could be tearing your clothes off and losing myself in that fabulous body of yours.' The control which Leo had thought he'd brought to the table disappeared fast under her willing submission, which was more of a turn on than he had ever imagined possible. He couldn't quite get his mind round that. Women had always been submissive when it came to him, hadn't they? So why did this feel so special?

They made it to his bedroom, just, tiptoeing past Daniel's room and pausing to hear the slow, steady rhythm of his breathing as he peacefully slept with the door very slightly ajar.

By the time they were in his bedroom, Leo was barely able to contain himself. He shut the door quietly behind them and then pushed her against it, ridding her of her clothes with as much urgency as she was intent on ridding him of his, standing so close to her that the accidental touch of their bodies seemed to generate an unholy heat inside him.

He was shaking as he reached down to cup her breasts, feeling the weight of them in his hands, sending her into orbit as he rubbed the pads of his thumbs over her stiff nipples while simultaneously grazing the side of her neck with his lips. He was desperate to see her, to feast his eyes on her beautiful body, but instinct told him that to switch on the light might frighten the inexperienced Heather off, and there was just no way that he was going to jeopardise what was proving to be the most erotic experience he could remember in a long time. Instead, he led her to his king-sized bed. She was fascinated by his nudity, by his impressive size. He could sense her eyes on his body even though he couldn't make out the expression on her face.

'I haven't, um, done this for a while...' Shorn of her clothing, Heather wrapped her arms protectively around her. She wasn't getting cold feet, far from it, but it was beginning to sink in that she was now in physical competition with all the sophisticated, urban, brainy, impossibly glamorous women he had bedded in the past.

'I like that...' He slowly and deliberately pulled her hands down to her sides and remained holding them, trying to keep his body in check as his eyes did a leisurely and enjoyable tour of her naked body.

Acutely self-conscious now, Heather blushed furiously under his lingering inspection, just thankful that he had been thoughtful enough to keep the lights off, although the curtains in the bedroom had not been drawn, and the silvery moonlight was sufficiently bright for him to clock that she was neither tall, slender or fashionably flat-chested. In fact, she was the opposite.

'You're perfect,' Leo surprised himself by saying, and Heather lifted her eyes to look at him hesitantly.

'Don't tease, Leo. There's no need. I'm not ashamed of how I look or anything like that, but I'm pretty realistic about my body.'

'No, I mean it. You're perfect,' he told her urgently, then, overwhelmed by the impact she was having on him, he backed her towards his bed until she found herself with the soft, downy duvet puffed up around her.

Her eyes had grown accustomed to the semi-darkness and she could easily make out the lean, athletic muscularity of his physique, the perfection with which his broad shoulders tapered down to his waist, the length of his powerful legs. The sight of him made her feel faint and excited at the same time, and the appreciative way he was looking at her revived her flagging self-confidence, introducing a spark of wantonness that she hadn't known she possessed. Where had that come from? Hadn't he told her that he thought she was *perfect*?

Of course, she wasn't a complete fool. She had a very limited time to bask in the accolade, because his attention span when it came to the opposite sex was brief by his own admission, but he had been sincere in the compliment and it had done wonders for any lingering doubts she might have been nurturing.

'So are you,' she murmured boldly as he stepped towards the bed.

Those three small words fired him up in a way no litany of compliments from his other lovers ever had. He lowered himself onto the bed and confessed, shakily, that it was going to be a real challenge to make their love-making last, to give her, without rushing, the most memorable experience she would ever have.

'I'm just so turned on,' he further admitted, straddling her and then sealing any more conversation with his mouth as he kissed her into a state of heated abandon, without so far laying a finger on any other part of her body aside from her face. In the end, she guided his hand to her breast, but he laughed softly in her ear and told her, 'Not yet.

'Ever heard of tantric sex? Shall I show you how sexy words can be? I can get you so close to the edge without touching you that you'd tip over if I just breathed on you. Would you like that? Or are you too hungry for me? Your choice.' He laughed softly, loving her compliance underneath him, knowing that she would have plenty of opportunity to show him her fire. He parted her legs and ran his fingers along the moist crease until she groaned loudly, begging him to take her.

When he had imagined her begging for him he had envisaged feeling a sense of triumph. If he did feel triumphant now, it was lost in the power of his answering emotion, a mixture of hunger, need and uncontrollable craving.

He was beginning to get an idea of what people meant when they said that they just couldn't help themselves. In the past, he had always been contemptuous of any such notion, figuring that when excuses were in short supply that was the inevitable lame fallback. Now he wasn't so sure. He might be in the driving seat but he wasn't too sure if he was steering the car.

'I want you,' Heather breathed huskily. 'And I can't wait.'

'Music to my ears.'

Heather watched with indrawn breath as he kissed his way down and finally paused at her heaving breast where he began ministering to one stiffened nipple, first teasing it with the tip of his tongue until she could bear it no longer, then pressing his head down so that he could take the engorged disc into his mouth, suckling on it while he continued to caress her other breast, leaving her breathless and whimpering and arching up under him so that she could feel the hardness of his erection against her.

It was exquisite torment. He had promised not to rush, and he was true to his word. When she could contain herself no longer, and made to touch the honeyed dampness between her legs that was driving her crazy, he caught her straying hand and responded by hauling himself up into a kneeling position, all the better for her to taste him and feel his big body shudder as she licked and caressed his rigid length.

It was a massive turn on to raise her eyes and see this powerful, unbearably sexy man shorn of his control, his head flung back as she lavished all her attention on pleasuring him.

When he curled his fingers into her hair and pulled her away from him, she knew it was because he was only a whisper away from losing control completely and she stilled as his raspy breathing steadied.

'Bad girl.' He grinned wolfishly down at her. 'Now I'm going to have to punish you…'

The punishment was tactile and verbal as he explored every inch of her restless body, murmuring smouldering, sexy endearments that made her turn to liquid. No one had ever talked dirty to her before, and it was amazing how primitive and erotic it could be. By the time he trailed his tongue along the flat planes of her stomach, Heather felt that the merest whisper of a breath could send her spiralling out of control.

He gave her a few seconds for her body to reach some semblance of calm, before nudging her thighs open with his hand and lowering his head between her legs so that he could breathe in the essence of her.

Heather felt a flare of panic at this shocking act of intimacy. Her experience when it came to men was strictly limited to her ex-husband, who had never had a great deal of interest in the concept of foreplay. She squirmed away from Leo's inquisitive mouth, but he was having none of that.

'I've never…' She stumbled anxiously over her words and he soothingly ran his hand along her thigh. He was incredulous that there were such huge gaps in her sexual knowledge. To have been married and not explored the glory of making love seemed to him a crime, and an indictment of the kind of man she had chosen to hitch her carriage to. If she had been married to *him*…

Closing his mind to a concept that had become totally alien to him after his own bad experience, and disconcerted that he had even been thinking along those lines, Leo resolved to show her just what she had been missing.

She quivered uncontrollably as he parted her womanhood so that he could run the tip of his tongue along her, gently honing in on her most sensitive bud. He felt her draw her breath in sharply as he began teasing it.

It felt unbelievably good to be pleasuring her in this way, giving her the first of what he wanted to be many new experiences. Even this brief flash of life with a woman planned ahead was something to be shoved away. He concentrated on driving her wild, lost himself in her body as she bucked and arched against him, her hands clutching at the duvet as his tongue continued to pleasure her.

He had told her to lie back and enjoy. But at the moment, with his dark head burrowing between her legs and his tongue sending her into rapturous response, lying back was the last thing Heather was capable of doing. Her body was seized by spasms of sheer, sensuous, wanton pleasure. She could hear the blood coursing hotly through her veins, and she had zero control over her own charged limbs as she raised her pelvis to his mouth.

She moaned when she was rocked to an explosive orgasm, and she hadn't even surfaced from that earth shattering experience when Leo drove into her with a grunt of satisfaction, picking up a grinding rhythm that sent her hurtling back to climax for a second time.

She was breathless when they eventually came down from their passionate heights, and was suddenly overcome by a wave of shyness so that she rummaged to draw the duvet around her.

'Bit late for modesty,' Leo murmured wryly. He propped himself up on one elbow and tilted her face so that she was looking at him. What he wanted to ask her was *was that the best sex you've ever had?* And this surprised him, because Leo didn't do insecurity, not on any front and certainly not on the physical front.

'And don't even think of telling me that it was all a mistake and you're never going to come near me again.' He reached over to plant a delicate kiss on her thoroughly ravished lips. 'And don't drape that duvet over you.' He yanked it off and let his eyes boldly roam over her flushed body. 'You have a fantastic body. Curves in all the right places.' He trailed one long finger along her waist and then over her breasts, circling her nipples and laughing softly as the tiny buds tightened under the feathery caress.

'Since when are curves fashionable?'

'You don't really believe that, do you?'

'I guess not.' Heather laughed and then looked at him seriously. She wanted to touch him so badly that it hurt, but she had to have the big 'what happens next?' question answered. 'Although I came pretty close to it when I found out that my beloved husband had been having affairs behind my back. Affairs with very skinny women who didn't embarrass him by doing something so uncool as *eating*.'

'Remind me never to bump into that creep,' Leo said. 'I might be tempted to send him on a one-way trip to Mars courtesy of my fists.'

'That's very gentlemanly of you,' Heather said, astonished, and Leo flushed darkly and shrugged.

'I have no time for married men who fool around. I might play the field, but I have certain codes of conduct, believe it or not.' He rolled over onto his back and stared up at the ceiling.

'Does your code of conduct permit one-night stands?' Heather asked lightly.

Leo turned to look at her. 'Is that your way of asking me whether I want more of you?'

'Maybe you should be asking me whether *I* want more of *you*.'

'You're kidding, right?'

Which was a sharp reminder of just how he saw her, Heather thought. He might wax lyrical about her body, but to him she was an amusing interlude, a break from his normal routine, someone who should be happy and grateful that he had found her attractive. She wasn't going to feel sorry for herself, though. She had made her choice—which didn't mean that she was going to jettison her pride.

'No, I'm not kidding.'

Leo tensed. Had he been thinking *long term*? No. That wasn't his style. Been there, done that. But he had been thinking longer than a night. Having been put in a position where he wasn't calling the shots, he was uneasily aware of a feeling of impotence and he didn't care for it.

'Don't think,' Heather said carefully, 'that because I've slept with you, that I've dumped all my principles about waiting for the right guy…' Some primitive instinct for survival kicked

in, making her realise that the last thing she should do was
hand over all control to him. 'I haven't, because you were
right about not confusing sex with love.'

Leo knew that he should have been relieved at that, but why
was his relief taking the form of irritation? Why was he
thinking that that just wasn't what he was in the mood to hear?

'Are you trying to tell me that you're just using me for
my body?' He could hear the dark edge to the lightly
spoken statement.

'It's a very nice body.'

'But you're still waiting for Mr Right.'

'And he's going to show up one day.'

'But, meanwhile, why not give in to a little temptation?'
This was all good, he told himself. In fact, it couldn't have
been better. 'Suits me.' He cupped her face possessively, stirring into response as her breasts brushed his arm. 'Now, why
don't I show you what a long way a little temptation can get
a girl?'

CHAPTER EIGHT

HEATHER had had no real idea where she imagined their relationship heading. She had given in to wild impulse, to a driving desire
to fling herself into the maelstrom of living with her emotions
and not just with her head. That had been two weeks ago and
now, as she sat in the quietude of her studio—which Leo had
had transported to Katherine's house with breathtaking speed
and efficiency—she allowed herself a little time to contemplate
the ramifications of her well-intentioned lapse of judgement.

Overall, not that good.

She picked up her paintbrush and began the delicate work
of daubing colour onto the meticulously drawn illustration she
had been working on for the past few days, but her mind was
a million miles away.

She wondered how, in the space of only fifteen days, her
harmless little fling had become her all-consuming obsession.
Since when could a fling become such a big deal that she
couldn't actually see beyond it? Wasn't it actually called a
fling because it was something passing, something from which
the recovery prospect was good—a bit like the common cold?
And, that being the case, why was it occupying her every
waking moment in what she could only think was a very unhealthy fashion?

She gave up on the illustration and instead swivelled her chair so that she could look out at the peaceful sunlit view through the windows, which had been flung open to allow in the balmy breeze.

With surprising astuteness, Leo had singled out the most appropriate room for her in which to paint. It was in the attic, a small space with a sloping roof and two generously sized ceiling windows, as well as the two long windows now open. The quality of natural light was unbelievable, and Heather had been quietly chuffed at his unerring instinct in sizing up the one place which she would be able to slot into with alarming ease.

In actual fact, she had been quietly chuffed at a surprising number of things in connection with Leo, starting with his choice of studio space for her, and ending with the amount of time he had devoted to being in the country—even though she knew that he probably had a heck of a lot of commitments in London, which he had doubtless put on hold so that he could be around for Daniel.

He had become a regular visitor to the hospital, where his mother was making a good recovery, and hadn't blotted his copybook once with his son.

The debatable upside of all this time spent being the perfect son and father was that he had been around a lot more than she had anticipated. Often, they had breakfast first thing, and then he would shut himself away in his office while she retreated to her studio to paint. Except that the painting was often interrupted by the soft pad of his steps on the stairs, by the feel of his body as he bent to look over her shoulder at whatever she happened to be working on, by the brush of his lips when they inevitably found the curve of her shoulder.

They made love with an insatiable hunger that thrilled and frightened her at the same time.

Under the onslaught of his continual presence, she felt herself becoming deeper and deeper embroiled in a situation that was as far from being a fling as chalk was from cheese.

And now there were further complications which had been thrown into the mixture, complications which she would have to mention to him when he returned from London later that evening.

If things felt a little crazy, then she had no one to blame but herself. She had allowed a situation to develop and now what had been an exciting white-water ride had become a whirlpool which was sucking her down faster and faster. The worst of it was the shocking realisation that she wanted to be sucked under, she *wanted* to give herself totally and completely to him, and she wanted to do that because she had fallen in love with him.

She had blithely ignored all the warning signs which now rose up to stare her accusingly in the face. She had thought nothing of the way he had taken over her thoughts; the way he could make her laugh and relax in his company; the way she was tuned in to his presence before he even entered a room; the way she had found herself waking up in the mornings with a spring in her step and a song in her heart, like a character from a corny romantic movie.

Now, of course, with that missing jigsaw piece firmly in place, she could see just how and why her safe, cosy life had been first undermined and then dismantled. She felt sick at the prospect of picking up all the pieces once he disappeared back to his London life, with its glittering social whirlwind of high-level meetings and chic cocktail parties full of those sophisticated, glamorous power babes with whom he claimed to be bored. At the time, she had been thrilled to bits by that unguarded snippet of information.

Now, she reflected on *why* it had been so easy to be swept away by every small thing he had said. Hijacked by love, she had been pathetically quick to believe what she wanted to believe. He'd told her that the skinny, beautiful barristers bored him, and she'd guiltily translated it into meaning that *she* uniquely captured his attention. He'd told her that she made him laugh, which was rare for any woman, and she'd invested it with a significance which it really didn't have. He hadn't played any mind games with her because he hadn't needed to. She had managed perfectly well on her own in undermining her pragmatic view of what they had.

She spent the rest of the day working on automatic while her mind went wild, freed from the constraints of pretending to herself that she was in control. By the time she sat with Daniel and supervised his prep, fed him and settled him into bed—noticing the way he now asked after his father when a couple of months ago the mere mention of Leo would have been enough to raise a scowl—her head was spinning.

She couldn't remember ever feeling like this, as though she was entering scary, unchartered territory, even when her marriage had been at its lowest and she had realised that she would have to walk away from it.

Daniel had asked her when his father was due to return, to which she had replied vaguely, 'Some time later, maybe around ten or so.' In fact, it was shortly after eight when she heard the slam of the front door from where she was pouring herself a glass of wine in the kitchen while doing her best to get involved in a rather silly television-sitcom.

Leo was still ridding himself of his jacket as he strode into the kitchen. Most unlike him, he had hurried his meeting along, politely declining the usual drink afterwards to celebrate successful completion of a deal, and had spent the entire trip back to his mother's house in the grip of a disconcerting type of eagerness. He had even been tempted to stop en route when he had happened to drive past a particularly charming florist in one of the nearby villages so that he could personally pick out a bunch of flowers for Heather. But he had managed to resist the extraordinary impulse. What the hell did he know about flowers, after all? His secretary usually saw to that type of thing. Except he knew rather more now about horticulture than he ever had before, having listened with amusement as Heather had acquainted him with all the flowers in her back garden, laughing when he'd told her that it was a sorry state of affairs for a woman in her mid-twenties to know the Latin names of plants.

He smiled when he saw her, his eyes roving possessively over her luscious body, and then he smiled some more when he saw the faint tinge of pink flood her cheeks at his hungry appraisal.

But first things first. He poured himself a glass of wine to join her and asked after Daniel.

'Is he asleep yet?' He extracted football tickets from his pocket and dangled them in front of her. 'Ever seen gold dust? I give you these.' With his eyes still trained on her, he placed the gold-dust tickets on the kitchen counter and lazily reached to pull her to him, murmuring into her hair that he had been thinking about her all day.

This, she thought, was how her defences had been so thoroughly overhauled. His softly spoken words and the feel of his body pressed against hers were lethal weapons. She shivered, wanting to break free, but stupidly clung to him with the glass of wine still in her hand.

He removed it from her, placed it next to his on the counter and did what he had been wanting to do since he had left the house at the ungodly hour of five-thirty in the morning. He kissed her with a thoroughness that had her whimpering and cleaving to him, and hating herself for doing both, when firstly she wanted to talk to him and secondly she knew that she was just digging herself deeper into a hole.

But he turned her on! He undid three buttons on her shirt and slid his hand expertly to cover one of her breasts. She made no move to stop him. The air felt as though it was being sucked out of her lungs; it always did the minute he laid a finger on her. She moaned as he began to play with the jutting nub of her nipple. When he licked his finger and returned it to her roused nipple, she could feel the dampness there race to every part of her body, until she felt like a rag doll that had to be propped up for fear of falling.

'The gold dust might have to wait until morning,' she said shakily, edging apart from him. Her breast was still exposed from where he had fished it out of her shirt, the big, pink disc of her nipple gleaming slickly from his wet fingers. She hurriedly did up her buttons and moved to rescue her drink from the counter. 'I wasn't sure what time you were going to be back, so I told him it was better not to wait up.'

'I got here as quickly as I could,' Leo admitted roughly, thinking back to the unholy haste with which he had dispatched his legal team and headed for his car parked in the basement of his vast office in Central London. He took a sip of his wine and shot her one of those wolfish smiles that could make her toes curl. He walked to the kitchen door and quietly closed it. 'Usually, I wrap up a deal with a slap-up meal with the team. Tonight all I could think about was getting back here. Explain that to me, if you will.'

The old Heather, the one that had existed yesterday, would have basked in that lazy, sexual appraisal that had her pulses racing and her heart beating like a hammer inside her. She wouldn't have cared less about explaining anything. She would have strolled over to where he was still standing by the door, watching her with proprietorial hunger. She would have reached up on her tiptoes as she melted against the hard muscularity of his chest, tilted her face to his with her eyes half-closed, and she would have let her body give him whatever answers he wanted to hear.

The new Heather, however, sidled towards the Aga and busied herself concentrating on the pasta sauce which she had earlier prepared for herself, having thought that he would most likely be eating out in London before returning to the country.

'There was no need for you to rush back,' she said indistinctly to the thick Bolognese sauce. 'I mean, I do understand that you have a job to do in London, and that job is going to prevent you from being here a hundred percent of the time. Don't forget, I was married to a workaholic.' She didn't dare turn round, because she knew that her will power would be threatened the minute she saw him standing there, lean, mean and sexy beyond belief. Stirring the sauce was her cowardly way of buying time.

Leo frowned. This was hardly the rapturous response to which he had become accustomed and which he now took as a given. Maybe she was having an off day. He crossed the room, vaguely noticing the way she stiffened, and dismissed that fleeting observation as a trick of the light.

'You were married to a creep,' Leo asserted. He slipped his arms around her and nibbled the side of her neck. She was all creamy curves, and the knowledge of what lay under those clothes was a fierce turn on. When they had first slept together, she had been wildly aroused but still unsure of herself. She was out of practice, she had later confessed, and she had virtually apologised in case she had been a let down. Leo had been touched by that lack of self-confidence. Since then, with all her barriers truly down, she'd been the most passionate, most satisfying, *hottest* lay he had ever had. He couldn't get enough of her. He frequently interrupted his working day so that he could seek her out and lose himself in her voluptuous body. When he wasn't around her, he caught himself looking at his watch and projecting his thoughts to when she would be back in his arms.

Heather didn't reply. Lust fired through her like a raging furnace, and her eyelids fluttered as she leaned back into him and stopped stirring the sauce, thereby losing whatever thread of helpful distraction it had offered her. She heard her own soft moan which caught in her throat as his hands began wandering the length of her body, unbuttoning her shirt to free her bare breasts which hung full and ripe and waiting to be touched. She gave another low moan as he began to caress her. She was barely aware of him easing her away from the Aga so that he could lean against the counter and continue to slowly manipulate her body from behind, notch by exquisite notch, towards a place of no return.

He was whispering into her ear, shredding her ability to think clearly as he began telling her what he wanted to do to her, where he wanted to touch her, how he wanted to touch her. By the time he slipped his hand under her gypsy-cotton skirt, her body was screaming for satisfaction, but he stopped her from turning around so that she could minister to him the way he was ministering to her, and she was too far lost in her own sensual pool to find the energy to resist him. She parted her legs and his fingers found the wet, slippery core of her and began stroking.

Her feverish response was an unstoppable force against which she had no resistance. She arched back, barely able to breathe, and when she eventually came her orgasm seemed to last for ever as she was tipped over the edge with shocking abandon. It seemed ages before she was once again earthbound, then she swivelled round to look at him, her face still flushed and her nipples still stiff and rosy with arousal.

'This wasn't meant to happen,' she said unevenly, and Leo grinned at her.

'Since when?' Instead of taking her right here and right now, he would wait until later when they were in bed. He would savour the moment. 'We're combustible when we're together. I like that.'

'Yes, well…' Her eyes skittered away from his lazy, searching gaze. 'We—we need to talk, Leo.'

Leo frowned. 'Talk? Now? What about?'

Heather could see that talking was probably the last thing he wanted to do.

'There's been a bit of an awkward development.'

'What kind of awkward development?' Alert to the nuances in her tone of voice, Leo was instantly on his guard as he rapidly sourced in his head what *awkward development* she might want to discuss with him. 'Do I need to sit down for this?' he asked abruptly. He didn't like the way she was looking at him with that cautious, shuttered expression. He didn't like finding that he had driven like a maniac to get here only to find his expectations of the evening going so drastically off-course. It struck him with unpleasant force just how much he had become accustomed to a certain pattern of behaviour between them, and how much he had come to enjoy that pattern.

For a man who had tried the whole domesticity thing and found it wanting, had fashioned a personal life that managed to escape the debilitating tedium of routine and the unacceptable consequences of commitment, Leo was unnerved to acknowledge how much routine had seeped into his relationship with Heather.

He couldn't pinpoint when that had happened. He just knew that he enjoyed having her available for him, enjoyed the smile that lit up her face every time he looked at her.

'If you like.' Heather shrugged. Now that sex was off the menu, she could tell that he wasn't best pleased. Wasn't it the driving force behind their relationship, as far as he was concerned? That *combustible* passion that flared up whenever they were around each other?

He refilled his glass with wine and headed towards the sitting room. Already one thought was forming in his head, a suspicion which took shape and was fully developed by the time she closed the sitting room door quietly behind them.

'Tell me.' He walked towards the bay window and stared outside for a few seconds before turning round to face her. 'That there hasn't been a mistake.'

'Mistake?'

'Don't play dumb with me, Heather,' Leo intoned rawly. 'You know what I'm talking about. We were careful all of the time.'

'*Most* of the time,' Heather corrected. She could see now where his mind was going, and the horror that would be unleashed should she tell him that she had accidentally fallen pregnant. Leo wasn't in it for the long haul, and if she had ever needed proof positive of that fact then she had it now. She felt as though she was being sliced open, but she remained outwardly calm. 'But I'm not pregnant, so you can breathe a sigh of relief.'

Having envisaged the worst, Leo was left oddly deflated by her denial. 'Good,' he said flatly. 'Then what is it?'

'I went to visit your mother in hospital today,' Heather

said slowly. 'She's spotted that there's something going on between us. She's been skirting round the subject the last couple of times I've been to see her, asking me what I thought of you, but today she asked outright.'

'And you told her…what?'

'I really did try to change the subject, but she wouldn't let it go, and in the end I may have mentioned that…that we've become involved over the past couple of weeks.'

'And that's a problem because…?'

'Because she believes that it's more serious than it is.' Heather thought it wise not to mention the extended conversation she had had, during which Katherine had poured her heart out about her misgivings over Leo's first wife, about the rift Sophia had driven between the brothers, a rift that had already been in the making. She had told her all sorts of personal stuff—regrets she harboured that her eldest son had somehow grown to feel shut out over time from the family unit, which he had seen as indulging his younger brother, while from a young age failing to acknowledge the achievements of the older. Her misguided faith that the *relationship* between Leo and Heather, the wonderful changes she had seen in him, would signal a new beginning for Leo had had Heather scuttling out of the room, appalled at Katherine's deductions.

'Of course she doesn't,' Leo denied dismissively. 'You're reading way too much into the whole thing. And, now that that's out of the way, why don't we pick up where we left off in the kitchen?' He moved towards her and Heather looked back at him with stubborn determination.

'You weren't there, Leo.'

'I don't need to have been. My mother has always known, since my marriage collapsed, that long-term relationships aren't my thing.'

'She's a romantic. She's clung to the notion that you've just been in search of the right woman. She said that Sophia wasn't right for you and that you've just been waiting to open yourself up.'

'To *you*?'

'I'm only repeating what Katherine said.' She could feel tears sting the back of her eyes.

Leo instantly recognised his mistake. He could see the hurt spread across her face, even though she made an effort to hide it, and an apology formed on his lips. But he remained silent because just the thought that other people might be playing around with notions of permanence on his behalf was an error he needed to correct. He had no intention of remarrying. If he hadn't said so outright to his mother, then he had always assumed that she had got the message, or why else would he have spent all these years happily playing the field?

He wondered uneasily whether Heather was right, whether his mother had been storing up misguided ideas about him waiting to find 'the right woman'. What was it with women and their pointless belief that a perfectly satisfactory life wasn't possible unless there was some kind of soulmate hovering in the background?

'So what do you suggest?' he asked heavily. 'And stop standing there by the door! You're making me feel uncomfortable.'

'Well, we can't have that, can we?' Heather said acidly, but she took up position on one of the chairs. 'I don't know what to suggest, except that we can't carry on deceiving Katherine.'

'We're deceiving no one!'

'Maybe *you* don't see it that way, but *I* do.'

'So, in other words, we either break things off right now or else we…what? Get engaged? Start looking for wedding rings?' Just when he had got used to having her around, he could sense her gearing up to take flight. Again. What was it about this woman?

'Of course not,' Heather muttered. She harboured a warming image of Leo asking her to marry him. For her, he was her one and only love. The situation into which she had drifted with Brian had been based on what other people had expected of them. This was the real deal.

'You'd like that, wouldn't you?' Leo said softly, narrowing his eyes on her pinkened cheeks. Something was telling him to back away from this conversation; he ignored it.

'I…I don't know what you're talking about,' Heather stammered as the ground threatened to open up under her feet.

'It would have been easy to laugh off Katherine's romantic notions. You could have shrugged your shoulders and told her that we were just having a bit of fun, nothing serious. My mother might well want to see me welded to *the right woman*, and I wouldn't know about that because she's never mentioned that to me, but she wasn't born yesterday.' Leo paused. 'I don't imagine she would be shocked at the reality that a man and a woman, sharing the same house, might have been attracted to one another, might have initiated a relationship. But maybe you didn't *want* to bring her up to speed with the truth. Did it suit you to let her think that there was something serious going on between us?'

'No!' Had it? Had she been unable to conceal her starry-eyed response to Katherine's scrutiny? She had tumbled like a blindfolded idiot into love with Leo, and had his mother spotted that even before she herself had?

'Are you sure about that, Heather?' He was very slowly coming to terms with the inescapable truth that she had invested a great deal more into their relationship than she had cared to let on. He had originally thought that their mutual physical attraction was just too powerful for her to resist, had forced her down from her moral high-ground and ambushed all the goody-goody principles she had been so keen to spout when they had met. She had mouthed assurances that it was all about the physical attraction because he wasn't her type, and, since that had made perfect sense to a man who was physical deep down to the core, he hadn't stopped to question the apparent ease with which she had embarked on their affair.

Now, of course, he knew that she was not a woman to whom sex was the be all and end all of a relationship. Her principles were deeply ingrained in her, and only now was it dawning on him that she had fallen in love with him.

He should be running scared. This was the very last thing he wanted. Indeed, in the aftermath of his failed marriage, he had made a determined effort never to find himself in a situation such as this. He wasn't scared—in fact, he felt weirdly pleased—but common sense put an immediate stop to that feeling.

'I'm not up for grabs,' he said in a cool, matter-of-fact voice. Leo could remember having this conversation before. There had been the occasional woman who had wanted more than he was prepared to give, and he had had to do the let-down speech, although by the time that had happened he had felt nothing. Frankly, by then, he had usually seen the signs of over-dependency and had dealt with the inevitable with a certain amount of relief. Not so now, although he wasn't going to analyse that, because the net result was the same. He was shot through with bitter regret that he would have to forgo the splendours of her body. He was ashamed to admit to himself that he wasn't ready.

Heather was mortified. 'I know that,' she said quickly.

'Do you?'

'Of course I do!'

'Then why did you allow yourself to fall for me?'

Heather sought divine inspiration, but the ground refused to comply by opening up and swallowing her. Had she been that transparent? Humiliation spread through every part of her. She knew that her face was bright red, a sure giveaway that he had hit the jackpot with his remark.

'You're wrong,' she whispered, looking everywhere but at him, although it was pointless, because she could feel those amazing eyes boring straight through her.

'You knew the rules of the game.'

'The game? *The game?* Since when is a relationship a *game?*'

'You know what I mean, Heather.'

'I didn't see it as *a game.*'

'But you *did* tell me that you were in it for the sex. If I recall, you didn't think that we had anything in common except, of course, lust.'

At this point, Heather was faced with two options. The easy one would be to agree. To strenuously deny all his accusations, to somehow manoeuvre a strategic backtrack and just enjoy the very little remaining time that they had together. Katherine was due out of hospital at the weekend. It would signal Leo's return to London, and why shouldn't she just have her fill of him before he headed back down south? Why should she be held captive by her emotions? Okay, he had guessed the truth, had guessed that she was a lot more involved than she had let on. But just because she had admitted that what they had hadn't been a game to her, didn't necessarily mean that she was looking for love and marriage. At least, not if she talked her way out of his assumption.

When she looked at her future without Leo, all she could see was a gaping, black void. Wasn't a couple of days of happiness worth it? She would be picking up pieces for the rest of her life, so why start now when she had the choice of putting it off just for a little while longer? Was she a masochist? Did self-denial win medals for anyone?

'I did think that,' Heather told him quietly. 'At the time. I mean, when we first…when I… Well, I thought it was all about physical attraction, but then I got to know you.' It was getting tricky, looking everywhere but at him, and eventually Heather raised her eyes to his face. His expression was still, shuttered. She knew that this would be a nightmare for him but she wasn't going to skirt round the truth because it was easy. If he didn't like what she was about to say, then tough.

'Or maybe,' she continued thoughtfully, 'I was just kidding myself. Maybe I felt that pull towards you even before I realised—before I realised that I had feelings for you.' She smiled weakly. Even in her discomfort, she was agonisingly aware of his potency, of that strong, masculine pull that emanated from him in dangerous waves. It made her feel giddy, breathless and horribly, horribly weak. She had to draw in a deep, steadying breath before she could continue in the face of his stony silence.

Leo bitterly regretted having brought the subject up. Frankly, he hadn't expected her to confirm his suspicions. Any other woman would have taken refuge in denial, making sure that the way was clear for a dignified exit. Not so this woman— but hadn't he already come to the conclusion that she was a one off?

Unfortunately, the more she said, the faster she would bury what they had. Did he want it buried? Strangely, no. Not that he wanted commitment. He just didn't want things to finish quite yet, and he was hellishly annoyed that she was the one doing the finishing. Role reversals and learning curves were two things he considered pointless in so far as they pertained to him personally.

He raised his hand to stop her mid-flow.

'There's no need to do the whole psychoanalysis thing,' he interrupted, pacing the room, his brows knitted into a frown as he tried to marshall his thoughts. Not for the first time in her company, they were proving strangely rebellious.

'Yes, there is. For me, at any rate.' Mortified as she was, Heather was determined to stand her ground and speak her mind. Things left unsaid meant that closure was never achieved, and besides, why shouldn't life be a little uncomfortable for him? Why should she slink away with a phoney smile and pretend that her heart wasn't breaking?

'Why?' Leo stole a scowling, frustrated glance at her and raked his fingers through his hair.

'Because I like honesty? Because I'm not going to pretend that I haven't fallen for you? I have.' She looked at him defiantly. 'I know it doesn't suit you to hear me say that, but it's the truth. I haven't told Katherine that, so you needn't worry on that score. In fact, I didn't encourage her to think that there was anything serious between us, despite what you said. I know this isn't what you bargained for, but believe me it isn't what I bargained for either.'

She stood up and began edging towards the door. 'I also know that it makes things a little uncomfortable between us at the moment, so I'm going to transfer back to my place tomorrow. You'll have to stay here with Daniel until your mother returns.' She collided with the door and paused, licking her lips nervously, willing him to say something instead of maintaining a silence from which she could deduce nothing whatsoever. Maybe, though, his continuing silence was preferable to his mockery or contempt.

Looking at her as she backed towards the door, Leo had been overcome with an angry, urgent need to stop her in her tracks. The inevitability of this outcome hit him like a sledgehammer. He didn't know what he wanted to say, but he damn well wasn't going to remain in tongue-tied silence. But before he could utter a word she was holding up her hand. The other hand had already turned the door handle.

'I don't want you to say anything. We both knew that this was going to end, anyway, for whatever reason.' There was a silence that lasted only a heartbeat. 'But, before I go, I mustn't forget to tell you: your brother's coming home. He'll be here on Saturday. In time for when Katherine arrives back from the hospital.' It was good to have the conversation back onto a prosaic level. It helped her diminishing self-control and reminded her that this wasn't some great romantic drama, just an everyday story of two people who weren't destined to be together. He would move on and she would too, eventually.

'Goodbye, Leo.'

She fled. He could hear her retreating footsteps, and he knew that she wasn't heading back up to her room because he heard the slam of the front door. It was as final as a full stop at the end of a sentence.

CHAPTER NINE

HEATHER looked at her reflection in the mirror. She could feel the flutter of nerves in her stomach and it was making her feel sick. Was she wearing the right thing? Was she giving off the correct message? What exactly *was* that message anyway? Some could argue that, having declared your love to a man who had a stone for a heart, there was no appropriate message that could be achieved with an outfit.

She had spent the past three days unable to eat, concentrate or do much of anything apart from think, and her thoughts had been very poor company. She had barely glanced at her work, which she had stolen back from Katherine's house, furtively having made sure that Leo was nowhere around when she had been inside the house. She had, however, checked her mobile phone every other second, or so it seemed, and had wished against the odds that she would hear the distinctive beeping sound of a text message from him. When they had been together he had often texted her, and she still blushed when she remembered the content of some of his messages. But she had not heard a word from him and, while that was precisely what she had expected, the pain of missing him was still unbearable. She had got the closure she had wanted, except it had done nothing to put her on the path to recovery.

And now she was about to see him again—when she still felt raw, bruised and vulnerable.

Katherine had returned from hospital—in fine fettle, although still unable to walk without the aid of crutches—and with the help of Marjorie, the lady who came in to clean the house during the week, she was hosting a dinner in celebration of her son returning from foreign shores.

Heather knew all this because she had been invited to the little dinner party, which was going to be a cosy affair. Just family. And Heather. No amount of helpful suggestions along the lines of, 'Wouldn't it be nice to have some time with your sons on your own? To catch up?' had managed to rescue her from the horror of having to face Leo again.

Which brought her right back to her outfit: casual. Nothing that would indicate that she might, in any way whatsoever, be attempting to attract him: a pair of grey trousers and a black tee shirt with a simple black cotton jacket flung over it, and some plain, black flat shoes. No one, she decided, could accuse her of wanting to draw attention to herself when she was dressed in the most background colours known to mankind. Colours that, coincidentally, were great for bolstering her confidence, because they made her feel utterly sexless. All she needed was the addition of a briefcase, and she might have been going for a job interview at a bank.

Not that she felt in any way confident as she left her house fifteen minutes later. In fact, she felt about as confident as a prisoner being led to the guillotine. She had decided to walk and, the closer she got to the big house, the slower her pace became until she was standing in the cool early evening, staring at the house in front of her, searching out the little attic window from which she had looked down, only days ago, to a breathtaking view of open fields and sky. Leo's car, the gleaming, silver Bentley, was parked at an angle in the large, gravelled courtyard, as was a small, red runabout which Heather knew belonged to the housekeeper who had come for the evening to prepare the meal and do the dishes. Close to the front door was a black motorcycle which looked as though it had seen better times.

Heather took a deep breath and forced herself on with the cheering thought that the evening wouldn't last for ever. In fact, she was determined to stay for as little time as humanly and politely possible.

Also on the plus side was the fact that they wouldn't be alone together. Alex, Katherine and Daniel would all be there as well, and chances were high that Leo would barely notice her presence at all.

In all events, he wasn't there when she entered the house. Where was he?

'He had to rush off to London this morning,' Katherine said, smiling from the sofa where she was sitting with a drink in her hand. 'He hasn't even had the opportunity to see his brother again!' Which drew Heather's eyes to the man sitting next to Katherine—no doubt the owner of the battered motorcycle parked askew outside the house.

Alex had the same set of features as his brother, but without the sharp edges, and with none of the power and arrogance that stamped the contours of Leo's face, giving it its own distinctive brand of sexual potency. When he stood up smiling to shake her hand, she could see that he was a little shorter than Leo and with the wiry body of a cyclist. He didn't threaten her in any way at all and Heather liked him immediately on sight.

Without Leo around her anxiety faded, and as introductions

were made and a drink pressed into her hand she felt herself begin to relax. If Leo had gone to London, then it was unlikely that he would be returning any time soon. She didn't have to be on the lookout. She could give herself over to listening to Katherine and Alex as they chatted animatedly with one another, Alex telling them about his travels, and Katherine chastising him gently about the risks he took living rough on the other side of the world.

Daniel's eyes were like saucers as Alex regaled them with tales of high adventure, teasing his mother that as soon as she was back on her feet she would have to ride pillion with him when he next took off.

'Although,' he mused as they went in for dinner, an informal meal served in the kitchen, 'being here, I kinda think that it might be time to find me a steady wife and settle down…'

'Just what I wish your brother would do.' Katherine sighed, taking her place at a table which had been optimistically set for five. Leo's empty space spoke volumes for his absence. Now that his mother had returned, he had clearly returned to his bad old ways of putting work first, Heather thought.

She noticed that, at the mention of Leo, Alex's face became closed, but the impression lasted only a second then he was back to smiling and joking, involving Daniel in the conversation with a warmth and ease that brought a smile to Heather's face—although, as the spectator watching the mother-son interplay, she couldn't help but feel a strong pull of sympathy for Leo. He had from a young age felt locked out of the family unit, Katherine had confided, felt less loved than his brother and less appreciated for his efforts.

'What he couldn't have understood,' Katherine had told her thoughtfully at the hospital when they had had their heart to heart, 'was that Alex had always just needed more looking after. He never seemed to really know himself the way Leo did. He had always needed reassurance.'

Now she thought about Leo and the way he had pulled back over the years from his family until now, when Daniel and then Katherine's fall had brought him back into the fold. Not entirely, but life, after all, was a gradual process of growing and learning.

She felt momentarily faint, thinking how much she would have loved to be by his side over the years, learning and growing alongside him. Instead, not only had he disappeared but no one seemed entirely sure when he would return.

'You must be really disappointed.' She turned to Alex when there was a lull in the conversation over dinner. 'Having travelled all the way over here to find that Leo's been called away on business.'

Next to her, Daniel was all ears as he demanded to know the gory bits of his grandmother's operation: 'What do you think it looked like, all that blood and stuff? Couldn't you have asked them to take a picture?' All those pressing questions which he had obviously felt constrained not to ask when Katherine had been in hospital, and which Katherine was now strenuously trying to evade, although Heather could tell from the expression on her face that she was close to laughing.

'Leo's always being "called away on business",' Alex told her in a low voice. 'It's his modus operandi. Haven't you noticed? The fact that I have turned up here like a bad penny would have sent him running for cover even faster than usual.'

'But why?' On one side, Katherine was now trying to divert Daniel away from the intricacies of hospital procedure and towards the more harmless topic of the dessert which had been placed in front of him, but Daniel was as stubborn as his father and was having none of it. In a minute he would be off to bed, and he was determined to make hay while the sun shone.

'Call it his way of showing brotherly love,' Alex murmured bitterly.

'Well, this is none of my business,' Heather told him, closing her fork and spoon on her dessert.

'Isn't it? I thought… Mum said that…'

Heather felt her face flame with unbidden colour, but her voice remained steady as she shrugged and gave a little laugh of dismissal. 'Oh, *that*,' she whispered in a shifty voice. *What on earth had Katherine said?* Okay, so it didn't take a genius to hazard a pretty good guess. Leo had clearly said nothing to his mother about recent events, and Katherine still believed that Heather and her son were an item. There had been no opportunity to talk to her, and when Heather thought about the awkward conversation that lay ahead—because she knew that she would have to disabuse Katherine of her romantic daydreams sooner rather than later—she felt a little nauseous.

'That…was nothing.' She gave a nervous, tinkling laugh and took refuge in a large mouthful of dessert.

'Now now, no need to be coy. I think we've known each other long enough for complete honesty. Mum's said Cupid's been busy with his little arrows.'

'You're awful!' But she was laughing, although she could feel the hysteria of tears welling up just below the surface. Thankfully she was spared any further embarrassment by Katherine standing up and excusing herself.

'Daniel needs to go to bed now,' she said, ignoring her grandson's pleas that it was the weekend, that he wanted to see his dad, that no one in his class went to bed before ten on a weekend. 'And I'm feeling rather tired,' she admitted, clasping Daniel's hand affectionately. 'Now,' she said, turning to Daniel, 'are you going to be the perfect gentleman and help an old lady up the stairs?'

'Mum, I'll walk you up.' Alex was already on his feet, but was being waved down by Katherine, who wanted the young things to enjoy getting to know one another.

'I'm just sorry that Leo couldn't be here, but he'll be back home first thing in the morning.' She looked at Heather warmly. 'There's an awful lot for him to return to.'

Heather smiled wanly. She could feel a thin veil of perspiration break out, but this was not the right time for revelations, not when Katherine looked all in and Daniel was yawning and coming over to wrap his thin arms around her for a hug. Furthermore, she thought, why should she be the one to break it to Katherine that the hot item had turned into a damp squib? Hadn't she been put through the wringer enough?

She would stay for a quick cup of coffee with Alex and then she would retreat and leave it to Leo to fill his mother in. After all, she thought bitterly, when it came to letting women down his experience was second to none.

'So tell me everything,' were Alex's first words as they sat on the sofa in the sitting room, he with a glass of port—because, he had told her, travelling the world had deprived him of that one small pleasure—and she with a cup of coffee which she cradled in her hands.

'Shall we start with age?' Heather sipped her coffee. 'Height? Vital statistics? Occupation?'

'All very interesting, of course, but I'm thinking more along the lines of you and Leo. What's going on there? Mum's over the moon. She thinks he's a changed person and it's all down to you. Actually, she's all but bought the hat.'

Heather groaned and sat back. 'I don't want to talk about Leo.'

'Yes, you do.'

'Why,' she asked, half-exasperated, half-amused at his persistence, 'are you and your brother just so damned *stubborn*?'

'You mean I have something in common with Leo?'

'You don't have an awful lot of time for him, do you?'

Alex wagged an admonishing finger. 'Uh-uh. No way. You're not getting off that lightly.'

Heather compressed her lips and stared down at the sensible black pumps which in all events had been an unnecessary gesture. Leo hadn't even bothered to turn up. He'd been that horrified at her admission that avoidance had been his chosen way of dealing with the prospect of seeing her again.

'How long are you here for?'

'Another attempt to change the subject. Things must be bad. 'Course, if you really don't want to talk about it then I'm happy to chat about your occupation, but it's always better to get things off your chest. Or else you risk ending up like Leo.'

It wasn't so much his tenacity as the sympathy in Alex's voice that did it. The tears that had been threatening like black clouds on a summer day came in a sobbing rush that frightened her with its intensity. She hunched over on the sofa and buried her head in her arms. When she felt Alex's arms enfold her, she turned to him blindly, thankful for his silent, accepting compassion. For the past few days she had kept her feelings locked up inside her, and now it was a relief to have someone else share the burden.

When she felt the handkerchief thrust into her hand she grabbed it gratefully, and after a while the racking sobs subsided to the odd hiccup until she was able to draw back and make an attempt to gather herself.

Unburdening herself of her feelings about Leo was like shedding herself of a great weight, and once she had started the need to tell everything was an unstoppable force, helped by the fact that Alex was an excellent listener. There were very few interruptions. As her words trailed off into silence, he told her that she needed a brandy, and she nodded in agreement even though she had never touched brandy in her life before.

He was still holding her hand. Every so often, he patted it sympathetically. His voice was a low murmur, which was very soothing, although she wasn't really taking in a word he was saying. She was back to thinking about Leo, thinking about the love she had confessed to, wondering what he was doing right now. Would work keep him away all night or would he be filling the space she had left behind with another woman? Just the thought of that made her clutch at the handkerchief again.

Neither of them noticed the figure in the doorway. The overhead light hadn't been switched on, and the light from the small lamp on the table by the mantelpiece barely managed to reach the far corners of the room.

The sound of Leo's voice, ice-cold and forbidding, shocked them into springing apart. Heather felt the blood rush to her face and she stared helplessly at him. His face was in shadow, but there was no mistaking the angry tension of his stance.

'Am I interrupting something?'

Alex was the first to react, leaping to his feet with a grin on his face, but Leo stayed where he was, making no effort to move forward and take the hand which was outstretched towards his in a gesture of welcome.

'I was about to leave,' Heather muttered, lagging behind with the response. She was finding it hard to drag her eyes away from Leo's face. She was mesmerised by the long lines of his muscular body, the same body which had covered hers in love-making. She looked at his mouth, the same mouth which could do things to her that no man ever had, and overwhelmed as she was she still couldn't stop her body from its purely physical response at all that remembered passion. Her nipples tightened into sensitive buds and she felt hot moisture dampen her underwear.

'We were just getting to know one another.' Alex's hand had dropped and he was eyeing his brother cautiously—as well he might, Heather thought, because Leo looked fit to kill. She felt a slow, burning anger begin to curl in the pit of her stomach.

Leo might have done his best to avoid her, might be enraged that she was still hanging around when he thought that the coast was clear, but that didn't give him the right to vent his anger on his brother.

'What exactly were the pair of you up to?' Leo asked in the kind of soft, sibilant voice that sent a tremor of apprehension racing up and down her spine.

'*Up to?*' Alex countered the preposterous question with a laugh, but Heather could hear the nervousness behind the laughter and her heart went out to him because when it came to everything there was no contest between the brothers: physically, verbally… Leo would always be the winner and right now, for reasons she couldn't understand, he looked very much as though there could be no better thing than taking on his brother.

'Leo! What on earth are you talking about?' Heather made to move towards him, but fell back at the glance he shot in her direction.

What am I talking about? The innocence of the question was like a red rag to a bull. 'I'm talking about finding the two of you huddled on the sofa like love birds,' he bit out, taking a step towards her, although what he really, really wanted to do was cover the distance between himself and Alex and show him who was the boss. Respect for his mother kept him from fulfilling the desire, but if he kept his fists clenched to his sides this was still a war that had been a long time coming.

'Leo, please,' Heather pleaded in growing confusion. Was he jealous? Those were the enraged, possessive remarks of a jealous lover, but since when had Leo been either possessive or jealous? There was also something else going on here. The air felt thick and heavy with threat.

'*Love birds?* You must be joking, Leo! I told you, Heather and I were just talking.'

'About what? What conversation is so intimate that it requires you to be entwined with one another?'

'We weren't *entwined*,' Heather protested, while her heart continued to beat out an erratic tattoo.

They had leapt apart like guilty lovers, Leo thought irrationally, and the more they defended themselves the more culpable they seemed to him. Rage was coursing through him like a toxin. He didn't know where it was coming from. He could almost taste it in his mouth, and he had to breathe deeply to regain some of his formidable self-control.

Was it his imagination or did she look ever so slightly tousled? This was the woman who three days ago had confessed her love for him, shocking him with her honesty. He had felt as though a gauntlet had been laid down, and it had not been one which he had been inclined to take up. He had never given her the slightest inclination that there could be a future between them. Not only had she chosen to disregard that glaring point of truth, but she had stubbornly refused the two options which had been left open to her—either slink away with a discreet lack of fuss, or else put aside her silly dreams and continue their relationship, which would have been his preferred path. She must have known, he had told himself repeatedly, that to fling all her cards on the table would put him in an untenable position.

He was a man who was not fashioned for long-term relationships. Hadn't he made that perfectly clear to her during the time they had spent together? More than with any previous woman, he had actually opened up to her under direct questioning, and had told her certain things about his marriage which had previously been kept in his own private terrain. Of course, he had not told her everything, but combined with everything else—and no one could say that he hadn't been upfront from the start—the least she could have done was take the hint.

Women, the very few who had ever dared to nurture inappropriate ambitions as far as he was concerned, always but always took the hint.

He had spent three days telling himself that he had to be ruthless when it came to this one woman who had dared to crash through the barriers he had carefully, over time, constructed around himself.

He had decided that he would have one final conversation with her, clear the air.

The last thing he had expected was to walk in on her and his brother cuddled up on his mother's sofa in virtual darkness.

Thinking about that now, Leo banged on the lights and proceeded to look first at her and then at his brother.

'I didn't think you would be back tonight.' Heather filled the awkward silence with the worst choice of explanation and the taut lines of Leo's face darkened further.

He hadn't expected to find her still at the house, and this was the last thing he needed to hear. Was this how she was managing to deal with her unrequited love? He was besieged by a host of unpleasant, conflicting emotions. He had never before been aware that he was a man who had a comfort zone, a place which was inaccessible to the rest of the human race. He was now keenly aware that she had managed to barge right into it, because he didn't feel himself, and it wasn't because his brother was back on the scene.

Leo found that when he tried to think about it his brain seemed to shut down, leaving him floundering in a morass of weirdly unanswerable questions. He didn't like it. It distracted him from the purity of his rage, forced him to ask *why* exactly he was so enraged. Was it just the thought that she might have declared her love for him—and she hadn't been lying about that, because hadn't he been the one who had sensed it, probably even before she had herself?—only to find herself in thrall to his brother, of all people?

'Where did you think I would be?'

'Katherine said that you had gone to London. It's so late; I thought you might have stayed there overnight.' Even with his face stony cold and her emotions all over the place, Heather was vitally aware of that leashed power and grace that was so hypnotic. His impact on her was so powerful that it made her feel giddy. 'I…I should leave. You and your brother probably have a lot of catching up to do.'

In his mind's eye, Leo was tormented by the picture of them sitting together in a darkened room, so close to one another that you couldn't have put a cushion between them. Normally adept at eliminating anything that threatened to disturb his much-valued equilibrium, he was finding it impossible to erase the distasteful memory from his head.

He made himself look at Alex. By active choice, he had only seen him a handful of times over the years and it struck him that, yes, his brother was a man who might seem to him lightweight but to some women could easily appear appealing. He looked vaguely unruly, just the sort to ride his battered motorbike around the world. Just the sort to be on Heather's wavelength. A free spirit. His tension ratcheted up a notch and a sense of purpose crystallised inside him like a block of ice.

'Yes,' Leo agreed, unsmiling. 'But, first, let me apologise

for misunderstanding a situation.' He turned to Heather and forced himself to smile. 'You'll have to excuse a lover for being a little jealous.'

Lover? Wasn't *ex-lover* a more fitting description of their current status? She looked at him in total bewilderment. *Jealous?* She would have been more capable of appreciating that startling sentiment if she wasn't presently feeling as though she had somehow been transported to a parallel universe.

'But—but—' she stammered in utter confusion as he began walking slowly towards her. She glanced across to Alex, who seemed as perplexed as she was, and then back to Leo.

So she had confided all in his brother. Leo caught that exchanged glance, and at once read the situation as it really was. She had been pouring her heart out to Alex. The jealous rage that had swept over him had been misplaced. She loved *him*. The certainty of that knowledge, while frustrating—because he could have spared himself his momentary lapse in self-control—was surprisingly soothing. For once he didn't mind being wrong about a situation.

'A lover's tiff,' he threw at his brother while moving to curl his long fingers in Heather's hair. It felt good. Better than he would have imagined possible. It also felt right, which was odd, considering he had spent three days building up a strong case for talking to her without the interference of emotions about where exactly she had gone wrong in trying to pin him down.

He felt himself harden, and it was an effort to bring himself down from that sudden surge of hot arousal. It was her proximity, the tempting fullness of her half-opened mouth.

Unable to resist, he lowered his head and took her mouth with his. 'You've been crying,' he murmured against her lips. 'Was it because of me?'

'Leo, no…' Heather pushed him, but she was trembling so

hard and he was an immovable force. He caught her fluttering hands in his and repeated his softly spoken question, demanding an answer, and when she gave an imperceptible nod he was momentarily overwhelmed by a surge of pure, primitive triumph.

Heather couldn't bring herself to meet his eyes, but she could sense his satisfaction at her miserable, grudging surrender, and she pulled back angrily. She forgot that Alex was still in the room. Leo could do that to her, make her forget everything, and he was doing it now. For what? To prove that he *could*? He didn't love her and he didn't want her, but maybe he just didn't care for the thought of her wanting someone else. He was a man who had become accustomed to absolute and supreme control. His high-octane, hugely successful financial acumen had won him an army of yes men, and his ludicrously powerful sex appeal had enabled him to snap his fingers and have any woman sprinting in his direction. So now that same desire to control would doubtless dictate that she pine for him.

She glared up at his arrogantly smug face and stamped down on her body's weak, automatic response to his proximity. She was shaking as she wrenched herself away from him.

'I fell for you, Leo,' she told him, keeping her voice low, controlled and steady. 'And, sure, right now I'm a little down in the dumps. But I won't be crying for you for the rest of my life. I've already cried over one failed relationship.'

'Don't even *think* of putting me in the same bracket as your ex! I've already told you that the man was a creep!'

'We were too young when we married, and he was weak. Since when are *you* any different?'

'I'm a one-woman man,' Leo responded comfortably, still riding high on the notion that she had been crying over him.

Of course, he abhorred the thought of her being unhappy—but being unhappy on his behalf was a hell of a lot better than flinging herself into someone else's arms as a method of recovery. 'I don't play the field when I know that there's a woman keeping my bed warm for me.'

'You're a one-woman man for just as long as it suits you,' Heather flung back at him, taking another step backwards and folding her arms. 'You talk a lot about making sure never to give a woman the wrong idea, but I think you quite enjoy the thought that you can get them into a position where they'd do anything for you. 'Course, that gets boring after a while, but when you walk away you can always remind them that you never promised them anything.'

'That's called being *fair*.'

'That's called being *a creep*. You're just a different kind of creep, Leo!'

Leo flushed darkly, outraged at having had what he considered to be his impeccably fair reputation dragged down into the dirt in the matter of a single sentence. Against his better judgement, he began to rapidly revise his satisfied acceptance that what he had confronted in the sitting room was a distraught Heather offloading on his no-good brother. What if she had already been subconsciously comparing him to Alex? Was Alex a creep? No. To her, he would have seemed as wholesome as freshly baked bread with his 'let's hold hands and discuss our feelings' approach.

Jealousy and possessiveness, two weaknesses he had always prided himself on not having, rose in him like a red mist. To top it all off, his brother at that very instant had the barefaced cheek to tell him, 'Perhaps you should take time out and, hey, maybe listen to what someone else has to say for a change?'

'And maybe *you* should listen, little brother. She's off-limits.'

'Hello?' Heather interjected furiously at Leo's ferocious verbal warning to his brother. 'Are you talking about *me*? Because, if you are, I just want to remind you that I'm not your *property*, Leo!'

'You're in love with me!'

Heather fell silent, cursing the one, wild moment in time when she had been drawn to be honest with him. Now, he was using her love against her. Tears of hurt and betrayal stung the back of her eyes, and she looked down at her feet, willing herself to fight against the temptation to really let the side down by crying. Once, in front of Alex, had been quite enough.

And I'm not about to let you go. That thought sliced through Leo's consciousness like a razor blade, shearing away at his fundamental acceptance that the chosen path of his life was to remain free of the encumbrance of a woman tied to him by a band of gold. He had his son. It was enough. He was not even aware that he had spoken his thoughts out loud until Heather, standing as still as a statue, asked him to repeat what he had said.

'You're right,' he told her, walking towards where she had managed to field him off by edging towards the mantelpiece. He was no longer aware of his brother. It was as if a genie in a lamp had magically made him disappear. There was a roaring in his ears, but still he felt good. Calm. 'I'm a different kind of creep.'

'Wha...?' The whole parallel-universe thing was happening again. She wanted to move out of Leo's reach, but her feet stubbornly refused to oblige. What had he been talking about when he had said that he refused to let her go? Had she heard correctly? Her heart was beating so fast that she felt faint. Or maybe it was just the way he was staring at her, his fabulous eyes reaching down into the depths of her and stirring everything around. It was so unfair that this was what love was all about: allowing someone in who had the power to scramble your brains.

'I am prepared to make a commitment to you,' Leo announced with largesse.

'You're "prepared to make a commitment" to me?'

'Correct,' Leo asserted.

'What sort of commitment?' Heather asked faintly.

'Are there different kinds?' He frowned, just a tiny bit thrown by her lack of a suitably rapturous response.

'Yes, there are different kinds!' Heather was compelled to point out, because her mind, which had turned to cotton wool for a moment, was finally cranking back into gear and warning her that their definitions of commitment would almost certainly not coincide. Leo's idea of commitment would be, in his opinion, to generously allocate a few months rather than a few weeks to a relationship, and to maybe tone down the tenor of his remarks when discussing any plans that stretched beyond a two-day time limit. Accept that, her mind was telling her, and she would be no better off than she was now. In fact, she'd be worse off, because she would have longer to fall even deeper in love with him.

'How so?' Leo demanded, but cautiously.

'You know how I feel about relationships,' Heather told him quietly.

'Then maybe,' he said in an undertone, 'we should get married.' He was gratified by the alteration in her expression. After everything he had been through over the past few days, he had never expected to land up in this place, and from the look of it neither had she. It was as if suddenly he was released to have her, and any misgivings about finding himself in such wildly unexpected terrain were wiped out by the knowledge that she was now his.

Predictably, he felt his body harden as his imagination ran amok, conjuring up pleasurable images of exploring her naked body, tasting her, losing himself in her fabulous curves. His eyes smouldered in anticipation of touching her, but for the moment he interrupted her stupefied, gaping silence to say quietly, 'I'll leave you to think about it, hmm?' He reached out and curled a finger into her hair, and admitted what he had been so strenuously denying for days—that, yes, she took his breath away. 'Because now there are things that have to be said between my brother and me.'

Think about it? Heather was in a daze. She felt as though, if she probed too deeply into his extravagant proposal—which seemed so out of keeping with everything she had assumed about him—then it would disappear like dew on a hot summer day.

'But—'

'No *buts*.' He kissed her parted mouth, a kiss that was both chaste and deeply, deeply sexy at the same time.

'Okay.' Heather sighed when his lips finally left hers.

'And we'll talk…later.'

Afterwards, a mere three hours that felt like three decades, Heather wondered what that promised land would have looked like had fate not decided to show her, had not guided her foolish steps back to that sitting room with two mugs of coffee to find that the door was ajar, just a slither. Just enough for her to overhear a conversation that was as destructive as a hammer shattering a pane of glass.

Sitting in her cottage while the clock chimed midnight she wished she could cry, but she was all cried out for the moment—although she suspected that, when the tears finally came, they would never stop. She would just drown in her own self-made misery.

CHAPTER TEN

THE past three hours had been cathartic for Leo. Indeed, he felt as though he had been sucked into a whirlpool, spun around at dangerous speed and then spat out. He had been stripped of his cynicism; of course it would return in time, because that was part and parcel of his personality, but right at the moment he felt weirdly exposed.

He also still had to talk to Heather. He was looking forward to it. In fact, he couldn't wait.

Having become accustomed to her being under the same roof as him, it was only when he was virtually outside the door to the room she had used while she had been in his mother's house that it struck Leo that she wouldn't be there. She naturally had returned to her cottage. He spun round on his heels and took the stairs two at a time, leaving the house as quietly as he could and choosing to walk to her place, giving himself a head start on collating his thoughts.

Although it was after two in the morning, he didn't feel in the least tired. In fact, he felt fantastically alive, and filled with a driving sense of purpose. Although it made more sense to wait until morning, because she would probably be fast asleep at this hour, Leo felt compelled to see her as soon as was physically possible. He didn't doubt for a single second that she would feel exactly the same way about seeing him.

As expected, her cottage was in complete darkness, but he didn't hesitate to ring the doorbell, and was slightly surprised, although pleasantly so, when she answered the door within minutes. Nor did she look as though she had been dragged out of bed. In fact, she looked as alert as he felt, which was great.

Leo grinned and stepped forward. 'I didn't wake you, did I?'

Wake her? Not much chance of that when she had spent hours replaying in her mind those stolen snippets of revealing conversation which she had overheard before she had fled. No, she had had no more chance of sleeping with so much on her mind than if Daniel had set up camp in her bedroom to play his drums.

Besides, it seemed a moot point whether he had woken her or not, because he was already inserting himself beyond the door, shouldering his way into the cottage.

Heather cravenly wished that he would just disappear, leaving her some more time to sort out in her head what she was going to say to him. When fate decided to play games, she thought, heart beating a frantic tempo, it certainly didn't cut corners. Leo was the opposite of the disappearing man— he was standing in her hallway, one hundred percent vital, insanely sexy male.

'I'm glad you came.' Heather found her voice and made it sound as cool as possible, although her fingers were knotted nervously behind her back as she watched him remove his weatherbeaten, tan leather bomber-jacket and sling it over the banister.

In the cold light of reality, she had taken time to consider his extraordinary marriage proposal. It had been the last thing she had expected, and she was ashamed now at how eagerly she had allowed herself to believe that he had really meant it.

Leo had never once talked to her about a future, not even when their relationship had been at its rosiest. In fact, he had been positively scathing about such a concept applied to him and any woman. Nor had he given her any inclination, when she had told him about his mother's assumptions—when she had *confessed her love*—that he was willing to commit to what they had and give it a fair go to see where it ended up. No, he had been more than willing to walk off into the sunset, leaving her to deal with her broken heart.

She was retrospectively incredulous that she had succumbed to his phoney, soft voice and honeyed words and had actually believed that he had come to some kind of wondrous realisation. She couldn't now comprehend how she had been so stupid. The man didn't love her, never had and never would. Really, how on earth could he have come to a wondrous conclusion that he had made a mistake, that he wanted her in his life? Even when he had uttered that preposterous proposal he had significantly failed to say anything about love. She had let herself believe what she'd wanted to believe, and it wouldn't be the first time she had made that particular mistake around him.

'We need to talk,' she told him in a stilted voice, solving the problem of looking at him by turning her back and walking towards her sitting room. She waited as he followed her in, but when he sat down, patting the space next to him, she remained standing by the door until he finally caught her mood and frowned.

'You are upset because I should have come sooner,' he said as an apology. 'There were things that needed to be said between my brother and myself.'

'Yes. I know.' Heather swallowed hard. She was so alive to his presence that it hurt. It was like being high up on a mountain where the air was thin and breathing normally was impossible. It was not how she wanted to feel, not now, and she had to make a big effort to keep her voice level and her thoughts as clear as possible.

'Sometimes,' he carried on, 'family situations can take longer than anticipated.'

'Yes. I know.'

'Is that all you're going to say? And why are you standing all the way over there by the door when there's a much more comfortable spot right here next to me?' *Where you belong*, was the unvoiced postscript to that remark, and incredibly he didn't try and rail against it.

'I've been thinking about what you said, Leo—about marriage—and it doesn't make any sense.'

Leo's deep, grey eyes, which could be as cold as slate when he was angry and as dark as coal when he was aroused, swept over her cautiously.

'You see,' Heather continued, pushing herself away from the door and sidling sideways, crablike, to collapse onto the chair facing him. 'I happened to overhear a bit of what you and Alex were talking about.'

'How is that possible?'

'I came back; I thought the two of you might want some coffee. The door was open and I heard…stuff.' The 'stuff' had become a jumble of words that had crystallised into a lethally destructive bomb threatening to explode in her head.

'Stuff that made me realise that you don't give a jot about me,' Heather told him. She was hanging on to her self-control, but only by a thread, and if he couldn't hear the angry tremor in her voice then *she* certainly could. 'You didn't ask me to marry you because you had decided that you wanted to build a future with me. You asked me to marry you because Alex was in the room and you felt the need to exercise your rights over a possession. Because there's a lot of muddy water under your bridge, isn't there, Leo? Would you ever have told me if I hadn't found out on my own?'

'You should not have stood out there listening to a conversation that was private!' Even as the words left his mouth, Leo was chillingly aware that there were more holes in that line of argument than a colander. Of course she would have listened, probably caught by the mention of her name, or maybe just by the urgency of their voices. She was only human. He felt out of control, and he didn't like it, but then again when had he felt completely in control since he had met her? He could no longer remember that happy state, nor did he have any inclination to return to it.

'That's not the point. The point is…' She heard the wobble in her voice and took a deep breath. 'I was just a bit player in a revenge game for you, Leo.' Big, fat tears were welling up and she swallowed hard.

'You're getting hysterical.'

'I am *not* getting hysterical!'

'No? Because your voice is getting higher and higher. Why don't you let me explain?' A lifetime of self-control made it possible for Leo to outwardly contain all nuance of emotion in his voice, but already he was considering the possibility that one overheard conversation would be the conclusive nail in his coffin, and a thread of panic was beginning to filter in. He wanted to go over to her, close the distance between them, but he knew instinctively that the result would be either fight or flight, and neither was acceptable.

'Explain what?' Heather asked him jerkily. 'How it is that you let your ex-wife destroy the relationship you had with your brother? With your son?'

The silence stretched between them, thick and tense. Heather wondered whether he would say anything. He was a deeply private man, and having her raise the spectre of a past he probably would have preferred to keep under wraps, she half-figured, would make him simply stand up and walk away.

Leo heard the scathing, incredulous criticism in her voice and for the first time in his life he found himself lost for words. The very basic foundation of his life—which was that essentially he didn't much care one way or another what someone else might think of him—deserted him.

'What you overheard has nothing to do with you.'

'How can you say that?' Heather asked. She stared at the man sitting opposite her and wondered who he was. There was no expression on his face. He wasn't going to explain anything to her because she just didn't *matter* enough. Since when should that thought hurt her? she wondered. It wasn't as though it came as any blinding surprise.

Since when had she ever really mattered to him? Even when he had been covering her body with kisses, touching her in her most intimate places, tasting her in ways that could send her into orbit, he had never let the barriers down. He lived life the way people might play a game of chess, always coolly conscious of needing to make just the right move. Wasn't that why he was so phenomenally successful in business? Leo did nothing unless it suited him. At that particular point in time, it had suited him to make a big song and dance of claiming her in the most irrefutable way he could think of.

'Alex and I were having a private conversation,' Leo said heavily. 'And one that was perhaps overdue.'

'*Perhaps?*'

'Sophia destroyed many things, and I allowed it.' For someone as open and as upfront as she was, she would find these dark secrets abhorrent. But he needed to explain before he could even begin to find out whether he had missed his chance with her, as he knew he probably had. 'I never questioned what she expected out of me, but I knew very early on that I was failing to deliver—too much time spent at work, not enough interest in going out to clubs or partying. My wife, in short, discovered that the man she married wasn't the fun-loving guy she wanted. It escaped her that I needed to work in order to earn the vast sums of money she enjoyed spending.'

'You don't have to tell me any of this if you don't want to,' Heather said. She was painfully aware that the words were wrenched out of him. While he maybe thought that the very least she deserved was clarification from *his* point of view, of things that had been said, she still shied away from causing him any discomfort. She could feel her tender heart reaching out to him.

Leo looked briefly at her and then vaulted to his feet so that he could pace the small room, a tiger forced to withdraw its claws and leash its primitive urge to dominate. Which made her no less conscious of his immense, restless energy. Even in thoughtful contemplation he still managed to overwhelm his surroundings and make her acutely aware of her fascinated response to his physical impact.

In that single sentence—*you don't have to tell me any of this if you don't want to*—Leo thought that he could identify her retreat from him. Why else would she show such little interest in a story that was so revealingly intimate? He hadn't thought that he had loved her. Hell, who knew what love was? His experiences in that field had been blighted, to say the least. How was he supposed to know, belatedly, that this powerful urge to be with her, the way she had filled his head, had been more than just a passing inconvenience? He had never had a problem compartmentalising women before. How was he supposed to recognise that his inability to do the same with this woman was an indication of feelings that were as alien to him as breathing air was to a fish?

He gave an elegant, casual shrug in the hope that it would conceal his desperation to make her understand.

'I don't pretend to have been a saint. I was away more often than I should have been, but returning to the house was like returning to a hell hole. Even after Daniel was born the arguments continued. In fact, they became worse, because added to the general gripe that I didn't pay her the attention she deserved was her resentment at being housebound. Even with nannies at her disposal her freedom of movement was curtailed, by her standards, and she didn't like it.'

Having heard only the bare skeleton of her eavesdropped conversation, Heather was silent at this unexpected fleshing out of the detail.

'Well?' Leo prompted, because her silence was unnerving. She was a woman who had opinions on just about everything, up to and including things which were outside the boundaries which he had silently but firmly laid down between them.

Heather looked at this clever, complicated, beautiful man who had stolen her heart without even trying, and she did her best not to be utterly transparent.

'Was that when she…um…?'

'Decided that an absentee husband wasn't good enough? Realised that infidelity was just the thing? Began screwing around?' Leo gave a short, humourless laugh. 'No idea. The end result was the same, and thrown into that wonderful hotpot was Daniel. She was determined that I not get close to him. I don't think she could stand the thought that there reached a point when I just didn't really give a damn about her any longer. I wanted my son, but as far as I was concerned she could have disappeared off the face of the earth. When I told her that I wanted a divorce, she went crazy, and she went even crazier when I didn't react.'

Heather had no difficulty in imagining the scenario. Leo, at the height of his indifference, was a formidable sight. She shivered. Was this story just a prelude to telling her why he had asked her to marry him? She could feel herself clinging to the miserable hope that he must care something for her if he was going to all this trouble, divulging details he had probably never shared with anyone else in his life before. She firmly squashed the feeling.

'You know what happened next, don't you?' Leo was finally standing in front of her, a towering presence that sucked the breath out of her. Heather nodded slowly, because 'what happened next' had been the very first words she had accidentally overheard. Leo dragged the small, up-holstered footstool across so that he could perch on it. A big, brawny, muscular man on a dainty pink footstool—it was a comical sight, but the last thing Heather felt like doing was laughing.

Giving in to feelings of sympathy that were beyond her control, she reached out and rested her hand lightly on his shoulder, although it seemed an inadequate way of express-ing her compassion. Which, it struck her, he may or may not even want.

How else could she let him know that she was appalled at the wickedness that had motivated his ex-wife to take Daniel to the furthest reaches of the universe, and not before she had constructed her cleverly woven lie that the child wasn't Leo's?

'She was evil, Leo. I realise you probably don't want to

hear this cliché but the past is over and done with, and today and tomorrow are all that matter.'

'Sometimes clichés can be very helpful.' He looked directly at her, and as their eyes tangled she felt her breathing sharpen into staccato bursts; typically, she thought, ambushing the cool demeanour she was so intent on portraying. 'It's unforgiveable that I have waited this long to confront my brother, but then that was probably what motivated Sofia to tell me that Alex was Daniel's father. She knew that it was the one thing I would find impossible to deal with, although I carried on attempting to maintain contact. Three times I made elaborate attempts to visit, and three times Sofia made sure that she went AWOL with Daniel. Then came the pictures of her and Alex, supposedly playing happy families behind my back.'

He released one long sigh, closed his eyes and swept his fingers through his hair. 'History now. Alex was there all right. He was in Australia, passing through, apparently, on one of his many "let's see as much of the world as I can" escapades, and he managed to corner her to find out what the hell was going on. At which point she played for the sympathy vote and implied all manner of things.'

'I'm…I'm really glad that you sorted everything out with your brother, Leo.' In fact, whilst it had taken time for him to warm to his son, big bridges had been built, and they had a relationship which she suspected would only get stronger and stronger.

She made to pull her hand away but Leo prevented her from doing so, placing his on top, a warm, heavy weight that made her pulses race. In a minute, Heather thought that he might pat her gently on her arm and give her a fond, brotherly peck on the cheek before sending her on her way.

'But I still think it was pretty inconsiderate of you to stick me in the middle of your argument. I guess when you were still of the mind that he had slept with your ex-wife that was just your way of telling him that he wasn't about to take what was yours again—but, hey, I was *never* yours.'

'That's not the impression you gave me a few days ago when you told me that you—'

'I don't want to talk about that!' Heather looked away, her cheeks flaming under his searching, narrowed eyes.

'Why not?'

'Because…'

'Because confession, you now realise, is not necessarily good for the soul? Because you've finally realised that love is an overrated option that comes with too many unpleasant side-effects? Because you've met Alex and realised that the world is full of more suitable candidates?'

'What does Alex have to do with anything?'

Leo's mouth tightened. He stood up, his body language speaking volumes for his tension. He wasn't sure how to manoeuvre the conversation to a place that felt more comfortable. He had just told her things which he would never have repeated to another woman in a million years, but how was she supposed to know that? In her world, people were honest and open and didn't have secrets that they kept to themselves for years on end, allowing lives to be damaged.

'I am nothing like my brother.' Leo shoved his hands into his trouser pockets and scowled darkly at the ground as he paced the floor. 'Alex has always been the *sensitive* one.' It was a description which, over the years, Leo had fine-tuned into an insult. Now, he was beginning to see the positives behind it.

'Some guys are,' Heather said softly.

'And no doubt you find that very endearing.' He paused to shoot her a frown.

'Are you *jealous*…?'

'I'm not the jealous type,' Leo grated, but dull colour slashed his high cheekbones. 'Did he try anything on when he was busy listening to you and providing a handy shoulder to cry on? No, scratch that question. I never asked it.'

'You *are* jealous!' Heather breathed, hardly daring to explore that wonderful concept too hard just in case it shattered under scrutiny.

Leo sat back down, because pacing up and down was making him feel even more like a caged animal, and decided to bite the bullet.

'I have a problem thinking of you with another man,' he admitted in a driven undertone.

'Why?'

'Why do you think?'

Heather struggled to find a suitable answer to that demanding question, but the drag of her senses to the man now staring down at her was wreaking havoc with her thought processes.

'Some people, some *men*, have a dog-in-the-manger attitude towards women,' she ventured uncertainly. 'Even if they don't want a woman, they don't want anyone else to have her.'

'That theory doesn't just apply to men. Anyway, you're wrong.'

'Why, then?'

'I didn't ask you to marry me because I wanted to assert proprietorial rights over you.' Leo side-stepped the direct question in favour of taking a more leisurely path to what he needed to say. For once, the preferred direct route with which he was accustomed to dealing with everything and everyone was not working for him.

'Why, then?' She was no longer trying to squash that little bud of hope that had taken root and was squirming steadily upwards.

Between them, the silence vibrated. Leo flexed his fingers and looked down at them before raising his eyes to her face.

'I never thought that I would love a woman. I'd been through hell on earth with Sofia, and as far as I was concerned commitment was for the birds. When you told me that you loved me, I didn't stop to think. I just assumed that it wasn't on the cards. Only…' He thought back to the way she had continued to prey on his mind, the way he had thought up excuses for contacting her again, the way he had subconsciously never contemplated a future without seeing her in it somewhere.

Heather was holding her breath.

'When I saw you there on the sofa, I saw red. I didn't stop to think, and even when I did I still couldn't stand the thought of you being in a two-metre distance of Alex. I figured that he was more your type than me.'

'He's a sweet guy, but he's not *you*, Leo. I didn't want to fall in love with you but I did, and there's no way I could ever fall out of love with you, no matter who else comes along.'

'No one else is going to come along,' Leo told her, locking his eyes to hers with fierce possession. 'Will you marry me, Heather? As soon as possible? Tomorrow?'

Heather laughed, light-headed with happiness, and she flung her arms around his neck and pulled him to her. This was one dream she was not going to be letting go of any time soon…

'As soon as possible' turned out to be four months. It would have been cruel, she gently told Leo, to deny Katherine the chance of really enjoying the day, not to mention Daniel, and of course Alex, who had decided at long last to put down roots. *Literally* roots, as he was in the process of opening a garden centre just outside the village with the help of his mother and, naturally, Leo, whose financial acumen would be essential to its success, he had asserted the minute the idea had first been broached.

Their wedding had been a quiet affair and afterwards had come the process of moving. Although thankfully, as far as Heather was concerned, not to London but to a village slightly more accessible for road and rail links and not very far away from Katherine so that Daniel could continue at his school.

Heather hadn't believed Leo when he had told her that he was a changed man, that his workaholic days were over, but he was true to his word, and only left the country when absolutely necessary. She felt blessed to be on his learning curve with him as he forged deep bonds with his son, finding shared interests in the most unlikely places.

And now…

She looked at the kitchen clock and her heart gave its familiar little lurch as she heard the click of the front door opening. When he walked into the kitchen, bringing with him that wonderful scent that was so peculiarly him, she walked straight up to him and curved into his open arms. Two whole nights away from him because he had had to go to New York to close a deal. Nearly three nights, when you worked out that it was almost ten in the evening.

'Next time you're coming with me,' he growled, smothering her in kisses, feeling as though he was finally coming home where he belonged as her body pressed against his. He tenderly unbuttoned her shirt and sighed with gratification as he saw that she wasn't wearing a bra.

'Don't you want to eat first?' Heather breathed, blissfully happy when he said that he had other things on his mind to eat that had nothing to do with food. The passing of time had not diminished their craving for one another, and their bodies were so finely tuned to each other's needs that his light touch against her thigh had her parting her legs, offering every inch of her body for his exploring hands.

'No panties,' he murmured into her ear. 'Just the way I like it…' He had long ceased to marvel that every time he touched her he felt as aroused as if he were touching her for the first time. Sometimes they could not even make it to the bedroom, and tonight was one of those times.

'You and Daniel,' he said with raw honesty, 'are the lynch-pins of my entire life.'

'And soon you'll have another…' The news which she had been hugging to herself for the past day brought a radiant smile to her lips. 'I'm pregnant.'

A new life beginning, a new journey, and there was no one in the whole world she would rather share both with.

MILLS & BOON

MODERN

Power and Passion

Prepare to be swept off your feet by sophisticated, sexy and seductive heroes, in some of the world's most glamourous and romantic locations, where power and passion collide.